# Seven Minutes Later

Bonnie Kistler is an American author. She received a degree in English literature from Bryn Mawr College and a law degree from the University of Pennsylvania, and she practiced corporate litigation in Alaska, Arkansas, and finally Philadelphia before becoming a full-time novelist. She is the author of *House on Fire* and, as Bonnie MacDougal, several other thrillers. She and her husband now divide their time between Florida and the Blue Ridge Mountains.

# SEVEN MINUTES LATER

## BONNIE KISTLER

**10 CANELO**

First published in the United States of America in 2022 by HarperCollins

This edition published in the United Kingdom in 2022 by

Canelo
Unit 9, 5th Floor
Cargo Works, 1–2 Hatfields
London, SE1 9PG
United Kingdom

A CIP catalogue record for this book is available from the British Library.

Print ISBN 978 1 80032 523 4
Ebook ISBN 978 1 80032 522 7

Look for more great books at www.canelo.co

Printed and bound in Great Britain by Clays Ltd, Elcograf S.p.A.

MIX
Paper from
responsible sources
FSC® C018072

# Prologue

The fog hovered high over the city, invisible in the cold night sky except for the diffused reflection of the urban skyglow. The only surface it touched was Marketplace Tower, the city's newest and tallest office building, where it painted a coat of rime over every sparkling facet of the spire. If anyone could see it, they might imagine a sugar-frosted fairyland. But no one could, in the fog, in the dark.

Down on the street, a van stopped at the entrance to discharge a crew of three men. As they unloaded their machines from the back and wheeled them to the door, one of the men, the new one, paused on the pavement and looked up, and up some more. The thirty stories that loomed over the street were dark except for two gauzy glimmers on the topmost floor. He craned his head back farther. The two lights glowed on opposite sides of the building, and as the fog drifted through the sky, they dimmed and brightened like lighthouse lanterns warning of two separate hazards.

In the building's lobby, a guard sat at a security console that faced the three sets of revolving doors. CCTV videos lit up four screens in front of him; on the fifth he was watching the game. Behind him stretched the bank of elevators, five cars on either side with a destination dispatch console between them. Their doors were etched with a gridwork of black bars, an homage to the old cage-style elevators of the Edwardian era.

The three men buzzed for entry, and the guard looked up and pushed a button to release the lock. They signed in and stowed their coats in an empty office off the lobby, rubbernecked the TV, and asked for the score. Twenty-two-nothing, the guard told them. They whistled, then started up their machines and tugged on their headphones to listen to the game as they worked. The lobby floor was Siena marble inlaid with geometric diamonds of onyx, and the polishers glided over it like Zambonis.

Thirty floors up a woman stood very still at her office window. On a clear day she could see the Manhattan skyline. Tonight she saw nothing but her own reflection. She was in her early forties, slender and petite, with alabaster skin and faded blond hair cut in a stylish swoop. Although it was a Sunday night, her makeup was flawless, and she was dressed for a workday, in a silk blouse and tailored trousers and pointed-toe heels with the distinctive red soles that marked them as a high-three-figure purchase. She gazed at herself in the darkness, her face utterly still, until at last she turned and picked up her coat and pulled her office door shut behind her. A beep sounded as the electronic lock engaged, and she headed down the corridor.

At the far end of the same floor, on the side without a view, the other point of light shone over a different desk. Its surface was covered with stacks of paper flying flags of multicolored tabs on the margins and topped with Post-it notes. In the shadows six feet away stood a different woman, six inches taller and ten years younger. She looked even younger with her sloppy ponytail and pale bare-skin face. She, too, was dressed for a workday, though not in designer wear, and she, too, stared at her reflection in the glass, but her face wasn't still. A muscle twitched at the corner of one bleary eye, winking on and off like a semaphore. She'd been at her desk for more than fourteen hours. Wearily she turned, slid some papers into a battered canvas bag, and picked up her coat. There was no lock on her office door, and she left it standing open.

As she trudged to the elevator, a hush swelled through the penthouse corridors, broken only by the abiding hum of the building's mechanicals. They wheezed like a hospital ventilator on a comatose patient.

When she arrived at the elevator bank, the older woman was already there. She didn't respond when the younger woman spoke to her. The center elevator arrived. The doors slid open. The women stepped on. The doors closed.

911. What's your emergency?

We're stuck in an elevator. The power's gone out.

Okay. Can you tell me your name?

Shay Lambert.

What's your location?

Marketplace Tower. We're stuck in the elevator. The power's completely out. I pressed the alarm button, but nothing happened. The intercom isn't working, and the air compressor's out, too, I think. We're in total darkness.

Is someone there with you?

One other person. Lucy Carter-Jones. This is her phone I'm calling on.

Is she all right?

I'm not sure. She seems pretty upset.

Let me talk to her.

Okay. Hold on. I have to turn on the phone light so I can see where she is. Okay. There. They want to talk to you. [*pause*] I'm putting the phone to her ear.

Hello? This is the 911 operator. Can you tell me your name?

[*no response*]

Hello? Are you all right?

[*no response*]

Hi, it's me again. Lucy's not talking. She seems really out of it. We need to get her out of here.

The Fire Bureau has been dispatched. Please stay on the line.

I don't know. This phone's about to die. It's got like one percent charge left.

Stay on the line. Rescue workers will be there soon.

No. I better conserve the battery. I might need the flashlight again.

Best if you stay on the line, ma'am.

No. But thank you.

Hello? Hello?

*Part I*

# Chapter 1

The motor started up with a chug of gears that sounded like teeth gnashing. The lights flashed on, and I scrambled up off the floor and charged for the doors. The elevator plunged beneath my feet, so fast it felt like free fall, but I didn't care. I wanted down, I wanted *out*. In seconds we reached the lobby level. The doors opened and I burst out—into a semicircle of waiting men. They were a blur of uniforms: policemen, firefighters, security guard, men in coveralls with oval name patches on their chests. I stopped and stared at them, but they were all staring past me, into the elevator.

I turned. Lucy Carter-Jones was sprawled in the corner of the car. Her eyes were open inside raccoon circles of mascara, and she had a hole in her left cheek so neat it looked like someone had taken a paper punch to her face. On the wall above her was a splatter of blood and gore, and on the floor beside her was the gun, a snub-nosed revolver in a matte black finish.

I felt sick, and then I *was* sick. I doubled over and heaved out a stream of yellow bile all over the gleaming marble floor.

Two men lunged at me from either side, and they hoisted me up, their hands tight on my elbows and wrists. My toes dragged the floor as they propelled me across the lobby and through a glass door into an empty office. It was furnished only with a metal desk and a chair and a coat rack hung heavy with winter coats. I looked around for my own coat before I remembered it was back there, on the floor of the elevator, near the gun.

I looked down. My suit jacket started out that day as a solid boring beige; now it was leopard-print, or cheetah, or some other predator splattered with the blood of its kill. The sight of it made me want to vomit again. I tore frantically at the buttons, and the two men jumped to restrain me until they saw what I was doing. They helped me remove the jacket, and one of them bore it away as the other pressed me down into the chair.

"My coat," I said. "My things." I tried to remember what else I'd left behind. My briefcase. My purse.

"They're being secured," he said.

The first man returned and handed me a plastic cup of water. He wore the uniform of a police officer. I turned to the other man and saw that he did, too. The cup trembled in my hand, and the water sloshed from side to side like waves lapping at a dock. I gulped a mouthful and swirled it around my teeth and spat it back into the cup. My hands were shaking badly. I stared at them, then at my fingernails. They were torn and ragged, and I remembered how I'd dug my fingertips into the crack between the elevator doors, how hard I'd pulled and strained to open them. I'd broken every nail, and the door never budged.

"What happened?" one officer asked, while the other said, "What's your name?"

A different uniform came through the door. This one was a firefighter, and he stayed only long enough to shake his head.

One of the officers stepped out into the lobby. I twisted around to watch through the glass door as he spoke into his shoulder-mounted radio. My brain wasn't working right. It took until that moment for me to realize what the firefighter's head shake meant. With a gasp, I spun to the remaining cop. "She's dead?"

He watched me closely and didn't answer, and that told me what the answer was.

"Oh, God." I dropped my face into my hands. "I should've tried—I don't know—could I have saved her?" My voice was strained and muffled against my palms. I looked up again. "It was dark," I said. "I couldn't see where she was hurt. Or even *if* she was hurt. I don't know what I could have done. What should I have done?"

"What happened?" he said again.

I took a breath to steady myself. "She had a panic attack," I said. "I guess that's what you'd call it. When the elevator stalled and the lights went out. She was making these sounds—I don't know—like a dog panting. I tried to get her to calm down. I told her that building security had to know what happened. We'd be out in no time. But it was like she didn't hear me. The intercom wasn't working, and it didn't seem like the alarm button worked either, so I called 911. I told her help was on the way. But she didn't respond. She was definitely hyperventilating by then. I was afraid she'd pass out. So I turned the phone light on to check on her. That's when I saw the gun in her hand."

I closed my eyes and took another deep breath. "I couldn't believe she had a gun. I didn't know what she meant to do with it. Shoot her way out? But then she was turning it, pointing it under her chin, and I realized she meant to shoot herself. I shouted '*No!*' and I grabbed for the gun. But she fought me. She fought me so hard. And then—and then—" I stopped and took another swallow of water from the paper cup, but it tasted of vomit, and I hurried to spit it out.

"She killed herself, you're saying."

I squinted at him. Did I not make that clear? "Yes!"

He took out a notepad. "Do you know her name?"

"Yes. She's Lucy Carter-Jones."

"Lucy Jones," he said, jotting.

"No, Carter-Jones. With a hyphen. It's one of those double-barreled British names, you know?"

He looked up, blank-faced. "Friend of yours?"

"She's the HR director of our company."

"What company's that?"

"CDMI." When he looked blank again, I explained: "Claudine de Martineau International. The fashion giant? We own most of the major labels around the world. Our design headquarters are in the city, but our administrative headquarters are here." I pointed upward. CDMI occupied the top five floors of the building.

"What's your name?"

"Shay Lambert. I work in the Law Department."

His eyes narrowed. "You're a lawyer?"

I nodded.

The other cop returned to the room. "CID's been alerted."

His partner pointed at me. "She's a lawyer," he said.

The two men exchanged a look, and as one gave a nod, the other pulled a laminated card from his pocket and began to read: "You have the right to remain—"

"Wait." My eyes darted between the two men. "You don't think—? No—she killed herself!"

He kept on reading in a monotone. "—silent. Anything you say can and will be used—"

"I tried to *stop* her!"

His partner left the room again and went into a huddle with two newly arrived uniformed officers. The three of them went through the revolving doors to the street.

"Yes, I understand my rights," I said when the officer was done reading. "I waive them. I'll tell you everything. I tried to *stop* her."

"Wait here."

He exited the room, but he didn't go far. He stopped and stood just outside the door. He was standing guard, I realized. He was standing guard over me.

# Chapter 2

The principal residence of J. Ingram Barrett, Jr., was in Rye, a classic white Colonial, three stories tall, its facade uplit with a dozen well-positioned landscaping spots that made it look like the star of the street. Another set of lights shone on the fountain in the middle of the circle drive that looped around to the front entrance. Thanks to a submersible heater, the water cascaded all through the winter.

In the master suite on the second floor, Barrett slept in a California king with his phone under his pillow. The phone was equipped with a bed-shaker ring, like those in alarm clocks for the deaf. This allowed him to receive middle-of-the-night phone calls without disturbing Melanie, asleep on the far side of the bed. Running a company with production facilities in Southeast Asia meant he often received middle-of-the-night calls, and Melanie wasn't pleased when it happened. As much as she enjoyed the income that came with his position as senior vice president and general counsel of CDMI, she resented any reminder that he had to work for it.

The phone shook him awake, and he pulled the blanket over his head before he looked at the screen. The caller wasn't on the other side of the globe. It was Jack Culligan, and since he was head of corporate security for CDMI, a call after midnight had to mean a crisis.

Barrett slipped out of bed and stole into his separate bath and through to his dressing room before he answered. "I'll call you back," he whispered, and disconnected.

He left by the other door directly into the hall and past the four empty bedrooms that nominally belonged to his children, though they seldom occupied them. He trotted down the helical staircase and skidded when his foot met wet floor at the bottom. "God damn it," he snarled as he caught himself on the newel post of the banister.

The maid was on her hands and knees scrubbing the travertine floor tiles in the foyer. "Sorry, mister. So sorry!" She crouched back on her haunches and cowered behind her upflung arms.

"Oh, for God's sake," he said. He would have preferred the cleaning to be done while he was at the office, but he knew that Melanie ordered the wet work to be done during the wee hours of the morning so as not to interfere with any of her activities during the rest of the day. "Relax," he told the maid. "I'm not mad."

He picked his way across the damp floor and into his office and closed the door before he called Culligan. "What?" he snapped when the man answered.

"Barry. It's about Lucy."

"Oh, fuck." He circled around his desk. "What'd she do?"

"Nothing. She's dead."

"Jesus." He sat down hard in his chair. "Where?"

"The office. In the elevator. Gunshot to the head."

"Oh, God." Were there warning signs, people always asked, and Barrett tried to think. There were certainly signs that she was bent on destruction, but he'd thought it was the company she was out to destroy, not herself. *I could burn this place down*, she'd threatened, which left him no choice but to remind her what the consequences would be if she tried.

"Did she say anything?" he asked Culligan. "Before——?"

"No. By the time they were rescued, she was already dead."

"Wait. *They?* Rescued from what?"

"She was trapped in the elevator with one of yours. Shay Lambert."

Barrett stood up abruptly. "Can we get to her?"

"Too late. The cops have her sequestered. And she's already made a statement."

"Saying——?"

"Claustrophobia. Panic attack."

"Okay." He digested that. "Where are you getting this?"

"Night guard chatted up one of the beat cops. By the way, they left me a voicemail asking for access to search Lucy's office. And Shay's."

Barrett thought for a moment. "Stall them. Get to Lucy's office. Look for a note, anything on her computer, anything. I'll go to her house and prep the husband. Send Lester to meet me there. We'll need to search there, too."

"Got it."

"Jack?"

"Yeah?"

"Did she give you any idea…"

"No. At least—no more than you."

Barrett bristled. "I didn't have a clue!"

"Then neither did I."

He didn't care for the CYA subtext in that remark, but now was not the time. "Report back after you've been through her office."

He disconnected and got dressed in the middle-of-the-night-crisis clothes he kept hanging in his office closet for occasions like this. Not that there'd ever been an occasion like this. *I could burn this place down*, Lucy had threatened, and maybe now, through her death, she'd done it. If so, the flames wouldn't stop with the company. They'd incinerate him, too.

He started for the garage, but before he reached the mudroom, he turned and went back to his study and opened the wall safe. Inside, under his passport and some cash and jewelry, was a single unopened pack of cigarettes. He'd quit nearly a year ago but kept the pack here as a test of his willpower. He was a man who liked to be in control at all times, even of himself. Especially of himself. But not tonight.

He slit the cellophane seal and tapped out a cigarette, then tapped out two, then put the whole pack in his pocket and closed the safe.

He lit up as soon as he reached the garage.

# Chapter 3

I tried to calm myself. A woman was dead. Obviously the police would have questions, and as the only witness, I was the only one who could answer them. The reading of the Miranda warning was nothing more than a patrol officer being overly cautious until the detectives arrived. And even then he probably read it only because I was a lawyer. I was stupid to mention that. Cops always went on their guard when dealing with lawyers.

I watched the proceedings through the glass door of the little lobby office. Two other cops assembled some panels into a screen and set it up in front of the open doors of Car 3. It was a crime scene screen, I realized. They were treating the elevator as a crime scene. But suicide wasn't a crime in the state of New York. Homicide was.

Another cop was herding three men in janitorial coveralls through the lobby. He had them sit on the floor at least twenty feet from one another. The witnesses were being sequestered.

Yet another cop was still standing guard outside my door. The suspect was being detained?

No. Of course not, I tried to convince myself. I was a witness, not a suspect. I was being sequestered, not detained. All of this was completely routine.

But my lawyer's brain was too analytical to overlook the obvious. There were only two people in that elevator and only two possibilities—suicide or homicide. The police wouldn't accept the first until they eliminated the second. That meant it was my job to convince them that I didn't do it. I needed to prove that negative.

I waited and watched, and everyone else seemed to be waiting and watching as well. In the long silence I became aware of the ringing in my ears. I wasn't sure whether it just started or whether it was only this moment that I noticed it. I remembered the sound of the gunshot so close to my ear. The blast had been deafening in that tiny space, swelling until it took up every cubic inch of the elevator car.

Car. Why did they call them *cars*? Elevators weren't cars. In a car you were in control. You could stop, pull over, get out, walk free. They should call them what they were. *Cages*. That was what it felt like when I was trapped in there, in the dark.

My hands weren't shaking anymore. Now it was my mouth that trembled, though if I clamped my jaws shut, I could hold it still. At the same time, though, the ringing in my ears was growing louder and louder. I wondered if my hearing might be permanently damaged, then I wondered how I could worry about something like that when I was lucky even to be alive. Our struggle over the gun had been ferocious—it was astonishing how fiercely such a small woman could fight—and it easily could have fired on me instead.

My hands started to shake again, and I clasped them together and held them tightly on the desk in front of me, like a schoolgirl. The best little girl in the class, that was what I always was, always attentive, always ready with the answer and my arm thrust in the air. Back in the days when that was all I needed to succeed.

Another image flashed through my memory. Lucy's eyes as I wrestled her for the gun in the crazy kaleidoscope of light that played up from her phone on the floor. Her wild animal eyes. Lucy had a face like fine porcelain— smooth and utterly immobile. But during those last awful moments it shattered into a million tiny shards.

New voices rumbled from the lobby, and I looked out as two men came through the revolving doors. One was young and short and wore a topcoat and a racing cap. The other was old and tall and wore a parka and a pair of ancient rubber galoshes. All the other men seemed to snap to attention at their arrival. These two must be the detectives. They were the ones I had to convince. My jury of two.

They stopped and spoke to the uniformed officers, and all of them turned and looked at me. The younger man was Latino, I thought, while the older one had the florid complexion of an Irishman. Or a drunk. Or both.

They ducked behind the crime scene screen into Car 3. They were in there a long time. When they came out, they talked to the security guard at the desk. The young one took notes; the old one stood and listened with his hands in his pockets.

They moved on to the janitorial workers sitting cross-legged on the lobby floor. The first one rose to his feet as the detectives approached. The younger detective did all the talking, much of it in Spanish, and he took all the notes. They moved on to the next worker and the next, with the younger one taking the lead each time. When they'd finished with all three, they said something to the officer standing guard outside my little room, and he came in and pulled the coats off the rack. He didn't speak to me or look at me but went back and passed out the coats to the janitorial workers. They shrugged them on, unplugged their machines, and wheeled them out to a van waiting at the curb.

Another van was unloading its crew outside. Men and women, two of each. Black and white, also two of each. They pushed through the revolving doors hauling big aluminum cases of gear after them. They suited up in Tyvek coveralls and booties and, after a brief conference with the detectives, disappeared behind the screen. They were the medical examiner's team, I guessed, or the crime scene investigators. The detectives stood and talked to each other for a few moments, then they went into another huddle with the uniformed officer standing guard over me, then at last they came in to see me.

They introduced themselves. The old, tall one was Detective Riley; the young, short one was Detective Cruz. I leaned in to their shields as they held them up for inspection. The letters swam in my eyes and I had to blink before I could make out their names. Riley was Joseph; Cruz was Carl. CRIMINAL INVESTIGATIONS DIVISION was emblazoned on both shields. CID.

"Ms. Lambert, is it?" This was the younger detective, Cruz. He was in his thirties, I guessed, and he had a neatly trimmed goatee and big liquid eyes like a waif in a Margaret Keane painting.

"Yes."

"Do you need any medical attention? We can get an EMT in here, or take you to the hospital. Whatever you need."

"No. No, I'm fine. Well, I mean—I don't need medical attention."

"Anything we can get for you?"

A few hours ago I was faint with hunger and almost delirious with exhaustion, but there was no way I could eat or sleep now. I shook my head.

"Is there anyone we can call for you?"

I shook my head again.

"Not your husband?" Cruz was staring at my wedding ring.

"No." I folded my hands on my lap. "He's—um—he's not reachable."

"We could send a patrol car for him," he offered.

"No. No, you see—he works nights. But thank you."

"Any friend we could call?"

"I wouldn't want to bother them. Not at this hour."

"Any other family?"

"No." When he seemed to wait for more, I added: "My mother's dead. I never knew my father. And I was an only child."

He gave a sympathetic nod. He didn't seem to be treating me like a suspect, or even like a witness. It was almost like I was a victim. In a way maybe I was.

The older detective, Riley, planted his hip on the edge of the desk. Up close I could see that he was much older. The skin under his eyes sagged like wet teabags. The hair on his head was gray, and so were the little tufts sprouting from his ears and nose, but his eyebrows were strangely black. They crawled like caterpillars across his brow as he studied me. "Can you tell us what happened?" His voice was an octave lower than Cruz's and sounded like a rusty rowboat being dragged over a rocky beach.

I'd had sixty minutes—maybe ninety; I didn't have a watch—to calm down and organize my thoughts and not blurt it out as I'd done before. My voice shook a bit, but I was able to relate the events coherently, from my arrival at the elevator bank on the thirtieth floor until the moment the doors finally opened on the ground floor.

Cruz absently stroked his goatee as he listened. "That musta been awful," he said when I was done. "You sure we can't call somebody for you?"

"No. But thank you."

He pointed to the two Tyvek-clad women hovering outside the door. "Some folks here need to come in and get you a change of clothes and take some photos. If that's all right with you?"

I hesitated. A victim would have no reason to refuse, and neither would a witness. Only a suspect would object, so obviously I couldn't. "Of course. That's fine."

The detectives left, and the women came in. They wore caps over their hair and face masks over their mouths and noses. It was like they were wearing hazmat suits, and I felt a reflexive shame, like I was contagious or contaminated. One of them had a camera, and the other was carrying little plastic containers. "If you'd put your hands on the desk, please," the first one said.

I spread my hands out, and she photographed them palms up and palms down. Then the other woman opened one of the plastic containers and removed a disc that she pressed against my right hand. It had adhesive backing, and I realized it was meant to collect gunshot residue.

The moment of the gunshot flashed in my memory. I could hear the roar and smell the odor and see Lucy's crazed animal eyes all over again. I could feel the heat, too, the hot metal of the barrel searing against my hands, and I knew that the test would be positive for GSR.

The technician returned the disc to the container and sealed and labeled it, then repeated the procedure with my other hand. "Stand up against the wall, please," the woman with the camera said.

Shakily I pushed back from the desk and stood where I was told. I tried not to blink as I was photographed again, full body this time, front and back.

"If you'd remove your skirt and blouse, please, and your shoes."

"What?"

"If you would, please."

*Cooperate*, I reminded myself. I had to seem cooperative.

They blocked the view from the door as I stripped down to my underwear, then they handed me a gray sweatshirt and sweatpants. These must have been their all-purpose, one-size-supposed-to-fit-all garments for anyone who couldn't come up with their own change of clothes. Apparently they didn't have any all-purpose shoes. Instead they gave me a pair of Tyvek booties like the ones they wore on their own feet. Then they bagged up my clothes and shoes and labeled them.

"Open your mouth, please." A swab brushed the inside of my cheek and around my gums. Finally they rolled my fingerprints and packed up their kits and left the room.

I sat back down at the desk. The clothes were too big for me, and the hood trailed down my back like a monk's cowl. The paper booties were meant to go over shoes, so they were too big as well, and rough against my bare feet.

I wasn't shaking anymore. The adrenaline was finally wearing off, and fatigue was creeping in behind it. I'd been up since, what, four thirty this morning? I'd arrived in the office at six thirty, and now it was—what? I looked around for a clock. I didn't even know if it was still today.

I felt a tremendous urge to put my head down on the desk and close my eyes, just for a minute. But I couldn't. I had to stay alert. I had to be on guard. There were only two possible scenarios of what happened in the elevator. Either Lucy killed herself, or I killed Lucy. Now that I'd been photographed and swabbed and fingerprinted and processed in every way like a suspect, I couldn't avoid the obvious anymore. No matter how sympathetic the detectives seemed to be, unless they were utterly convinced of suicide, they were going to default to murder.

I could see them out there in the lobby, conferring with the crime scene specialists. They kept glancing at me as they spoke. At last they returned to the room.

"Forensics won't help," I blurted as they cleared the doorway. "We both had our hands on the gun when it went off. So I probably do have residue on my hands, and the gun will have my prints and DNA, too."

Riley shrugged. "They're just routine tests."

"We have to go notify the victim's family now," Cruz said. "But we'd like to pick up our conversation when we get back. If that's all right with you."

"Of course. Whatever I can do to help."

"It's best if we talk over at CID," he said. "If you wouldn't mind riding over there and waiting for us."

"Riding?"

"In a patrol car. The uniforms will take you to CID and get you settled until we get back."

"All right."

"It shouldn't be more than an hour or two."

"That's fine."

That meant two more hours of waiting, after however many hours I'd waited already. But it would give me time to recover, time for the tinnitus to fade, time to shut down the strobing replay of Lucy's face. I'd have time to gather my thoughts and time to prepare my opening statement, my presentation of the evidence, and my closing argument to my jury of two. By then I'd be ready for them.

# Chapter 4

Lucy's kitchen was immaculate. All the hard surfaces were polished to a high gleam, with not a smudge on the stainless, not a crumb on the granite. She had a housekeeper, of course, but Barrett was certain that the state of this room was all down to Lucy. She was equally as anal at the office, with never more than a single document on her desk and often not even that. Likewise all the surfaces here were bare. The spices were alphabetized, the cans in the pantry organized by expiration date, the knives precisely lined up like miniature samurai swords on the magnetic rack. This was Lucy, all right. She was too fastidious for her own good.

Barrett's phone buzzed. It was the call he'd been waiting for. "Anything?" He kept his voice low. The husband was in the next room and the children asleep upstairs.

"Nothing in her office," Jack Culligan reported. "Nothing on her computer. Nothing unusual on the video."

Lester Willard came down the back stairs, ducking his head to clear the ceiling. He was all in black, skin and clothes, even down to his black latex gloves. Barrett directed the same question to him. "Anything?"

"No, sir."

"You got everything in place?"

27

"Yes, sir. House and car."

Barrett put Culligan on speaker so Lester could hear, too. The three of them comprised his entire crisis response team now that Lucy was gone. CEO Phil Duvall should have been here with them, too, but he'd made it clear that he didn't want to be consulted, updated, or even blind-copied. Plausible deniability were his watchwords.

"We can't rule out her briefcase and handbag," Culligan said. "But our man on the desk watched the cops search them at the scene, and they didn't react like there was any kind of note inside."

"Okay," Barrett said, but he knew it wasn't okay. It wasn't enough that Lucy hadn't left a note confessing everything. It wouldn't shut down the questions. A woman with no history of mental illness, successful in her career and happy in her home life, didn't kill herself for no reason. People would go looking for that reason. They'd ask questions, and other people would start to remember things, like how upset she'd seemed after that last trip to Myanmar, or how strangely she'd behaved at that seminar last month. Somebody would put it all together. He'd done all the damage control he could think of, but it wasn't enough. He reached for a cigarette and flicked his lighter, and as the flame burst out, he imagined the feel of it, licking at his feet. *I could burn this place down.*

"One more thing," Culligan said. "Our man overheard something. The gun? It was a ghost gun."

"What the fuck's that?"

"Homemade. They sell these DIY kits online, and any bozo with basic machining skills can put it together."

"Jesus. Is that legal?" Barrett said. Not that he cared, but as a lawyer he always liked to know.

28

"Legal to build, legal to own. It's only illegal to sell to somebody else. But Barry, here's the thing. There's no serial number. There's no registration."

"You mean—it's untraceable?"

"Almost always."

Barrett blinked. Suddenly there was an earthquake in his landscape of possibilities. "Hold on a minute. Let me think." He held up a hand at Lester, a crossing guard's command to halt even though the man hadn't moved. If Barrett could have a superpower, this was what it would be: the ability to freeze a scene and all the other players in it. Then he could take his time to think and strategize, maybe even peek into the others' files, and, when he was ready for them, snap his fingers and bring them all back to life.

He didn't need a superpower with these players, though. They worked for him. Lester froze where he stood, and Culligan remained obediently silent on the phone.

"Hey, listen, Jack," Barrett said finally. "What if it wasn't suicide?"

"What?" Culligan's voice crackled over the line.

"She didn't leave a note and it wasn't her gun. And she wasn't alone in that elevator."

"Huh."

"Lester," Barrett said abruptly, and the tall man snapped to attention. "Do we have to worry about Lambert? Anything she could do or say?"

"No, sir. She never broke protocol. Not once."

"But what's her motive?" Culligan asked.

"I'll take care of that." Barrett had long known that the secret to being a good lawyer was the ability to define the issue and thereby direct the avenue of inquiry. Instead of wondering why Lucy killed herself, people would wonder why Lambert killed her. They'd go looking in the other direction, and he could control what they found.

"All right, then," he decided. "That's our play. Everybody got it?" He didn't wait for them to answer. "Jack, any ETA on the cops?"

"They left here ten minutes ago."

"Okay. Lester's heading back in now." Barrett pointed him to the back door. "Pull all your background on Shay Lambert," he said to Culligan. "Pull the video. I'll meet you in Tech in an hour."

The call ended, but Lester still stood there in the kitchen, shifting uncomfortably from foot to foot.

Barrett pocketed his phone. "Is there a problem?"

"Sir." Lester cleared his throat. "She's a nice girl. She didn't do nothin' wrong."

"I know." Barrett heaved a sigh. "It's a damn shame. She was just in the wrong place at the wrong time."

Lester bowed his head, and after a moment, he gave a nod and slipped soundlessly out the back door.

–

Elliott Gutman was in the living room, slumped on the low-slung silk-covered sofa. He wore a turquoise brocade robe that Lucy probably brought back from one of her trips to Asia; it was far too flamboyant for a tweed-and-elbow-patches guy like Gutman. He looked like the academic he was—stoop-shouldered and concave-chested, with frizzy gray hair in a Dershowitz do and steel-rimmed glasses in need of some polishing.

Barrett cleared his throat as he entered the room, and Gutman looked up, his eyes red and brimming behind the smudged lenses.

"The police are on their way. Are you up for this, Elliott?"

"I—I don't know. What—what do I need to do?"

"Just tell the truth." Barrett took a seat on a chinoiserie chair. Lucy's decor was nothing like the English-country look one might have expected. Instead of cabbage-rose florals, there were embroidered jewel-tone silks; instead of cherry flooring, teak; instead of mahogany case goods, bold red lacquerware. If he didn't already know how far she'd renounced her British heritage, he could have guessed by this room. Displayed on the fireplace mantel was a collection of blue-and-white porcelains amid photographs of their two sons. "And the truth is," Barrett said, planting his elbows on the bamboo armrests, "Lucy never would have wanted to leave you and the boys."

"No. No, she wouldn't."

"She had a happy home and a good life."

"Yes—"

"Nothing was bothering her. Not at home. Not at work."

"Well—"

"Nothing out of the ordinary. She had a high-stress job. But she coped. She always did."

"Yes, but Barry—"

"Here's the thing, Elliott." Barrett sat down beside him and put a hand on his shoulder. "The police are going to be looking for an easy way out. All they want to do is clear their cases and close their files. So they're going to default to suicide, I guarantee it."

"Oh."

"I can't emphasize enough how important it is that you not let them close this out as suicide. Because that won't end it for you. Everyone will go looking for reasons. What drove her to do it? Was she mentally ill? Was her husband having an affair?"

"No! My God!"

"But people will speculate. They'll ask questions. And in ten years your boys will be asking those same questions."

Gutman winced.

"If the police think there's any chance the gun was Lucy's? That'll clinch it in their minds. They'll swallow this panic-attack nonsense and close their file. And you and your boys will have to live with all those questions for the rest of your lives."

"No, I can't let that happen—"

"You need to protect your children, Elliott. They've already lost their mother. Don't let their memories of her be ruined, too."

"No. But—"

"And not to be crass, but you're their sole provider now. You have to think of that. The company policy on Lucy won't pay out in the event of suicide. That's ten million dollars, lost forever."

Gutman's red eyes went wide.

The doorbell rang. Barrett gave him a reassuring pat on the back as he stood. "You can do this, Elliott. Do it for Lucy and your boys."

Barrett went to the front door and opened it. Two plainclothes cops were on the semicircular brick porch, one a sad-sack white guy and the other a dapper young Puerto Rican. Barrett sized them up instantly. A has-been and a never-will-be. They held up their shields and pronounced their names. "Is this the residence of Lucy Carter-Jones?" the younger one asked.

"Yes. Please come in."

"Are you her husband?"

"No. I'm a family friend." He stepped aside to admit them to the foyer. "Lucy's husband is just in here." He waved them into the living room and made the introductions. "Elliott, these are Detectives Riley and Cruz. Detectives, Elliott Gutman, Lucy's husband. Widower," he amended.

Gutman made a noise and buried his face in his hands.

Cruz looked at Barrett. "I take it he's already been notified?"

Barrett nodded.

"By—?"

"Building security. Is that right, Elliott?"

Gutman cleared his throat. "Right."

"Please. Have a seat," Barrett said.

They each sat gingerly in a chair facing Gutman. Barrett stayed on his feet, poised to swoop in if he had to. But he didn't.

It was an ordinary quiet weekend, Gutman told them. Their boys had a swim meet at the club that afternoon, and they all went out for pizza afterward at Vinnie's in Greenwich. After dinner Lucy went to the office to take an overseas conference call. No, she didn't own a gun. Neither of them did. She'd never even fired one. No, she didn't suffer from panic attacks, and she wasn't claustrophobic. No, she had no history of depression or substance abuse or any other mental illness. They had a happy marriage and two young children; there was no way she'd take her own life.

He broke down at that last part, the timing so perfect Barrett could have scripted it for him.

"I'm very sorry, sir," Cruz said. "How long were you married, if I might ask?"

Gutman swallowed hard. "Twelve years."

"She was British, is that right?"

He nodded. "Yes. Though she was born in Malaysia. Her family used to own property there. But she was educated in England and started her career there."

"How'd you two happen to meet?"

"I was speaking at a conference at LSE—"

"Louisiana State?" This interjection came from the older detective, Riley.

"The London School of Economics," Gutman said, pained. "Lucy came up afterward with some follow-up questions, and we continued the conversation over dinner, and we kept in touch as best we could after that. I was teaching at Princeton at the time, and she was in the London office of CDMI. After she was promoted to the headquarters office here in New York, we started seeing each other."

"What'd you talk about?" Riley said.

Gutman swung a bewildered look his way. "The usual things you talk about when you're dating."

"I mean at the conference. What was your speech about?"

"Oh. Monetizing human capital in the global economy."

"What's that mean? How to put a price tag on your workers?"

"No, no, no," Gutman sputtered, indignant. "Human capital refers to the skill sets of the workforce and their value or cost. I developed some metrics for use in making a comparative valuation in different parts of the world. But what's this got to do with Lucy's murder?"

The two detectives exchanged a look, and they stood up and pocketed their notepads and offered their condolences.

"Mind if we have a little look around?" Cruz said, like it was an afterthought.

Barrett would have allowed it, but before he could speak, Gutman shot to his feet, suddenly ferocious in billowing silk turquoise. "Yes, I damn well do mind. My children are asleep. They've lost their mother. Show some goddamn respect."

The detectives murmured their apologies and Barrett showed them to the door. But Gutman wasn't done with them yet. He called after them, "You're holding her, right? The woman who did this? You won't let her get away!"

They didn't answer him, just murmured their good nights and left.

Barrett closed the door after them and turned back to Gutman with a nod of approval. "You're a good dad, Elliott," he said.

# Chapter 5

They put me in a room marked Interview A, which I suppose was fitting for a girl who spent her whole life striving for A's—the perfect report card, GPA, SAT and LSAT scores, bar exam results, all the way through employee evaluations. Because where did all those A's lead me to but here, this narrow windowless room where I would soon be interrogated as if I were a murderer. I sat on a cold stainless-steel bench anchored to a cold stainless-steel table. Facing me was a six-foot expanse of mirror that I knew was a mirror on this side only. A video camera was mounted above it and aimed straight at me. I couldn't tell whether the camera was recording, and I couldn't guess whether anyone was watching on the other side of the mirror, but I assumed both were true. *Always conduct yourself as if people are watching you,* Mrs. Casco used to say, and this time it might literally be true. She'd been my guidance counselor, and she'd guided me from seventh grade all the way into law school, so I was inclined to follow her advice.

When I was first ushered into this little room, I asked for and received a cup of black coffee. I drank it straight down, laid my head on the table, and took a caffeine nap. I woke fifteen minutes later, exactly on schedule. But I felt only marginally refreshed. The technique used to work like a charm when I was at the Jackson Rieders firm. I worked a lot of late nights in those days—overnights, too—often enough that I learned to always keep a complete change of clothes in the office. But that was five years ago. My old trick wasn't working now.

On the end wall of Interview A was a large video screen. Above it was a digital clock. Two hours had passed, according to the glowing green digits. It was tomorrow.

On the other end wall of Interview A was the door into the corridor that led to the CID bullpen. I didn't know whether the door was locked, and I was afraid to try the knob. If anyone were watching from behind the magic mirror, they'd take it as a sign that I was being uncooperative.

But after two hours I almost wondered if they'd forgotten me. Something else was going on here in police headquarters. Something big. When I was ushered into my little room, the CID bullpen was a hubbub of activity. Uniformed officers were escorting young women to and from the desks of the detectives. Other officers were frog-marching shady-looking men in handcuffs. There was a babel of voices, mostly in foreign tongues.

I guessed that it was the aftermath of a news story I'd read online at the office this morning. Or—yesterday morning. According to the article, a multi-jurisdictional task force had conducted sweeping raids on dozens of motels and massage parlors in the tristate area. Operation Super Bowl, it was called, because the motels and massage parlors turned out to be pop-up brothels catering to the visiting football fans—men who were out for a good time every way they could get it. Some news accounts called the women in question prostitutes, while others called them victim workers. Which explained why the women looked both frightened and combative as the detectives questioned them. They weren't sure whether they were being held as victims or witnesses or suspects.

I could commiserate. Which one was I? If I were a victim, the police would have taken my statement at the scene and driven me home. If I were a witness, they would have taken my statement at the scene and let me go, just as they did for the janitorial workers. Those men weren't fingerprinted or photographed or swabbed for DNA. But I was.

*You decide who you want to be*, Mrs. Casco often told me, *then be that person. Visualization*, she called it. *Visualize yourself as the person you want to be. When you see yourself that way, others soon will, too.* In seventh grade, I knew only that I didn't want to be what I was—the late-in-life accidental child of a beer-swilling, chain-smoking, spandex-wearing, good-time-girl wannabe. But with Mrs. Casco's guidance, I soon figured out what I *did* want to be, and she taught me how to visualize it. I pictured myself as a superstar, smart, athletic, popular, the girl everyone wanted to know. By the time I reached ninth grade, everyone else saw me that way, too.

Now? Now I wanted to be a witness, only a witness, so that was what I would be.

Only a witness but also—the *only* witness. I alone could tell the police what happened in that elevator. I was here as a good citizen, a volunteer to help them sort through the evidence and arrive at the truth of the matter. I wouldn't be defensive or cagey, and I wouldn't be weepy or shaken, no matter how I might be feeling. My account would be the only one they would ever get. So long as it was plausible, so long as I was straightforward, they'd have to accept it as true. History was written by the victor, or so they said. I wouldn't exactly call myself the victor, but I *was* the survivor, which meant I was the one to write the history of what happened in that elevator.

The image flashed again in my memory, of Lucy's eyes in the seconds before her death. Eerily lit by the cone of light shining up from her phone, they were the crazed eyes of a caged animal. The smooth lacquered shell of her everyday armor was completely shattered.

I felt sick again with the memory, and I had to swallow back the bile and blink hard to clear away the image. I couldn't afford to be sick now, or weak. I needed to keep my own armor up until this was all over.

At 2:35, finally, a knock sounded on the door. It was nothing more than two taps, a warning that the door was about to swing inward. Still I called out "Come in!" Stupidly, like I was a lady in her parlor receiving callers.

Detectives Riley and Cruz entered the room. They'd shed their overcoats. Riley wore a rumpled brown suit that sagged at the knees and elbows. Cruz wore a sleek gray suit that was a little too tight through the arms and chest and thighs. He had the body of a fitness buff and clearly wasn't shy about showing it off.

"Sorry to keep you waiting," Cruz said as they took their seats opposite me.

"That's all right," I said. "I'm here to help."

Riley leaned back in his chair, while Cruz leaned forward and opened a folder. He stroked his goatee between his thumb and forefinger as he sorted through some papers. It was a habit I'd noticed earlier; I thought that the goatee must be new and unfamiliar to his touch. He took out some papers and slid them across the table. "Just a few formalities, if you don't mind." He slid a pen at me, too.

I picked up the forms and read them. One bore the full text of the Miranda warnings, followed by a waiver of my right to remain silent, a waiver of my right to counsel, and separate signature lines for each. I signed it. The second form was a consent to all the tests already done by the forensics team at Marketplace Tower.

"Just routine," Cruz said.

A retroactive consent wasn't routine. They were dotting every *i* and crossing every *t*, and I didn't know whether they were being so careful because I was a lawyer or because I was a suspect. Regardless, I signed that one, too.

The third document was a consent for a search of my residence. I hesitated over this one. I thought about the state of the apartment when I'd last seen it. I thought about David and whether he'd be there and what he might do or say if he was. "What would you even be searching for?" I asked.

"It's just routine," Cruz said again.

"But what specifically?"

He shrugged. "Anything that might connect you to the deceased. Your phone. Your computer. Anything that might connect you to the gun. Ammo, a gun safe. This is all just routine elimination work."

"The gun was Lucy's," I said. "Didn't you check the registration?"

"It's not registered. It's a ghost gun."

I peered at him. "A goat gun?"

"Ghost," he said, exaggerating the enunciation. "Homemade."

"Wow. Really?"

"So far we can't tell whose it was."

"You should tell the lab to check for fingerprints on the remaining bullets in the cylinder. That'll tell you who loaded it, which would establish who it belonged to."

Cruz glanced at Riley, who lifted one shaggy eyebrow. "Sounds like you know your way around guns," he said.

I saw the trap and sidestepped it. "No, but I read a lot of mysteries. You pick things up."

"Yeah, right," Riley said. "Between that and *CSI* and *Law and Order*, everybody's an expert."

"Anyway." Cruz looked uncomfortable with Riley's sarcastic tone, almost apologetic. "It turns out the cylinder was empty. And there aren't any usable prints on the spent casing. Or on the trigger."

"Oh." I considered that. No registration. No fingerprint evidence. Nothing to point to me as the owner or the shooter of that gun. "Well, it wasn't my gun," I said. "You won't find anything in my apartment to connect me to it. Or anything to connect me to Lucy beyond the fact that we work for the same company." I dashed my signature across the bottom of the last consent form. "But feel free to look. The key's in my purse. You have that, I think?"

"Thank you." Cruz put the forms in the folder and closed it. "Need anything before we get started? Something to drink? A bathroom break?"

"I'm fine."

He reached under the table, and a green light began to glow on the camera above the mirror. Recording must now be under way. The camera was pointed over the shoulders of the detectives, so that their faces—and their facial expressions—would remain off-camera. Only their voices would be recorded, and they'd be sure to keep those perfectly neutral, while my every expression, down to the smallest tic, would be captured on video. The face I wanted the detectives to see was cooperative, compliant, and above all innocent, and that was the face I tried to show them now.

Cruz established the preliminaries—time and place, persons in the room, consent form signed and acknowledged. He was doing the spade-and-shovel work of this interview, while Riley sat back and looked bored. I could see the dynamic of their partnership. Cruz was the young up-and-comer, eager and disciplined and by the numbers, while Riley was probably cruising through the second or third extension of his mandatory retirement date, doing little more than punching a clock until he punched out for good.

Cruz asked me to state my name, then my address, and when I named my street in the Bronx, I could see his surprise. He'd expected me to live somewhere better. So had I, once. Married? Yes, to David Lambert, and I could see his surprise again. Professional women of my generation typically used their own names.

"What's your maiden name?" he asked.

My birth name, I thought, but this was not the time to school him on gender politics. "Chance."

"Chance? Like *gamble*?"

*Like possibility*, I used to like to retort, but not this time. I nodded.

Next he asked about employment, and I confirmed that I worked for CDMI, in its Law Department, and yes, I was a lawyer.

"Where'd you go to law school?"

"In the city. Columbia."

"When did you graduate?"

"Two thousand six."

"Wait." He flipped some pages. "You're thirty, right?"

"That's right."

"Most people don't finish law school until they're twenty-five. You were twenty-three?"

I shrugged. "I skipped a couple grades."

"Wow," he said. Then, "Where'd you go to undergrad?"

"Brown. That's in Rhode Island?" I wondered if next he was going to ask for my résumé and two letters of recommendation.

"Ever work in a machine shop?"

"What?" I said, baffled. If we were in court, I would have said, *Objection. Relevance?* But I was here to cooperate. "No."

"Any experience in machining?"

"No. I'm not even sure what that means."

"Working with metal parts. Cutting, boring, assembling."

"Then definitely no."

"What about your husband?"

"David?" I couldn't help a short laugh. "No."

"You went to the office this morning—I mean, yesterday morning—at what? Six thirty?"

"About that, yes."

"And stayed until nine p.m."

"Yes."

"Long hours."

"Yes."

"And on Super Bowl Sunday."

"I don't really follow sports."

"What was the big crisis that made you work—what, fourteen hours?—on Super Bowl Sunday?"

"It wasn't any crisis. It's just a big case. And I'm still new to the company. I want to make a good impression."

"What's the case?"

"*Palmer v. Duvall*. It's a shareholder derivative action against the company's top executives, alleging waste and mismanagement in the operation of our overseas production facilities. The company's only a nominal party, so we're not exactly defending against the lawsuit. The executives have their own outside counsel for that. But we—the company, that is—have to respond to discovery requests, and that's what my assignment is. To go through all of the documents from the factories in Southeast Asia and organize them to produce to the plaintiffs' attorney. It's kind of a massive undertaking."

That was more than Cruz wanted to know. He stroked his beard while he skimmed his notes. "When did you start working at CDMI?" he asked next.

"Just last month. January second."

"Did you practice law anywhere before that?"

"Yes, at Jackson Rieders LLP."

"That's the big law firm on Wall Street?"

Big law firm, period. It had a roster of Fortune 500 clients and offices all over the world. "Yes," I said. "When did you start there?"

"September fifth, 2006."

"Until?"

"December nineteenth…" My voice trailed off.

"Twenty thirteen," he finished for me.

"No, 2008."

"Five years ago?"

"Yes."

"Where'd you go from there?"

"I took some time off."

Cruz paused and shuffled some papers. "What time did you arrive at the office yesterday?"

*Asked and answered*, I would have said if we were in court. Instead I said: "About six thirty a.m."

"Who else was there in your office?"

"No one."

"Were you planning to meet someone?"

"No."

It seemed he wasn't going to return to my five-year gap in employment. He didn't register how significant it was. An Ivy League–educated lawyer, hired by one of the top law firms in the world, didn't simply take off five years at the start of her career. There were no parking pads on that road to success. I glanced at Riley, but he didn't seem struck by it, either. Neither of them thought to ask: *What happened on December 19?*

# Chapter 6

*Don't be nervous*, David said.

But did he? He couldn't have, yet I could hear him speak the words so clearly. I could feel his lips nuzzle my ear and his arms wind around my waist as we stood at our floor-to-ceiling windows. I could feel the smile on my face and see the sun in its sparkling ascension over the towers of the city. Sparkling, everything was sparkling— the bright light of dawn, the polished wood floors of our brand-new apartment, the gleaming stainless steel in our gourmet kitchen, the decorator-designed Christmas tree in our living room, the platinum rings on our newlywed fingers.

This was how we greeted each day, beginning with our very first morning in the apartment, even before our first stick of furniture was delivered. We made love on the living room floor that night and slept there with our limbs entwined, then rose naked to the dawn and stood hand in hand with all of the New York paradise spread out before us. We were primordial man and primordial woman, I thought. We were Adam and Eve basking in our garden of earthly delights. I didn't say it out loud because David would think it was silly. But it was worse than silly. I knew that now. It was a jinx. Because Adam and Eve fell, didn't they? They lost everything.

*Don't be nervous. You're a star.* I could hear him say it, but he couldn't have, not when he was passed out cold in the sagging beanbag chair with his legs sprawled out so far I had to step over them to get from the bed to the tub.

Cold. The whole room was cold. I banged on the radiator, and it let out a single gasp before it lapsed into silence again. It was like the death rattle of a corpse. Three more steps to the kitchen, and I turned on the oven and opened the door and waited for a shimmer of heat to radiate out before I moved to the tub. At least the boiler was still working. The hot water met the chill air, and a cirrus cloud of steam wisped through the tiny studio apartment.

David flung an arm over his face and snorted once before he fell silent again. It sounded like the death rattle of another corpse.

*Don't be nervous*, he said, but he didn't. Not today. I was hearing an echo from five years ago. Time was all mixed up in my head today. My first callback in over a year and it had to be on December 19? How could it not be a jinx?

*Don't be nervous*, he said on that other December 19, but I wasn't. Not then. I had no reason to be. *You're a star*, he said, and I knew it. I woke up that morning early and eager, a rising star poised to accept all the accolades I was certain to receive in my annual performance review that afternoon. Certain because each of my supervising partners had taken me aside to tell me so. They'd even shown me the glowing evaluations they'd submitted to management. Their reviews were the equivalent of a 4.0—top marks, they said, the best evaluation they'd ever given. They wanted to stroke my ego, to show me how much they appreciated my work. The associates were all competing against one another for these evaluations, but the partners were engaged in their own competition, too—to snag the best of the associates to work on their cases. After all, a lawyer was only as good as his team. The law was a business with little value in the way of hard assets. Human capital was everything, and among the class of third-year associates at Jackson Rieders LLP, I was the capital capital.

I leaned back in the tub and submerged to rinse my hair, then stepped out into the cold and huddled under a towel in front of the oven.

If only the interview weren't today. Today of all days.

*Don't be nervous*, David said, but I wasn't then. It was he who was. He'd been nervous for six months and verging on panic the last three, ever since Lehman Brothers collapsed into the biggest bankruptcy filing in history. September 15, 2008. A date that will live in infamy. Already Wall Street was calling it the day the world ended. The Dow plunged. The housing market tanked. Unemployment spiked. The credit markets dried up, which meant that the merger and acquisition work that David's investment bank depended upon was dead. His bonus wouldn't be as lavish this year. His assured promotion from associate to VP would doubtless be delayed. He'd never worried about money before, but now he did, constantly. We'd overpaid for the apartment, he fretted; our student loan debt was crushing. Our liabilities hung like a black miasma over his head.

But I was sanguine. I was a litigator, after all, and my work wasn't threatened by the Recession, no matter how Great. When times were bad, the first thing anyone wanted to do was sue somebody. Litigation was as inevitable as death and taxes. My own year-end bonus would surely have enough fat to offset the lean in David's, and with a little belt-tightening, the bump in my base salary would carry us through until he made VP the following year.

That was what marriage was about, right? Pooling resources. Sharing the burdens. Neither of us could have afforded the apartment on our own, but the bank was happy to make the loan when we applied for it together. And we'd done a brilliant refinancing of our combined student loans: by cosigning for each other, we'd reduced the interest rate by two points, which made a huge difference on a half-million-dollar debt. *Joint and several obligation* was the legal term. We each owed the whole amount individually, but we also owed it all together, because that was what marriage was all about.

The law of unintended consequences: in five years our debt would be all we had in common and the only thing that kept us together.

–

My beige suit, sponged and pressed last night, hung from the clothesline that stretched across the room. I stepped carefully over David's prolapsed legs to reach it. I'd worn it with a black shirt for my first interview at CDMI, so today I'd wear it with a white shirt and hope nobody would notice it was the same suit. Once I had a closet full of designer clothes, but I'd sold them all, on eBay and in consignment shops, piece by piece, like an impoverished royal selling off her jewels. And realized almost nothing for them. It turned out designer clothes were like new cars. They lost half their value the minute you wore them off the lot.

I turned off the oven and pulled the blanket from the bed and spread it over David and tucked it up to his chin. I wished he'd wake up and say it again. *Don't be nervous. You're a star.* This was the first callback I'd had for a real lawyer job in over a year. I was fighting not to let myself hope, to steel myself against the pain of another disappointment. But hope sneaked in anyway, and the more I hoped, the more nervous I became.

"Say it," I whispered, but he slept on.

–

We met at a merger. two midsize law firms aimed to increase both their prestige and their average profit-per-partner numbers by pooling their personnel. I was on the litigation due-diligence team for Firm A; David was on the financial due-diligence team for Firm B. The closing was attended by more than thirty lawyers and accountants and investment bankers, and the conference room buzzed with a dozen separate conversations, live and through headsets.

David was busy running numbers on his laptop, and I was occupied with the closing document inventory. Still, I noticed him across the crowded room. I noticed the mop of golden hair, the square jaw, the nice bulge of biceps inside his shirtsleeves. I didn't usually go for pretty boys—*You be the pretty one*, Mrs. Casco always told me; *find somebody smart instead.* But I could tell he was smart, too, by the way the other men on his team listened when he spoke, the way they nodded when he corrected them.

But what I noticed most was that he was noticing me. It was more than noticing. He recognized me, and I, him. We could each see the glow of ambition that burned like a signal fire in the other. We could see in each other a clear front-runner in the meritocracy race. No legacy admissions for us, no family connections, no quota assistance. We came from nothing but were certain one day to have everything. We were self-made in the self-making. Golden boy, meet golden girl.

The merger closing was followed by a celebratory dinner, and the same thirty people exchanged the conference table for a long banquet table at an uptown steakhouse. We sat in the same scrimmage lines we'd occupied during the day, but after the starter course, David pulled off a sleight-of-hand shuffle that landed him into the seat next to me. As a dozen increasingly drunken and raucous conversations roared around us, we bent our heads low and spoke only to each other while our neglected rib eyes oozed red blood over our plates.

We swapped résumés but it was like reading our own. Both raised by single mothers always teetering on the edge of poverty. Attended public schools where we not only survived but prevailed: we captained teams, won popularity contests, and graduated first in our respective classes. Then on to college, Brown for me, Harvard for David, paid for in small part by merit scholarships and in enormous part by student loans. Then Columbia Law for me and Harvard B-school for David and another layer of student loans on top of the first. And now here we were, a first-tier law firm for me, a major I-bank for David. *Not bad for poor white trash*, he said, and I threw my head back and let out a laugh because I knew we would have the last one.

Before dessert, we found ourselves in the restroom, his pants down, my skirt up, our bodies coming together with the inevitability of water seeking its own level.

We never returned to the table. Instead we grabbed our coats from the hatcheck girl and ran laughing out into the street. A fine mist was in the air, and it beaded on our faces like dewdrops. David threw up his arm, and a cab cut in to the curb. "Shall we do yours or mine?" he asked.

I turned and looked down the avenue. The streetlamps, the traffic lights, the illuminated storefronts, the shimmering facets of the spire on the Chrysler Building—they danced and sparkled in the swirl of the mist. "Neither," I said, and lifted my arms like a maestro to take in all the dazzling beauty of the city. "Let's do ours."

He knew what I meant. With a smile, he waved off the cabbie and took my hand, and we plunged together into the night.

We wandered the empty streets for hours, talking, laughing, sometimes singing. Sprinting through red lights and splashing through puddles, stopping to kiss at every tourist landmark in the city. Manhattan was ours, and we were hers. We made our way south, like homing pigeons, to the Financial District. He pointed out his building, and I pointed out mine, and we heel-toe-walked the distance between them and declared we were practically neighbors. The night was ending by the time we reached Battery Park, and we ambled along the Esplanade as the stars winked out and the sky turned from black to gray and the boats glided ghostlike through the harbor. When the first fingers of sunlight began to steal out over the water, I leapt onto the base of a lamppost and swung circles around it while I crowed an exultant greeting to the dawn.

I expected David to laugh. I hoped he would join in, but he did neither. I turned and found him gazing up at me with a look of disbelief on his face. I felt suddenly ridiculous. I'd let my guard down. He'd seen too much of me. I climbed down.

"Eight million people in this city," he said slowly. "I never thought I'd find it. But you're it, aren't you?" His eyes were full of wonder, and I realized he hadn't seen too much of me at all. What he'd seen was himself. His perfect match. And I, mine. "You're the one, aren't you?" he said. "The one I've been looking for—"

"My whole life," I finished for him, and he threw his head back and let out his own cock-a-doodle-doo until I stopped his mouth with a kiss that lasted until the world lit up all around us.

We never went home that night, to his or mine. We were both at our desks by nine. But within a month his home was mine. Within a year we were married.

—

I pulled on my coat and glanced up at the window, where a parade of legs passed by. This was how I checked the weather each day, gauging the temperature outside by the proportion of bare legs and the precipitation by the splash of feet past the window. We didn't have a TV or Internet connection or even a landline telephone. Those were all things that were hard to get after your credit was destroyed by million-dollar debts. "It's like we're Amish," I joked the day we moved into the basement studio, but David didn't laugh. He didn't find me funny anymore. Or anything else.

It shouldn't have been so hard to be poor again, not when we'd been rich for only a tiny fraction of our lives. By balance-sheet measures, we'd never been rich at all, or even solvent. But poverty was harder the second time around. Crueler. To have things, then to not have them. To be admired, then ignored. To be full of promise, then empty of everything but regret.

–

I watched the feet of the world pass by. Men and women striding purposefully to work, to shop, to learn, to prosper. Everyone else had recovered from the Great Recession. They'd been retrained, landed new jobs, had their debts forgiven. The banks and insurance companies and automakers were bailed out to the tune of $700 billion. Too big to fail, they were called.

But I was small. Small enough to fail, and I did, spectacularly.

Outside, the legs were sloshing through puddles, and I picked up my umbrella and left.

–

That other December 19. We bounded out of our building hand in hand into the bright cold morning. The shopkeepers and doormen waved and smiled at us as we strode down the block. We were the golden couple of Chelsea, and so alike, David with his sun-bleached hair, me with my two-hundred-dollar highlights, he in his Hugo Boss topcoat, me in my belted alpaca from Barneys. At the corner we hailed a cab for our commute down to Wall Street, and one obligingly stopped beside us, our chariot awaiting. We got on our phones as we rode, David texting, me talking, our free hands entwined on the seat between us. My stop came first. A quick kiss goodbye, then he said it again. *Don't be nervous.*

I should have realized then, but I didn't, not until I arrived home in the middle of the afternoon. I unlocked the door and stopped short when I heard music playing in the living room. Bags of shopping sat on the kitchen counter, a magnum of champagne, a wheel of Brie, a dozen red roses.

"Hello?" I called thickly, my throat burning with unshed tears. I came around the corner to find David on a stepladder, hanging a banner across the wall of glass. *Congratulations, Shay!* it read. *You're a superstar!*

The tears came then. He jumped down from the ladder and held me close as I sobbed out my devastating news. "I'm sorry, babe. I'm so so sorry," he choked. It wasn't until I felt his arms trembling around me that it occurred to me to ask: "What are you doing home at this hour?"

We were alike in every way. He'd been laid off, too, way back in October.

For Wall Street, the world may have ended on September 15, but December 19 was the day it ended for us.

# Chapter 7

"I wonder if you can help us out with the timeline," Detective Cruz said.

I nodded. "If I can."

The detectives had excused themselves about twenty minutes earlier. When they returned, Cruz was carrying a computer tablet. He set it on the table in front of him. "Your building's equipped with CCTV, did you know that?"

I nodded again. "There're cameras in the lobby and in the elevator banks on every floor. In the elevators, too. Motion-activated, I think."

"Right. Well, building security gave us the feed from the thirtieth floor."

"Okay."

He touched the screen on his tablet, and as it lit up, so did the big TV screen on the end wall of the room. A video started to play, and I recognized the elevator bank on the thirtieth floor of my office. A blond woman walked into the frame, turned her back to the camera to face the etched gridwork of the elevator doors, and pressed a finger to the destination touch screen. The date and time stamp appeared in the upper-right corner of the video.

Cruz paused the playback. "Can you identify that person?"

"Yes. That's Lucy Carter-Jones."

"Arriving at the thirtieth-floor elevator at nine-oh-two last night?"

"And thirty seconds, if the time stamp's accurate."

"Any reason why it wouldn't be?"

"Not that I know of."

He resumed the playback, and I watched myself enter the frame. I looked a little unsteady on my feet, and I remembered how weak I felt last night. How tired. On-screen I glanced at Lucy, then I turned to face the elevator doors as well. Cruz paused the video again.

"Can you identify the next person to arrive?"

"That's me."

"You arrived at nine-oh-four?"

"That's what the time stamp says. It sounds right."

"Ms. Carter-Jones was already there when you arrived."

"Yes."

"What did you say to her?"

"Nothing."

"No? Look here." He rewound the video. "Right before you turn. See there? You look at her and your lips are moving."

I peered at the screen. "Oh. Well, I guess I said *hello*."

"It looks like you said *I know*."

"Does it?" I leaned in as he played it again. "I think it looks like *hello*."

"What did she say to you?"

"Nothing."

"Even after you might have said *hello*?"

"I'm not sure she knew who I was."

"She was the head of HR. Wasn't she the one who hired you?"

"Well, she extended the offer and did the paperwork. But I only met her then and one other time, briefly. It's a big company. She could have forgotten me. Anyway, she seemed preoccupied, so I just left her alone."

Cruz closed that video file and opened another. "This is the feed from the camera inside the elevator."

This video showed us both stepping onto the elevator, turning toward the doors, and standing in opposite corners. He froze the image there. My expression was impassive. But Lucy's face... Her mouth was open, her eyes dazed, her features frozen into a tight mask. She looked terrified.

"Let me ask you again," he said. "What did you say to her?"

"I told you. *Hello* or *how are you*. A casual nicety."

"Nice?" Riley spoke up. "And she reacts like that?"

"She wasn't reacting to me. I don't think she even noticed me. She obviously had other things on her mind."

"Obvious, why?" Cruz said.

"Because she was contemplating suicide."

He raised an eyebrow. "Before you told us she killed herself out of a panic attack brought on by the power failure. Which hadn't failed yet."

"But she must have been thinking about it. She had a gun in her purse."

"If she did," Riley said.

"She did." I tamped down the impulse to shout. I mustn't be antagonistic. I reminded myself—I was here to help.

Cruz resumed the video playback. It showed us facing the doors until the cage went dark and the camera cut off. The last time stamp on the display was 21.04.55.

"The 911 call was received at nine-twelve."

"Okay."

"Almost seven minutes later."

"Okay."

"Walk us through what happened during those seven minutes." I described it. How I groped for the emergency call button and pressed it. That I said something to Lucy—*Looks like we're stuck*—but she didn't say anything. How I pressed the button again. That I thought someone was supposed to answer through the intercom, but no one did. How I banged on the doors and shouted for help. How I even tried to prize them apart.

"What was Ms. Carter-Jones doing while you did all that?"

"It was dark. I couldn't see her. But I could hear her breathing. It sounded—labored. I asked her if she was okay, but she didn't answer. I tried the emergency button again, and I banged on the doors again. And when it was finally obvious that no one was responding, I called 911."

"On Ms. Carter-Jones's phone."

"Yes."

"Which you got out of her purse," Riley put in.

I swiveled his way. "No. No, she took it out. We were in the dark the whole time I was trying to get help. Then there was a sudden glow of light behind me. I turned around and saw that she was staring at the screen. *Oh, good idea*, I said. *Call 911*. But she just kept staring. Her mouth was open, it was like she was panting. *Okay, let me*, I said, and took the phone out of her hands. And then I called 911."

Cruz resumed the lead. "How much time passed from the 911 call until the gunshot?"

"I don't know. I couldn't even guess. It seemed like we were in there for hours." Hours before the shot and hours after the shot, too. It was those hours afterward that stretched out the longest in my memory. Trapped in that cage with the smell of smoke and blood.

"You had her phone. You didn't glance at the time?"

"No. I turned it off. The battery was almost depleted." I thought for a minute. "The guard, the other men in the lobby—didn't they tell you when they heard the shot?"

"Unfortunately, no. The janitors were running their floor polishing machines, and they had headphones on. The guard was watching the game on TV. Nobody heard a thing."

"Oh." That possibility hadn't occurred to me.

"So we don't know when the gun was fired," Riley put in. "How long after the 911 call. If it *was* after the 911 call."

"What? You think—?" My mouth dropped open. "No! Obviously she was still alive when I made that call. You could hear her in the background!"

"We listened to the 911 tape," Cruz said. "She never spoke."

"No, but— Well, I put the phone to her mouth. She must've— She was hyperventilating. You must have heard that!"

"We heard somebody."

"That was Lucy! She was alive when I made that call. I tried to get her to talk to the operator, but she was already in full-blown panic."

"Okay, so you made the call. Then what?"

"I turned the phone off, like I said, to conserve the battery. I told Lucy that help was on the way, but by then she was definitely hyperventilating. I tried to calm her down. *Take slow breaths*, I said, or something like that. *In and out, nice and deep and slow.* But she didn't seem to hear me. I reached out to touch her, to stroke her arm or pat her back or something. I kept trying to calm her down. I said, *Help's on the way. We'll be out of here in no time. Everything's fine.* You know, like that. But her breathing just sounded worse, and then it sounded like she was gasping, you know? And I turned her phone back on to use the flashlight to see how she was. She was reaching into her purse. I thought maybe she had an inhaler. Maybe she had asthma. But it was a gun."

"She had a gun in her purse."

I nodded. "I kinda reared back, you know? She was staring at it in her hand. I said, *Oh, no,* or *Put that away,* or something. Then she put it under her chin."

"Show me."

"Like this." I mimed a gun with my thumb up and index finger out, then turned my hand until the finger touched the underside of my chin. "I screamed *No!* and I dropped the phone and lunged for her. I grabbed her hands, and I pulled the gun out from under her chin. But she fought me. She fought me so hard. And she twisted her arms around, and my arms, too, and then it was like the whole elevator exploded."

"The gun fired."

"For a second I didn't know what happened. The phone was still lit up on the floor, and then she was on the floor, too, with her eyes wide open and a hole in her face and everything behind her splattered with blood. I think I screamed again. And then the battery died and everything went black."

I closed my eyes as the scene looped through my memory. As terrifying as the fight was, as much as Lucy's crazed animal eyes haunted me, it was even more frightening to be plunged into darkness, alone in the cage with her, while the roar of the gunshot reverberated through my skull.

"Then what did you do?"

"I don't know," I said. "Nothing. I should have checked for a pulse, I guess, or given her CPR? I don't know. I guess I was in shock. I pressed myself back into the other corner and stayed there until I heard the elevator start up. Until the doors opened."

There. I'd told the whole story now. I took a deep breath and let it out slowly. Cruz powered down the tablet, and the TV screen went black, a clear signal that we were done. I'd been holding my back straight the whole time, but now I let my spine relax.

"So here's my question," Riley said.

I turned a startled look his way and sat up straight again.

"Why didn't you call 911 yourself? On your own phone? The one we found in your purse."

"Oh. That? It's a pay-as-you-go, and I'd forgotten to top it up."

"Why didn't you top it up right then? You had a signal. All you had to do was add some money, and you could have kept the line of communication open until help arrived."

"I guess I didn't think—"

"And why are you carrying a burner phone anyway?"

"A—what?"

"You know what a burner phone is. Disposable. Anonymous. Untraceable. The criminal's best friend."

"It's nothing like that—"

"Then you must be on that dating app—what d'you call it—Timber."

"Tinder," Cruz quietly corrected him.

I felt my face flush. Cruz's questioning had been neutral, almost gentle. He was the good cop, and now Riley was stepping in to play bad cop. "I'm not on any dating app," I said. "I'm married."

"So what's the burner for? Drug deals?"

"No!"

"And where's your real phone?"

"I don't have—" I checked myself before I started to shout. "Look—" I checked myself again. For five years shame had kept me from ever disclosing my financial situation to anyone, but suddenly I could see that it might work to my advantage. Besides, if they hadn't already run a credit search on me, they soon would. "You can't get a real phone without credit," I said finally. "And I don't have any. So I use a pay-as-you-go. That's all there is to it."

Both detectives leaned in at that. "You're saying you're broke?" Cruz asked.

"Worse than broke, I'm drowning in debt. Student loans, a mortgage deficiency judgment, credit card debt. So, yes, I'm in some financial difficulty. Or I was, until I got this new job."

"So this job," Cruz said slowly, fingering his beard, "it must be pretty important to you."

I lifted my chin. "It's the most important thing in my life. I would never do anything to jeopardize it. I am eternally grateful to the people who hired me. And that includes Lucy Carter-Jones."

–

I was pretty pleased with my delivery of that last line, and when the detectives left the room immediately after,

63

I thought I might have scored a direct hit. They were probably out there at their desks right now running a lien and judgment search. They'd confirm that I was in debt and that I had no motive to kill Lucy. I was simply in the wrong place at the wrong time.

I thought of that old mystery-novel trinity of motive, means, and opportunity. The detectives had to check off each of those boxes before they could seriously consider me a suspect. Obviously opportunity was a given in this case—I was right there beside her, after all—but there was no way they could link me to the means—that is, the gun—and I'd just established that I had no motive to kill Lucy.

Quite the opposite, in fact. It was ironic that I had to pull out my poverty and desperation to do it. Those were circumstances that I usually went to great lengths to conceal. But it made sense, and it had the added benefit of being true. I *was* desperate for this job. I *was* grateful that I'd landed it. It was only the eternal part that wasn't true.

–

It was a scant twenty minutes before Cruz returned to the room. Without Riley this time, and he didn't sit down. "We appreciate your time, Ms. Lambert," he said.

His tone was more than cordial; it was warm. He wasn't just playing good cop. He liked me, I could tell. Not *liked me* the way cops on TV shows pegged their target perp, and not *liked me* in a leering, lascivious kind of way either. He liked me the way a nice boy in junior high liked the most demure good girl in the class. He wanted to carry my books and maybe introduce me to his mother. It was sweet.

64

"We'll be in touch if we have any more questions," he said. "You're free to go."

"Oh!" I surged to my feet, elated. I'd done it. I'd convinced them. But before I started my victory lap, I had to hurdle some practical concerns. "Can I get my clothes back? And my purse?" I had no car, no money for a cab, and I was wearing oversize sweats and paper booties on my feet. "And my briefcase!" I really needed to get my briefcase back.

"Sorry," he said. "We can't release any evidence until the investigation's over."

I peered at him. "It's not over?"

"Well—no." He seemed apologetic. "We still have to execute the searches, and run down the manufacturer of the gun kit, and interview the family and friends—" He caught himself as he seemed to realize he'd been too quick to share their investigative game plan with me.

And I'd been too quick to assume victory. I hadn't convinced them yet. I wasn't exonerated, and the case wasn't closed. They were simply sticking a pin in it for now.

I was due back at work in a few hours. Everyone there would soon know that Lucy was dead, and they'd soon hear that I was the only one with her when she died. If they didn't also hear *suicide* and *case closed*, I'd have to get through the day with a storm cloud of uncertainty hanging over me. And what if the detectives changed their minds? They could swoop in and arrest me at the office, probably during the pitch of morning arrivals or evening departures when the maximum number of coworkers would be there to watch them snap on the handcuffs and march me to the elevator. I wouldn't even get to clear out my desk this time. As humiliating as it was to be marched out of Jackson Rieders five years ago, this would be a million times worse. No, *free to go* wasn't good enough. I couldn't leave until I heard the words that mattered: *exonerated, not a suspect, simply a witness to a tragic suicide*— any of those would suffice.

"You know what?" I sat back down. "I think I'll stay."

Cruz looked flummoxed.

"You may think of other questions," I said. "I may remember additional facts. Either way, I'll be here."

He tilted his head to one side. "I gotta ask. Why are you being so accommodating?"

"Because I have nothing to hide."

He wasn't buying it. "Your run-of-the-mill bystander has nothing to hide, either, but they can't wait to get out of here. After what you've been through, I'd think you'd be champing at the bit to go home. So how come?"

He seemed sincerely curious, so I answered him sincerely. "Because it's a zero-sum game, right? There were only the two of us in that elevator. If she didn't do it, then I did. The second that gun went off, it became my job to convince you that I didn't do it."

He shook his head. "The burden of proof's always on us. Come on, Counselor. You know that."

"Not this time. This time the burden's entirely on me." I folded my hands on the table like I was putting down stakes. "As long as your investigation's still ongoing, I'm staying right here."

He winced a little. "It could be a long night."

"I'm used to long nights," I said.

## Chapter 8

It was good to be nervous, I decided, because nervous energy was better than no energy at all. I'd put in a full shift at Cubby's bar the night before, gotten home at four, and tossed and turned, waiting for David to stumble home before I finally fell asleep. I should have been exhausted, but nervousness triggered adrenaline, and adrenaline kept my eyes open and my feet moving briskly out the door and up the steps to the street. It was a ten-minute walk to the Metro-North station and a forty-five-minute train ride to White Plains, and I stayed awake and on edge through it all.

The Bronx scrolled by through the rain-streaked glass. Apartment blocks and no-name storefronts. Concrete abutments adorned with elaborate graffiti showing polychrome swirls, 3D effects, portraits big enough to rival Mount Rushmore. I marveled at the artistry. How wonderful it must be to have a talent like that, one you could exercise all on your own, needing nothing but a blank wall and a can of paint, no office space, no computer network, no conference rooms or business cards or HR departments. Whatever my own talent was, it was worthless without clients and a support staff.

The graffiti gave way to the cemetery. It seemed to go on for miles, 150 years' worth of dead bodies, many of them interred in ornate mausoleums that must have cost a fortune. *You can't take it with you*, the saying went, but somehow these rich people managed to, or at least managed to ensure that no one else would get it. Rich people could manage anything.

It was raining hard by the time the train pulled into the White Plains station. I stepped off and looked around for a clock and found it on the station wall. I was way too early. I'd left plenty of time to avoid any possibility of being late, but I should have come later and saved the peak train fare surcharge.

I lingered under the roof in the station and read the front-page headlines at the newsstand until it was time to go. I flipped up the hood on my parka and hurried past the taxi line and across the street. The rain fell in planes that flapped with each gust of wind like sheets on a clothesline. At least it wasn't snow, I thought for a second until David's voice spoke inside my head: *Stop being such a fucking Pollyanna.*

I wasn't a Pollyanna. I always knew how bad things were. But I also knew that David was spiraling too fast. I had to find some way to slow his descent. So I labored to find the silver lining in every setback, searched to find some way to put a positive spin on the negatives. It all backfired, though. Now David believed not only that his life was ruined but also that he'd married an idiot.

I *was* an idiot. An idiot to waste money on train fare for a job I'd never get. To shiver through the cold and wet for a job I'd never get, risking another bout of bronchitis for which I had no health insurance and no prescription plan. To miss my weekly plasma donation appointment this morning. That was twenty-five dollars, lost forever. To miss an extra shift at the bar this afternoon that might have earned me enough in tips to pay the electric bill this month. All for an interview that was a mere courtesy. At best. At worst it was window dressing for HR to conceal the fact that the job was already promised to someone with insider connections. I should have given up months ago, years. David had. But somehow I couldn't stop trying. Maybe he was right. Maybe I was a Pollyanna.

My first interview at CDMI was in November, a twenty-minute meeting with a low-level lawyer named Seth Salway. He was brusque and unsmiling throughout, and when a month went by with no follow-up, I had to assume it was a pass. Nobody bothered with polite rejection letters anymore. Nobody bothered to acknowledge receipt of a résumé, either, not even by a simple email. Unless I sprang for certified mail, I never even knew whether my application had arrived. It was like launching a message in a bottle into a vast and roiling ocean and hoping someone somewhere might come upon it.

But this time I got a call back. This time I had a shot, and my hands trembled inside my pockets as I stopped at the corner and waited for the light to change. A car turned in front of me, too close and too fast, and spewed a tidal wave of water onto the pavement. I danced clear of it and hurried on.

Marketplace Tower loomed ahead, thirty stories of glass, steel, and concrete. I pushed through the revolving doors. A two-story Christmas tree stood in the lobby, and at its foot, like an array of wrapped gifts, was a quartet of Victorian-garbed choristers singing carols to serenade the workers to work. I pulled off my coat as I passed them and presented my ID to the guard at the security desk.

He found my name on the visitor list and handed me a pen to sign the registry. "I found this on the floor over there," I said, handing over my coat. "Would you put it in your lost and found?" He'd probably give me the side-eye when I came back later to reclaim it, but my name was inside; he'd have to let me have it. And meanwhile I wouldn't have to disgrace myself by showing up in a frayed parka at a company that owned the best fashion labels in the world.

The building was a glitzy Art Deco revival, and the stainless-steel elevator doors were etched with a gridwork of black bars, an homage to the metal cage elevators of yesteryear. The back wall of the elevator lobby displayed a piece of mosaic artwork so tall I had to crane my head back to take it all in. It depicted men and women sowing seeds, turning wheels, hoisting timbers, packing crates— a workers-of-the-world-unite mural fractured into thousands of glittering glass tiles. If I hadn't been so nervous, I might have laughed at the irony of mounting it here, in a building that was practically a paean to capitalism. Standing between the banks of elevators was a high-tech destination dispatch console. It prompted me to enter my destination floor, then ran some kind of algorithm to calculate which of the ten cars should open for me.

"Car Three, please," a robotic voice intoned.

The doors slid open, and I stepped on. The interior walls were paneled in mahogany, and the interior doors were mirrored. The control panel beside the door didn't have any floor buttons, only emergency alarms. Above the doors a news chyron scrolled the morning headlines: *Global Stocks Surge After Fed Tapers Bond Buyback. 80 Injured in London Apollo Theatre Ceiling Collapse.* Christmas carols played in here, too, through invisible speakers in the elevator walls. There were probably invisible cameras as well. Nonetheless, as the elevator rose at warp speed, I pushed my shoulders back and lifted my chin and put my game face on. I visualized it. Alert, eager, self-confident, but not self-important. The kind of person any captain would want to pick for his team.

Then I gave myself a pep talk. Mrs. Casco taught me how to do that, too, way back in middle school; it was her advice for every new challenge I might face: *Tell yourself you can do this, because you can. Tell yourself you're the best, because you are. Tell yourself you own the room, because you will.* Mrs. Casco thought I could do anything, and back then I thought so, too.

I stopped answering her emails four years ago.

But I gave myself the pep talk now. It was my pre-interview mantra: *You're still a star; you can do this; they'd be lucky to get you.* I didn't believe a word of it, but it was like "Now I Lay Me Down to Sleep." The cadence alone had some effect, and when the doors opened on the thirtieth floor, I stepped off with a purposeful stride.

Another Christmas tree stood in the reception area of CDMI, this one decorated with a double helix of faux white doves. The white dove was the corporate logo of CDMI, and it appeared liberally on labels in fine clothes and emblems on sportswear. There were more white doves, real ones this time, in a glass-walled aviary behind the reception desk. They perched on the branches of make-believe trees and looked as bored as the young woman behind the marble-and-onyx desk. She was flanked by two female mannequins, one dressed all in white, the other in black. The receptionist was dressed like the mannequins, too, in black and white. She was Korean, I thought, and could have been a walking—

sitting—advertisement for K-Beauty. Or maybe she was Japanese. Whichever, she could have been a model for one of CDMI's premier labels. She was willow-thin, with full red lips and skin like glass.

The call to schedule today's interview had come from somebody's assistant, and I'd been too startled to get her name. So when I arrived at the reception desk, I asked for the same young lawyer who'd interviewed me last month. "I'm here to see Seth Salway?"

The receptionist's long black lashes curled up like an Akita's tail. They blinked. "I'm afraid Mr. Salway is no longer with us," she said sadly.

I blinked, too. No longer with us? This was fate's cruel joke on me, to kill off my only hope at landing a job. Or was it the company's cruel joke? Maybe this interview wasn't a smokescreen; it was a prank. "Oh," I said. "Well, I'm Shay Lambert—"

"Oh, Ms. Lambert." She perked up. "Of course. Please have a seat. Someone will be right with you."

I stanched the flow of relief before it could spread through my whole body. I mustn't let my hopes rise. I strode past the white leather banquettes to the windows and pretended to admire the view. The city was out that way, somewhere behind the wall of fog. Once it was the only place I considered working—Wall Street, the center of the legal universe—and I wouldn't work for anything less than a mega-firm with branch offices throughout the country and a few international offices to boot. Now here I was, desperate for a job in the suburbs, for a position in a corporate law department I would have sneered at before.

Hubris. I'd been lousy with it.

I could have collected unemployment, but I never bothered to apply for it, so certain I was that I wouldn't

72

be unemployed for long. Besides, unemployment was only welfare for losers and meth heads and fat slobs who watched TV all day. I had my image to think of. I also didn't bother to apply for any jobs at second-tier firms because I was certain to be hired again by a first-tier firm, and again, image. But that year and the next, the first-tier firms were hiring only the newly minted lawyers right out of school, the shiny bright graduates with no shadows on their résumés. The years of experience I'd already acquired, all my stellar evaluations, counted for nothing against the fact that someone had once found me disposable.

I landed a job, finally, doing document review for a litigation firm defending a Big Pharma company against thousands of product liability claims. It was trained-monkey work and nothing I could ever put on my résumé. I sat in a subbasement in Newark with dozens of other unemployed young lawyers all scanning medical records for certain keywords. The documents numbered in the millions, and each new batch was brought in by forklift. We sat at long communal tables and punched timecards like factory workers. *I can't believe I got a law degree for this*, my coworkers groused to one another. But they should have kept their mouths shut. We were all laid off when the work was outsourced to India later that year. The year after that, the Indians were laid off, too, displaced by robots.

My hubris was gone by then. I took any work I could find. I lied about my education and experience and pretended to be a young mother returning to the workforce. That landed me some clerical positions, then retail jobs, and finally warehouse work. But my loan defaults trailed after me like a bloodhound. Within weeks of starting each new job, a wage garnishment order was served on my new employer, commanding it to turn over ten percent of my gross pay. It never went over well. Nobody liked to employ a deadbeat, and besides, the garnishment paperwork was such a headache. My services were always dispensed with shortly thereafter.

The only solution was to work off-book, and that was what I'd been doing for the past year. My hubris was gone and so was my pride. Now I worked for tips only, serving drinks and getting my ass fondled night after night in a dingy bar. If Mrs. Casco could see me now.

"Ms. Lambert?"

Another woman materialized in the reception area. This one was older but just as stylish as the three mannequins out front. Her hair was cut in a sleek silver bob, and she wore what looked like a Chanel suit but was more likely a CDMI derivative. She introduced herself as Mr. Barrett's executive assistant, Marcia Post. Mr. Barrett was just finishing up his morning call to Paris, she explained with sublime composure, and would join me shortly in the conference room. If I didn't mind waiting?

J. Ingram Barrett, Jr., was the senior VP and general counsel of CDMI. I never expected to get a meeting with him. The hope rose like gorge in my throat, so thick I was afraid I might vomit. I smiled broadly. "Not at all."

I was like a stage actor, performing the same role in interview after interview, always a new audience but the lines were the same, and I could deliver them on cue and with opening-night enthusiasm. Actors might be jittery with nerves backstage, but when the curtain went up and the lights came on, they revved themselves up and dazzled the audience night after goddamn night. That was me in a job interview.

The woman escorted me to a conference room, apologized again for the delay, and closed the door behind her as she left. I sank into a chair and let my smile collapse. Ingram Barrett. I was meeting with Ingram Barrett. I mustn't blow this. I had to input everything I knew about him and calculate the optimal approach. I had to be smart.

I wasn't smart before, and neither was David. He was in finance, I was in law, so between us, we knew all the ins and outs of indebtedness. We should have been smart enough to figure the best way out of our troubles, or at least smart enough not to compound the damage with bad decisions. We should have been a check on each other's worst impulses. Instead we were each other's enabler and rationalizer.

That fall we'd booked a winter vacation in Bali, and after the ax fell, we convinced ourselves to go ahead with it anyway. *We'll lose our deposit if we cancel*, I said. *We need to keep our spirits up*, David said. Job hunting required self-confidence, and self-confidence required lots of self-care. That was the way we rationalized keeping our gym memberships and my monthly appointments at the hair salon. We dined out often, lunch, drinks, and dinner, because networking was critical, and again, spirits.

Our credit card debt snowballed. The co-op fees went unpaid, and so did our mortgage and student loans, and when we finally faced the fact that our debts were insurmountable, we convinced ourselves that the best course wasn't to contact our creditors and negotiate forbearance plans but, instead, to walk away from all of it. We moved out of the apartment in the dead of night and left no forwarding address.

The banks found us anyway, and they seemed to take our flight personally: they didn't merely foreclose and call it a day, as banks everywhere were doing with other borrowers. No, our banks pursued us personally for the deficiency and obtained judgments that would hang over our heads for decades.

My hands were trembling again. I clasped them together and took a deep breath and rose to my feet to survey the conference room. The wall of windows showed the same gray fog I'd viewed from the reception area. The other three walls were hung with enormous TV screens. Most of them were playing videos of runway shows from the latest collections of the company's major labels, but on the center screen, a digital slideshow of Claudine de Martineau was playing.

Photo after photo slipped past of Madame de Martineau back in her supermodel days, before she became one of the iconic fashion designers of the late twentieth century, before she founded CDMI. The photos showed a big-eyed girl with spiky lashes and teased-up hair. Her age was a fiercely guarded secret today, but the clothes and makeup she wore in the photographs were classic 1960s styles, which probably placed her well into her seventies. I knew from my research that Madame de Martineau now lived in virtual seclusion somewhere in the Loire Valley, but she still reigned as chairman of the board of CDMI. She was universally known as *Madame*, though no one knew whether or whom she'd ever married.

The slideshow lingered on her most famous photo, the one that once adorned posters in thousands of dorm rooms. She was nude, with her arms strategically folded over her nipples and a white dove perched on one shoulder. I studied her face closely. In each photo she seemed to adopt a different persona. In this one, a waif; in that one, a vixen; in the next, a warrior. She was a woman who'd reinvented herself in real life, too, from walking mannequin to celebrated designer to corporate titan. At every turn of time and tide, she'd been smart enough to take the temperature of the world and navigate the best route to the top.

I hadn't been smart at all, but I needed to be now, smarter than I'd ever been. I needed to process everything I knew about Ingram Barrett and navigate the best route to a yes. So what did I know? I'd studied his photo in the company's annual report and knew that he was balding and wore Clark Kent glasses. I'd studied his bio in *Martindale* and knew that he was Harvard-educated, the clichéd white-shoe, country-club corporate attorney with a big-bucks practice on Wall Street until he left it to become general counsel here. He still made big bucks—according to the SEC filings, he had an eight-figure comp package—but even so, not many lawyers in his position would give up the power and prestige of the practice he'd already enjoyed. He was probably on the speed dial of a couple dozen Fortune 500 CEOs. Why would he leave that to answer to a single board of directors and some notoriously litigious shareholders?

The answer to that question might be the answer to mine as well. I needed to figure out what factors made him take this job, then build the same factors into my own profile. If he could see himself in me, I'd be his ideal employee.

I left the wall of screens for the wall of windows. The fog was starting to clear over Manhattan, and I took myself there, back to my old firm, to my office on the sixty-seventh floor, to the library carts of client files that lined my walls and the phone console with half a dozen lines, the lights sometimes blinking on all of them. I remembered all of it, and I formulated what I prayed would be the winning strategy.

The door swung open, and Ingram Barrett entered the room. I turned with a practiced smile. "Mr. Barrett." I held out my hand. "It's a pleasure."

He was more attractive in person than in his photo. Power did that for a man. He wore a black suit and black shirt with no tie. He must have retired all his pin-striped suits and repp ties when he came to work for a fashion company. He shook my hand with a broad smile. "Please. Call me Barry. Everyone does." He waved me to sit as he took the chair at the head of the table. "I have to apologize for not getting back to you sooner. We had some personnel shifts recently, and your résumé got lost in the shuffle."

*Personnel shift.* A corporate euphemism for getting shit-canned. That might explain the departed Seth Salway.

"It wasn't until I happened to run into Joel Edders at a function last week that it came back to me." He slapped his forehead to show what a dunce he was.

Joel Edders was one of my supervising partners at Jackson Rieders, the one who gave me the highest marks he ever gave any associate, or so he told me. He was the only one to drop by my office on that other December 19. I'd been given an hour to clean out my desk while a security guard hovered nearby to prevent theft or sabotage. As recently as that morning I'd been entrusted with our clients' million-dollar secrets; with the stroke of a pen, I was recast as a common thief.

Joel came by to tell me why. AT&T had yanked their business, he told me dolefully, a client that accounted for ten percent of our billings. Unless the firm made some drastic cuts, the partners might face reductions in their draws. They already had permanent offers out to ten of last year's summer associates; they'd get some serious bad press if they tried to revoke them. So it was the current associates they had to cut, and third-year was the sweet spot.

As for why me, with my top marks and twenty-five hundred hours billed? Well, they couldn't lay off Matt or Jeremy, whose fathers sat on the boards of two of their biggest clients. Or Justin, with a baby on the way; they weren't monsters, for God's sake. And if they laid off any of their diversity hires, at least three other clients would yank their business for failure to meet their requisite quotas. *You, my dear,* Joel confided, his hands spread helplessly, *are a victim of affirmative action.* I never knew if that was the real reason or if Joel was simply a racist. Maybe both were true. *Keep in touch,* he said, but months later, when I finally forced myself to make the call, he didn't take it.

"Joel," I said warmly to Barrett now.

"He tells me you did some work on that derivative suit in Rand."

"Some?" I smiled. "I wrote the winning brief that got the case dismissed."

Barrett chuckled. "So he said. I read that brief. It showed excellent scholarship, which of course I'd expect from anyone in your shop. But it had that something extra, I don't know what to call it—" He waved a hand as if to catch the missing word out of the air.

"Conviction," I supplied.

"Yes!"

"You can't hope to persuade the court unless you first persuade yourself."

"So you believed in Rand's position."

79

"I always believe everything I need to for my client to prevail." Barrett leaned back in his chair with a satisfied smile. "I think you were up against Mark Ivins in that case?"

"That's right."

"Ever meet him?"

"Yes, many times."

"Any insights you could offer? We're up against him in a case now."

Mark Ivins was famous—or, in some quarters, infamous—for filing shareholder derivative lawsuits. Rumor had it he kept a stable of potential plaintiffs on tap, friends and neighbors and maybe even passersby who together owned nominal holdings in virtually every public corporation in the country. This enabled him to file suit within hours of any report of corporate malfeasance and thereby win the race to the courthouse. He was married to a DuPont, and the couple appeared often in the New York society pages. His wife was a painfully thin blonde with hair pulled back tight and skin pulled back even tighter. Ivins had a full head of gray hair and a dazzling smile. He was one of those men who shone with sexual self-confidence well into their fifties and didn't hesitate to flirt with much younger women. I'd been on the receiving end of his charms a few times.

"Mark likes to think he's playing you," I said. "He's enormously proud of his own wiles. And that's his Achilles' heel. He never realizes that you're actually playing him until it's too late."

Barrett laughed. "Like jujitsu."

"Exactly. Use what he considers his greatest strength against him."

"What I don't understand," he said, suddenly serious, "is what made you leave Jackson Rieders."

I leaned forward to show my eagerness to answer. I could make myself believe whatever I needed to prevail, too. "I did some pro bono work for the Innocence Project while I was at the firm," I said. "And one case in particular really seized me. A death row case down in Georgia. The evidence convinced me that the man was innocent, but none of the staff attorneys agreed, at least not strongly enough to take on the case. So I really felt I had no choice but to go full-time at the Innocence Project and handle it myself."

"What happened?"

I lifted my chin in a gesture designed to look both proud and defiant. "It took five years, but today he's a free man."

"Good for you. Good for you. But I have to wonder, with that kind of success, why not stay on and do it all again?"

"Truthfully? My heart was all in for that man, but not my mind. The work wasn't an intellectual challenge. I needed to get back to the complexities of corporate law."

"Then why not return to Jackson Rieders?"

"I always planned to," I said. "But when the moment arrived, I'd realized something. All that time working exclusively for one client made me appreciate the value of maintaining that kind of single-mindedness. Never suffering any conflicts of interest or divided loyalties or competing priorities. In my time at Jackson Rieders, I worked on a hundred and forty different client files. Sometimes as many as twenty at a time, all vying for my wholehearted attention. It took some serious juggling to handle it all. In fact, I wrote a software program to help me prioritize my work, factoring in deadlines, time required for completion, relative importance of clients based on billings, and so on. I'd input all that data, and the program told me what I should work on first, second, and third."

Barrett's eyebrows went up. "Genius idea! Where do I sign up?"

"Sorry." I smiled. "I wrote it on firm time, so it's proprietary to Jackson Rieders. I hear they're still using it today. My point is, working exclusively for Mr. Gibbons convinced me that I want to be all in for one client, and one client alone. A position in a corporate law department ticks every box for me. Intellectual challenge and undivided devotion."

"That kind of loyalty is worth a lot around here," he said. "We're in the middle of a big lawsuit."

"The Palmer case. Yes, I read about it. A shareholder's derivative action like my Rand case."

"Yes, and also brought by Mark Ivins. But this one really strikes close to home."

"Because they're challenging executive compensation. Of course. No one wants to be put in the position of justifying his own salary. It's like having to blow your own horn." I laughed. "Like in a job interview."

He laughed with me, heartily, and slapped his knees as he rose from his chair. "Shay, sit tight a minute, would you? I have to make a call."

He left the room, and for the next fifteen minutes, I was certain he was searching for his assistant to show me the door. I'd blown it with that interview joke. Or was it the Innocence Project? What corporation wants to hire a lawyer who's done nothing but criminal law for the past five years? But it was right there on my résumé; they knew it before Barrett himself decided to meet me.

No, it must have been something I said or the way I looked. My suit wasn't fashionable enough for this place; it wasn't fashionable at all. My wardrobe used to be the height of fashion, before I sold it, back in the days when I thought I could stave off ruin if I could just raise enough cash for this month's mortgage payment. Not that those clothes would have been fashionable anymore. They were all five years old or older.

A knock on the door. It was Marcia Post, Barrett's assistant, here to escort me from the premises. "If you'd follow me, please?" she said. At least it wasn't a stone-faced security guard this time.

She led me back to the reception area, but she didn't make the expected turn to the elevator bank; she continued down a corridor on the other side of the building. I sent a confused look backward. The receptionist was watching, and she showed a small smile when I saw that I'd been caught.

"Here we are," Marcia said, stopping beside a closed door. "Let me just see if she's on the phone." She tapped once and ducked her head into the office.

I stared at the nameplate beside the door. *Lucy Carter-Jones*, it said. *Vice President and Director of Human Resources.* The door swung wide, and an attractive, middle-aged blonde rose from behind a spotless desk. She smiled.

In the five seconds it took me to step in and shake her hand, the hope swelled up and crashed over me like a tsunami. It was happening. I was getting the job. We'd have a real income for the first time in five years. We could move out of the basement to a bigger apartment; we could hire a bankruptcy lawyer and discharge the mortgage deficiency judgment and work out a payment plan on all the rest; I could get some help for David; we'd get our lives back; we'd be ourselves again.

"Hello, so nice to meet you," I said.

# Chapter 9

A crew was at work Monday morning installing a metal detector in the lobby. Too little, too late, Ingram Barrett thought as he sidestepped them on his way off the elevator. Car 3 was still barricaded with yellow crime scene tape, and the office workers streaming in from the street stopped to gawk at both of these new developments. Some of them were getting out their phones on the spot to Google the news and find out what had happened.

He'd have to get a press release out soon. The Communications Department put together a draft overnight, but it was far too equivocal for his taste. After this morning's meeting, after things were settled, he'd take a stab at writing it himself.

The company limo was just pulling up to the curb. Barrett would have preferred to summon the detectives to his office for this meeting, just as he'd already done with the building manager and the elevator company representative. But Jack Culligan said it would play better if they went to the police instead. Culligan was retired FBI, so Barrett supposed he should defer to him in matters like this.

Lester Willard was behind the wheel of the limo. Driving wasn't one of his regular duties, but Barrett thought it best to keep a tight circle on this operation. The only ones who needed to know were the ones who already knew. These three plus Phil Duvall. It still rankled, Duvall's insistence on keeping his hands clean. As if he weren't the one who worked his magic to make the numbers jibe. But his role was limited to changing figures on a spreadsheet. It was Barrett and Culligan who had to do the dirty work. And Lucy, of course.

Culligan jumped out of the front seat to open the rear door for Barrett. As always, he wore a suit right off the rack. He was making some serious money here at CDMI, but he still dressed like a GS-13. Barrett liked that about him.

"Got the video?" he asked as he settled into the back.

"Got it."

The city complex was only a few blocks away. They could have walked there if the sidewalks weren't land-mined with patches of ice and sooty slush. Lester pulled over at the entrance to City Hall, then carefully backed up and edged in beside a dry stretch of pavement. "Stay close," Culligan told him as he and Barrett got out. Lester nodded, eyes straight ahead.

The metal detector was already in place in this building, along with a conveyor belt for their briefcases. They passed into the elevator bank and rode up two floors to the Criminal Investigation Division. The space was drab and utilitarian, cinder-block walls and industrial carpeting all in the same dull gray. CDMI paid a monumental sum in taxes to the city, but the lion's share must have been skimmed off to line somebody's pockets; they sure weren't spending it on office decor.

Culligan knew his way around. He spoke their names to the cop behind a glass window, passed through their business cards, and asked to see the detectives handling the Carter-Jones homicide. After a phone call and a long

86

delay that had Barrett tapping his foot with impatience, the cop buzzed them through.

A little fireplug of a woman bustled up to greet them. She was fifty-plus, with permed hair dyed an unnatural shade of red. "Linda Mayes, police assistant," she said in an officious tone. "Detectives Riley and Cruz are busy just now, but if you want to wait—"

"We'll wait," Culligan said.

"For a bit," Barrett clarified.

She showed them into a room marked Interview B. After she left, Barrett pointed to the mirror on the wall. "Is that what I think it is?"

Culligan nodded and pointed to the camera above it. They took their seats and took out their phones and didn't speak another word to each other.

In fifteen minutes, the detectives came in. They were the same pair who'd visited Elliott Gutman last night, which meant they must have been racking up some serious overtime. Culligan shook their hands and told them his name and title, and Barrett started to do the same.

"We met already, Mr. Barrett," Detective Riley said, putting his hands in his pockets. "Funny you didn't mention then that you were Ms. Carter-Jones's boss. *Family friend* is all you said."

Barrett was unfazed by the dig and mildly amused by the snub of his handshake. "That's because work didn't even cross my mind at the time. Lucy wasn't only a colleague; she was a dear friend. This tragedy really hit hard."

"Of course." Riley made a sad face. "How long had she been depressed?"

Barrett suppressed a laugh at the old cop's feeble attempt to trip him up. "It wasn't suicide," he said. "Shay

Lambert killed her. And we can prove it. Gentlemen, please." He waved at the chairs opposite him. "Have a seat."

Riley and Cruz rolled their eyes at each other in a *can you believe this guy* look, but they pulled out their chairs and sat down.

"You've already seen the CCTV from building management?" Culligan said.

The cops nodded like the effort was costing them something. *You clowns work for me*, Barrett felt like telling them. But he held his tongue as Culligan opened his laptop and hit a button. "CDMI has its own surveillance system in all the public areas of our space," Culligan said as an image opened on the screen. "This is the corridor outside Lucy's office."

Cruz leaned in to read the time stamp. 02.02.14 20.36.48. "About eight thirty last night?"

"Correct. Watch."

Culligan pushed another button and launched the video. The detectives leaned forward to watch as an office door opened. "It's motion-activated," Culligan explained.

On-screen, Shay Lambert stepped out of the office into the corridor and closed the door behind her. She sagged against the wall with her hands over her face. The image resolution wasn't perfect, but when she took her hands away, tears were visibly rolling down her cheeks. She drew a breath and scrubbed her fists across her cheeks, then she hurried down the corridor, turned a corner, and disappeared.

Culligan paused the video.

"Lucy had just terminated her employment," Barrett said. The detectives leaned back in their chairs. Cruz folded his arms over his chest. "How do you know that?"

"Because I told her to do it."

"Because—?"

"I discovered that Shay lied on her résumé. We had plenty of highly qualified applicants for this position. I hired Shay for one reason and one reason only. Her résumé listed a clerkship with Judge Wendell Arnold on the Second Circuit. Judge Arnold had an amazing knack for picking the best and the brightest and training them well. All of his clerks went on to brilliant careers. I know because I was one of them."

"But she wasn't?"

Barrett shook his head in disgust. "The judge passed away last year, and we had a memorial for him Saturday night in the city. Fifty of us former clerks made the trip, from all around the country. I asked Shay if she was going, but she said she had a prior engagement. At the party there was a slide show of all of Judge Arnold's clerks through the decades, and when Shay wasn't in it, I went looking for answers. Turns out she never clerked for Arnold. No one had ever even heard of her. She made it up to get her foot in my door. So I called Lucy at home yesterday. I wanted this impostor out before the workweek began."

"We knew from Lambert's keycard swipe that she was in the office yesterday," Culligan said. "So Ms. Carter-Jones agreed to go in and take care of it."

Cruz looked at him. "You're the security chief, right?"

"Right."

"And you involve yourself in personnel matters?"

"It's protocol in a discharge situation. I had a team standing by."

"Not close enough, it looks like," Riley said.

Culligan looked appropriately abashed. "She was supposed to call me if she ran into any trouble."

"We'll need a copy of that video," Cruz said.

Culligan pulled out the flash drive and slid it across the table. At the same moment Barrett pulled a document from his briefcase. "Affidavits establishing authenticity and chain of custody," he said.

Riley looked askance as Cruz took the documents. "You really wrapped this up with a bow for us, didn't you?"

"We want justice for Lucy. We'll do whatever we can to accomplish that."

"We'll need to see the rest of your surveillance from last night, too," Cruz said. "Where Lambert went after that, what she did, where Carter-Jones went. Movements of both of them from eight thirty-six until they stepped on the elevator."

Barrett looked to Culligan, who nodded. "Like I said, the system is motion-activated and only in the public spaces, so it won't be continuous. But we'll pull it together."

Barrett nodded and got to his feet, a signal that the meeting was adjourned. But Cruz was giving him a skeptical look. "She'd have to be an idiot," he said. "To pick that moment to commit murder. Stuck in an elevator with no escape route."

"Or a genius," Barrett said, "if she sells you guys on suicide."

"Genius enough to sabotage the elevator, too?"

He shrugged. "Talk to the elevator company. Their engineers tell me the power went out because a breaker tripped. That happens. But the emergency backup system failed, too. That shouldn't have happened. It was a software malfunction, they tell me. And Shay's a software whiz."

"C'mon," Cruz scoffed. "She hacked the system?"

"Maybe. She wrote a software program for her old law firm that they're still using today. She's a smart girl, Detectives. You shouldn't put anything past her."

# Chapter 10

It wasn't simply a job that I was desperate for. I was desperate to work. I wanted to release the parking brake on my career, put my brain back in gear, and stomp my foot all the way to the floor. That was Mrs. Casco's analogy. *Your brain is a high-performance engine*, she used to say. *You need to open it up and let it roar.* For the past few years it had been more like a hand-pushed lawnmower. My biggest workday dilemmas had been *paper or plastic* or *cash or card*. So now I couldn't wait to hit the gas and see how fast and far I could go.

But I had to wait. When I reported for duty bright and early January 2, the CDMI reception area was dark and the desk unattended. Behind the glass wall of the aviary, the doves perched with their beaks tucked to their breasts and their eyes closed. I hovered uncertainly beside the all-white mannequin. After ten minutes the elevator chimed, and when two men in suits strode off, I stepped out with a bright "Hello?" One mumbled "Morning" and walked on. The other nodded and walked on.

I moved to the all-black mannequin and hovered there awhile until I gave up and sat down on the white leather banquette. My new-hire form listed January 2 as my start date, but nowhere did it mention my start time. I'd obviously arrived too early.

When the elevator chimed again and discharged a trio, I rose to my feet with an expectant smile, but they all walked past without acknowledging me. I sat back down.

At ten o'clock the K-Beauty receptionist finally arrived, weaving an unsteady path from the elevator to her desk. I would have blamed her razor-thin stilettos for the wobble, but when she turned around, I could see that the slit of eyeball showing between her Akita lashes was bloodshot. Her New Year's Eve celebration must have lasted all the way through New Year's Day. She sat down behind the desk with a moan and stared at her computer as if waiting for it to turn itself on.

I stood up. "Hello. I'm Shay Lambert. I'm starting here today?"

The girl slowly blinked her gaze upward. "Uh, starting what?"

"Employment. I'm a new hire in the Law Department."

She stared. "Huh. Where are you supposed to go?"

"I'm not sure." I spoke pleasantly; I knew better than to antagonize the staff by showing impatience on my first day. "Perhaps you could ask Mr. Barrett's assistant?"

"Oh. Right." The girl picked up the phone and stared blearily at the keypad before tapping in some numbers. "Somebody's here," she said into the phone. "Says she's a new hire?"

She hung up, and when she spoke again it was with the assurance of an actor reciting a well-rehearsed line. "Please have a seat. Someone will be with you shortly."

I stayed on my feet, and soon Barrett's assistant rushed into the reception area. It was Marcia Post, the woman who'd displayed such elegant composure on my last visit. Now she seemed flustered. Her silver hair was frizzed, and her suit jacket was askew. There was one solitary button up top and one solitary buttonhole gaping loose at the bottom.

"Ms. Lambert—Shay—I'm so sorry! Mr. Barrett was unexpectedly called to Kuala Lumpur over the holiday, and I'm afraid—well, it was all so sudden—I'm afraid he didn't leave any instructions for—for"—she let out a nervous laugh—"well, for what we're to do with you."

"Oh."

The woman looked at her watch. "And of course, he can't be reached in KL at this hour, so I'm afraid—" She spread her hands helplessly.

"Oh," I said again. I wondered if I was supposed to go home. I wondered if I'd still get paid for today if I did.

"It says here"—behind Marcia Post, the receptionist was struggling to focus on her computer screen—"that she's going to be in 3018."

"Oh!" Marcia Post gasped with relief, as if everything was now solved. "Your office! Of course. Let me take you there."

She led me in a long circuit around the perimeter of the floor to the east-facing side of the building. The office doors were closer together along this corridor, and a faint buzz hummed from behind some of them. Worker bees, I thought, all toiling in their cells in the hive. But at least they had cells. At least they had work.

The woman stopped beside a closed door. An empty nameplate bracket was mounted to the wall beside it. "And here we have your new home away from home," she said, and with a bright smile swung the door inward.

The door met resistance halfway through its arc. A stack of file boxes stood in its path. The office was prison cell–size, and the desktop, windowsill, and most of the floor were taken up with stacks of boxes.

"Oh, dear." The woman's smile fell. "It hasn't been set up. Or cleaned," she added with a recoil at the layer of dust on the desk and windowsill. "I'll have to call someone…" Her voice trailed off.

Once I would have been dismayed, too. But I looked past the dust and the clutter and the obvious fact that the space was in service as a storeroom. I looked past it all to the window. The glass was grimy, but through it I could see out over the city from a height of thirty stories. It was my window. This was my office, and they were going to pay me to come and work here every day, and I loved it as much as I once loved our sparkling Chelsea apartment.

"No need," I said, crossing the threshold. "I'll take care of it. I'll take care of everything."

–

I found the supply closet and the cleaning products and an empty office next door that I could shift the boxes to. They all bore international shipping labels, from such exotic locales as Kuala Lumpur and Yangon and Chiang Mai. After I wheeled them on a handcart to their new home, I unsealed one for a peek at its contents. Up rose a musty, spicy scent, like stale chai or a perfume gone rancid. But there were only documents inside, in English mostly, invoices and purchase orders and inventory spreadsheets. Routine business documents from factories abroad.

I polished my desk and dusted the windowsill and foraged through the supply closet for a stapler and tape dispenser, pens and legal pads. The office wasn't yet equipped with a computer or even a telephone, but within an hour my desk was otherwise set up. I adjusted the chair height and tried it out. It squeaked when I rolled back, so I returned to the supply closet for some WD-40 and flipped the chair upside down on a mat of paper towels. I was on my knees behind the desk when Marcia Post reappeared at the door.

"Oh," she said, stopping abruptly. "My."

I looked up from the floor. "Yes?"

Her suit jacket was buttoned correctly now, and her hair was smooth. She'd regained her composure. "I've heard from Mr. Barrett. He does apologize for all the confusion, but he's gotten it all organized, even though it's midnight in KL." Her tone was one of admiration that anyone could accomplish so much at such an hour. "Tomorrow the IT staff will be here to install your phone and computer, and here's your employee manual"—she placed a three-ring binder on the desk—"and meanwhile you have a full schedule of orientation activities ahead." She placed a memo on top of the binder.

I scanned it. "Beginning tomorrow."

"Yes. So there's no need for you to stay here today."

"I wonder…" I got to my feet. "Perhaps I could go around and meet some of the people in the Law Department?" There were a dozen other in-house lawyers I knew of, specializing in such fields as real estate transactions, securities compliance, trademark enforcement, and labor law. It was like its own mini law firm.

"Oh, there's no need for that. Since you'll be working directly with Mr. Barrett on the Palmer case. So feel free to go home. Start fresh tomorrow." With a parting smile, the woman glided away.

I stayed at my desk. I didn't like the idea of a false start. It made me nervous, as if the job might disappear if I didn't get my hooks solidly into it today. I read the employee manual from cover to cover, then cast about for something productive to do. I recalled seeing copies of the company's annual reports in the reception area, and even though I'd already studied the public filings online, I went out and fetched the glossy publications from the coffee table and brought them back to my office to read again.

Lunch was an apple, sliced, spread with peanut butter I carried in a little tub. The cover of the latest report showed a white dove swooping over Planet Earth. Inside was a photo of the chairman of the board, Claudine de Martineau. It wasn't one of her flashback modeling photos, but it wasn't recent, either. Her hair was black, and her lips were full and red, and she stood next to a dressmaker's dummy with a tape measure around her neck.

Page after page showed glossy photos of beautiful people in beautiful clothes, interspersed with glossy photos of clean and modern manufacturing facilities. Then came the matte pages with no photos, only numbers and charts with lines moving in the wrong direction. There'd been some losses over the last several quarters, the board acknowledged in its letter to shareholders, but significant steps had been taken to cut costs, and management was confident the losses had been stemmed. Principal among the cost-cutting moves was the recent closing of Paradis sur Terre, the company's manufacturing facility in Myanmar. Not only would that slash expenses dramatically, but they'd been enormously successful in selling off the equipment and inventory and other capital items from that facility, realizing much more than the original cost. The printed materials included a press release to that effect, in which Madame de Martineau was quoted as saying, "We've turned the proverbial sow's ear into a silk purse. Which is nothing less than you'd expect from a fashion giant like CDMI."

The Paradis sur Terre facility was much ballyhooed in the three annual reports preceding that one. The standard business model in the garment industry was to sub out production to independent contractors, most of them small sewing factories in Southeast Asia. Many of them were notorious sweatshops. CDMI was determined to break that mold and to end the abhorrent conditions by eventually moving all its production in-house.

Paradis sur Terre was the first step in that plan. It was designed to be a world-class manufacturing facility carved out of the jungles of Myanmar, incorporating the latest technological advances in equipment. It was also designed to be a model for the best practices in employee well-being. Because the factory was so remote from any town or village, the company built on-site dining halls and dormitories for the workers that were so clean and modern—and air-conditioned!—that they almost rivaled some of the seaside resorts in the region. When the job postings went up, the company was flooded with applicants. As a result it was able to hire the best, most skilled workers, two thousand of them, who all happily relocated to Paradise on Earth. They even brought their families with them; many of the photos showed young children sitting with their parents at the long communal dining tables.

I thought it sounded wonderful. It was grand and experimental and could have become a paragon of manufacturing for the future. It should have been allowed more time to get established and eventually turn a profit. But the stockholders were a short-sighted bunch. Many of their grievances in the Palmer lawsuit focused on the losses at Paradis sur Terre. The shareholders attacked management for green-lighting the factory, complaining that it was nothing but a vanity project for Madame de Martineau. That it was a drain on company resources. They wanted quick returns, not long-term advancements, and their greed had doomed this little piece of paradise.

I had to laugh at the thoughts in my head. Already I was living up to my interview hype and believing whatever I needed to believe for my client to prevail. But I was fine with that. If it meant I could work again, I was more than happy to drink the CDMI Kool-Aid.

Some of the file boxes I'd wheeled next door had been shipped from Myanmar and labeled PsT. Now I realized that referred to Paradis sur Terre. If so, those files might be relevant to my work on the Palmer case. I could get started right away.

I went next door and unsealed the boxes. Inside the first several boxes were expense reports—invoices and payroll records and utility bills and the like. Another set of boxes held capital cost documentation reflecting the purchase and installation of factory equipment such as pressing machines, robotic cutting machines, and many hundreds of industrial sewing machines. Heavy equipment was in there, too—conveyor systems and speed rails, generators, forklifts, trucks. There were also thick binders of the closing documents for a number of real estate transactions. It seemed that CDMI had purchased the tracts of land for the PsT site from the local military establishment.

A third set of boxes held reports titled "Liquidation Proceeds 2013," and the attached backup included bills of sale for the factory equipment and more closing documents for the various parcels of real estate, including all improvements and fixtures thereon. The documents in another box reflected the sale of raw materials and of inventory, finished and unfinished.

Also in that box were charter contracts with an air carrier called APU Transport, and I could see at once that they'd been misfiled. These documents had nothing to do with the sell-off of company assets. Instead they showed the company's outlays for passenger transport from PsT to various other points in Southeast Asia over several weeks in the fourth quarter of 2013. Apparently the company had chartered private jets on six occasions for one-way trips from its airstrip in PsT to Songkhla and Chiang Mai in Thailand and to Pontianak in Indonesia. Attached to each charter contract was a passenger manifest listing scores of Asian names.

I started to refile the air charter contracts where they actually belonged, with Expenses, in the first set of documents. But I checked myself. There might be some reason I couldn't guess for filing them where they were. I put them back in the Liquidation Proceeds box, but just to be safe, I made copies and tucked them into one of my desk drawers for easy access should anyone ever question why the charter documents weren't filed correctly.

I had a sudden worry that I might have already disturbed the filing system. Although the boxes seemed to have been haphazardly stacked in my office, it was possible that whoever had put them there had some kind of order in mind. Again, just to be safe, I took a legal pad next door and made a complete inventory of the contents of every box. It wouldn't be a wasted effort if these boxes turned out to have anything to do with the Palmer case, and in any event, it consumed the rest of the day.

At seven o'clock, I switched off the lights, closed my office door, and headed for the elevator. It was the end of my first day of real employment, and when I stepped on the elevator, I gave a proud, happy smile to the mirror.

–

The first item on my orientation schedule the next day was IT training at the Tech offices in the center of the twenty-seventh floor. I felt certain this would be a waste of my time. I already knew how to do everything I needed to do. Or so I thought. It turned out that technology hadn't stalled along with my career. It had galloped ahead during the last five years, and there was a lot I had to learn.

A young Tech employee named Jason was my instructor for the day. He couldn't have been twenty-five yet, but he was already losing his hair. His high domed forehead made him look smart, I thought, and I wondered if that was where the term *egghead* came from. He walked me through everything that was new since 2008: network security shields, virtual meeting platforms, collaborative tools for creating and editing documents online, even social media dos and don'ts.

"And here's our pièce de résistance," he said with a flourish as he brought out some kind of electronic box. "This is your virtual assistant. In honor of our founder, we call her Ma Belle." He mugged a grin. "Get it?"

I smiled on cue. The box was black and silver and roughly the size of a four-slice toaster. On the outside were a video screen, a microphone, and a speaker. On the inside, Jason explained, was an artificial intelligence device. It operated the phone and the electronic calendar. On voice command, it would place a call and set alarms and reminders. It took dictation, autocorrected the text, and sent it to the nearest printer. To make it do any of those things, I had to first speak its name. Or rather, her name, since Jason was emphatic that the machine was a she.

"Go ahead, try it," he said.

I felt a little silly. "Ma Belle, connect me to Mr. Barrett," I said, and to my horror, Marcia Post's voice responded: "Mr. Barrett's office."

Jason covered for me. "Hi, Marcia. This is Jason in Tech. Just testing the system."

"Very good," she said, and rang off.

"So it—she—wakes up when I say her name," I said. "But doesn't she have to be awake and listening already? Or she wouldn't hear me say her name."

He bobbed his domelike head. "She's always listening. Always recording, too. That's how she learns. She reviews what she hears and uses it to make herself more responsive. For example, if you regularly ask about, I don't know, the weather in Springfield, the first few times she'll ask if you mean Springfield, Massachusetts, or Springfield, Illinois. But if you always mean Massachusetts, after a few more tries, she'll go right there without asking for clarification. See, 'cause she's learning."

"Cool," I said. "But aren't there some privacy concerns? If she's always listening in."

"Not at all," he assured me. "The recordings are automatically zipped to remote servers on a cloud campus in Virginia. They can't be accessed. They're not searchable by any human being. They're just there for the system to review and learn from. And eventually they're all overwritten."

Next he told me about the Ma Belle mobile app, which allowed us to take her with us wherever we went. He offered to download the app for me and asked for my phone. "Sorry, I left it at home," I said. I didn't have a smartphone, of course, but even if I did, I would have refused. I could control what the device heard at work. I couldn't at home.

When I returned to my office at the end of the day, there on the desk was an ergonomic keyboard, a supersize monitor, and my very own Ma Belle. I sank into my chair with a happy sigh and raised my fingers to the keyboard like a concert pianist. When I logged onto the company network, I felt like I'd been given the keys to the kingdom. For five years I'd been pressing my nose to the glass of this world, but now I was on the other side. I was In.

My elation lasted all the way through the train ride back to the Bronx, all the way through a fierce wind-driven walk to our building, and all the way down the squalid stairwell to our apartment until I opened the door.

David was there.

It was weeks since we'd spent more than a few waking moments in each other's company. Sometimes he was simply passed out; most times he wasn't home at all. Christmas Day had come and gone with no sign of him, and the same was true of New Year's.

But he was here now, legs spread wide in the beanbag chair, hands folded over his abs. Or what used to be his abs before he became so gaunt.

"When's payday?" he said the moment I stepped through the door.

I closed the door and hung up my coat. "Salaried employees are paid monthly."

"You work all month, and you don't see a fucking paycheck until February first?"

"February tenth, actually." I banged on the radiator and waited for the hiss of steam before removing my suit jacket.

"Fuck." With an effort, he hauled himself to his feet. "Six weeks' work without pay? What the fuck are we supposed to live on until February tenth?"

I'd known about this lag time since my hire date, and I'd planned for it as best I could. I'd worked double shifts at Cubby's every day from December 20 through New Year's. Customers' wallets were looser during the holidays, and I'd been able to set aside a decent amount in tips. I couldn't tell David that, of course. The money was well hidden from him.

What did it say about my life, I wondered, that a hidey-hole in a dive bar seemed safer to me than my own home?

"I thought I'd sell my laptop and printer to tide us over." I unzipped my skirt and hung it up with the jacket on a hook over the radiator. "I won't need them anymore now that I have office equipment."

"And what I am supposed to use? Huh?"

I didn't answer. I couldn't remember the last time I'd seen him use a computer.

He grabbed his suit coat and stuck his arms in. He'd kept all of his beautiful suits and still wore them every day. At first I'd found that dashing, the way he'd put together an expensive suit with an open-necked shirt or tee, like he was some kind of dissolute rake, a young noble slumming his way through his gap year. But five years was too big a gap. Now the seams were frayed on his jackets, and he no longer filled out the shoulders. The pants were bunched up at his waist and cinched with a belt that had too many extra holes punched in it. Now he looked like a homeless man. He seldom bothered to shave anymore, and his beach-boy hair had turned to straw.

"Why even take the stupid job?" he ranted. "The bank's gonna be in there with the garnishment by end of month. You'll get fired before you collect your first paycheck."

"I already talked to the payroll people about that. They said it's no big deal. They've got a whole procedure set up. Apparently they have lots of student-loan defaulters." They were the *Creatives*, the man in Accounting had confided to me, and they always seemed to be caught by surprise that anyone would expect them to repay their loans.

"Oh, great." David curled his lip. "So basically you'll be working for the bank."

"They only take ten percent." I unhooked my bra. "They're paying me enough that we'll barely notice it." I'd already calculated my net pay to the penny, including the deduction for the fee charged by the check-cashing company. I didn't have a bank account anymore; I couldn't, not with our judgment creditors lining up to seize it. Still, the net-net was a decent number. We'd get by.

He pulled on his topcoat. It hung below his knees now. Somehow he'd lost height along with everything else. "You act like this is actually gonna work out for you," he sneered.

"For us, David."

I was naked by then, a state that used to bring him across the room as if pulled by a tractor beam. Tonight he didn't even glance at me on his way out. "Yeah, right," he said, and slammed the door.

# Chapter 11

*Free to go*, Detective Cruz had told me five hours ago, and now I realized I should have taken him up on it. It was a mistake to insist on staying. I was pretty sure the police were inclined to clear me, but there was no way they'd do it in the middle of the night. They'd want to wait for the forensics, and I doubted the lab worked the third shift. They'd want to search my apartment, and they'd probably wait until dawn to do that. They'd want to search my office, too, and Lucy's, and they'd have to wait for business hours to get access. No matter how far they were leaning my way, they wouldn't close their file before they checked off all those boxes.

Of course, I'd also hoped that staying would signal my cooperativeness and gain a few points in my favor. But I may have miscalculated there, too. The officious little woman who'd been checking on me since the start of her shift that morning seemed nothing but annoyed by my continued presence. *Aren't you tired of just sitting here?* she'd snapped at me the last time she came in.

Now, though, at 9:45, I could hope that the end was in sight. By now the police should have been through the apartment, and I knew there was nothing there to link me to the gun and nothing to suggest any reason I'd want to kill Lucy. By now they might have searched our offices, too. I couldn't hope for a suicide note on Lucy's desk or computer, but at least I knew they wouldn't find anything incriminating in my office.

When they finally returned empty-handed to Interview A, I'd turn on the full strength of my persuasive powers. I'd make them see that without any evidence of means or motive on my part, there was no reasonable basis for concluding that Lucy's death was anything but suicide.

I prepared. I organized my thoughts and rehearsed my phrasing. When the bossy little woman escorted me to the bathroom, I splashed handfuls of cold water on my face. I accepted a cup of coffee and a glazed donut. I was caffeinated and my blood sugar level was restored. I was ready to wrap this up.

At 9:45 Cruz and Riley came in, and instantly I knew something had changed. Cruz didn't look at me as he took his seat. His jaw was clenched tight, and he all but slammed his computer tablet down on the table. Riley looked like a wrung-out marathoner who'd finally spotted the finish line ahead. Something had happened. They'd found something incriminating. My mind raced through the possibilities.

Cruz switched on the recording equipment and went through all the preliminaries again—time and place, persons in the room, rights waiver acknowledged, and signature identified.

Then he looked at me. His eyes weren't soft and liquid anymore. "When I first heard the name Shay Lambert," he said, "I thought you came from money."

"Yeah, and Shay Chance sounds like a snooty French restaurant," Riley cracked.

This was new. No more *help us out here*. Now they were being snarky, needling me, trying to get under my skin.

"Then I heard Brown and Columbia and Wall Street," Cruz said, "and I was sure of it. But that was all a big act, wasn't it?"

"I don't know what you mean," I said slowly. "That's all true."

"But that's not who you really are."

"I told you I was raised by a single mother," I said. "I told you I was deep in debt."

"You didn't tell us how deep," Cruz said. "A million and a half?"

"You're so far underwater you're already drowned," Riley said.

"I told you. That's why I was so grateful to get this new job."

"Grateful?" Cruz said. "Or desperate?" His tone made it clear he didn't like me anymore.

"Extremely grateful," I said.

He scoffed and changed gears. "You told us your husband works nights."

"Yes—"

"I knew a girl once. Told me her dad worked nights. I pictured him stocking shelves at the corner bodega. Turned out he played the cello for the New York Philharmonic."

I gave him a weak smile. "David doesn't do that."

"No? What does he do?"

"Odd jobs. Whatever he can get."

"Funny. He told us he's unemployed."

"Oh." I cleared my throat. "He was there?"

"Hey, don't worry about it. No reason you should have known. It's not like you're speaking to each other or anything."

I stared at him.

"Yeah, he told us. Your marriage is over. You're just roomies now until one of you has enough money to move out."

I couldn't figure out the new hostility. Okay, so they knew how deep my debt was, they knew my marriage was in trouble, but why would they go on the attack this way? I wondered if this was simply an interrogation technique. Instead of good cop/bad cop, they did nice session/mean session.

Cruz touched the tablet, and the big screen on the wall lit up. "Your company has its own CCTV system set up in its internal space. Were you aware of that?"

"I guess I noticed some cameras. I never really thought about it."

"Motion–activated, right?"

"Okay."

"Watch."

A video started to play on the screen. It was me, emerging from an office into the corridor. I watched myself close the door behind me. Then I put my hands over my face and collapsed against the wall. When I dropped my hands, tears were rolling down my cheeks. Then I took a deep breath, wiped my eyes, and hurried down the corridor.

"Look familiar?" Cruz said.

"Yes, of course." I hadn't realized my reaction was so obvious, but I remembered that moment perfectly. It was right after Lucy had extended the job offer and I'd accepted and signed the new–hire paperwork. I'd been delirious with relief and joy.

"That's you, right? Coming out of Ms. Carter-Jones's office."

I nodded. "But why are you showing me this? It was long ago."

"Eight thirty last night was long ago?"

"No, this is from last month. December nineteenth."

He rewound the clip and played it again. "Look at the time stamp."

I squinted at the screen. The digits in the corner read 02.02.14 20.36.48. "Wait," I said. "That's not right." I looked at Riley and back at Cruz. "Where did you get this?"

"Last night you had a meeting with Lucy Carter-Jones that upset you so much you left crying." Cruz tapped the tablet and left a freeze-frame of me up on the screen. "And thirty minutes later you got on an elevator with her."

Then it hit me. Hard. Someone had altered the time stamp. Someone had manufactured evidence to show I had a motive to kill Lucy. This was why the detectives' attitude had changed so dramatically. Someone was trying to frame me for murder, and they were buying it.

"No!" I burst out. "This wasn't last night. This was the day I got the job offer. Lucy had me come to her office to do the paperwork, and I was so happy when I left—"

"Look at what you're wearing," Cruz said. "Those are the same clothes you wore last night. The exact same clothes."

My face burned. "I only have the one suit."

"It's the same shirt, too."

"I only have three. I rotate them."

"So it's just a coincidence."

"Yes! I didn't go to Lucy's office last night. I had no reason to."

"Except that she summoned you there. And fired you. And that's why you were crying when you left."

"What? No! Why would she fire me? I'm doing fine. Better than fine! I've been putting in eighty-hour weeks. My work has been first-rate." I jabbed a finger at the screen. "Somebody doctored this. That's not the right date. Somebody's trying to set me up!"

From the moment that gun went off, I knew I'd have to work hard to sell my version of events. But it never occurred to me that someone would be actively trying to sell the opposite version of events. Someone who'd scoured the surveillance archives to unearth that clip, then changed the time stamp.

Cruz looked down at his notes. The image of me crying was still up there on the screen. Apparently he intended to leave it there. "What was your first job out of law school?" he asked.

The sudden change of subject caught me off-guard. "Jackson Rieders. I told you."

"Not clerking for Judge Wendell Arnold?"

"What? No—"

"Then why did you say that on your résumé?" He slid a plastic-sleeved sheaf of papers across the table.

I looked down. The text was hazy through the plastic cover. "I— What?"

He reached over and tapped a line on the page.

I blinked and the words came into focus: *Law Clerk, the Honorable Wendell Arnold, Judge of the United States Court of Appeals for the Second Circuit.* "What is this?" I said. "This isn't my résumé. I never clerked for Arnold."

"No," Cruz said. "You didn't. But your boss did, and you knew it would get your foot in the door if you said you did, too."

The second shoe dropped. Here was the someone who was framing me. My boss. I tossed the packet of résumés aside. "You got these from Barrett, didn't you?" I could see it all now. Barrett coming to the police with the doctored video and the made-up résumé, serving my motive up on a silver platter.

"Nope," Cruz said. "We found them in our search of your apartment this morning."

I stared at him. "That's impossible."

"A whole stack of them, right there in your dresser drawer. Your husband—or ex, whatever—he was very helpful. He showed us where you keep your papers."

My hands trembled, making my wedding band wink against the light. I pulled them off the table and folded them in my lap.

"He told us you ditched your laptop. But it looks like you forgot to get rid of the printouts."

"My laptop? I didn't ditch—"

"The judge is dead. You thought you'd never get caught, but your boss found out you lied."

"No, it's Barrett who's lying—"

"He told Ms. Carter-Jones to fire you. That's why she came into the office last night."

"No—"

"That's why you were crying outside her office. You were wrecked. After all you'd been through. Trying so hard to succeed. Working eighty-hour weeks. And with your marriage breaking up, and living in that awful apartment, and over a million dollars in debt. You were desperate for this job. It was the only thing that could save your marriage. It was the only thing that could save *you*."

"It mighta worked," Riley said, "if Barrett didn't stumble on the truth about Judge Arnold."

"So you got fired," Cruz picked up.

"It musta been awful," Riley said.

"And only got worse when you got trapped in an elevator with the same woman who fired you."

They were tag-teaming me, and I shook my head wildly as my gaze darted from one to the other.

"And you killed her."

"No! That's not true. I didn't lie on my résumé and I didn't get fired. I had absolutely nothing against Lucy. And even if I did— I'd have to be stupid to kill her in a stalled elevator."

"Or a genius," Cruz said. "If you could convince us it was suicide."

"If you killed her in the office, you knew it would look like murder," Riley said. "But in a stalled elevator? You could go with the panic-attack story."

"I had no idea the elevator was going to break down!"

"No?" Cruz gave an enigmatic smile.

I squinted at him. "No. How would I know?"

"Because you broke it. You and your mad techie skills."

"My—what? I'm not a techie."

"You wrote a software program for your old law firm that's so good they're still using it today."

I froze at the echo of my own words. If I hadn't been certain before, I was now. Ingram Barrett was the only person I'd ever told about that. He was the only one who could have packaged this whole story for the detectives. I had to give him credit. In only a few hours he'd come up with a totally plausible scenario. So plausible that parts of it were even true. Here was the risk with fabrications. I'd been tripped up in a tangled web of my own weaving. I stopped to think how best to play this. "That's not true," I said finally.

"You're saying your boss lied?"

"No," I admitted with a sigh. "I did. In my interview. I made it up to get the job."

"The same way you lied about clerking for Judge Arnold."

And here was the risk in confessing to one fabrication. Everything else fell into doubt, too. "No, I didn't lie about that—"

"The same way you lied about those missing five years."

He caught me off-guard again. "What?"

"You told us you took five years off, remember? Rather than admit you're a criminal defense lawyer."

"I'm not—"

Cruz snatched the packet of résumés from my hand and jabbed a finger at a line farther down the page: *2009–2014. Staff Attorney, The Innocence Project.* "You worked there for five years." He was seething. "Overturning convictions. Learning all the tricks to outfox the cops and the prosecutors. Exactly what you've been doing here."

I squeezed my eyes shut. Here was the real reason he'd turned so hostile. It wasn't the video surveillance. It wasn't the clerkship or the software hacking. It was the Innocence Project on my résumé. He was the kind of cop who saw criminal defense lawyers as his mortal enemies, so that was what I was now. I wasn't sure how to deflect this charge. Admitting to another lie would be disastrous. But finally it came to me. I opened my eyes.

"Let me see if I understand your theory, Detective." I leaned forward, my elbows on the table and my hands clasped together again. "You think Lucy fired me at eight thirty last night, and I spent the next half hour planning to kill her, including how to hack the elevator system. Carefully premeditated, right? That's your theory?"

Cruz set his jaw and folded his arms over his chest.

"And what exactly would that have accomplished? I'd still be fired, right? Unless you think I hacked into her files and unfired myself? But what good would that do if Barrett's the one who ordered me to be fired? I guess I'd have to kill him, too, huh?"

"You were desperate. You weren't thinking straight."

"But straight enough to figure out how to shut down a state-of-the-art elevator system?"

"That does sound pretty far-fetched," Riley said. He ignored the hot look Cruz shot at him. "But so does your theory. Which depends on Barrett lying about your résumé. Lying about firing you. And getting somebody to doctor the time stamp on the CCTV. All just to make it look like you killed Ms. Carter-Jones."

"Yes," I said. "That's how it must have happened."

"Oh, I get the *how*. What I can't see is *why*. A bigwig like Barrett's gonna go to all that trouble—break the law—to cover up a suicide? What for? Just to spare the husband's feelings?"

Cruz nodded. "It doesn't make any sense that he'd do that."

"I don't know what his motive was," I said. "But I can disprove mine. Your whole theory turns on the idea that I was fired for résumé fraud. This"—I struck my palm on the sheaf of papers—"is not my résumé. And I wasn't fired. And I can prove both of those points."

Cruz snorted and threw his pencil down. It did a cartwheel across the table, and I snatched it out of the air and held it aloft like a conductor's baton.

"You think I made up the clerkship to impress Barrett, right? But if the résumé was tailor-made for Barrett, why would I print out a stack of them with the same lie? I would've only needed the one. And I didn't even need that anymore. I already had the job."

"Oh, so somebody planted them, huh?"

I ignored the sneer in his voice. "Yes. Check the pages for fingerprints. You won't find mine. Because I never touched these papers. I never even saw them before."

Cruz's eyes shifted slightly to Riley.

"I can prove I wasn't fired, either. What's the first thing they do when you get fired? It's all spelled out in their employee manual. They have a whole protocol. They take away your keycard and have security escort you back to your office to clear out your desk. Right? To make sure you don't sabotage the place on your way out or sneak back in later. Do you see any security officer in that video? No, because nobody escorted me anywhere. And guess what else? I still have my keycard. Or you do. It was in my purse when you bagged it up last night. Go and check." I shot the pencil like a torpedo across the table and leaned back and folded my arms. "I'll wait here."

Riley was studying me with a look of bemused interest. But Cruz set his jaw even tighter. They both got up and left without saying another word.

After they were gone, I let my game face collapse. I hadn't anticipated any of this. I could blame my failings on the shock of the gunfire, the ringing in my ears, my utter exhaustion, but the plain truth was that I'd been outwitted.

Funny. A month ago I'd thought Barrett was my savior. Now he was my worst enemy.

I looked at the clock on the wall. A minute had passed since the detectives left the room. By now they could have slipped into the room behind the mirror. They could be watching me, gauging my reaction to all these new revelations. I folded my arms on the table and hid my face inside them before I let myself think about the other development that I'd failed to anticipate.

"Oh, David," I whispered into the shield of my arms. "What have you done?"

# Chapter 12

*January 4, 2014*

My third day on the job coincided with a company-wide sexual harassment training session, and Barrett had neatly shoehorned that into my orientation schedule. Attendance was mandatory for all non-executive employees, and the Manhattan-based staff was bused in for the event.

The program was held in the company auditorium in the interior of the twenty-eighth floor, a space labeled *Theater* on the office floor plan. Since it was an all-day affair, lunch would be catered in. I was looking forward to that part. Despite how carefully I'd budgeted for forty days of no income, I'd forgotten to factor in food. I was used to living on all the free snacks that went with my barmaid job, but there was no free lunch in the corporate world. Today, though, there *would* be free lunch, and I brought my briefcase with me. With a few furtive moves, I might be able to stash some extra food for later.

The theater looked like the auditorium in an exclusive prep school—small but with all the highest-end appointments. I took a seat near the back and watched as the busload of employees from Manhattan strolled in. These were what the Admin employees referred to as the Creatives—the designers and illustrators and pattern-makers, of course, but also the publicists and copywriters and even the fit models. They were immediately recognizable by the yards of scarf they unwound from their necks as they did slow revolutions to take in the room. They were a United Nations of races and ethnicities, yet all wore the same uniform, narrow pants and wide glasses, and the same affectation—an air of supreme boredom.

"You're the new litigator, right?" A woman slipped into the chair beside me. She was African American, perhaps forty, and her sensible shoes marked her as an Admin, not a Creative. "I'm Cheryl Fitts, labor and employment."

"Shay Lambert." I smiled and shook her hand. Here was my first new workplace friend. My first new friend, period. Unless I counted the bartender at Cubby's, I hadn't made a new friend in five years. Or kept the old ones. "It's nice to meet you," I said. "I've been hoping to meet the rest of the Law Department."

"No point, though, right?" Cheryl said. "Since Barry told us to keep our mitts off you."

"Did he?"

"I guess you're his prize catch. No sharing allowed."

"Huh."

"Anyway, welcome," she said as the lights dimmed throughout the auditorium.

A giant screen descended from the ceiling at the front of the room. Music sounded in a little fanfare flourish as an image of a white dove fluttered across the screen. A disembodied voice announced: "Please welcome our senior vice president and general counsel, J. Ingram Barrett, Jr., appearing with us live from Kuala Lumpur!"

There was a short burst of applause as Barrett appeared on-screen. He was seated at a desk with a bookcase behind him and his well-manicured hands clasped together on the blotter. There was an expanse of glass to his right, and through it we could see the night sky of KL dotted by a hundred pinpoints of light.

"Good morning," Barrett said with a broad smile. "I'm sorry I can't be with you in person today, as planned, but the show must go on, as they say. So, from the other side of the world, let me welcome all of our CDMI family to this important instructional session."

Cheryl leaned over and whispered to me: "All of the family except the ones who need it most. How'd management weasel out of this?"

"As you all know," Barrett was saying, "CDMI has a zero-tolerance policy for any form of sexual harassment. Our workplace must be a safe place for every single one of us. And that means not only unwelcome advances but a hostile work environment, dirty jokes, so-called locker-room talk—"

"Fuck, yeah," guffawed a man in the row behind us.

"Even consensual relations, if they impinge on a healthy work environment. We exist to nurture our talent to reach his or her or their highest potential." He seemed to be reading, and I wondered if he had a teleprompter or if someone off-camera was flipping through cue cards. "We won't tolerate anything that impedes that. I want to assure all of you that here at CDMI we take sexual harassment very seriously."

"I take it seriously, too," spoke the same voice behind me. "That's why I practice it every single day."

Snickers rippled through the seats around us. "Tom Canto," Cheryl hissed in my ear. "Staff photographer and resident perv."

I stole a glance: in the seat behind me was a man with a three-day scruff who looked very pleased with himself. He was surrounded by young people, boys and girls watching him with expectant smiles—fawning interns, I guessed, all waiting for their next cue to laugh. He held a camera on his lap, right at his crotch. He grinned at me, and the shutter whirred before I could whip forward again.

"I don't even know why I need to attend sex training," he said loudly. "I'm already damn good at it."

Cheryl raised her voice as the interns giggled. "Ignore him. He's terrified that people might think he's gay. It's typical over-compensation."

The man let out a belly laugh.

Barrett was winding up on-screen. "So now let me turn the program over to our much valued director of human resources. We are extraordinarily lucky to have her on our team. Everyone, please welcome Lucy Carter-Jones."

"You met Lucy?" Cheryl whispered.

"Briefly."

"I work with her on our EEOC cases. She's great. Fascinating bio, though, right?"

"Hmm?"

"She comes from one of those posh English families, you know? Who made all their money in the Atlantic slave trade. When that was outlawed, they went into tea plantations in Asia and basically did the same thing there."

The video screen levitated back into the ceiling, and Lucy Carter-Jones stepped onto the stage to a smattering of applause. When I'd met her on December 19, I'd been too overcome to take much notice of her, but now I could appreciate how elegant she was. She was impeccably dressed in ice-blue wool, with not a hair out of place and not a muscle, either. She moved carefully to the lectern and stood very still before it, as if she'd broken a bone or was afraid she might. But I guessed that she was simply reserved, self-contained inside a hard lacquer shell. That was probably an asset in a job where people regularly broke down in her office or tried to milk her sympathy.

"Good morning," she said into the microphone. "Thank you all so much for coming today." Her accent was British, with precise consonants and BBC vowels.

"Like we had a choice," the photographer carped behind me.

If Lucy heard that, she ignored it as she introduced the presenters/facilitators, a male-female team from an outside vendor who specialized in putting on such programs.

"They're still filthy-rich today," Cheryl whispered. "But Lucy wanted no part of it. She walked away—from her family, the money, all of it."

Lucy was walking away at that moment, too, as she turned the lectern over to the presenters and retreated to a chair at the back of the stage.

"Now she devotes her life to ensuring fair labor conditions." Cheryl's eyes glowed. "It's so inspiring."

The facilitators began with a PowerPoint lecture about the definition of sexual harassment and its various workplace manifestations. They explained that they would be screening a series of short videos in which actors portraying office and factory workers would reenact various situations designed to stimulate audience discussion.

"I'm stimulated already," snickered the photographer. His interns tittered. Cheryl shot him a glare. "I've about had it with this asshole," she hissed.

The giant video screen descended again, and the moment the auditorium lights dimmed, the phones and tablets came out. I didn't own a smartphone or a tablet, but inside my battered briefcase was a ream of printouts that I was itching to work on. I glanced right and left, and when I confirmed that almost no one was watching the program with more than half an eye, I pulled the papers out.

These were the discovery pleadings in the Palmer case. I'd devoured all the public filings long before my start date, but discovery requests and responses weren't filed with the court, and it wasn't until I logged on to the company network late yesterday that I'd been able to access them. When Mark Ivins filed his complaint, he made only generalized allegations of misfeasance and malfeasance on the part of CDMI management. His discovery demands should give me a better idea of the shareholders' specific grievances.

While the slick videos played on the screen at the front of the room, I flipped through pages and pages of interrogatories and document requests. The first batch of questions focused on executive compensation and sought details about every senior executive's comp package and the decision-making process that went into it. Ivins was also seeking the names of every board member who'd participated in that process, probably with a view toward taking their depositions, a move that would upset most board members and increase the pressure they might bring on senior management to settle the case.

"Oh, dude, she wants you bad," the photographer groaned from the row behind me. I glanced at the screen, where a petite Asian woman was trying to break away from a male coworker's grip.

Cheryl twisted in her seat. "Would you shut up?" she growled.

The interns looked abashed, but the photographer only laughed.

I returned to my papers and read on. Ivins's second batch of questions homed in on operating losses at certain CDMI manufacturing facilities, particularly Paradis sur Terre in Myanmar. So I'd guessed right about those exotic-smelling file boxes I'd inventoried on Monday, and I congratulated myself for getting a good head start on the case.

"Oh, Mr. Man!" Now the photographer was speaking in a Suzie Wong falsetto. "You so big and handsome. Take me home with you. I give you plenty good sex. I be good slave for you."

"That's enough!" Cheryl jumped to her feet and whirled on the photographer. He leaned back with a smirk and snapped another photo from his crotch.

"Excuse me?" the moderator called from the front of the room. "Is there an issue?"

"Yes, there's an issue," Cheryl yelled. "I want to register a complaint against this—this person—who's creating a hostile work environment at this very moment!"

The lights came up in the auditorium, and people's heads came up from their phones and tablets. Voices started to buzz. The program leaders turned to the back of the stage and looked expectantly at Lucy Carter-Jones, who shook her head slightly. They turned back to the audience. "Perhaps you could raise this issue through appropriate channels at a later time—"

"I'm sorry, but no, I can't. Lucy!" Cheryl called. "His behavior is outrageous. It's illegal!"

Lucy got to her feet and reluctantly took the microphone that the speakers were thrusting at her.

"He's not only making gross sexual innuendos," Cheryl said, "he's making racist ones as well!"

"Perhaps we could address this—"

Cheryl spoke over her. "I mean, come on, Lucy—how can you sit by while he makes jokes about slaves? You of all people."

Lucy's face froze, her mouth still open. After a moment she closed it.

"I mean—" Cheryl faltered. The room was suddenly very quiet. "I only meant given your own country's sordid history with the subject. That—that is—" She was stammering now. "Your country of origin, I mean."

The photographer leaned back with a big grin, obviously relishing his accuser's discomfiture. Lucy moved, finally, but only to exit stage right. Cheryl's hand flew to her mouth, and she hurried to the rear exit of the room amid a whipsaw of whispers through the audience.

The episode ended with that. After a moment, the lights dimmed again, the video play resumed, and everyone went back to work.

I went back to work, too. Barrett would be returning from KL next week, and it was critical that I make a good impression—a dazzling impression—from the get-go. I figured that once I proved my value to the company, once I made myself indispensable, a little résumé padding could surely be overlooked.

A few minutes later I noticed Cheryl steal back into the auditorium and take a seat off by herself. Her head was bowed. I worried that my new friend had disgraced herself.

But in the next moment I forgot her and went back to work. Because who was I kidding? We were never going to be friends.

# Chapter 13

The Ma Belle virtual assistant on Barrett's desk kept a running tally of his incoming phone calls; the names crawled across the video screen like subtitles in a foreign film. Callers were holding on all of his lines: his wife, Melanie; security chief Jack Culligan; the *avocats* in Paris; Graziella, the company's premier luxury label designer; and finally, the Hollywood agent for that movie star, Luke Rafferty. Each of them was far more important than the Communications director Barrett was currently talking to. She was giving him some serious pushback about his redraft of the press release.

"I just think it's overstating things to say that a suspect is now in police custody," she said.

"I don't agree," Barrett said. "They have her, and I suspect her."

"But this implies that the *police* suspect her. And that she's been arrested, and that's not my understanding of the facts." She was a Sarah Lawrence English major who probably dreamed of working for a big publishing house and editing somebody like Margaret Atwood. Instead she was copyediting prospectuses and catalog text. And now a press release about the shooting death of the company's director of human resources.

"We don't really know the facts, do we?" he said.

"Then we shouldn't say anything at all. Just that the investigation into the shooting continues."

Obviously that wasn't good enough. He thought for a minute. "*Police are questioning a former employee of CDMI in connection with the shooting.* There you go. It's absolutely factual."

"All right. I guess." She still sounded reluctant.

"And add some stuff about how valuable Lucy was to the company and how much we all mourn her, blah blah blah. Got it?"

"Got it," she said with a sigh.

He disconnected and punched the call from Paris. "*Je te rappelle,*" he told the lawyers, and disconnected that call as well. His missed calls also crawled across the Ma Belle screen, each one requesting an immediate call-back: his broker, reminding him of the margin call; his banker, ditto; Ingram the Third, once known as Trey, now Tripp because it was "edgier," no doubt pleading for another loan to start up another start-up; and daughter Chloe calling from St. Moritz to complain about daughter Courtney, currently in Cap Ferrat. Culligan had dropped off the line by then, leaving only Melanie, Graziella, and Luke Rafferty's agent on hold. Barrett knew which call took priority.

"Darling! How are you?" He stood and routed the call to his headset, and with a cigarette in hand, he opened the door to the balcony. A cold wind pushed its way inside.

"Infuriated, that's how," Melanie said. "I just had to fire Lin."

"Oh?" An inch of pristine snow coated the floor of the balcony and the teak furniture outside. He leaned as far as he could through the door opening and lit up. Much as he relished a smoke, he couldn't abide the after-smell in his office. It was like the scent of a woman's genitalia: he enjoyed it well enough during but couldn't wait for her to shower after. "What'd she do?"

"She ran the vacuum cleaner. While I was on the phone!"

"Oh, dear. Something important, was it?"

"Of course it was important. I was talking to Jan!"

He took a long drag on the cigarette. Jan was the latest in a line of Melanie's *life coaches* who was training her in *self-care*. He wouldn't have thought she needed much help in that department. Her days consisted entirely of beauty and health treatments, shopping, tennis and swimming, and sessions with her therapist, all under the rubric of self-care. While his own days consisted entirely of caring for others. For women it was all about choice, but for men like Barrett there was no choice. From the cradle his fate was set: to work every day of his adult life to support a household—or two, as it turned out—of other people who could then be free to amuse themselves or express themselves or do whatever the hell they felt like doing. Or not doing, in the case of his layabout son Christian. These were the expectations with which every man of his age and race and class had been raised, and they were passed down from generation to generation. If a man wasn't more successful than his father and his father before him, he was a failure. And Barrett was responsible not only for his families but for all the employees in this office and the one on Seventh Avenue and the studios in Tours and Milan, not to mention the factories on the other side of the world. This, he thought, was the true white man's burden.

"She can't follow even the simplest instructions, Barry."

"I'm sorry you had to go through that, darling."

"Send somebody to come get her, would you? And you need to get me a new housekeeper, Barry. Today! Someone who speaks a modicum of English this time."

"I'll get right on it. Love you!"

Graziella was next; her fall line would be unveiled on the runway at Lincoln Center in just four days. Always high-strung, she was close to snapping under the pressure of Fashion Week. Today's crisis was the detention of six of her models at JFK. Customs and Border Protection had the gall to question the purpose of their visit. The girls had done what the foreign models were always instructed to do: pretend to be tourists or students. But they'd made the mistake of traveling together—what to call a group of models? he wondered—and CBP couldn't help but be suspicious of such an *anorexia* flying into New York on the eve of Fashion Week.

"We'll handle it," he assured her. Visas had always been Lucy's bailiwick, but he could shunt this off on Cheryl Fitts, his labor and employment go-to. "Graziella, while I have you." His voice took on a wheedling tone. "Any cancellations come in?" Melanie was desperate to attend the runway show, preferably in a front-row seat. He couldn't make her understand that the shows were put on for buyers and the fashion press, not the wives of corporate executives. Or that the design team spent months coaxing big-name celebrities to occupy those front-row seats.

"Certainly not." Graziella sniffed and hung up.

He sighed out a cloud of smoke. "Marcia," he called above the roar of the wind. "Any idea what Mr. Hollywood's calling about?" His assistant's prim voice floated through the speaker. "Oh, dear, yes. It was in the paper this morning. Mr. Rafferty was arrested in New Jersey yesterday and charged with"—she hesitated—"soliciting prostitution."

Barrett groaned. Luke Rafferty was the face of Martineau pour Homme, the company's premier fragrance line for men. "Part of that Operation Super Bowl sweep?"

"Hmm. It seems he was caught on video with a young woman." Barrett flicked the stub of his cigarette into the snow, where it hissed and died. Rafferty could have any woman he wanted, and apparently what he wanted was a blow job from a twenty-dollar hooker. Barrett closed the door and, back at his desk, punched Line 4. "Sid."

"Barry! Thank God! We need you to put out a statement. Something about supporting Luke and asking people to respect his privacy. You know the drill."

"Hmm. I was thinking of something a little different. Like: *In view of the fact that Mr. Rafferty has engaged in conduct tending to shock, insult, or offend the community or outrage public morals or decency, his services are no longer required.*" He was quoting from the morality clause in Rafferty's contract.

"Barry, come on! You don't want to do that."

"I recall we had a liquidated damages provision in there, too. Disgorgement of all monies received during the preceding year, is that right?"

"No, come on. Let's be reasonable here. Luke sells a lot of cologne for you guys."

"He's giving off a different stench now."

"It was entrapment!"

"Tell it to the tabloids, Sid."

"No, come on. This'll all blow over in no time. It'll be yesterday's news, and Luke'll still be a big action star."

Barrett reflected. The agent was probably right about that much. Still, Rafferty was in a tough spot today, and that was always the best time to strike a better deal. "I could try pleading your case with the board," he said finally. "But I can't go to them empty-handed. If Luke agrees to cut his fee—let's say by fifty percent—I might be able to persuade them to stick by him through this sordid affair."

"Twenty." The agent's tone was sullen.

"Forty. Final offer. And no statement to the press."

The deal was struck, and Barrett finally returned Culligan's call. "Jack. What is it?"

"Elliott Gutman's being interviewed over at the police station."

"What?" Barrett shot out of his seat. "When?"

"Right now. He's been in there thirty minutes."

"Christ! How'd you miss this?"

"They sent a patrol car out to get him. So we didn't pick up anything on the phone tap or the vehicle tracker."

"You didn't have anybody watching the house?" he shouted.

Culligan was silent a moment. "We discussed this," he said. "You agreed on the electronics."

"Well, obviously that's not good enough. Jack, I don't need to remind you that you stand to lose as much as I do."

This wasn't precisely true. Culligan's comp package was only a sliver of Barrett's. Still, it was ten times what he made as a GS-13 at the Bureau. "No," he said quietly. "You don't need to remind me."

"Get somebody on the house. ASAP. And get somebody to grab Gutman when he comes out. Tell him we have some papers for him to sign, or Lucy's belongings to collect. Whatever. I don't care. Just bring him straight to me."

"Got it."

"Oh, Jack. One more thing."

"Yeah?"

"Send somebody out to my house. Melanie's recycling maids again."

# Chapter 14

*January 14, 2014*

Ingram Barrett was back from Kuala Lumpur—KL, I reminded myself to call it—and he'd put a ten o'clock meeting on my electronic calendar for today. He'd also sent me an email. It was the first one I'd received that wasn't a company-wide blast, and it gave me a little thrill to see the *To: lamberts@CDMI.com* at the top of the message. *I want to bring you up to speed on Palmer,* he wrote.

Up to speed? By then I was already cruising at about ninety miles an hour. I'd read through the Palmer pleadings so many times I could recite key passages by heart. I'd boned up on the law on shareholder derivative actions and executive compensation and the business judgment rule, and I'd learned everything I could about the companies' factories in Southeast Asia. I'd even spotted grounds for dismissal of one of the plaintiffs' claims—something outside counsel had missed—and I took it upon myself to draft a motion to dismiss.

I arrived at Barrett's office suite at the stroke of ten with my shirtsleeves rolled up to the elbow to show how ready I was to dive into work. Marcia Post was manning the sentry station in the antechamber to Barrett's corner office. "I'm afraid he's in a meeting just now," she said as I came in.

"Oh." I tried to hide my disappointment. This ten o'clock slot was mine; I had electronic evidence to that effect. "Do you want to ring me when he's free?"

She pursed her lips, and instantly I knew I must have committed some kind of office faux pas. "He'll expect you to be waiting here when he's free," she said.

"Oh. Of course."

"Please have a seat."

I perched on the white leather chesterfield and waited. The door to Barrett's inner sanctum was closed, but I could hear a low rumbling voice within, punctuated now and then by a sharp-pitched interjection. Their words were indistinguishable until a single exclamation burst out. "They were never supposed to come here!" That was a woman's voice. A deeper, gruffer voice replied: "It's too late now." That was Barrett.

Marcia tilted her head to one side, like a dog hearing a whistle, a posture that struck me as peculiar until I noticed her chrome headset. It blended perfectly into her sleek silver bob. "Certainly, Mr. Barrett," Marcia said, and picked up the phone. "Very well," she said and placed it down again.

Thirty seconds later the door swung open. Lucy Carter-Jones rushed out, and I hurried to my feet. "Oh, hello, Lucy!"

She stopped and looked right through me. Her shell-like face was utterly blank. I was afraid I'd committed another office faux pas by using her first name. But Barrett had said to call him Barry and he certainly outranked the HR director. Maybe Lucy had simply forgotten who I was. "I'm Shay Lambert? The new addition to the Law Department?"

"Oh." Lucy blinked and her face came back to life. "Yes, of course. How are you getting on?"

"Just fine. Thank you."

She gave a perfunctory nod and left.

"You can go in now," Marcia said to me.

Barrett's office door was still ajar. I pushed through into an expanse of glass—floor-to-ceiling windows on two walls, glass shelving on the other two walls, a huge glass-topped desk, and a glass coffee table between the facing sofas. The effect was so overwhelmingly empty that it took me a moment to realize the office was also empty of Ingram Barrett.

"Have a seat. I'll be with you in a minute," he called from behind a different door. "Do you want anything to drink?"

"No, thank you."

"Coffee, tea, water?" he shouted. "Sparkling or still?"

"I'm fine, thanks."

I took a seat in front of his desk. The visitor chairs faced the windows, and one of the windows was a door. It led to a private glass balcony that was cantilevered off the face of the building thirty stories above the city. On it was an arrangement of snow-covered cubes and rectangles— patio chairs and chaises that looked like summer cottage furniture covered with dust sheets until Memorial Day.

A row of framed photos lined the edge of his desk, turned not inward where he could see them but outward for his visitors to admire. One was his wedding photo: a recent one, judging from his appearance, and on his arm was an elegant blonde. The second Mrs. Barrett, I assumed, since she was too young to be the mother of the twentysomethings captured with Barrett in half a dozen other photos. She might have been a twentysomething herself.

Another sound came from behind the interior door—a toilet flushing with the high-speed whoosh of a jet engine. Barrett had his own washroom, I realized. A private balcony and a private washroom—even the most senior partners at Jackson Rieders didn't have such luxuries. These must have been among the perks that had lured him from Wall Street to the executive suite of CDMI.

He emerged with a smile. "Let's talk over here," he said, and settled comfortably on one of his white leather chesterfields.

I got up and hurried over to the facing sofa.

"Settling in, are you?"

"Settled. And anxious to get to work."

"Good, good. Glad to hear it. First things first." He jerked his chin at a multipage document lying front and center on the coffee table between us. "I need you to sign the NDA."

I picked it up. *Nondisclosure Agreement* was the document's title. "I don't remember seeing this in the new-hire packet," I said, flipping pages.

"No, this isn't from HR. This is my own creation for my troops here in the Law Department. Obviously we handle a great deal of confidential and sensitive information. We need extra protections here."

The bar rules governing client confidentiality should have given him all the protections he needed. But as I skimmed through the pages, I saw that he was going far beyond the bar rules. This NDA covered any information about the company or its employees that I might acquire during the course of my employment, whether or not such information was confidential or privileged. The penalty for disclosing any such information would be the automatic entry of a judgment against me for any and all damages caused by such disclosure, which I was required to stipulate were equal to the sum of at least $1 million.

There was no way this NDA would hold up in court. I knew it and Barrett certainly knew it, too. He must have drafted it solely for its *in terrorem* effect. It didn't scare me, though. I already had over $1 million in judgments entered against me, and any subsequent judgment would come behind those. CDMI would wait in line an eternity before it could ever collect a penny. Not that I had any intention of disclosing company information. I picked up the pen on the coffee table and dashed off my signature.

"Good. Thanks," Barrett said. He spread his arms wide over the back of the chesterfield. "So. The Palmer case."

He proceeded to give me a ten-minute summary of the case. It was nothing I didn't already know, and in some instances know better, since he mangled a few of the details. But I listened and nodded and attempted the occasional interjection: "Yes, I saw that in the file" or "I was struck by that, too, when I read the judge's opinion." He spoke over me, cordially, but in a tone that made it clear my only job was to sit and take it all in.

Opposing counsel Mark Ivins was a showboat, Barrett declared, and the Palmer case was nothing but a publicity stunt. Ivins was attacking the business judgment of the company's executives, alleging malfeasance in the operation of its manufacturing facilities abroad, but that was only a smokescreen for his real grievance: executive compensation. He'd been going after companies all across the country in case after case, complaining that executives were grossly overcompensated, that the average CEO raked in three hundred times the amount of the average

American worker. Executive overcompensation was his pet crusade, something he thought would endear him to the public and make them overlook his own lavish lifestyle.

Unfortunately, Paradis sur Terre was an easy target. A vanity project, Ivins called it, a money pit. I'd already read every media piece I could find about PsT, and I'd also watched a feature-length documentary about what the filmmakers called the *Miracle in Myanmar*. But I sat and listened while Barrett waxed poetic about the company's grand experiment in the jungle, its vision for what an ideal manufacturing facility could be. He described the state-of-the-art engineering and the near-utopian conditions for the two thousand employees recruited to work there. "Of course, it lost money in the short run," he said. "If we'd had only a couple more years, we could have shown the world a way to be both profitable and humane." But the shareholders had no patience, and the board felt it had no choice but to shut down PsT.

Then a second miracle happened: the sell-off of the Myanmar assets proved to be so phenomenally successful that the operating losses were more than wiped out. The real estate appreciation was enormous, since the company made such enormous improvements to the property, bringing in electricity, water, and Wi-Fi, and building the factory, dormitories, dining hall, not to mention the roads and the airstrip.

"Yes, I was curious about the airstrip," I said, recalling the misfiled air charter contracts.

He ignored me. "There was actually a bidding war for our equipment, as everyone hoped to reverse-engineer it—it was that cutting-edge."

"Wow," I murmured.

"So—" He leaned forward, elbows on knees, and rubbed his hands together. "What contribution can you make?"

I sat up straight. At last, my moment to shine. "I've given that a lot of thought," I said. "I think the *Raul* decision out of Delaware last year gives us a clear basis for knocking out the third cause of action in the complaint. I took the liberty of drafting—"

"No. No." Barrett waved a dismissive hand. "Our outside counsel can take care of all that."

"But they didn't include that in their—"

"What we need you to contribute—"

Too late I realized his question was merely rhetorical. My cheeks flamed, and I sat back again.

"—is the collection and review of the documents we have to produce to Ivins in discovery. He's demanded all the company's documents showing income and expenses at each of our facilities. We objected, of course—it's obviously a fishing expedition—but the judge is a spineless idiot, and she ruled we have to comply."

I made a sympathetic noise.

"So we've had all the documents shipped here from our factories as well as from our various Asian law firms and brokers, et cetera. I need you to go through them, sort out what's responsive and what isn't, and get them to our outside counsel to deliver to Ivins."

"Okay." I tried not to show how deflated I was. "Although— Well, typically that's more a paralegal's function?"

"Yes, and you'll have one." Barrett tilted his head back and spoke to the ceiling. "Marcia, get Lester up here."

"Certainly," the woman's voice replied.

I looked around the room for the microphone and speaker, but they were well hidden. I wondered if the intercom was always open or if Barrett's assistant was voice-activated. Like the virtual assistant on my desk, Marcia's wake word was her own name.

"You'll need to review the documents for privilege—I assume you know how to do that?"

"Of course," I said stiffly. This was Document Production 101.

"And indexed—"

I'd already made a start on that task my first day on the job, when I went through the boxes that had been haphazardly stored in my office. "Of course," I said again.

"And organized according to which document request they relate to—"

These were insultingly basic tasks. I couldn't believe he was paying me the salary he was to do work that a paralegal or even a document clerk could have done. But thoughts of my salary made me keep my game face on. I was being paid, well paid, to do this, and I would do it well. Perhaps after this project, he'd realize he was wasting my talents and assign me something more meaningful.

"And one more thing. There may be a number of documents pertaining to our employees at PsT, their medical conditions and so forth. We have a duty to safeguard that kind of private information. So you'll need to pull those as well."

A knock sounded on the door. "Here's Lester," Marcia Post announced, and stepped aside to usher in a tall Black man in a navy-blue blazer. He strode up to the seating area, and I scooted aside on the sofa to make room for him. But he made no move to sit. He assumed a military at-ease posture, with his hands clasped behind his back.

"Shay Lambert, Lester Willard." Barrett made the introductions with quick finger jabs. "Lester will act as your paralegal on this project," he said to me.

I looked up at him. And up. He must have been six-six. But his height was the least of my surprise. Paralegals were typically young white women, not middle-aged African American men. I was impressed with CDMI for breaking the stereotype this way. I stood and extended my hand, and after a fleeting recoil, Lester unclasped his hands from behind his back to shake it.

"Lester, you'll show her where everything is?"

"Yes, sir."

"Then I'll leave you to it. Marcia," Barrett called to the ceiling as he stood. "Get me Yves in Tours."

It seemed our meeting was over. I turned to mumble some closing remark, *thank you* or *see you soon* or something, but Barrett was already strolling to his wall of windows with his hands in his pockets.

"The documents are on the twenty-ninth floor," the man named Lester said.

I followed him through the antechamber past Marcia and into the corridor and halfway around the floor to the elevator bank. "How long have you worked here?" I asked him as we waited for the elevator to arrive.

He didn't answer me. I was taken aback until I realized he was listening to someone else. He had a coiled wire at his ear, like a Secret Service agent.

"Sorry, what?" he said as the elevator doors opened.

I repeated my question as we stepped on.

"Here at headquarters, two years. With CDMI, for eight years now."

"Where else?" If the Law Department had auxiliary offices in, say, Paris, maybe someday I could transfer there. The prospect was tantalizing. Not the glamour. Just the idea of making a fresh start somewhere else, where everything could be new and shiny again.

"Southeast Asia, mostly," Lester said as the doors opened and he led the way off.

"Oh?" I had to lengthen my stride to keep up with him. "I wouldn't think there'd be much paralegal work to do over there."

"I'm in Securities," he said, and stopped at a door in the center core of the building.

That was even more puzzling. If he worked on SEC filings and the like, he'd be either in Washington or here at Admin head-quarters.

He swiped a keycard to open the door, and at that moment I realized he hadn't said securities. He'd said Security.

"Why would Corporate Security get involved in a document production?"

He hit a switch, and cool white lights came on over a vast, windowless, and nearly empty space. All of it was blindingly white. White walls, white ceiling, white concrete floor. White worktables lined the perimeter of the room, and every surface was covered with towering stacks of white paper.

"I wouldn't know, ma'am," he said, and shut the door behind us.

## Chapter 15

Elliott Gutman came into Barrett's office like a man in a trance. He was wearing a tweed jacket over what looked like a pajama shirt, and his hair was even more frizzed than usual. Barrett put an arm over his shoulders and steered him to the sofa. "Elliott, what can I get you? Coffee, tea?"

"Coffee, I guess." Gutman put his elbows on his knees and dropped his head into his hands.

"Marcia, coffee for Elliott," Barrett called to the ceiling. "You should eat something. Croissants?" Gutman didn't answer. "Marcia, croissants, too."

"Right away, Mr. Barrett."

Gutman whispered something.

"How's that?" Barrett bent lower to hear.

"I said, I had to ID her."

"Oh, Elliott. You shouldn't have done that on your own. I told you to call me first if the police contacted you. For anything."

"There wasn't time. They just showed up."

"Next time—if there is a next time—you keep them waiting and you call me. Understood?"

"She looked... perfect. You couldn't even tell—"

Barrett gave him a moment before he spoke again. "Elliott, think carefully now. What did the detectives ask you?"

Gutman lifted his face from his hands. "Barry. They think it's suicide."

Barrett's breath caught. "Why would they think that?"

"They have her phone. They had me unlock it—"

"And you did?"

"Well, I could hardly refuse. How would that look?"

Barrett gritted his teeth. "No, you're right." Whether Gutman had unlocked it or not, the police would have gotten into it eventually. Culligan had warned him of that and said he was on top of it. "Go on. What makes you think they're leaning toward suicide?"

"They wanted to know why I was so worried about her last night. Why I texted her and called her so many times."

Barrett eyed him. "How many times are we talking?"

"Oh, I don't know. Here." Gutman reached into his breast pocket and came out with two folded sheets of paper. "They printed it out."

Barrett took the pages from him and smoothed them out. The first was a printout of Gutman's unanswered texts to Lucy:

> Sunday 7:27 PM
> Are U OK?

> Sunday 8:12 PM
> Call me

> Sunday 8:48 PM
> Please come home

She hadn't responded to any of them. Her only outgoing text appeared at the bottom of the page. Barrett already knew about that one, because she'd sent it to him.

He shuffled to the second page, which was a printout of the missed calls to Lucy's cell phone. Between eight thirty and midnight last night, Elliott had placed six calls to her cell. Barrett already knew from the internal phone system that Elliott had placed another six to Lucy's office line.

"Elliott—what the hell?" He chucked the pages onto the coffee table.

"I was worried, okay? She was so upset yesterday. For weeks, really, but yesterday—I don't know. It scared me, the way she was acting. I told her to stay home, relax, watch some TV, but she insisted on going to the office. And when she didn't answer, I got even more worried. So I kept on trying. Hoping she'd answer. Until you called"—Gutman sucked in a big breath—"and I knew not to hope anymore."

He clapped his hand over his mouth and nose and held it there so long that Barrett almost wondered if he might suffocate himself. And if so, why he hadn't done it a few hours earlier.

"Did you tell them why she was upset?"

"They said we must have had a fight!" He lifted his hand from his mouth and raked it through his wiry hair. "They actually implied I was having an affair—"

"Elliott. What did you tell them?"

"Well, I wasn't going to stand for that accusation! So I told them she was a little blue about something she read

145

in the newspaper that morning. She is—was—a tender-hearted person. When bad things happen to people, she takes it to heart."

"Is that it?"

"Well, they pressed me on it. What specifically did she read in the paper. Barry, they had her briefcase there. She had the Sunday *Times* in it, turned to that exact page. So I could hardly deny it."

Barrett stared at him. He knew what page Elliott was talking about. He knew what the article had reported. A typhoon in the South China Sea had caused an entire Thai fishing fleet to sink. More than thirty boats were lost, and something like five hundred men drowned.

"What did *they* say?"

"They wanted to know why bad weather on the other side of the planet would make her so upset that I'd call her so many times. So I explained—"

Barrett held his breath.

"I explained that it happened off the coast of Malaysia, so it wasn't the other side of the world, as far as Lucy was concerned. It was her homeland. She felt a connection to those people."

"That's it?"

Gutman nodded.

"Okay," Barrett said, and let his breath out again. "Okay. You did fine, Elliott."

"But then the old one, Riley, started asking questions about you."

"What about me?"

"About you and Lucy, specifically. How you worked hand in glove. How you traveled together a lot. He insinu-ated the most outrageous—"

"He was trying to rattle you. It's the oldest trick in the book."

"He said—he said—*Obviously something was going on in her life that made her so unhappy and guilty that she couldn't even medicate it away.* I said, *What are you talking about?* And he said the medical examiner found an undigested tablet in her stomach, and they'd sent it to toxicology, but he guessed I knew what it was. So I told him Xanax."

"Jesus, Elliott! He was lying. They haven't even done the post-mortem yet."

"How was I to know? So I told him she had a high-stress job, and a little Xanax now and then got her through the day. And he said—he said—" The Adam's apple bobbed in the man's throat. "*That's one of those ads I hear on TV, isn't it? Side effects may include thoughts of suicide.*"

He moaned and dropped his head in his hands. Barrett pushed to his feet and walked to the windows and studied the low-hanging gray clouds in the sky until Gutman could pull himself together. In a few minutes Barrett heard a loud sniff and turned to see the man take his hands from his face and rake his fingers through the frizzle of his hair.

Barrett spent another fifteen minutes testing Gutman's memory, seeing if he could dredge up anything else from his police interview. Nothing worse came out of his efforts, but nothing better, either. When he was finished, he called Marcia to arrange a driver to take Gutman home, and walked him to the elevator bank.

"This is it, isn't it?" Gutman stared straight ahead at the grid-work of bars etched into the stainless-steel doors. "This is where she stood. This is where she got on."

"Try not to think about it," Barrett said. Fortunately the doors of Car 5 opened at that moment, so he didn't have to muster up any more comforting words. Gutman stepped on, the doors closed, and Barrett all but sprinted back to his office.

"Jack," he said when Culligan answered. "They have her phone. Are we ready with the rest?"

"Ready."

"Then let's get them over here ASAP."

He disconnected and picked up the printout of text messages again. There, at the bottom of the page, Lucy's final words, texted to Barrett at 8:45 last night.

I can't do this anymore.

# Chapter 16

My alarm went off in a whisper, set to the lowest possible volume, and still I flew out of bed to tap it silent. I held my breath and peered into the darkness until I could make out the shape of David sprawled in the beanbag chair. He hadn't stirred at the sound. I breathed again.

My hours had changed dramatically since I started my new job. When I worked at Cubby's, I seldom made it home before five, and I'd usually find David already asleep. But now I tried to be in bed by eleven, and he was never home at that hour. That first night he stumbled home at two and couldn't find his key—or maybe he couldn't find the keyhole. He yelled, _Open the fuck up!_ and pounded the door so hard it rattled. I hurried to let him in, but not before he woke most of the other tenants in our building. They swarmed the hall in various stages of dress, all of them upset and clamoring for silence. One of them called the cops.

I made David hide under the bed when the officers rang the bell, and I answered the door and apologized for making so much noise. They gave me the once-over and sniffed my breath and warned me not to let it happen again. When they were gone, I whispered to David to come out, but he was already asleep. That was where he spent the night, on the floor under the bed.

Ours was not the kind of neighborhood where you could leave your apartment door unlocked overnight, but after that incident, that was what I did. The first night I lay for hours with my eyes open and my fists clenched, ears straining for any sound of an intruder, until I finally fell into an exhausted sleep so deep I didn't even hear David when at last he came home.

So this was our new routine. The alarm went off at six, I rolled over, and there David was, asleep in the chair. It was months since we last shared a bed, and many more months since we last made love. No, that wasn't right. It was months since we last had sex, years since we last made love.

I slipped out of bed and tiptoed around him and picked up the spoon he must have dropped on the floor. I turned on the oven, and when I looked back, I found him sprawled in the beanbag with a smile on his face and the needle still in his arm.

The shock slammed into me, and I froze there in the chilly kitchen.

He'd never brought it home before, even in the early days, when it was only coke. It was a workplace thing then, something to help him to supercharge his battery so he could power through the day. Cocaine was the young financier's drug of choice, and it carried none of the stigma of other drugs, not the meth upstate nor the heroin downtown. It almost had a certain elite panache, like drinking Cristal. David would do a couple bumps during the day when the numbers were flying fast and furious, every deal bigger and more precarious than the last.

I never needed it myself. The law was a more contemplative profession than finance. Poise was valued over speed. Yes, my ability to think on my feet was an asset, but the truth was, there were seldom any surprises in court. I already knew what the evidence would be, because I'd already exchanged all of it with my adversary. The surprises, when they came at all, came to the office, where I had time to react, to deliberate, to strategize.

But even though I didn't indulge, I didn't object to David's use back then, so long as he didn't bring it home and he was careful about where he got it. And he was—his dealer was the compliance officer at his investment bank.

He gave up cocaine after the Fall, even though that was when he could have used the energy boost the most. Instead his weed usage went up as he spent his days drifting between couch and bed. His alcohol usage went up, too, as he spent his nights drifting between bed and couch.

I could handle his drinking. I'd grown up with drunkards, and everybody I'd ever known had an alcoholic somewhere in their life. They dealt with it and so could I. But then David started disappearing at odd hours of the night, and I started to notice things disappearing, too—a piece of jewelry, the oil painting we bought from a chichi gallery in SoHo, money from my wallet. For a long time he let me pretend it was only alcohol he was abusing. He'd even slosh a little whiskey on his clothes for effect, sip a little to scent his breath. It was our unspoken pact: I'd enable his habit if he'd enable my pretense.

He didn't bother anymore; he didn't try to hide it. But still it was a jolt to see the truth laid out so starkly.

I lifted his wrist and checked for a pulse and found it. He might be dead to the world, but he wasn't dead to me. Not yet, anyway. Carefully I slid the needle from his vein and untied the rubber strap from his arm. I searched each of his pockets, and he didn't stir, even when I slipped my hand underneath him. In the back pocket of his pants I found his stash: three little baggies of a fine powder. I flushed it down the toilet and wrapped the needle and strap in a garbage bag and put it by the door.

I found his wallet in his other back pocket. There were only a few bills left in it, not enough to do any damage on their own, but I took them anyway. I'd started to put the wallet back when the photo sleeve fell open and I got my second jolt of the day.

My own face looked up at me. It was my last professional portrait, a head-and-shoulders shot in front of a shelf of law books, taken for the Jackson Rieders website. There I was, the golden girl of yore, wearing salon highlights and a Theory suit and a supercilious smile.

I hadn't realized he was carrying around this old photo. The discovery might have charmed me or made my eyes well up. But it didn't. It only made me jealous of that other girl—the one who didn't exist anymore, the only one he'd ever loved.

I took the photo out and tossed the wallet on the floor. On my way out the door I picked up the garbage bag and dropped it in a dumpster two blocks away. I threw the photo in after it.

–

One month in, my routine was well established at CDMI. Every morning I went to my own little office first, checked my voicemail and email for anything from Barrett or any company-wide blasts—those were the only two possibilities—got a cup of coffee, then took the stairs down to the document room.

In my mind I called it The Lab—it was that sterile and that secret. According to Lester Willard, the paralegal-cum-security guard, the room was to remain locked at all times. Only the two of us were permitted entry, and he had the only key. None of the documents were to be removed from the room. A copier stood in one corner of the vast white space, and all photocopying was to be done on that machine and that machine only. The same machine would be used for Bates-stamping to place identifying numbers on the documents that eventually would be produced to Mark Ivins.

On one of the tables was a computer for my use in indexing the documents. It was a standalone unit without Wi-Fi and not connected to the company LAN. The only other furniture in the room was a single chair on wheels for me to roll from table to table as I did my document review, and a stationary chair for Lester that he kept by the door.

All the documents in the room, all those stacks of pure white paper, were photocopies. The first day I asked Lester where the originals were, and he replied, "I wouldn't know, ma'am," which soon became his default response to every question I asked. He worked the copier whenever I gave him a stack of documents, but otherwise he spent the day in his chair, reading the paper and mostly watching me. He was my paralegal-cum-babysitter.

Some of the documents I'd seen before. They were copies of the original papers I'd found in the file boxes in my office the first day on the job. None of these elaborate security measures were in place then, probably because the boxes arrived without warning after Barrett was unexpectedly called to KL. It was pure accident that I'd stumbled upon them, and now I was glad I'd taken such care in resealing the boxes. It was obvious that Barrett considered them to be highly sensitive.

My marching orders from Barrett were to identify any privileged or confidential documents among these towering piles of papers. The privileged documents were easy to spot, since they almost always involved communications to or from a lawyer. As soon as I developed a roster of pertinent lawyers' names, I was able to breeze through that part of the job. Identifying confidential employee information was a little harder, with thousands of people in the company's employ, but once I came upon the payroll records, I was able to create a database of employee names.

All of this was routine work in preparing documents for production to a litigation adversary. But nothing about The Lab and Lester was routine, and that tipped me off: there had to be something far more sensitive than attorney letters and employee records among these documents.

One day last week I thought I'd found it.

I came upon a stack of employee medical records. Apparently every new hire underwent a medical assessment upon arrival at PsT, to screen out any serious or infectious diseases. The doctors' notes were there, in English, listing DOB, height, weight, BP, temperature, pulse rate, respiration rate, then a handwritten *OK to work*. It was the DOB that jumped out at me. Some of them were as young as ten, yet the doctor's note was the same: *OK to work*. I cross-checked the children's names with the payroll records and confirmed it. Those children photographed in the dining hall at PsT weren't family members of employees, as I'd thought. Or at least not only family members. They were employees, too.

Okay, so CDMI used child labor. They weren't the first Western company to exploit Asian child labor, and the practice didn't violate any local laws. But it would be an enormous black eye for the company if the media found out, and I could see why Barrett was worried.

More to the point, I could see that the medical records were not remotely responsive to Mark Ivins's document request. There was no legal requirement to produce these files to him, and hundreds of reasons not to. Hundreds of employees under the age of sixteen.

So I pulled all the employee medical records, placed them in a box, sealed it, and told Lester to deliver it to Mr. Barrett, for his eyes only.

I thought that might be the end of the DEFCON 1 level of secrecy, but the next day I got an email from Barrett: *Shay, good work flagging those confidential employee documents. Might still be more. Stay alert! Barry*

–

Today I discovered the real smoking gun.

It was Saturday, but I came into the office anyway. I did every day. It was warm there, and the coffee and Internet were free. Besides, there was nothing to do at home but worry about David if he wasn't there and maintain silence if he was.

Lester had agreed to come in on his day off but not until after lunch. I couldn't work on the documents without my official escort into The Lab, but I kept myself otherwise busy. I read the news online, focusing especially on the fashion features and anything coming out of Southeast Asia. I drafted some of the boilerplate language I would use in responding to Mark Ivins's document requests, and I updated the forms I'd developed during my time at Jackson Rieders. I found some hanging file folders in the supply room and organized the drawers in my desk.

In the bottom of one drawer I found the documents I'd copied from the file boxes my first day on the job, the air charter contracts that had been misfiled with the asset sale documents. Also in that drawer was the legal pad containing the handwritten index of the boxed files I'd prepared that first day. As it turned out, it was a wasted effort, since I had to start from scratch to prepare the same index down in The Lab. I tossed the legal pad in the wastebasket, but as the pages fanned out in a cascade of words and numbers, one of the entries caught my eye.

I pulled the papers back from the trash. The notation was my summary of the sale of one of the real estate parcels at Paradis sur Terre. I'd listed the sale price as $2.4 million, but I felt certain the settlement sheet I'd seen in The Lab listed it as $4.1 million. Maybe I was remembering wrong, but I didn't think so. Or maybe I'd made an error in the entry, either here or downstairs. But again, I didn't think so.

I wasn't allowed to take any documents out of The Lab, but nobody said I couldn't take any documents in. I photocopied my handwritten index, and when Lester called to let me know he'd arrived, I tucked the pages inside the waistband of my skirt. They crackled a bit as I walked downstairs to The Lab, but Lester didn't seem to notice. He swiped his keycard through the lock and let me in.

I set him to work Bates-stamping a few thousand pages that I'd already cleared for production to Mark Ivins. Once he was occupied with the machine in the corner of the room, I pulled the photocopies from my skirt and smoothed them out on the table. Then I sat down at the computer and opened the document index I'd been creating here in The Lab. It took only a moment to confirm that my recollection was correct. My hand-written notes showed proceeds of $2.4 million for that particular parcel of real estate. The entry on the computer screen showed proceeds of $4.1 million.

I wheeled my chair across the room and located the settlement sheet for that transaction. The sale price that appeared there was also $4.1 million. Okay, I thought, so I made a mistake in my handwritten notes. But I didn't believe it.

I did a side-by-side comparison of the index on the screen against my handwritten index. I went through every asset sale from PsT—real estate, equipment, raw materials, and finished goods. In nearly every instance, my notes from the original documents in the file boxes showed a much lower sale price than the copies in The Lab. A forklift sold for either $15,000 (per my notes) or $25,000 (per the computer screen). A sewing machine for either $1,495 or $2,799. It went on and on. Cafeteria tables, trucks, air compressors, mattresses, cutting machines—all the sales proceeds were greater than what I'd recorded from the original documents in the file boxes.

I scooted my chair across the room to the table where the closing binders and bills of sale were stacked, and I double-checked the sales figures against those documents. They all matched the numbers I'd entered into the computer; so my mistake, if I'd made one, hadn't been made in The Lab.

But it wasn't one mistake. It would have been a mistake in recording the sale prices of literally hundreds of assets.

One mistake I could admit, but two hundred? No.

The documents in The Lab were copies. The documents I'd indexed from the file boxes were originals. The conclusion was inescapable. Someone had altered the copies to inflate the sales proceeds of the PsT assets.

Madame de Martineau had boasted in her annual letter to the shareholders that CDMI had sold off the assets so successfully that it had turned the proverbial sow's ear into a silk purse. Somebody, at her behest or Barrett's, must have doctored the sales documents to support that boast.

Reality check: CDMI couldn't just make up numbers. It was a publicly held company with certified public accountants doing regular audits. If there'd been a discrepancy between the reported sales proceeds and the actual monies received into the company's bank accounts, the auditors would have caught it. And the documents couldn't have been altered just for purposes of the lawsuit. Mark Ivins had access to the audited financials, and he'd catch any discrepancy, too.

That had to mean the company actually did receive the total amount it was claiming, but not from the asset sales in question. So what else did it sell to arrive at that silk purse?

The answer was obvious: drugs. Deep in the jungles of Myanmar, CDMI had turned to drug trafficking to save its bottom line. The idea wasn't far-fetched. That was exactly what John DeLorean was accused of doing years ago in a last-ditch effort to save his failing car company. CDMI could have used the drug proceeds to shore up its balance sheet, but it had to disguise the source of that money. So what it did was inflate the proceeds of its legitimate asset sales.

Now I understood The Lab and Lester and all the elaborate security measures. I stole a glance at him. He was still busy at the copier, but he clocked me with a side-wise glance as I wheeled my chair back to the computer. I picked up a random file and pretended to study it. I needed to look and act normal for his sake. I couldn't let him guess what I'd stumbled upon. He might very well have been part of the drug trafficking business when he was stationed in Southeast Asia. That would explain his assignment here. He'd know to be on the lookout, and he'd be especially vigilant where those doctored sales figures were concerned.

Now I understood something else—why, against all odds, I'd been hired. Barrett must have figured out how desperate I was for a job, and how desperate I'd be to keep it. He knew he could count on me to keep my mouth shut.

I didn't go near the asset sales files for the rest of the day, but they weighed heavily in my thoughts. I was working for a drug trafficker. Covering up for a drug trafficker.

I tried to rationalize it away the same way I had when I'd discovered the company was exploiting child labor. I tried to convince myself that none of this was my problem. I hadn't doctored those documents, and no part of my assignment required me to examine the numbers. I wouldn't even suspect they'd been falsified if I hadn't accidentally stumbled on the file boxes that first day. My assignment was simply to flag the privileged and confidential documents and organize the rest for production. That was the extent of my job. That was what I was being paid for, and that was all I was going to do.

–

It was snowing when I emerged from Marketplace Tower that night, and a couple inches already blanketed the pavement. Working all day in a windowless room made me oblivious to the weather until the cold reality struck. I flipped up the hood on my parka, but there was no way to protect my feet, and my pumps were sodden by the time I reached the station. My train was delayed, and I stood shivering on the platform for twenty minutes until it arrived. The heat wasn't working in my car, and my teeth were chattering by the time I reached my stop. I promised myself a hot bath the minute I got home, and I prayed the boiler wouldn't be on the fritz again.

I got off the train and ran the rest of the way home and down the stairs to our apartment. I unlocked the door and hit the light switch. And stopped dead on the threshold.

The apartment had been ransacked. Drawers were upended and dishes flung into shards. The mattress was pulled off the bed and ripped open. Stuffing erupted from the gash. Some of the Sheetrock had even been pried from the wall, exposing the studs and wiring and tufts of pink insulation.

*We've been robbed!* was my first panicked thought. But an instant later I knew it wasn't true. No one could be desperate enough to rob the poorest people in New York.

No, this was David's work. He'd been searching for his stash—or my cash. He'd done the same thing many times before. But this time was different. This time there was fury behind it. The only thing left untouched was the beanbag chair. He must have felt confident that I wouldn't be so bold as to hide anything in the very chair he was sleeping in. Or maybe he simply wanted to be sure he'd have a place to sleep when—if—he came back.

When he came back. I wondered if he'd still be in the rage that had caused all this destruction. Until now, even on our worst day, I'd never felt unsafe with him. I wondered if we'd finally crossed that line. I wondered if I should lock the door or go stay somewhere else.

But I had nowhere else to stay. And neither did he.

I picked up the broken crockery, slid the drawers back into the dresser and cabinets, hauled the mattress onto the bed, and pushed the stuffing back inside as best I could.

When I went to bed, I left the door unlocked.

# Chapter 17

*A sound mind in a sound body*. Mrs. Casco's advice wasn't always original, but it was always valuable. Case in point. The better I got at books and exams in middle school, the more I tended to shut myself up in the library, and the less I tended to move. It was Mrs. Casco who made me get outside and run and play and try out for sports and work as hard at exercise as I worked at studying. She helped me out with uniforms and fees and rides to and from practice, and she sat in the bleachers and cheered me on through the seasons, from hockey to swimming to lacrosse, from JV to varsity to team captain and MVP. Thanks to the campus gyms at Brown and Columbia, I was able to keep it up through college and law school, and after that I could afford to join the trendiest gym in Manhattan.

I was in the best shape of my life on the day I lost my job. In my first year of poverty, I gained ten pounds on cheap, starchy foods and lost all my muscle tone through lack of a gym. There was a reason why obesity was the scourge of the poor.

Salvation came only when I took up running. I ran for miles, hours, every day, through three of the five boroughs, through posh neighborhoods and poor, at all hours of the day and night, and I never once feared for my safety, because I knew I could outrun anyone who might threaten me.

These were the thoughts roiling through my mind while I jogged in place in Interview A. I'd been in this room now for twelve hours, slept for a few of them, and sat for the rest, until I realized that my brain was in danger of atrophying along with my muscles. If I hoped to have any shot at matching wits with Ingram Barrett, I had to keep my blood flowing. So I ran for an hour, did jumping jacks and burpees, and was just cooling down when Detective Cruz entered the room.

"Oh!" He stopped short. "Sorry."

I was standing on one leg with the other stretched out behind me in an arabesque. He looked embarrassed, as if he'd caught me flossing or worse. I lowered my leg to the floor and stood up straight. "Just trying to keep my blood circulating," I said.

"Sure. I get it."

Something seemed to have changed again. His eyes were once more soft, and his lip no longer curled into the sneer he'd worn during our last session.

He held up his arms. He had a big paper bag in one hand and a small paper bag in the other. The aroma of grilled meat was floating out of one of them. "I brought you some lunch," he said. "And some clothes from your apartment."

"Oh! Thank you!"

I couldn't say which one made me happier. He handed me the bags. I wanted to tear into the food, but not while he was standing there. I took a peek inside the larger bag.

"I don't know if I brought the right clothes." He shifted uncomfortably. "They were in the hallway outside your apartment."

I nodded. That was where I'd last seen them. Inside the bag were a sweater, jeans, socks. A bra and panties. I looked up at him.

He had the grace to blush. "I brought some shoes, too."

My running shoes were in the bottom of the bag. "Thank you. Thank you so much."

"You're still free to go, you know."

"I know. But you know why—"

"Yeah, I know." He nodded toward the bag of clothes. "Sorry I couldn't find a coat."

"That's all right." The only coat I owned was in his evidence lockup. "It's plenty warm in here."

"You may not be here much longer, though."

My gaze sharpened. "Oh?"

"Looks like your story checks out. Your keycard was in your bag, like you said."

"Thank you for checking."

"And, um, your prints aren't on those résumés. Nobody's are."

"Ah," I said. "Like somebody wore gloves."

He nodded. "We just need to nail down the source of the gun, and we can wrap this up."

"I see." I thought a moment. "Can't you run it through that federal database? What's it called?"

"IBIS, and we already did. The gun's never been used in any reported incident."

"Oh."

"And the maker of the DIY kit sold thousands of them, but none to Lucy Carter-Jones."

"Or to me."

"Or to you."

"So what else can you do?"

He hesitated, as if wondering how much more he could share with me, then went ahead. "We're searching her house this afternoon. Looking for a gun safe or ammo or even some metalworking tools."

"All the things you didn't find in my apartment."

"Right."

"But what if you don't find them in her house, either?"

He didn't answer. He turned to the door and put his hand on the knob, but he stopped there. "Even if we don't," he said without looking back—he spoke barely above a whisper, and I knew he was confiding something he shouldn't—"it looks like we found her suicide note."

He seemed to regret the words as soon as he spoke them. He wrenched the door open and hurried from the room.

I sat, stunned, after he was gone. Lucy left a suicide note? She actually did mean to kill herself?

Wow.

# Chapter 18

I can't do this anymore.

Lucy's text had landed last night while Barrett was out to dinner with two other couples. He'd glanced at it on his lap while Melanie harangued the waiter about the carb count of every item on the menu. Then he'd pocketed his phone and resumed perusing the wine list. It never occurred to him that *this* meant her life. His conscience was clear on that point. At the time it was the *anymore* that puzzled him. Because it was already done. He wasn't asking her to do any *more* than to keep her mouth shut about it. He needed to have another conversation with her, obviously, but at the time it also seemed obvious that it could wait until Monday morning.

Now, though, looking at the readout of the text synced through to Ma Belle, he had to wonder—should he have realized? Could he have prevented this awful tragedy?

It was a terrible loss, and he allowed himself a brief moment to mourn her. It may have been a stretch when he'd told the police she was a dear friend, but there was no question she was a valuable employee. There couldn't have been a more perfect interface with the company's wide and varied workforce. Her familiarity with Asian culture made her someone the factory workers could relate to; her upper-crust British accent was all it took to intimidate the Creatives and keep them in line; and her no-nonsense efficiency was everything the Admins wanted in an HR director. If only she'd been a little less fastidious. He mourned that as well.

The whole Admin team was currently mourning her in an impromptu gathering in Reception. CEO Phil Duvall was making one of his rare visits to Marketplace Tower, and when he sent out an office-wide blast that he'd be *receiving* in Reception, everyone felt entitled to abandon their work and flock around him like he was laying on hands or something. Barrett stayed in his office, door closed, and watched the proceedings on CCTV.

By all rights Duvall's office should have been here in the Admin headquarters. Not only because he was CEO but because the accounting office was here, and Duvall was also the fucking CFO. But he preferred to maintain his office with the Creatives on Seventh Avenue and another one in Tours so he could *liaise with Madame*. He liked to dress like the Creatives, one day in a turtleneck and beret, another in a dashiki and gladiator sandals. Today, for his visit to the hinterlands, he wore a tweed jacket and a pair of voluminous plus fours, as if golfing in the twenties or shooting pheasants in Derbyshire.

Barrett watched the Ma Belle screen as Duvall swanned around the employees, doling out two-grip handshakes and pressing forehead to forehead as if he could ease their grief with the power of his touch. Now and then he pasted on a brave smile and posed for selfies. Introducing himself to everyone as Phillippe, when Barrett knew for a fact that the name on his birth certificate was Philip. He even sported a little French mustache with waxed tips, like he was some kind of maître d'. Most of the Admin employees recognized him for the phony he was, but they treated him like visiting royalty. He was their only living conduit to Madame de Martineau. She might preside over the board meetings by telephone (audio only; no video hookup— *Vanity, thy name is former supermodel*), but she otherwise saw no one, spoke to no one, except Duvall. He was her official gatekeeper. No one—including Barrett, much to his resentment—could speak to Madame directly. Everything had to be funneled through Duvall.

Rumor had it that they'd once been lovers—a rumor Duvall did nothing to dispel. If true, it made him the only man in history to sleep his way to the top. At least the only straight man. At any rate, it worked. He started out as an accountant for Madame's fledgling design firm. A decade ago, she made him CFO, and five years later she named him as her successor. Today he held the titles of president, CEO, and CFO, though they were titles in name and comp packages only. Everyone in Admin knew it was Barrett who was doing all the heavy lifting in this operation.

The video feed on his Ma Belle screen showed Duvall heading this way. Barrett must be the last whistle stop on the papal tour. "Mr. Duvall's here," Marcia announced through the speaker as the office door swung in.

"Barry!" Duvall cried with a big shit-eating smile on his plump chinless face.

"Phil!" Barrett jumped up and met him for a handshake that they both held for thirty seconds too long. "Just wanted to say hello."

"So glad you did. Coffee?"

"No, no. Can't linger."

Under the tweed jacket, Duvall wore a waistcoat and a woolen tie. Barrett stole a glance down, expecting to find wellies on his feet. But no, only a pair of sturdy leather brogues.

"Just wanted to pop in and check that all's well."

"Glad you did."

"That brouhaha last night — that's all taken care of, is it?"

"In progress," Barrett said, tight-lipped. "In fact, the detectives are on their way over here now to review a few details. Be great if you could join us."

"No, no. Wouldn't want to step on your toes. Anyway, I'm afraid I have to be going. Off to Tours tonight!"

"Give my best to Madame."

"Yes, yes, and give my love to Andrea, won't you?"

Andrea was Barrett's first wife, divorced eight years ago. "I sure will," he said.

—

Barrett seethed for a full ten minutes after he left. *That brouhaha*. As if Lucy's death were some kind of minor dustup. He knew Duvall's game. By downplaying the whole thing, he thought he could maintain his *plausible deniability*. As if such a thing existed. If Barrett went down, so would Duvall. He was the one who got Madame de Martineau's blessing for the scheme, and he was the one who massaged the numbers to make it work, and Barrett had him on tape confirming all of the above. Or rather, on a digital voice recording that was now tucked into Barrett's wall safe at home under the cash and jewelry.

"The detectives have arrived, Mr. Barrett." Marcia's voice came through the speaker. "Mr. Culligan's assistant has shown them to the theater."

"Ma Belle, show me the theater," Barrett commanded the box on his desk, and instantly the screen lit up with a shot of the auditorium on twenty-nine. Detectives Riley and Cruz were waiting there, as he'd instructed. They were sitting in the front row, their butts sunk deep into the plush upholstered chairs. But they'd resisted any temptation to recline them: their seatbacks were in the locked and upright position.

Riley's eyes were closed, and they both looked like they were dead on their asses. They'd have to be, after fifteen hours on this case and without the benefit of the fear-induced adrenaline that was keeping Barrett alert. By now they'd be desperate to wrap this up. They'd be willing to accept any reasonable theory.

Time to check in on Culligan. "Ma Belle, show me backstage left," he said, and the video cut to Jack Culligan waiting in the wings. His lips were moving soundlessly, and beads of sweat dotted his forehead. He looked like he was rehearsing his lines. He was too nervous, and Barrett worried that he might be the next weak link in the chain. He'd need close watching.

"Ma Belle, connect me to Jack Culligan." Barrett watched as Culligan pressed the wire at his ear and the call connected. "All set, Jack?"

"All set."

"On my way."

He went downstairs and joined Culligan backstage. "Go ahead," he said, and Culligan pushed a button that lowered the jumbotron screen at the front of the stage. They entered from stage left.

"Gentlemen," Barrett said as Riley shook himself awake. "Mr. Barrett," Cruz called up. "We'd like a word alone."

"Of course. Whatever you need. But first—Jack has something to show you."

Culligan stepped forward. "When we met this morning, you asked us for the rest of our internal surveillance from last night. And for the hard drives off their computers. We've pulled all of that together for you. But there're a couple things we want to highlight. Let's start with Ms. Lambert's movements after she left Ms. Carter-Jones's office. These clips track her back to her own office."

Barrett and Culligan moved to the opposite wings of the stage as the house lights dimmed and a video began to play on the screen. The first sequence was the same clip they'd shown the detectives earlier, the one with Shay Lambert coming out of Lucy's office and clapping her hands over her teary face. But now it was magnified fifty times. Now they could see not only that Lambert was crying but that her whole body was trembling.

"We saw this already," Cruz called up to the stage.

Culligan nodded. "Now watch as she comes around the corner."

Another camera was activated as Lambert came into view. The time stamp on this clip read 20.40.32, about four minutes after the previous clip. She seemed to be walking in a normal gait in this one, with no obvious sign of distress.

"And here she is, coming into the corridor toward her own office."

The time stamp said 20.43.06, and she was striding purposefully, her shoulders back and her chin high. The camera followed her down the hall to an open office door. She went through, and although there was no audio on the footage, it looked very much like she slammed the door.

Culligan played three more time-stamped clips: Lambert emerging from her office ten minutes later; striding down the corridor; and rounding the corner to the elevator.

"Now I'll show you Ms. Carter-Jones's movements." This video clip showed the door to Lucy's office opening, and Lucy pulling on her coat as she came out. She turned and locked the door behind her. Another clip with another time-stamp jump showed her turning a corner and walking down the corridor, and the final one showed her turning in to the elevator bank.

"You've already seen the elevator surveillance, I believe," Culligan said, "but for the sake of continuity, I'll play that now."

The screen cut to the elevator bank and the image of Lucy's back as Lambert came up beside her. Lambert spoke some soundless words and turned to face the elevator. The doors opened and both women stepped on.

The next clip they'd also seen before: the two women standing inside the elevator. Lucy's face was a mask of horror, then the screen went blank.

"That look on her face." Barrett came out of the wings to stand silhouetted before the white screen. "I've never seen her look so scared. Obviously she was terrified of Lambert and what she might do."

"Then why'd she get on the elevator with her?" Cruz said.

"Who knows? A desire to maintain normalcy no matter the situation? Whatever, she soon regretted it."

"We'll need the raw footage."

Barrett nodded at Culligan, who trotted down the stairs on the side of the stage and handed Cruz a large manila envelope. "In there you'll find a flash drive with the video footage, along with affidavits establishing authenticity and chain of custody," Barrett said. "You'll also find flash drives containing the non-privileged contents of Lucy's computer, and the same thing for Lambert. Meanwhile, I want to draw your particular attention to this document that we found on Lucy's computer."

The screen lit up again with a supersize image of a form. It was a CDMI form, with the white dove logo in the upper left corner. *Notice of Termination* was the preprinted heading. Barrett used a laser pointer to highlight the first field. Lambert's name was typed into that box. Next he pointed to the either/or boxes farther down: *Without Cause* and *With Cause*. The second box had an X filled in. Below that was a blank for *Grounds*, and the field was filled in with the words *Falsified Employment History*. Barrett ran the laser to the bottom of the form, where there was a line for *Employee Acknowledgment*. It was blank. Below that was a notation that *Employee declined to sign*. He highlighted that for a long moment before he turned back to his audience.

"She was combative. She left in tears. But by the time she returned to her own office, you can see her resolve in her posture. She wasn't going out like a lamb."

"I got a question," Cruz called from his seat. "For you, I guess, Mr. Culligan. Doesn't company policy state that a terminated employee has to be escorted off the premises by security?"

Culligan glanced at Barrett before he answered. "It does."

"So why didn't you have a security officer on site?"

"It was Sunday. Super Bowl Sunday. No one was on duty—"

"And Lucy said it wouldn't be necessary," Barrett put in.

"Uh-huh," Cruz said, obviously not buying it. "Doesn't company policy also state that terminated employees must surrender their keycards?"

"Yes."

"And Lambert still had hers."

Barrett answered again. "Lucy's assistant was in charge of collecting the cards. She wasn't in the office last night, obviously, and I expect Lucy simply overlooked it."

"That's it? Mistakes were made?"

"What can I say, Detective? These policies are written in a vacuum for an idealized, perfect situation. In real life, mistakes are made. But you can see what happened. She was terminated, she refused to sign, she refused to surrender her keycard, she was clearly hostile."

"And Ms. Carter-Jones was clearly suicidal."

Barrett scoffed. "That's ridiculous."

"Her husband confirms it. She'd been anxious about something for a while. She was taking Xanax. She was especially upset last night. So upset that he was frantically trying to reach her. But she wouldn't take his calls or answer his texts."

Barrett shrugged. "That could mean anything."

"What does it mean to say *I can't do this anymore*?"

Slowly Barrett came down off the stage. "You're referring to the text she sent me last night."

"That's right. And if you'd like to do this in private—" Cruz nodded in Culligan's direction.

"No, Jack can stay. He's already acquainted with these facts. As I told you this morning, I directed Lucy to fire Lambert last night. I wanted her gone before the office opened this morning. Lucy was reluctant, I admit it. She wanted to open an investigation, give Lambert a chance to defend herself, paper up the file. But I wasn't worried about blowback. Lambert wouldn't dare sue us with that bald-faced lie on her résumé. Lucy didn't like doing it that way, though. It didn't sit right with her. If she was upset about anything last night, that's what it was. Now that I think of it, that's probably why she forgot to get the keycard back. In any event, that's what she meant when she said *I can't do this anymore.*"

"You can't know that."

"In fact, I can. She spoke the identical words to me on the phone earlier when I told her to fire Lambert."

"But she said she can't do this *anymore.* Like this wasn't an isolated case. This was something ongoing."

Barrett acknowledged it with a grim shrug. "Not ongoing, exactly. But it happened once before, with another young lawyer I wanted gone. That was on a weekend, too, and Lucy wasn't happy about the way that was done, either."

"Why'd you fire that one? Another case of résumé fraud?"

Barrett scowled at the jibe. "That one wasn't willing to do the work. Look, I'm a tough taskmaster. I make no apologies." He took a breath and let his expression relax. "But I did apologize to Lucy. I told her I wouldn't ask her to do it this way again. After this I'd follow protocol. She sent me that text to let me know she'd be holding me to that promise."

The detectives looked at each other. "Interesting spin." Riley hauled himself to his feet. "Let me give you another one."

Barrett spread his arms wide, like *Take your best shot.*

"Ms. Carter-Jones was having an affair. With you, Mr. Barrett. And the guilt was eating her up."

Barrett barked a laugh. He wished he had that super-power now: he'd freeze this scene until he could work it out. He had to wonder if that wouldn't have been a better play all around. It would have given Lucy a reason for suicide that had nothing to do with business. No one would go digging for any other skeletons in her closet if they could write this all off as a sex scandal. And it would have been a solution that didn't require the sacrifice of Shay Lambert. But manufacturing an affair? He couldn't do that to Melanie, not in their no-prenup marriage, and there was even the risk that the board might demand his resignation. No, better to stick to the course they were on. "That's absurd," he said.

"She was popping Xanax like breath mints," Riley said. "She was ducking her husband's calls. The guilt was eating her up."

"That's ridiculous," Barrett said. "Lucy was the consummate professional. Everything about her was above reproach. You can ask anyone."

"Oh, we will," Riley said. "You can count on it."

Barrett shrugged. "Fine. But it's Lambert's friends and family you really should be talking to."

"She doesn't have any family," Cruz piped up.

Barrett raised an eyebrow. "Is that what she told you?" The detectives exchanged a glance.

"Ahh, I see. Jack?" Barrett snapped his fingers, and Culligan came down off the stage with a folder in his hands. "Our security team does a background check on each of our new hires. Jack's handing you a copy of what he found on Lambert. Take a look, gentlemen," he said as

176

Culligan handed the folder to Cruz. "She's not who she says she is."

# Chapter 19

The lights flashed on in the apartment. David was back. He was tearing through the dresser drawers. He was hauling armloads of clothes out of the drawers and dumping them out in the hallway. My clothes.

I bolted upright in bed. "David! What are you doing?"

He wheeled on me. "I want you out of here! Get up. Get out!" He took my suit off the hook and flung it out into the hall.

"David, please—stop!"

He stooped to sneer in my face. "God, you make me sick. It makes me sick to look at you!"

I couldn't tell whether he was desperate for a fix or he'd already had one. I scrabbled away from him, backward on the collapsing mattress.

"I wish I'd never married you. I wish I'd never met you! You ruined my life! I had everything going for me! Everything! And then you came along. Acting like you were gonna be somebody. Amount to something. But you were nothing but a loser. A total loser. And you've done nothing but drag me down with you."

"David, no, sweetheart—"

"You acted like you were going places, but that's all it was: an act. You're nothing but a fraud!"

"But I have a job again. We're going to be okay now."

"A *job*," he sneered. "You think you're something, you and your job. But you're nothing but a worker bee, a little insignificant worker bee. A peon. A wage slave. That's all you are."

"Even so, it's a start. We can build from here. We can get our feet back under us."

"Don't you fucking hear me?" he yelled. "There is no *we*!"

He lunged across the bed and dragged me off the mattress and across the littered floor of the apartment. I struggled to stand up, and he grabbed the front of my T-shirt and almost lifted me off my feet. I was startled by the power in his grip, that he had that much strength left in him.

"You get out, and never come back. You hear me? Never come back!"

He shoved me into the hall, and I landed sprawling on the pile of clothes. He slammed the door and shot the deadbolt with a hollow thud.

The door across the hall cracked open, and a single eye peeped out at me. "Sorry," I whispered.

"You want I call the cops?"

"No! No, everything's fine."

The door closed.

I rummaged frantically through the heap of clothes until I found my purse and briefcase. I checked inside. My cash was gone, but I was relieved to find that everything else was there. I rose to my knees. "David?" I whispered through the keyhole. I knocked softly and whispered his name again, and when he didn't answer, I pressed my forehead to the door. "David, please let me in."

No response.

"David, please. We can fight this together."

When his voice finally sounded, it was also through the keyhole and as soft as mine. "I hope you die," he said.

I sank back on the pile of clothes. He was out of his mind on drugs. He couldn't mean it.

I looked around bleakly. I didn't know what time it was. Very late or very early. People might soon be stirring. I couldn't stay here. But I didn't know where else to go. I had nowhere to go.

No, I remembered. As long as I had a job, I had somewhere to go.

I stood up and hoped that no one else would crack their door open in the next five minutes. I peeled off my T-shirt and rooted through the heap on the floor for underwear and a blouse, then put on my suit skirt and jacket. My rail pass was still in my wallet. My keycard was still in there. I could get to the office. The only place left in the world to go.

—

It was a Sunday, and so early that I had the office to myself. I made a fresh pot of coffee and searched for any food that might be left over from Friday, but there was nothing. The vending machine was stocked up, and the candy bars and chips and crackers were tantalizing through the glass, but without money that was where they had to remain.

Lester wasn't scheduled to come in today, and I didn't have any work to do that wasn't in The Lab. I played solitaire on my computer. I read the news online. I read about Operation Super Bowl and the arrests of thirty sex traffickers and the rescue of seventy victim workers. I read about a typhoon in the South China Sea and the feared loss of an entire Thai fishing fleet. I did the *Times* crossword. Anything to keep from thinking. To keep from hearing those ugly words. *Loser. Worker bee. Wage slave. I never would have married you. I hate you! I hope you die!* They ricocheted inside my head.

One phrase kept haunting me—*You act like you're something, but it's all just an act*—because that much was true. It had always been true.

I worked another puzzle. I read another news website. I went for a stroll around the perimeter of the thirtieth floor, then kicked off my shoes and turned it into a run. I ran lap after dizzying lap, but it was no use. I couldn't drown out the words in my head.

Work. Work would occupy me more than any of these attempted distractions. I unlocked my desk drawer and took out my notes on the PsT asset sales. I started to plug the numbers into an Excel spreadsheet, but I realized that anyone in the company could access it through the server, so I deleted all of it and wrote it out on a legal pad. In the first column, I put a shorthand description of the asset sold; in the second column, I recorded the actual price received; and in the third column, I wrote the falsified price that was on the documents in The Lab.

I filled pages after pages with the data, and when I was done, I totaled up the difference between the actual and the recorded prices. The delta was over $20 million. Twenty million dollars' worth of drug money masquerading as asset realization. Twenty million dollars' worth of drugs going into addicts' bodies and destroying their lives.

And here I was, working for the people responsible for such devastation. And grateful for the chance. David was right: I was pathetic.

I went online again and logged on to lawjobs.com. It was a site I used to visit twice a day, sometimes all day, continuously refreshing the page in hopes that something new would be posted and that if I were the first to see it, I might somehow ensure that the job was mine. I'd hoped those days were behind me forever, but here I was again, desperately scanning the job postings for something, anything, that would get me out of here.

It was late in the day when I spotted my ideal job. I was weak with hunger by then and bleary-eyed from a day of staring at the computer screen, so at first I thought I might have hallucinated it. I couldn't be seeing right. I blinked hard to clear my vision, but it was still there when I looked again. My ideal job. I was perfect for it. I knew that because it was the job I currently held. The posting was identical to the one I applied for last fall.

CDMI had reposted my job. Ingram Barrett was replacing me.

I was a piece of single-use plastic, to be disposed of after the single use was over. Barrett couldn't risk having me around after my project was done. Even if I never figured out the drug connection, I might let something slip inadvertently. Better just to let me go and count on the nondisclosure agreement to keep me silent. So he'd told Lucy Carter-Jones to find a replacement, and she'd posted the job.

Everything David said was true. I was nothing. Less than nothing. A worker bee. A wage slave. Fungible. Disposable. Human capital, to be exploited. Human resources, to be mined like ore until the vein was exhausted.

I lost a few hours after that. I may have fallen asleep in my chair, or passed out from hunger, or simply zoned out. But when I came to, it was after eight, and the top of Marketplace Tower was shrouded with fog.

I would miss the last train out if I didn't leave soon, though I had no idea where to go.

I reached into the desk drawer for my purse. Beneath it were the air charter contracts I'd squirreled away weeks ago. I couldn't remember what had bothered me about them, but there was something, and I took them out now and read them through again. They were all signed on behalf of CDMI by Lucy Carter-Jones, director of human resources, and the passenger manifests listed a total of eighteen hundred names on six flights. I recognized some of the names, many of them, from the database of employee names I'd created in The Lab.

One of the chartered flights carried the underage workers I'd flagged earlier, and that discovery prompted me to scan through all the names on the manifests. The passengers were divided by age and gender. Two flights carried men only. Two carried women over forty. The last two carried the younger women and children. That struck me as strange. I wondered if it was some religious thing.

I looked back at my charts showing the inflated asset sales, then back at the flight manifests. The inflated numbers and the passenger names scrolled through my mind in intersecting loops, then the loops lined up into parallel reels and they started to spin like the symbols displayed in a slot machine until one by one they clicked to a stop and lined up to spell it out.

My breath caught in my chest like a fist squeezing. The asset sales weren't inflated to conceal drug revenues. It was never about drugs. It was worse than drugs. It was eighteen hundred times worse.

I sat frozen with horror. I couldn't say how long. Those words rang inside my head again. Worker bees. Wage slaves. Fungible. Disposable. We were all the same.

I had the proof, and slowly I pulled myself together enough to put it into a chronology that told the whole story. I labeled the contracts with Post-it notes numbered one through six. I labeled the table of sales figures as number seven. Then I slid the documents into my battered briefcase and grabbed my coat.

A hush swelled through the penthouse corridors as I made my way to the elevator, broken only by the abiding hum of the building's mechanicals. I didn't know where I was going. I didn't know where I could go, but my feet kept moving. It was like I was sleepwalking or in a dream. A nightmare.

I arrived at the elevator bank. Someone else was waiting there, and as I came up beside her, I saw that it was Lucy Carter-Jones, director of human resources. Director of human trafficking.

I stared at her. "I know what you did," I said.

The center elevator arrived. The cage door opened. We stepped on. I reached into my bag, and her face froze in a mask of horror when she saw what I brought out.

Everything stopped. Darkness descended.

## Chapter 20

Four hours passed before the door to Interview A swung in again, and instantly I could see that something had changed since I last saw the detectives. Riley now wore a stubble of beard that was shockingly white against the gray pallor of his skin. Cruz's Vandyke was neatly trimmed again; he must have kept a razor in his desk. But it was their expressions that had changed the most.

"What?" I said. "What happened?" They might have struck out on their search of Lucy's house. But they still had the note; that should have been enough.

Cruz didn't answer or even look at me. He sat down and turned on the recording equipment, and he droned out all the preliminaries again: date and time, persons in the room, consents and waivers duly executed.

Riley ignored my question, too. "Hold up," he said to Cruz. "You just said Shay Lambert's in the room."

"Oh, you're right," Cruz agreed. "Let me correct that for the record. I should've said Sharona Chance." He looked at me then, finally. "Isn't that right?" he said, and he opened a folder and shot a paper across the table like a hockey puck.

I didn't need to look at it. I knew what it was. As soon as he said Sharona Chance, I knew they'd gotten their hands on my birth certificate. The name was Barb's little dig against the man who'd knocked her up. "My

Sharona" was their song, and Fat Chance was the name she gave him after he took off and she found out he wasn't really Paul Getty. "It was a stupid name," I said. "I never used it."

*You can call yourself whatever you want*, Mrs. Casco told me, so starting in eighth grade, I signed all my tests and homework papers as Shay Chance. The school eventually conformed my transcripts, and by the time I reached law school, I made it legal. Later I switched out Chance for Lambert and made that legal, too. A birth certificate wasn't a public record in the state of New York. No one was ever supposed to see it.

"Makes you wonder, doesn't it?" Riley said. "About the kind of person who'd kill off her own mother?"

"We were never close," I said in a low voice. "We didn't have any kind of relationship."

"Yeah, so we gathered," Cruz said. "That call you made to her on Christmas Day was the first time she'd heard from you in years."

They'd opened my phone. They'd talked to Barb.

"She told us a lot more than that," he said. "Things that make us wonder if you told us anything that's true."

"I have—"

"*Poor me, I'm an only child*," he said in a falsetto.

She'd told them about Roger and Tommy.

"They're half brothers," I said. "They're a lot older than I am. I barely knew them."

"Or maybe you deliberately withheld their names because Roger's doing time in a federal penitentiary."

"No. I didn't know that. We haven't been in touch for years."

"You'll never guess what he was convicted of."

During the few years when I knew him, he was arrested for public drunkenness, retail theft, auto theft, and assault. "I have no idea," I said.

"Illegal firearms sales," Cruz said. "And you'll never guess what kind."

I stared at him.

"Ghost guns. Homemade. From DIY kits he bought online."

"No. I didn't even know what they were until you—"

"From the same manufacturer as the gun that killed Lucy Carter-Jones."

I shook my head. "I haven't seen or heard from him in almost twenty years. I don't know anything about any ghost guns."

"You brought the gun onto that elevator," Cruz said.

"No—"

"You'd just been fired," Riley said.

My head swiveled his way. "No—"

Cruz: "Your marriage was over."

Riley: "And there you are, trapped with the woman who fired you."

Cruz: "When the lights go out."

Riley: "It wasn't Carter-Jones who snapped."

Cruz: "It was you!"

I was spinning between the two of them, shaking my head wildly at each accusation. "No. No, it was Lucy—"

Cruz pushed back from the table. "Stand up."

"What?"

He came around behind me.

"No, honestly, you're making a terrible mistake!"

He grabbed me and pulled me to my feet and jerked my arms behind me. "Sharona Chance Lambert, you are under arrest for the murder of Lucy Carter-Jones."

I felt the cold snap of handcuffs around my wrists.

*Interval*

# Chapter 21

In Old Norse mythology, Valhalla was where slain Viking warriors went for their heavenly reward. In Westchester County, it was where pretrial detainees went when they couldn't post bail.

That was where I went, in a prison transport van. It had a latticework of steel bars behind the driver's seat and the acrid odor of urine everywhere. It might have been an animal control van except for the metal posts in the floor that my leg irons were shackled to. The cold seeped up from the steel floor and spread frigid fingers up my torso and down each coatless arm. Through the windshield I could see the slant of snow falling through the beams of the headlights.

Valhalla was for warriors, and that was what I had to become. Roger and Tommy had been in and out of jail throughout my childhood, and they liked to scare me with tales of kidney punches and toothbrushes sharpened into shivs. They delighted in teaching me about sodomy and wolf packs. So from the moment I realized I was actually going to jail, I started to prepare my game face. It was just like Mrs. Casco taught me: put on the face you want the world to see. I wanted to be seen as a warrior, and I practiced it on the drive to Valhalla, galvanizing my eyes into a hot stare, clenching my jaw into a snarling grimace, staring at my fellow transport prisoners with a look that said, *Go ahead, I dare you.*

But they weren't looking at me. Three of them were huddled together and whispering in a language I didn't know. Hookers, I guessed, though not the happy variety. If there was such a thing. My fourth fellow prisoner was a white girl trembling so violently her teeth clicked. From fear, the cold, or the drugs she'd ingested—take your pick.

Upon arrival at the Women's Unit, we were led shuffling into a holding cell where the white girl promptly vomited onto the concrete floor and started to cry for her mother. Successfully, as it turned out. In less than thirty minutes, a guard arrived to take her to her parents; her bail had been posted. The three Asian women were soon taken away, too. I was left behind with the puddle of vomit.

An hour later I was processed, a term that made me think of packaged meat. I underwent a cursory medical exam—stick out your tongue, say *ahh*, hold this thermometer in your mouth until we finally remember to take it out ten minutes later. This was followed by a less cursory strip search. I used to laugh when my personal trainer used the term *prisoner squat*, but that was when I was wearing Lululemon leggings. It wasn't so funny when I was wearing nothing.

A shower came next, and I was glad for it after a long day in the office and a second long day in the police station. They gave me a scrap of a towel to dry myself with, but no comb and certainly no blow dryer. My hair was going to dry in tangles—I'd look like Medusa. But maybe that was a good thing: one more mark of the warrior.

I waited with the scant covering of the towel clasped around me while a clerk eyeballed me for size. She issued me a white cotton bra and panties, a set of orange scrubs, a pair of canvas sneakers, and a white T-shirt and blue pants for pajamas. I changed as directed into the underwear and scrubs, and they bagged the clothes I'd been wearing. They bagged my wedding ring, too. I didn't have any other personal property to be checked; my coat and purse and briefcase were still being held by the police as evidence.

I was assigned an inmate number, fingerprinted and photographed, then led to another clerk, who peck-typed my data into a computer and had to backspace with a sigh at regular intervals. Full legal name, address, birth date. Contact person? I hesitated before I named David Lambert, same address. But when I couldn't provide a telephone number for him, the clerk heaved another sigh and backspaced to delete his name. I watched it disappear across the screen, letter by letter, until he was wiped from my profile.

I didn't have any money to deposit into my commissary account, a deficiency that made the clerk sigh yet again. Then it was time for my allotted phone call, my single chance to find someone to post my bail. Who could I call? Not my mother. Not only was she broke, she was the one who'd landed me here. Not any of my old friends. I'd ghosted them years ago so they wouldn't know how far I'd fallen. Imagine if they could see me now. And certainly not Mrs. Casco. She might never recover from the shock and disappointment of learning how her brightest hope had turned out.

"No, there's no one," I told the clerk.

A guard arrived, a middle-aged woman, stout, with a warrior face at least as impressive as mine. She led me into Pod C in the Women's Unit, past a long corridor of cells on either side. They had a gridwork of steel bars and doors that slid open and closed, and two bunks in each, top and bottom, all currently unoccupied. I followed the guard in a zombie walk with my arms stretched out in front of me, heaped high with sheets, a blanket, a pillow, the rest of my prison clothes.

The guard spoke over her shoulder as we walked, biting out the rules and the daily schedule. Roll call at six a.m., breakfast, then work—everyone was required to work, in the kitchen, the laundry, or one of the prison industries. Then lunch, yard time, another roll call, and back to work until dinner.

She stopped beside a cell, and when she stood aside and glared at me, I knew this must be where I got off. All day I'd been wondering where I would sleep tonight, and here was my answer. This cell was my new home.

*Cell*, I thought as I stepped inside. Why did they call them *cells*? They should call them what they were. Cages.

"Lights out in thirty," she said. "You can stay here or go to the common room till then."

I stayed where I was. I didn't know where the common room was, and I wasn't ready to make my prison debut just yet. I let my face relax as the guard left, and I turned a slow revolution to take in the tiny room. It had two metal bunks cantilevered on the wall like a pair of oversize steel bookshelves. Cantilevered on the opposite wall was a smaller metal slab, this one serving as a desk, with an attached metal chair. Mounted to the end wall were a stainless-steel toilet and sink.

Neither bunk was made up, and there were no papers on the desk, no photos or other signs of habitation. It gave me hope that I'd be spared a roommate. Or rather, a cellmate. No, a cellie. I needed to learn the lingo.

I made up the lower bunk with the rough-weave sheets and a pilled blanket. When I stretched out on the bed, I realized it was the first time I'd been horizontal since early Sunday morning. I tried not to think about the bedbugs and bodily fluids that might reside in the lumpy mattress. I tried to relax and let my muscles sink into the bed. But I could feel the metal slab under me. It was the proverbial pea, and I was the proverbial princess.

Hot tears pooled in my eyes. I'd felt like a princess once, in my sparkling tower apartment with my handsome husband-prince. And now here I was, in prison. Charged with murder.

I shivered with the cold and tugged the blanket up to my chin. The hard metal bunk wasn't a pea. It was more like a mortuary slab. *They've killed me*, I thought, and tears of self-pity streaked down my face.

Or I'd killed myself. Because, really, I did this to myself. *My mother's dead. I'm an only child. My husband works nights.* They were stupid lies, easily exposed. If only those hadn't been the cops' first questions out of the box. I wasn't ready for them yet, penned up in that little room off the lobby with the gun blast still bouncing around inside my skull. Denying my family was simply a reflex, as involuntary as breathing. I hadn't been thinking like a suspect yet. I hadn't foreseen the land mines awaiting me.

Then there were my job-hunting lies. The Innocence Project. The software program. Harmless embellishments invented solely to get through an interview, but they'd backfired on me, too. Now my credibility was shot. The cops would never believe what really happened.

—

No, my family did this to me. They'd been dragging me down all my life, and here they were, doing it again. Barb and her big mouth. Roger and his stupid gun-making business. (*You tell me, Miss Fancy-Pants Lawyer*, Barb had said during my idiotic Christmas Day call. *How come it's legal to buy the kits and legal to make the guns but not legal to sell them? What about the Second Amendment? Huh? Sure, Mom*, I'd answered. *The Constitution definitely guarantees the right to keep and sell arms.*)

I remembered Mrs. Casco driving me home after debate practice one day when I was about thirteen, and there they were— Barb and Roger and Tom, all of them splayed on the front stoop with beer cans in their hands, my brothers shirtless and paunchy and tattooed, my mother with her trademark orange smear of lipstick and a kaleidoscope of changing hair color. I froze in the passenger seat as tears of shame flooded my eyes. *Forget them*, Mrs. Casco had said. *They're nothing to you. Less than nothing. In no time you'll be far from here, living your own life your own way, and it'll be like they never existed.*

It worked for a time. For a long time. Certainly David never doubted I was all alone in the world. It would have worked still if they hadn't found my birth certificate or tracked down Barb through my phone. Once they found her, it was all over. She couldn't keep her mouth shut about anything.

But there was no point in blaming this on my family. Seeking revenge against them would be as pointless as suing a homeless person. It would gain me nothing.

I had a far better target for my revenge: J. Ingram Barrett, Jr. He was the one who really did this to me, and if I figured out how to bring him down, it could gain me everything.

I had a lot of nights ahead to work out how I'd do it.

I scrubbed away my tears. Enough of that. I had to be a warrior, not a princess. A princess would spend this time wallowing in self-pity, but a warrior would be planning her attack. Or, in my case, my defense. Vengeance would come later, after exoneration.

–

A loud buzzer sounded, and the corridors of Pod C suddenly swelled with a cacophony of shouts and cries and laughs and grunts. My fellow detainees were being herded back to their cells before lights-out. I lay very still on my bottom bunk, hoping they wouldn't notice me as they streamed past the open door of my cell. Their voices were guttural and their language foul. "Who da fuck dat?" I heard someone say, and I braced myself, but no one ventured in.

The clamor died down a bit. Someone started to sing, and someone else roared for her to *shut the fuck up*. Then the cage doors shut with a booming clash of steel up and down the corridor. A minute later everything went dark.

The night sounds in Pod C were softer. Sobbing, snoring, and sex sounds. And in my cell, a different sound that only I could hear. The hum of the wheels turning inside my brain as I worked through what I was going to do next.

Exoneration first. Then revenge.

–

I made my prison debut in the morning, after roll call, when the doors clanged open up and down the block. The women swarmed out of their cells, voices buzzing loudly as they made their way to breakfast. Theirs were a sea of brown faces, African Americans and Latinas. Not a white face to be seen, and I realized why. White women made bail.

I let them pass before I stepped out and joined the end of the line crowding into the cafeteria. I kept my face a tight mask, tamping down every reflex to smile or show interest or any other emotion. Supreme boredom was the look I was aiming for in repose. But when some of the women turned and stared at me, I ramped it up to that face I'd practiced in the prison transport van: fierce, fearsome, a force to be reckoned with.

The cafeteria—or mess hall? the barracks term was probably more accurate—was a long, low-ceilinged room with regimented rows of metal tables and clamped-on metal chairs. Raised voices bounced off the concrete floor and boomeranged through the metal furniture until the decibel level was high enough to rival a Tribeca dance club. I went through the line and loaded up my tray with dry yellow lumps of scrambled eggs, sausage patties floating in a pool of grease, and fruit cocktail out of a can. Then I looked around for a place to sit. There were no empty tables, but I spotted a table with two empty seats at the end, and I took one of them.

There were four other women at the table, and they all stopped eating to stare at me. I resumed my look of bored indifference and shoveled a lump of egg into my mouth.

The woman at the far end of the table suddenly leaned around the woman beside her and stabbed a fork in my direction. The three other women stopped eating to watch. The fork was plastic and didn't concern me, but the woman holding it did. She was small and dark, Latina, with a purple bandana over her hair and a hard, wiry body coiled tight with energy. Even if I hadn't noticed the deference shown to her by the other women, it was obvious to me that this one was the alpha female. "What are you?" she demanded, fork pointed like a laser.

Later I would learn that was a routine question meaning *What are you in for? Drugs, hooking, who'd you kill, or what'd you steal?* But I didn't know that yet. I still defined myself by my job, not my crime. "I'm a lawyer," I said with my eyes narrowed and my tone brutal. I said it like I was saying *killer*. Like being a lawyer *was* my crime, and a pretty heinous one at that.

A rumble of murmurs rolled around the table, then spread to the next table and the table beyond that one. Dozens of women twisted in their seats to gape at me. But they didn't look hostile. They had a gleam of interest in their eyes. I thought they must be struck by the novelty of seeing a lawyer on this side of the bars. Penitentiaries were full of lawyers serving hard time, but I doubted there were any here in pretrial detention, for the obvious reason that lawyers could post bail or had friends who could post it for them. As both a lawyer and a white woman, I had no business being here at all.

But as it turned out, it wasn't the novelty that drew their interest. It was my potential usefulness. The women surged out of their seats and swarmed around me, buzzing with questions. *How long till they have to give me a trial? Don't they have to let me go if my boyfriend says he did it, not me? Don't my mom have to bring my kids to see me?*

They must have all had lawyers on the outside, but public defenders were notoriously overworked and underpaid and stingy with their time. A lawyer on the inside would be a real asset. They pressed in close, jostling one another to gain my ear, calling out their questions from all sides.

I had to clap my hands over my ears to close out the clamor. "I can't hear when you're all talking at once," I shouted.

The bandana-wearing alpha woman put two fingers in her mouth and blew a sharp whistle. Instantly everyone fell silent. "Back the fuck off!" she shouted. She stabbed her fork at me again. "You know any of this shit?" she said. "You ain't no real estate lawyer or nothin'?"

I took a bite of sausage, chewed, and swallowed. "I know all of this shit," I said.

The woman's chin came up, and her eyes narrowed. Her name was Nina, I soon learned, and she ran Pod C. She ordered everyone back to their tables and announced that the lawyer would take their questions one at a time, by appointment only, beginning in the common room that evening. She, Nina, would be in charge of the appointment book. "How much time for each?" she asked me.

"Depends on the question."

Nina shook her head. "No. We gotta do this orderly-like."

"Then make it fifteen-minute slots."

"Okay, bitches," she hollered. "See me if you want an appointment."

The other women seemed to know enough not to clamor around Nina. They formed a line and waited patiently until she finished her breakfast and waved the first one forward. She wrote that woman's name on her napkin, then waved the next one forward.

I finished my own breakfast and mentally reviewed everything I knew about pretrial criminal procedure. I'd never actually been employed by the Innocence Project, of course, but I'd put in enough volunteer hours there to pick up a working knowledge of criminal law. Enough hours that the local office director was willing to let me claim it as employment on my résumé. Anyway, you didn't need to know the answers to be a good lawyer; you only needed to know which questions to ask. I had this.

It hit me then. I didn't have to pretend to be a warrior to survive here in Valhalla. Because a lawyer *was* a warrior.

—

A bell clanged at the end of breakfast, and the inmates filed off to their assigned jobs in the kitchen or the laundry or the workshop. A guard stood at the door scanning the crowd. Not a guard, I reminded myself, a CO. His eyes landed on me, and he crooked a finger. "You," he shouted. "Come with me."

He was a white man with a scrawny neck and an Adam's apple that protruded like a tumescent organ. I got up and followed him uneasily. He took me by the elbow, bony fingers digging in, and led me out of Pod C and down a long corridor. He stopped at an unmarked door. *A broom closet?* I wondered, and I wondered next if this would be my introduction to prison rape. I looked him up and down. I was pretty sure I could take him in a fight.

He opened the door. It wasn't a darkened broom closet; it was a small office under the glare of fluorescent tubes in the ceiling. Three women in street clothes sat at three of the four metal desks. One of them was on the phone and the other two were peering at the screens of their last-generation computers. Against one wall was a bank of gray metal filing cabinets.

"Here she is," the CO announced.

The woman on the phone clapped her hand over the mouth-piece. "Can you type?"

"Yes," I said, startled.

"Then sit there." She pointed to the empty desk.

The CO left, and I sat down. It seemed that my work assignment was to assist these clerical employees with typing and filing and photocopying. While the other inmates did the dirty work of the jail, I would spend my days here, in a comfortable chair, in a clean office, with the thermostat set to a balmy seventy-two degrees. My white-woman privilege might have been useless when it came to raising bail, but I knew it was the only reason I'd landed this plum work assignment.

It turned out that jail was a business, with business records to process. It issued purchase orders and received invoices and maintained inventories of supplies just like any other business. And because the jail workshops made products for sale, there were also finished-goods inventories and shipping documents and records of the payments remitted to the county. There was the prisoner payroll, too, such as it was, at an average wage of forty-five cents an hour. My own wages were set at sixty-two cents an hour, a nod to my superior skill set. It meant almost five dollars would be credited to my commissary account at the end of the day: enough, I hoped, to buy a toothbrush. The next day might even earn me a comb.

We broke for lunch. That was followed by exercise time in the yard. I'd been issued a polyester-blend coat but no boots, and the snow was six inches deep outside. I huddled against the wall and stamped my feet and tried not to inhale the periwinkle clouds of tobacco smoke that drifted through the yard.

Then it was back to the office for my afternoon shift, where I was able to dazzle my bosses with a few functions they'd never mastered on Excel. Then a dinner of meat loaf, mashed potatoes, and canned peas. It was bland but hot and filling. I'd had three hot meals today, something I rarely experienced outside.

I spent the evening in the common room. It was a space set up for cards and checkers at steel tables with four attached seats each. It struck me that throughout the criminal justice system, all the way from Interview A to here in Valhalla, the chairs were always bolted to the tables. I'd never thought of using a chair as a weapon, but obviously someone had.

One of the tables was reserved for me, with a pen and legal pad already set out. Nina pointed me to my seat, called out a name, and a young Black woman hurried into the opposite seat. She was the first of the eight "clients" I advised over the course of the evening.

Once I never would have dispensed legal advice this way. Whenever friends or strangers tried to wrest an opinion out of me at the gym or a cocktail party, I'd tell them to make an appointment and sign a retention letter, and I'd be happy to answer their questions. It had been drummed into me at Jackson Rieders never to give advice or receive confidences except in the context of an acknowledged attorney-client relationship. It wasn't just to assure a fee. It was for self-protection. Otherwise any off-the-cuff remark could be construed as legal advice and form the basis of a malpractice suit, even when given for free.

Destitution had released me from such constraints. Nobody would bother to sue me now. So I listened to their stories, gleaned the gist of their problems, and gave them a five-minute answer and a list of issues to raise with their public defenders during their next sessions.

There was a depressing sameness to all of the women's stories. Whether they were in for solicitation or possession with intent or larceny or even drunk driving, there was always a man somewhere behind it. A husband or boyfriend who put her out on the street, or who gave her a package to deliver, or who enlisted her to make a straw purchase of a gun or to drive the getaway car. It was their men who dragged them down, every single time. In a world without men, none of these women would be here.

My last appointment was with a pregnant nineteen-year-old who had two children now in foster care. She wanted conjugal visits with their father, and she didn't like the answer I gave her. Addicted to love, I thought as her face twisted into a snarl and she lunged at me across the table. Nina got between us, and the girl backed down. I didn't even know what her crime was, but it seemed clear there was a man at the root of it, just as with all the others.

At the end of the night, the bell clanged in a signal to return to the cells. I snatched up the pen and paper and joined the line shuffling out of the common room. After an evening of hearing their stories, I felt like one of them. I might be the only white face among them, for sure the only one with a graduate degree, but I'd been dragged down by the men in my life, too, just as they had. In a world without David, Roger, and most of all Ingram Barrett, I wouldn't be here either. I occupied the rest of my march to Pod C visualizing a world without Barrett.

But—exoneration before revenge. I needed to write to David and get to the bottom of exactly what he'd done to land me here.

In the early days we wrote to each other all the time. It was just a silly lovers' game, since we were living together and saw each other morning and night. But there was something so thrilling about opening my briefcase at the office and finding a hand-written letter from David tucked inside, an ode to our lovemaking the night before or a paean to my body, using terms that would be vulgar in the hands of a lesser writer. But David had the same way with words that he had with my body. I'd read his letter again during lunch and again on my evening commute, and by the time I got home I'd be hot for him all over again.

When did he write the last of those letters? I tried to remember. Probably September 15, 2008. The day the world ended. And when did I write the last of my own letters to him? Probably a year later, when I found one unopened in the trash and realized there was no point in continuing.

I reached my cell and stopped short. Someone else was there, up on the top bunk, tugging a sheet into place. All I could see of her was her upturned backside in the orange scrubs. Then she leapt to the floor and stuck her landing like a gymnast.

"Oh, hi," she said as she turned. She was tiny, Chinese, I thought, with long black hair held up in a high pony. She'd tied a knot in the hem of her scrubs shirt so that it hugged her rib cage and gave a glimpse of her navel. She could have been thirteen or thirty. She looked like a teenage pop star. "I think you my cellie?" she said.

"I'm Shay."

"My name Jingjing."

I took a seat at the desk and picked up the pen. I had fifteen minutes before lights out. *Dear David*, I wrote. *You may have heard—*

"I no criminal," the girl said.

"Me, neither."—*about what happened in the elevator.*

"I mean, I not charged with anything. I a *material witness.*"

"Oh?" That was interesting. I looked up from the page. Here was one more white-woman privilege for me to enjoy, a cellie who was merely a witness. "Witness to what?"

Jingjing spoke her next words carefully, as if from a script, and with barely a trace of an accent. "International sex trafficking."

–

My only visitor was my court-appointed public defender, Harold Watkins. He was fortysomething, seriously over-weight, and perpetually short of breath. He was more experienced than the PDs assigned to most of my fellow inmates—a murder charge warranted a more senior defender—but since it was only second-degree murder, I suspected he was only a second-stringer. In any event I found him wanting. Especially when he began every visit by pushing the idea of a plea. I didn't want to face trial, he warned me. The DA might knock the charge down to manslaughter, he thought—

I stopped him cold. "No deal," I said, and handed him a type-written page. By that time I'd earned enough goodwill from my work supervisors that I was allowed the use of the office equipment, and I'd used it to prepare a list of assignments for Watkins. The law entitled me to the government-paid assistance of counsel, and I intended to fully avail myself of it. I'd come a long way from the twenty-five-year-old who had too much pride to apply for unemployment benefits.

Watkins skimmed the page and looked up with a frown. "Hire a forensic video expert?"

"They've doctored that surveillance video, I know it. An expert can prove it."

"Maybe. For a fee. A hefty fee."

"Yes, you need to petition the court for expert funding." I handed him a motion I'd already drafted to that effect.

He skimmed those pages. "This is a real long shot."

"No harm in asking. And no skin off your back, since I've done all the work."

He scowled in a way that made me suspect I was his least favorite client. I didn't care. I wasn't out to make friends. Only to influence people. Specifically, I hoped to influence the assigned prosecutor, an ADA named Max Harper. Watkins was right that I didn't want to go to trial. I was counting on the charges being dropped long before that. I was dropping breadcrumbs and counting on Harper to follow them.

Watkins was still running down the assignment list. "A deposition of your brother," he said, wheezing with the effort of speech. "In Leavenworth. Kansas."

"He'll testify that he never sold or gave me a gun."

"Of course he will. Nobody would expect otherwise. Of your brother or a convicted felon." He took his pen and drew a line through that task. "A trip to Kansas? That is skin off my back."

My mouth tightened, but I moved on to the next item on my list: the release of my briefcase from evidence.

His brow furrowed in deep fleshy folds. "How come? What's in it?"

"Confidential company documents."

"Saying what?"

"Sorry. Privileged."

"You don't even work for that company anymore."

I shrugged.

"Besides, you'll get your briefcase back at the end of the case."

"I want you to file a motion now."

"Why?"

"To get their attention."

He chuffed a laugh. It sounded like a gasp for breath. "I think you got it."

"I want to redirect it."

He gave me a long look. "I wish I knew what you're not telling me."

"It's nothing you need to know." I moved on to the last item on my list: interview David. I'd written to him several times by then, but I'd heard nothing back. In lieu of an actual marital conversation, I needed my PD proxy to talk to him.

"We already tried that," Watkins said. "A couple times. Nobody's ever home."

"Try again," I said, and stood to adjourn the meeting.

Watkins sighed, or maybe he just breathed hard as he heaved himself out of his chair.

–

When he was gone, I shifted over to the next table in the attorney visiting room, where Jingjing was awaiting her own visitor. Hers wasn't a defense lawyer, though. Hers was an assistant from the DA's office who came regularly to talk to her and the other rescued sex workers about their anticipated testimony at the traffickers' trials. During her second meeting, she introduced me as her lawyer and insisted I be present at every interview. *This is highly irregular*, the ADA complained, but she let me stay.

Jingjing was walking a tightrope with the DA's office. She needed to feed them enough information that they would continue to see her as a potential witness and keep the protective custody arrangement intact—but not so much information that her pimps would be able to figure out where it was coming from. Today the ADA had a photo array for Jingjing to peruse. It included mug shots of dozens of men, both pimps and johns. She wanted Jingjing to pick out the ones she recognized.

"This is hard job," Jingjing said as she turned the plastic-sleeved pages.

"You told us you saw the boss men every day. You must know what they look like."

"You no get it. White people all look same to me."

The ADA rolled her eyes while I hid my smile.

"Wait." Jingjing suddenly pounced on one of the photos. "I know this man. I know him real good!"

The ADA spun the photo array back around to see where Jingjing was pointing and looked up with an excited gleam in her eyes. "Really? You can definitely identify this one?"

"Sure can." Jingjing leaned back and folded her arms across her chest. "I see all his movies."

The photo was of Luke Rafferty, the full-time actor, sometime john.

After the ADA packed up and left, Jingjing and I walked to the commissary. The ADA topped up her account at every visit, and Jingjing always made a beeline to spend it. She laughed about it as we shared a bag of chips on our way back to our cell. "They think they do awful thing to keep me here," she said. "But it way more awful out there." For the last eight years she'd slept on the floor in a back room of whatever massage parlor she was working that month. She'd boiled water in a microwave and stirred in rice and dry soup mix for her meals. "Here I got mattress and good food. And no gross men." She beamed a smile. "And a new bestie!"

Sometimes I almost felt the same way. In Valhalla I slept warm and enjoyed hot showers and a full belly every day. I got to exercise in the gym for free. Thanks to Nina and our legal aid clinic, I was in no danger from the other inmates, and I had a pleasant cellie. We'd become constant companions over the past month. More than that. Friends. The first one I'd made in over five years. The only real complaint I had about my current situation was the confinement.

That didn't bother Jingjing. She hadn't been free in her outside life, either. And her only alternative, according to the DA, was an ICE detention center, then deportation. She declared she'd rather spend the rest of her life in Valhalla than go back to her village in Yunnan. She didn't know whether her family was still there, nor did she care. They were the ones who'd sold her to the slavers in the first place.

Her only real complaint was boredom. Because she was in custody as a material witness and not as a pretrial detainee, she was excused from the work requirements imposed on the other inmates. Without a work assignment, and with me in the office most of the day, she didn't know what to do with herself. There were three other victim workers housed in the Women's Unit pursuant to the same material witness orders, and they were also excused from work, but Jingjing wanted nothing to do with them. "They Malay," she sniffed. She ate with me, exercised with me, and sat at my elbow during evening consultations and even took notes. "Maybe I can go to job with you?" she'd suggested after the first week.

"You'd be bored there, too," I told her. "Just watching a bunch of women work with numbers all day."

"Maybe I help. I good with numbers."

It turned out she was better than good. She was a whiz at double-entry bookkeeping. She was also good at scheduling, filing, and, if given a script to read from, telephone etiquette. Our supervisors raised skeptical eyebrows at first, but soon enough they were happy to bring in another desk for Jingjing.

"How'd you ever learn all this stuff?" I asked one night when we were alone in our cell. We often talked after lights-out as the clamor faded up and down the pod and the snow fell softly outside our window.

"Promise not tell?" Jingjing whispered from her top bunk.

"Of course I won't tell."

"'Cause could be big trouble if cops find out."

"Tell you what," I said. "Toss me down a Snickers."

"Oo-kay." Jingjing sounded skeptical, but a candy bar landed on my blanket.

"Now you've paid me a retainer, and I'm your lawyer, and you're my client, and anything you tell me is privileged."

"What this mean, privileged?"

"It means it's a secret I can never tell anybody without your consent."

"Oh. Good deal," she said.

For the first several years of her captivity, she told me, she was strictly a sex worker, confined to a small room where she turned as many as twenty tricks a day. But gradually she was able to impress the bosses through her facility with numbers. She'd work out the day's tally in her head and tell them her estimate, and it would be close enough to the actual take that the bosses decided to move her up front when none of them could be there to run the register. A guard was always stationed at the door, but he was muscle, not brains. So Jingjing was the one who greeted the johns as they came in, told them the menu of services and the fee for each, and took their money before directing them to a room. The bosses were pleased; she freed them up to do the important work of finding more girls for their operation. She seldom had to turn a trick again.

"So that mean I a pimp, too?" she asked.

"No," I assured her. "You don't need to worry. Even if the cops knew, they wouldn't charge you. You were still in captivity. And the bosses were still making money off you."

Jingjing hesitated. "But what if I make money, too?"

"How?"

Her whisper grew even fainter. "The men, they come in and ask how much for hand job, yes? And it twenty bucks, right? But sometimes I tell them forty. I know which ones will pay. The ones who come in already hard, they want back room bad, they not say no."

"Then you only turned over twenty dollars to the bosses?"

"Yes."

"And the extra twenty?"

"I have special hiding place. Then special friend, he come get it and put in bank for me." Her whisper went deep and husky. "I have twenty thousand dollar in bank."

"Wow," I said, then, "You trust this guy?"

"Oh, sure. He crazy for me."

"Then why doesn't he pay your bail and get you out of here?"

"I tell him not to. Boss men come after me if they think I testify against them. I safer here than out there."

"Jingjing," I said after a moment. "You're the smartest person I've ever known."

An appreciative giggle sounded from the top bunk.

"But this boyfriend," I said. "How'd you ever meet him?"

Jingjing's head popped over the edge of her bunk, and she gave me a disdainful look. "How you think?"

—

It was six weeks before I received any mail at Valhalla. It arrived in a thick manila envelope that had already been opened and clumsily resealed with cellophane tape. My name and the Valhalla address were printed on the front. I didn't recognize the handwriting, but the return address was my own street in the Bronx, so it had to be from David.

I carried the envelope back to my cell, ripped off the tape, and shook out the contents. They landed in a heap on my bunk, and I stared at them, all my letters to David.

"Is bad news?" Jingjing asked, watching my face.

"He returned all my letters."

"Prick," she said.

"No, wait." I sorted through the envelopes. One of them wasn't addressed to David. It was addressed to me, in the same hand-writing that was on the outer envelope. Inside was an itemized bill for the last month's rent and the damages to the apartment in excess of our security deposit. Also enclosed was a copy of the eviction notice, dated March 2. "It's not from David," I said. "It's from our landlord."

"So David no a prick?"

"I'm not sure." He couldn't have received any of my letters that arrived after the eviction, but I wondered about before, whether he just left them unopened on the floor for the landlord to find and forward. Or whether he was already gone before the first letter even arrived. He could have moved out the same day I was arrested.

Jingjing picked up the eviction notice. "So where he live now?"

I shrugged.

"And what he use for money?"

She really was the smartest person I knew. She'd homed in on the biggest question of all.

–

That afternoon we were both summoned to the attorney consultation room at the same time, me to see my PD and Jingjing to see the ADA.

"You okay on your own?" I asked her as we entered the room. Harold Watkins was at one table; the ADA was at another one across the room. "I can blow this guy off if you want me to come with you."

"No, you go talk to Mr. Lardo. I handle Ms. Bitch just fine."

She peeled off, and I sat down across from Watkins.

"I have news." A smug smile creased his fleshy jowls. "We lost the expert funding motion."

His announcement barely registered. I never expected to win that motion. That wasn't the point.

"I have news, too," I said. I slapped the eviction notice down on the table in front of him. "It would have been posted on the door. Your people would have seen it there."

Watkins frowned at the paper. "All they told me was nobody was home."

"They never even went," I hissed.

He had the good grace to redden. "I'll look into it, okay?"

"Have you filed a motion for the release of my briefcase?"

"There's no real point—"

"Here." I slapped another paper on the table. "I drafted it for you. File it."

"Listen." He folded his hands on the table and leaned forward. "They blinked. They want a deal."

I stared at the flesh of his ring finger where it swelled out around his wedding band. His other fingers were pink, but that one was white. The ring was cutting off the blood supply. He was heading for an amputation. "No deal," I said. "I told you."

"There's a lot of sympathy building for you out there. People understand what it's like to be trapped in an

215

elevator. On top of everything else you had going on? Anybody could flip out. The DA's willing to take all that into consideration."

"Tell them to consider this," I said. "I hadn't been fired, the video was doctored, and the résumé was planted."

He sighed a blast of air that could have come from a blacksmith's bellows. "The company framed you, you're saying."

"Yes! I've been saying it all along."

"They went to all that trouble just to cover up a suicide." He rolled his eyes.

"They have their reasons. Reasons that have nothing to do with me."

He threw his fleshy hands into the air. "Then tell me what they are!"

"File the motion. Get my briefcase back. Find David. Then I'll be happy to tell you, the DA, and everybody else." I stood up and looked around for Jingjing, but she'd already left the room. "You need to get that cut off," I said to Watkins.

"What?"

I pointed to his wedding ring, and he was still staring at it as I left.

—

My own wedding ring was bagged up with my street clothes in the jail lockup, but throughout my afternoon work shift, I could feel it squeeze around my finger like the phantom pain of an amputee. I stabbed at the keys on my computer in hot frustration. I'd been incarcerated for six weeks, and none of my get-out-of-jail-free strategies was working. If David couldn't be found, I couldn't prove that the stack of résumés had been planted. My motion for expert funding had been denied, but more to the point, it hadn't triggered the ADA to look more closely at CDMI's video footage.

This was the course I'd fixed on from the moment I realized my credibility was shot. They weren't going to believe anything I told them outright, so I would drop hints for them to pick up. If they thought they'd stumbled on the truth on their own, they'd believe it. But they weren't picking up on anything. My strategy wasn't working.

I shut down the computer at the end of my shift. Jingjing had never returned to her desk that afternoon, and when I trudged back to our cell, she wasn't there, either. My letters to David were still strewn across my bunk. I stared at them, wondering where Jingjing was, wondering where David was, my thoughts spinning furious somersaults until I finally threw myself down on my bed. I buried my face in the envelopes until the ink ran with my tears.

I didn't hear Jingjing return, but I felt her arms around me and heard her voice crooning softly, "I miss you, too. Big-time. But we still be friends. I write you letters every day."

I rolled over and looked up at her. "What are you talking about?"

"I tell you my phone number and you call me. We talk same as here."

I wiped my tears. My hands came away streaked with blue ink. "You're leaving?"

It took me a few minutes to pull the story from her and piece it all together. The government had decided that Jingjing's testimony would not be necessary at the traffickers' trials. Her material witness order was vacated, and she was free to go, with the government's gratitude.

"But what about ICE?"

"My boyfriend already coming to get me. I be gone before ICE know I free."

"What about the boss men?"

She grinned. "I no worry no more." It seemed that the government had filed its witness list, and Jingjing's name wasn't on it. She wasn't a threat to the traffickers anymore. She was only a missing asset, and she intended to stay missing. "I worry only for you, my friend," she said sadly.

Every time I thought I'd reached the bottom of my life trajectory, something came along to remind me I could fall further. Now here I was, being pitied by a onetime sex slave. I forced a smile. "Don't you worry about me," I said, and gave her a farewell hug before I got up to help her pack her things.

# Chapter 22

Barrett was on a call with the auditors debating *materiality* and exactly which of the company's potential liabilities had to be disclosed. Since the dust had settled from the elevator incident—that was how he was able to categorize it now, as an *incident*—he had time for the more mundane tasks of his position. He'd even been able to schedule a getaway with his children. They'd each been agitating for some "dad time," as they called it, and while they wanted it to be one-on-one, there was no way he could manage four separate getaways. Instead they'd all be spending the next seven days together. It would be the first time since the divorce.

He was pushing back against the bean counters and their insistence on red-flagging every little nuisance claim when Ma Belle chimed an alert on his desktop. He received dozens of these every day, and he gave the screen barely a glance. It was only a new filing on one of the dozens of civil case dockets he monitored. Then he looked again. This one was a new filing in a criminal docket. *State v. Lambert.*

The case had been quiet for weeks, and with Lambert safely out of sight in the county jail, he'd allowed her to fade out of mind, too. But when he logged on to the public access website, he saw that her public defender had filed a motion for the release of her briefcase from the police evidence lockup. It contained documents that were in no way relevant to the charges she faced, the motion argued, but were valuable to her. The motion didn't say what those documents were.

He ran through the possibilities. She'd been in the office all day that Sunday, but she hadn't been in the document room, and anyway, Lester Willard was certain she'd never removed a single piece of paper from those files. It was probably nothing. Collection letters from her many creditors, probably, or poetry she wrote on the train. Still…

"Let's pick this up tomorrow," he told the auditors, and disconnected. "Marcia, get Culligan up here," he shouted to the ceiling.

"Right away, Mr. Barrett."

"No, wait. Tell him to meet me in Tech in five minutes. With the video."

"What video shall I tell him?"

"He'll know."

Culligan arrived five minutes late, his face a moist pink. "What's up?" he puffed.

Barrett looked around the room. A half dozen young men sat at computer stations staring at their screens but probably listening to every word he said. "Which one's your guy?"

"Jason," Culligan said, and snapped his fingers. A bald kid in tight pants and high-top sneakers jumped up to join them.

Barrett drew them into a huddle and explained in a whisper: "We need to look at the footage from that night and see what she put in her briefcase before she left here."

Culligan scratched his chin. "I doubt that'll show up."

"It might," the Tech kid said. He went back to his terminal and inserted the thumb drive Culligan handed him. Barrett leaned in to watch the screen as the file loaded and the playback began. Culligan leaned in, too, and Barrett caught a whiff of Scotch. It was only eleven o'clock.

"There," the kid said. He paused on an image through the open door of Shay Lambert's office. She was standing at her desk and sliding some papers into the shabby canvas bag she called her briefcase.

Barrett squinted at the screen. Those had to be the papers she wanted back, the ones that were supposedly valuable to her. He couldn't tell what they were. "Can you blow this up?"

"Let's see." The kid hummed. He switched screens, hit some buttons, then switched back to the first screen. "There."

Barrett leaned in again. In a freeze-frame on the screen was a close-up of the stack of documents in Lambert's hand. The top page looked like a printed or typewritten form, but the text was too blurred to read.

"See? It's no use," Culligan said.

Barrett pushed the kid out of the way and put his face close to the screen. There was a Post-it stuck to the top page, and he just could make out the handwritten notation there: *All male employees.* "What the—?" He cut himself off as the logo at the top of the printed form came into focus. At first glance he thought it was the company's white dove. But no, it was a different bird, and with a jolt, he realized it was a Siamese fireback, the national bird of Thailand. "Oh, fuck," he hissed.

"What?"

"Look."

Culligan leaned in. "The bird?"

"It's the logo of APU Transport."

Culligan turned to stare at Barrett. "She has the charter contracts?"

"She *knows*."

–

"Maybe she doesn't know," Culligan said when they were back in Barrett's office. "I mean, these flights could've been anything."

"Of course she knows," Barrett snarled. This was his own fucking fault for hiring someone with her smarts. It wasn't even like the job required it. A good paralegal could have handled that document production. It was his own form of self-aggrandizement to always have the best and the brightest reporting to him. A stupid habit, and potentially self-destructive. "Why else would she have smuggled the documents out of the goddamn building?" That reminded him: this was actually Culligan's fault. "How the fuck did you let this happen? You were supposed to have a system in place. She wasn't supposed to take any documents out of the room."

"She didn't! These documents were never in the room!"

Barrett got up into the man's face. The smell of Scotch was now mixed with the stink of nervous sweat. "Well, she didn't get them out of thin air!"

Culligan's glistening brow furrowed. "She could've seen a reference to APU in the accounts payable. Then—I don't know—she did some digging on her own."

"*I don't know*," Barrett jeered. "I fucking pay you to know!"

"I'll go and see her. I'll find out what she knows."

"You do that, Jack." He stabbed a finger into Culligan's chest. "And you better hope the answer is nothing."

The man swallowed hard. "And if it isn't?"

"Then we'll have no choice. We'll have to bail her out."

Culligan's eyes went wide. He ducked his head and hurried out of the room.

# Chapter 23

Daffodils were erupting through the patches of old snow at the edge of the exercise yard. I was mystified that such a thing was possible. The concrete walls stored heat and created a microclimate that accelerated the growing season, I understood that much. What I couldn't understand was who could have planted the bulbs. Valhalla was for short-timers only. Nearly everyone who was in Pod C when I first arrived was gone now. Some to trial, most to plea deals. Some to freedom, most to Bedford Hills or one of the other correctional facilities for women. Nina was gone; her lieutenant, Danita, was running the pod and organizing my evening consultations. Two of the three Malay women were gone, presumably deemed immaterial witnesses, just like Jingjing.

So whoever had dug these bulbs into the earth must have known they wouldn't be here long enough to see them bloom. It was like the old man who plants a tree even though he'll be long dead before it ever casts any shade. He does it for future generations. Some inmate must have planted these bulbs for the women who would come after her.

Or a bird dropped them.

-

The one Malay woman who remained in Valhalla was my new cellie, Bulan. Three years ago she'd traveled to a job fair in Padang. She spoke some English and hoped that might land her a good office job. Instead she landed in a shipping container with two dozen other women and girls, all bound for prostitution in the United States. Since then she'd been transported from sea to dingy sea, from one motel or pop-up massage parlor to another. Like Jingjing, she was happy to be liberated from the boss men, but unlike Jingjing, she wanted to go home. She couldn't, though, because the government lawyers said she needed to be a witness against the boss men.

Bulan attached herself to me much the way Jingjing had. She followed me through the food line and claimed the seat beside me during meals. She hovered nearby in the exercise yard and sat at my elbow during my evening consultations. But I couldn't warm to her the way I did with Jingjing. For every degree in temperature that rose outside, I grew a degree chillier inside. Once my only hope was not to make enemies in Valhalla. Now I tried desperately not to make friends.

Bulan couldn't take a hint. After lights-out she lay in the bunk above mine and talked on and on into the night. She was like a twelve-year-old at a sleepover, spilling secrets in the dark. Jingjing never liked to dwell on the abuses and indignities her body had suffered, but Bulan recounted them in living color. She talked about the pimps and the johns and the other girls, she had a story for each of them, and I tuned her out when I could and clamped my pillow over my head when I couldn't.

–

The confinement always bothered me, but it bothered me even more after spring weather arrived. I could tolerate being penned up when there was snow on the ground and cold winds whipping through my too-thin coat, but now I hated every moment I had to spend indoors. Whenever I was allowed outside, I just stood there with my face to the sun, drinking it in through every pore.

Jingjing's letters didn't help. Her boyfriend had been as good as his word. He'd given her all her money and a roof over her head and a seat at his table. A place in his bed, too, but she didn't mind that. Her only complaint was that she couldn't get a job, at least not a legitimate one, with no papers allowing her to work in this country. But her letters were otherwise sunny. She wrote about walks on the beach, a cookout on George's back deck, a hedge of blooming yellow bushes around his tiny backyard, and I felt like I was in a straitjacket, my arms and legs bound so tight that I was going to explode.

It was my idea not to push for an early trial date. I'd been so sure that the government would pick up on one of my cues and reopen the investigation. I'd been willing to wait them out. But that was back when my hope sprang eternal, just like those daffodil bulbs. The government hadn't picked up on anything. I'd miscalculated badly.

The world was waking up outside and I chafed to be out there in it. So I was annoyed when a CO pulled me out of the line for yard time when I was only twenty feet away from the door. She was the same CO who'd taken me to my cell that first night. My warrior face had relaxed since then, but hers hadn't. "You got a visitor," she snarled.

There was only one name on my approved-visitors list—Harold Watkins, my PD—but this wasn't his day to visit Valhalla. If he'd made a special trip to see me, it had to mean something had finally happened. I did an abrupt about-face and led the CO at a brisk pace to the attorney consult room.

"Not there," she groused. "Here." She pointed down the corridor to the regular visiting room, where inmates saw family and friends. I'd never been in that room. "Who is it?" I asked.

The CO held out a business card, and I almost recoiled when I saw the white dove. Gingerly I took it. *John F. Culligan, Director of Corporate Security.* I'd never met the man, but I recognized the name. I went down the hall and peered through the square of glass in the door. There were a dozen people in the room, half of them inmates, the other half visiting women and children. The children had been planted in a corner of the room strewn with brightly colored plastic toys. They played listlessly while the adults whisper-argued with one another.

Culligan sat alone at one of the tables, awkwardly, with his tie loose and askew.

"How'd he get in here?" I asked the CO. "He's not on my approved-visitors list."

"Warden vouched for him personally."

Of course. Culligan had all sorts of law enforcement bona fides. I shook my head. "Well, I'm not meeting with him." This was one of the few rights that inmates had in Valhalla. We didn't have to see anyone we didn't want to, and I didn't want to see anyone who worked for Barrett.

The CO scowled and blocked my way when I turned to go.

"Okay. Tell you what," I said. "Let me borrow your pen." Still scowling, she handed it to me, and I wrote a note on the back of Culligan's card. *I'll talk to Lester. No one else.*

I watched at the door as she delivered my note. Culligan read it, then he looked up and across the room to meet my eyes through the glass. He nodded at me and held up a hand in a five-minute signal. Then he got up and left.

Ten minutes later, Lester Willard took his place, and this time I allowed the CO to take me in.

Lester was by far the biggest person in the room, but he looked even more nervous than Culligan had. He didn't meet my eyes as I sat down across from him.

"Okay, so what's the message?" I snapped.

He answered in a mumble: "They wanna know what you know."

Even when he was hanging his head, I had to look up at him. "About?"

"Those papers you put in your briefcase that night."

"Oh." I sat back. My motion had missed its mark. It didn't get the DA's attention, it got Barrett's. Now he knew that I knew. Now he could rationalize putting me here.

"You know why I agreed to see you, Lester?"

"No, ma'am."

"Because I'm curious. How much did you know?"

"About what?"

"The miracle in the jungle. How they turned the sow's ear into a silk purse."

He shook his head. "I wouldn't know about that, ma'am."

That was his default response to every question I ever asked him. "See no evil, is that it, Lester?"

His chin came up slightly. "I do my job. That's it."

"No matter how dirty that job might be."

He didn't answer.

Two children in the play corner started to wail. I couldn't tell which of the women they belonged to. None of the mothers or grandmothers broke off talking to even glance their way.

I pushed to my feet. "Well, you can tell your masters that I refused to answer. Because I do."

He shook his head. "You don't want me to say that."

"No, you're right. Tell them I said *fuck you*."

"Ma'am," he said sharply, and he stood up just as abruptly, all six-foot-six of him. "You need to be careful."

I scoffed. "They've already done their worst. They framed me for murder. What else can they do?"

He didn't answer, but he finally looked straight at me. There was dread in his eyes, and I felt a chill creep through me.

"They're not Mafia," I said. "It's not like they could put out a hit on me in here."

"Maybe not," he said. "In here."

—

That night after lights-out, I replayed the conversation in my mind while Bulan prattled on in the bunk above me. The only point of the motion for the return of my briefcase was to spur the prosecution to take a peek inside. I hadn't figured on Barrett taking an interest, too. It had never occurred to me that he'd be watching the court docket. It was a serious blunder on my part, and I wondered if I'd overplayed my hand.

And then there was Lester's cryptic remark—*in here*. It was as baffling as my PD's comment that there was a lot of sympathy for me *out there*. Because there was no *out there* for me so long as the murder charge remained. I would be *in here* until I was exonerated. Barrett couldn't do anything to me after that, so what was Lester alluding to?

Bulan was still droning on about her ordeal. It made me long for a cellie who repressed her traumatic memories like PTSD sufferers were supposed to. Tonight she wasn't even talking about her own trauma. This time it was about a big shipment of girls who arrived last fall. They were new to the life, very young, and terrified. Their only prior work experience had been in a sewing factory.

I sat up and listened to every word, and when it was more than I could remember, I got out of bed and took notes by the faint glow of moonlight through the narrow window.

–

The next morning the sun shone so bright through the cell window that the bars laid shadow stripes over the concrete floor. I couldn't wait for yard time. The old patches of snow would be gone. The daffodils would be up another inch. Till now their blooms had been held tight inside their little fistlike buds, but today they might start to relax. They might unfurl and dot the yard with pops of sunny yellow.

I was shuffling along, twenty feet from the door again, when the same CO called my name. I refused to turn around. I was desperate to get outside. "Whoever it is, tell them I'm not interested!" I shouted.

She pulled me out of line with a hard squeeze on my bicep.

I went a little crazy then. It was just like in the elevator. I felt such a swell of hatred in that moment that my heart started to thump, my head grew hot, my vision swam. I turned on her, hands up, claws out, ready to kill her if I had to.

"It's not a visitor, asshole," she snarled. "You made bail."

I backed off with a scowl. This was her idea of a sick joke. April Fool's. "Ha," I sneered. But when she only gave me a slow blink, I realized she wasn't joking. "I— what?" I said.

"You're bailed, idiot. You're free to go."

I didn't understand. Someone must have posted my bail. But I didn't have a single friend who could do such a thing. What I did have was an enemy. Finally I understood Lester's warning. I jerked my arm loose. "No. I don't want to go."

"You don't got a choice!"

The other inmates caught wind of our argument, and they circled around me, catcalling slurs. *Retard. Fucking moron.* They were right. Only an idiot would refuse to be bailed. And the CO was right. I couldn't refuse. Valhalla wasn't a hotel. I couldn't call the front desk and extend my stay. Even if I told them my life was in danger, even if they believed me, they wouldn't care. I was no longer the responsibility of the Westchester County Jail.

—

Outgo was the reverse of intake. A clerk peck-typed my discharge forms, then a CO stripped me out of my prison scrubs and tossed me a plastic bag holding the clothes I'd worn the day I arrived. I got dressed and laced up my running shoes. My wedding ring was there, and I slipped it in my jeans pocket.

A CO escorted me to the front gate. A buzzer sounded, a lock sprang open, and I walked out into the glare of the sun.

No one waited at the gate to claim me. I looked back at the CO. He shrugged. Not his problem anymore. He closed the gate, and an electronic bolt fell with a clang that echoed up and down the street.

The parking lot was in front of me, and rows of cars were lined up with their grilles facing the gate like they didn't dare turn their backs on the criminals inside. Beyond the parking lot was a two-lane highway, and beyond that a patch of woods. I visored my hand over my eyes and scanned the parked cars. There were a lot of older sedans, a few SUVs, and to my left, one sad rusted-out Chevy driven by an old woman with a passel of kids in the back.

None of the cars looked like the CDMI limo, but of course Barrett wouldn't have come himself. He would've sent Culligan to post my bail, and even Culligan would have taken off after that was accomplished. They'd farm out their dirty work to someone else. Wet work, they called it. I had to learn the lingo. What did a hit man drive? I wondered, and then I wondered—hoped—that maybe he wasn't here yet. Maybe I'd been processed out too fast.

I had twenty-two dollars in my jeans pocket, the remaining balance of my prison earnings. I could hail a cab if one came by, or I could take a bus. The jail was on a bus route—I knew because I'd mapped it out for David in one of my letters—but I didn't know the schedule, and I didn't know what time it was now. I could walk, but I didn't have a coat and wasn't sure how long I'd last, especially after the sun went down. And there was still the question of where to go. I no longer had either an apartment or an office. Jingjing would take me in, for a little while anyway, but she was in Cape May, New Jersey, which was more than twenty-two dollars away. I decided to find my way to the nearest pawnshop. I'd sell my ring. That plus twenty-two dollars should get me somewhere.

The grandmother in the rustbucket was backing out of her parking space. I considered flagging her down to hitch a ride, but I could see there wasn't a spare inch of room in her car. She ground the gearshift into drive, and half a dozen children pressed their faces to the glass as they passed me by. A black SUV zipped into the spot she'd vacated.

A parked car to my right was idling in its space, and I sneaked a sideward look at it. It was a big silver Mercedes with a cloud of cotton candy puffing out of its tailpipe. A man in a shirt and tie was behind the wheel, and beside him was a young woman. The rear windows were tinted black, so I couldn't see if there were any other passengers. Was the driver the hit man? Did a hit man travel with an entourage? Maybe the woman was the hit man. Hit woman.

I eyed the woods on the other side of the highway. I hadn't gone for a run in two months, but it looked like that was my only exit. I started to thread my way between the parked cars. The traffic was heavy in both directions on the highway. I'd have to bob and weave in my sprint to get across.

I heard a car door pop open. I threw a look right at the Mercedes, but its doors were closed, and the driver and the woman hadn't moved. I turned to the left as the driver's door opened on the newly arrived SUV. The sun glare made the windshield opaque, but a figure cleared the doorway, and as soon as he straightened and his head rose higher than the roof of the car, I saw that he was Lester Willard.

I hesitated between two parked cars. Lester was the one who'd warned me to be careful, who'd hinted that Barrett might post my bail to get at me. I gazed at him over the roofs of four parked cars. He gazed back. I couldn't guess whether he was here to deliver me from that fate or to deliver me to it.

Another car door popped open, and my head whipped the other way. The rear door of the silver Mercedes was swinging open. Someone was climbing out of that car, too.

I spun back. Lester stood waiting by the open door of the SUV, and the sun passed behind a cloud, the glint off the SUV windshield faded, and I could see straight through to the passenger seat. I could see Jack Culligan, waiting.

A shout came from the Mercedes.

Behind me was the jail. To my left was Jack Culligan, to my right the wet-work team in the Mercedes. My only hope of escape was to dash across the highway and run into the woods, but Lester was built like a running back, and I knew he'd catch me before I got fifty yards. I was trapped.

I'd definitely overplayed my hand.

*Part II*

# Chapter 24

Barrett huddled over a cigarette on the terrace while the wind beat against his back and the waves crashed against the rocks below. It was ridiculously early to open up the summer house. Yesterday there'd been snow squalls, and today it was only in the forties. The house was big and old and drafty, a delight in the mild Maine summers, but in April the chill was still embedded deep into the walls and floor and furnishings, and even with the furnace running nonstop, it hadn't shaken loose yet. The handyman and housekeeper who usually looked after the place were in Florida for the winter— Barrett needed to take a closer look at how much he was paying them—so he'd had to hire a crew from a temp agency, and they were proving to be wholly inadequate. He hadn't had a decent cup of coffee in three days.

But this first week of April was the only slot that all the children had agreed upon, and this house was the only place they were willing to convene. The house in Rye had too many bad memories, they claimed, despite the fact that they'd spent no more than a handful of weekends there since he bought the place. It was because it was Melanie's house, he knew that, and he also knew it was no coincidence that the week the children chose for this get-together was the same week Melanie would be at Canyon Ranch.

And after all that, they'd yet to spend more than a passing moment in each other's company. Trey—*Tripp*—and Chloe had each brought an unannounced date, and when they weren't holed up in their respective bedrooms, they were tooling around the coast in the jaunty little roadsters he'd leased for them. Courtney was in seclusion in her own room, nursing a broken heart and imposing strict instructions to leave her alone and deliver her meals on trays. While Christian, at twenty-four the baby of the bunch, was everywhere in the house and nowhere, wrapped up in a cocoon of marijuana smoke with a pair of headphones soldered to his ears.

As for Barrett himself, he'd spent most of the last three days on the phone in his study or outside smoking one frantic cigarette after another. Ever since he got that call from Culligan, ever since he learned that Lambert was stonewalling them, he'd been in full-scale crisis mode. Until that moment, she'd been nothing but a convenient scapegoat, and one he actually felt bad about. But now, now she was nothing but a threat. A bigger threat than tariffs, a bigger threat than taxes. Bigger even than Mark Ivins. She was the biggest threat this company had ever faced.

He'd spent the last three days making the arrangements. A stack of cash delivered to Culligan to pay her bail; another stack for Lambert to persuade her to get on the plane; an emergency passport in her name; a ticket to KL; and finally Tony Low waiting at the other end.

Tony was the broker who'd handled the special asset sales out of PsT last fall, and he'd done a fine job with the exception of that one shipment, the one that had sent Lucy over the edge. Nothing was supposed to happen in this hemisphere, that was always the rule, and Tony was clear on that now. This whole operation would take place on the other side of the world. He would meet Lambert's plane in KL, relieve her of her stack of cash, and deliver her to his customer.

In many ways, this was the best possible solution, and Barrett wished he'd set on this course from the start. Lambert would be presumptively guilty by virtue of having skipped bail, with no need for a trial or any airing of dirty company linen. Her case would be de facto closed. The inquiry into Lucy's death would be over. It would be an ideal outcome for the company.

It wouldn't necessarily be a bad outcome for Lambert, either. An attractive white girl was much in demand in the markets Tony frequented. She'd probably end up as the pampered concubine of a Hong Kong oligarch. Instead of spending her best years in prison, she'd spend them in the lap of luxury. When he looked at it that way, Barrett realized that he was doing her a favor, really.

That was assuming all went as planned. He was still waiting for the all-clear call from Culligan. He glanced at his watch. He'd hoped that they'd be on their way to the airport by now, though he honestly had no idea how long it took to post bail. Maybe Lambert had to go through a fumigation chamber before she could be released. He tried Culligan's number again, and again it went straight to voicemail. If his phone was off, it probably meant he'd been required to surrender it to jail security. It probably meant he was still doing the paperwork to process Lambert out.

Barrett took another deep drag on the cigarette and straightened enough to look out over the terrace wall. The sea and the sky were the same dull pewter gray, and the waves crashing against the rocky coast were the color of dingy sheets. His mouth tasted of tar and ash. As soon as this was over, he resolved, as soon as Lambert was safely on the other side of the world, he'd quit again. For good this time.

The French door cracked open behind him. "Daddy?" came Courtney's voice from inside his study. "Can we talk?"

He turned around. His youngest daughter had finally emerged from her bedroom. "Of course, sweetheart." He waved toward the pair of Adirondack chairs at the edge of the terrace.

She rolled her eyes. "In here," she said pointedly, and stepped back from the door. She wore a pink bathrobe and had her hair in a ponytail that made her look like she was twelve again.

He stubbed out his cigarette and followed her inside. When he closed the door, he could hear the sounds of pots banging in the kitchen and voices shouting in Spanish. He dreaded the thought of what the temps might concoct for tonight's meal. He'd probably have to take the whole gang out to dinner again, and again watch Tripp peruse the wine list until he found the most expensive bottle in their cellar.

"What's up, sweetie?"

She put her hands on her hips. "We didn't finish our conversation." Somewhere in their teens, both his daughters had acquired the habit of speaking in a deep, creaky voice, an affectation that he understood the linguists called a vocal fry. It made them sound like they were supremely bored by, and slightly disgusted with, everything around them. "About the apartment?"

"I thought we did finish," he said. Last year she and her ex-boyfriend went in together on a loft in San Francisco, with Barrett fronting Courtney's half to the tune of $1 million. Now that they'd broken up, she wanted to buy out her ex, and she wanted $1.5 million to do it. "Like I said, get me two appraisals of current market value, and I'll consider it."

"Why can't you just take our word for it? It's worth three million today."

He raised an eyebrow. "Is it? Or is he just charging you a half-million-dollar breakup fee?"

"I don't care! I just want this to be over. I can't have him in my life anymore. It's just too fucking painful."

Courtney wasn't as lucky as her sister in the looks department. *Potato Face*, Chloe called her, and admittedly there was a pasty lumpiness about her. Her eyes sometimes looked like currants pressed deep into a rising dough. When she was in high dudgeon, as now, her face became red and mottled and even more unfortunate.

"You told me he moved in with that other girl," he said. "So how is he still in your life?"

"He's still on the deed, isn't he? He still has the right to come and go whenever. How am I supposed to get over him if he can show up at any moment?"

"So put the place on the market, divide the proceeds, and you'll never have to see him again."

"Why should I have to give up my home? I love that place! It's the only thing I love in the world."

"No wonder," he said. "An apartment that appreciates from two million to three in barely a year must be pretty darn lovable."

She flung her arms out. "So it's the money you object to!"

"Of course it's the money. What else?"

"It's always about the money with you. That's all you've ever cared about!"

"A good thing, too. Considering how you and your siblings run through it."

She stared at him in horror, as if he'd just strangled a kitten in front of her. "I can't believe you said that," she rasped in her creaky voice.

His phone buzzed in his pocket. He dove for it. Culligan at last.

"Oh, sure," Courtney said. "Ignore me. Your work always comes ahead of us. It always did."

"Jack." He turned his back to answer. "Is it done? Is she out?"

Culligan's reply came a beat too late. "Oh, she's out."

His voice sounded strange. Even stranger than Courtney's. Barrett opened the Ma Belle app on his phone and switched on the dashboard camera in the company SUV. It was hidden inside the AC air vent, and it gave him an up-view of Lester at the wheel and Culligan in the passenger seat. Culligan had a silver flask in his hand.

"We were too late," Culligan said.

"What do you mean, *too late*?" Barrett's reflexive thought was that Lambert must be dead, perhaps knifed in a gang fight, if such a thing went on in women's prison. It would be a terrible tragedy, of course, but a cleaner solution than the one Tony Low proposed.

Culligan took a swig from the flask and swallowed hard. "She was bailed out before we got there."

"What?" Barrett gasped. This was even more shocking than a shiv in the shower. "Who the hell by?" His hands went numb when Culligan told him. "I'm heading in now," he said. He fumbled to disconnect and called

Marcia next. "Get me Harrington on the phone. And send the chopper for me. ASAP."

"Oh, sure," Courtney cried as he ran to pack a bag. "Abandon us. *Again*."

# Chapter 25

"Shay!" a voice called from the other side of the parking lot. "Over here!"

My head swiveled that way. A man was leaning out of the rear passenger door of the silver Mercedes. He had a full head of gray hair that ruffled in the breeze and a gleam of a smile in a sun-bronzed face. He waved an exuberant arm. "Shay!" he called again.

I stopped and stared. I knew him. He was the notorious class-action lawyer, the bane of corporate counsel across the country. Once my opponent, now my savior. Mark Ivins.

He stood braced against the door with a big welcoming smile. I glanced behind me at Lester and Culligan. They were staring at Ivins, too, with shock and resentment on their faces. I walked slowly toward the Mercedes. "Mr. Ivins?"

"Mark. Please."

"Am I to understand that you've posted my bail?"

He nodded. "I'm only sorry I didn't learn about all this sooner. It makes me sick to think you've been in here for—what? Two months?"

In the front seat, the driver was still staring straight ahead, but the woman in the passenger seat twisted around to watch us. "I don't understand," I said.

"Let's talk in the car, shall we?"

244

I hesitated. He'd posted my bail. He was offering me a ride, but I didn't have a destination to give him. "I—I don't have anywhere to go."

"I've arranged your accommodations." He put an easy hand on my elbow. "You'll be comfortable there until you're back on your feet."

"I don't understand."

"Let's talk in the car," he said again.

I threw one last look back as Lester got behind the wheel of the SUV and slammed the door.

I ducked into the Mercedes. The upholstery was soft and supple, like the dewy complexion of a young girl. It had that new-car smell, and also in the air were the scents of the woman's perfume and some dark-roast high-grade coffee. Luxury smells. I sank into the seat.

Ivins got in beside me, and the driver put the car in gear as the front-seat woman turned all the way around to smile at me. She was about my age, a beauty, with chiseled cheekbones and long dark hair as shiny as a sheet of black ice over asphalt.

"Shay, this is my associate, Phoebe, and Lonnie, my driver."

The driver gave a nod to the rearview mirror, while the woman reached a hand back. Her fingers ended in tapered nails that were polished in a high-gloss shade of blue-black. I shook her hand. It was as soft and supple as the upholstery.

The car rolled forward, and as the woman turned to face front, I sneaked a look behind us. The SUV was following us out of the parking lot. They'd come to bail me out, too, but somehow Mark Ivins had beaten them to the punch.

"I have to be in court," Ivins said. "But I'm leaving you in Phoebe's good hands until I get back to the office."

"Mr. Ivins—"

"Mark."

"If you're thinking I can help you with the Palmer case—well, you must realize I can't."

"Of course you can't. I would never ask you to betray a professional confidence or otherwise violate the Code of Ethics."

"Yes, there's that. Plus I signed an NDA."

His face darkened. "As a condition of employment?"

"I can't say. Obviously."

"Those sons of bitches," he muttered. "But nobody would expect you to honor that. After all this."

"I expect it of myself."

He turned to the window for a moment, and when he turned back, his expression held something like contrition. "It makes me sick, thinking of you languishing in there all this time. I should've bailed you out right away. But I only found out yesterday. I was out of town when the story broke, and my clipping service dropped the ball."

"I've replaced them," Phoebe said to the windshield.

"And I shut down all my social media accounts a while ago—too many trolls out there—so I didn't know about the Internet stuff."

"What Internet stuff?"

"I said I was sorry!" Phoebe sang out. "I didn't know you weren't seeing it!"

"But luckily," he said, "I ran into your former colleague—Joel Edders—at a reception last night, and he filled me in."

"Oh," I said, but I wasn't buying it. It was too much of a coincidence—that he just happened to hear about me and rushed in to bail me out only minutes before Barrett's henchman would have done the same. I didn't have that kind of luck.

"Of course I remembered you at once," he said. "You wrote the brief in *Rand*." He chuckled. "You really ate my lunch."

"So you think I'm a good lawyer," I said. "That doesn't explain this."

"I know you're a great lawyer. And I know Ingram Barrett is a lying bastard. I don't know why he's done what he's done to you, but I know that he's done it, and I'm appalled. I won't countenance it."

"You think he's set me up."

"Don't you?"

I was spared an answer by a vibration in his breast pocket. He pulled out his phone, and while he looked at the screen, I glanced through the rear window again. The SUV was three cars back, still following us.

"Excuse me, I have to take this," Ivins said as he answered the call. He listened, then said, "Phoebe, dial in," and she got on her phone, too.

What followed was a half-hour conference call about his upcoming hearing. I listened closely and pieced it together. Late last year he'd filed a shareholders' action against a company he called NSP. He'd recently filed a motion to certify the class along with an application that he be appointed as class counsel. But another law firm had filed a similar lawsuit and was now presenting a competing application to be appointed counsel on behalf of the same class. The judge had to decide which firm would be permitted to represent the shareholders. At stake was the potential award of millions of dollars in attorneys' fees. The competing lawyer was on the phone, proposing that they settle the dispute by agreeing to partner as co-counsel in the matter. Phoebe listened and took notes on her tablet, while Ivins spoke pleasantly, even charmingly, and committed to nothing.

"Sorry about that," he said when the call finally ended. We'd reached lower Manhattan by then, and Phoebe's notes were spooling out of a mobile printer on her lap. "That was my adversary in today's hearing. Ned Bartman."

"A Johnny-come-lately angling for a share of your spoils."

He laughed. "No, he was only doing the requisite dance. He actually wants the whole case to himself. Despite the fact that we did all the investigatory work, filed the first complaint, and have the case positioned for an excellent settlement."

"That's how you'll argue it today?"

He nodded.

"Who's representing Northstar? If I may ask."

He smiled, pleased but not surprised that I'd correctly deduced the name of the defendant by its stock symbol. "The Harrington firm."

"Ahh. The same firm that's representing Ingram Barrett in your Palmer case."

"So you know them."

"I knew them before, too."

I looked out the window as the roadside trees blurred past. Bright green buds were bursting free of the bare brown branches. It was strange the way my brain worked. I needed to be thinking about my own case. I needed to evade Barrett and his henchmen, and I needed to steel myself against whatever Ivins was up to. Instead my mind was humming with litigation strategy. I could almost feel the zap of the electricity snapping across the synapses in my brain. It felt good.

"What?" Ivins said, watching me.

I shrugged. "My guess? Harrington's done a reverse auction. And Ned Bartman was the low bidder."

Phoebe twisted around in her seat. "What's this?"

I explained it to her. "Obviously Northstar wants to see counsel appointed who's willing to settle for the cheapest amount. Harrington's MO is to negotiate privately with each of the competing plaintiffs' lawyers and cut a deal with the low bidder. Then they leak some morsel of information to give them the edge in the counsel fight. Thus making Ned Bartman look like he's the one who's done the real investigation. So he deserves the appointment."

Phoebe twisted to face Ivins. "That discrepancy in the fourth quarter—"

His forehead creased. "We always wondered how Bartman stumbled on that."

"Maybe he was led there," I said.

Phoebe chewed her lip. "Should we ask to adjourn pending discovery?"

We'd reached Foley Square, and as the driver pulled up to the courthouse, Phoebe handed back a silk tie, already knotted, and Ivins looped it over his neck and slid the knot up to his throat. She closed a briefcase on her lap and handed that back, too. "Good luck," she said.

"Thanks." He reached up to lay a hand on her shoulder, and she smiled up at him, and that was when I knew they were sleeping together.

"Thanks," he said again, this time to me. He hopped out at the curb to jog up the courthouse steps.

"What was that about *Internet stuff*?" I asked Phoebe as the driver made a U-turn and headed north.

"You don't know?" She smiled. "You're something of a sensation. There's a bunch of message boards debating your case, and the pro-Shay side is winning. You have your own hashtag. #FreeShay. And somebody even started a GoFundMe to raise money for your defense."

"What? Who?"

She shrugged. "Probably some dork in his basement who's fantasizing about you. But the thing is, it caught fire. I think it's raised close to fifty thousand dollars."

"What?" I exclaimed again, even louder. "Why?"

"Because your story's so compelling. It could happen to any of us—being stuck in an elevator with a suicide. And then getting blamed for it." She shuddered at the injustice. "And of course it helped how you looked."

"What?" I said again.

"Never underestimate the power of a good mug shot. It went viral, you know."

"No," I said. "I didn't know."

"Left up here, Lonnie," Phoebe said to the driver, and he nodded and turned the wheel. "I thought you'd like to get your hair and nails done first. I know that's the first thing I'd do if I—" She caught herself.

"Just got sprung from jail?"

She gave a wide-eyed nod. She had perfect winged eyeliner, so precise it could have been applied by a pinstriping machine in an auto factory. "Was it awful?"

I shrugged. "I made some friends."

She didn't know what to do with that information. "Oh, well," she said. Then, brightly, "Here we are!"

The driver pulled up beside a pink awning that flared out over the storefront windows of a swanky salon and day spa. I climbed out after Phoebe. A stylist was waiting at the door with a smile—"You must be Shay. Welcome!"—and so was a manicurist—"I'm a big fan!"

Over the next two hours I was draped and washed, foiled and trimmed, soaked and dried, clipped and polished, and served a Cobb salad and a glass of pinot grigio. All while my attendants chattered brightly about my ordeal, and how great I looked, considering, and how amazing I was going to look and feel when they were done with me.

It felt strange to be touched in a way that wasn't hostile. It had been two months since I'd experienced such a gentle caress. Longer.

"Relax," the stylist said, his hands on my shoulders. "You're so tense." From her nearby perch on a stool, Phoebe looked up from her phone. "I'm booking you a massage tomorrow," she said, tapping on the screen.

I felt ridiculous when the stylist whipped off my cape. There I was with my nails gleaming and my freshly high-lighted hair swinging in a glossy blunt-cut blowout—but wearing baggy jeans, an old pilled sweater, and a pair of worn-out sneakers.

"Don't worry." Phoebe brandished a credit card at the counter. I couldn't make out the figures on the register. My reference points were five years out of date, but I calculated that the tab came to five hundred dollars. Plus tip. "We'll get you some new clothes," she said. "Next stop is Saks."

"The Gap would be fine."

She shook her head. "We sort of have a dress code at our office. Not to be restrictive. Just that we all like to look good. You'll want to fit in."

"At your office?" I wondered, but she was already out the door. Lonnie was waiting at the curb. Phoebe got into the back with me this time, and we headed north again, to Saks.

It was a shopping mecca for fashion worshippers. I used to spend at least one Saturday every month wandering its floors. I used to stretch my budget to reach around every new collection. But it had been five years since I'd last stepped through its revolving doors on Fifth Avenue. The smell of luxury that first enveloped me in the Mercedes was magnified a thousand times as I followed Phoebe through the array of cosmetic counters on the first floor.

We stopped at a makeup counter where it seemed I was again expected. "Your skin's so dry," the artist said, and troweled on some moisturizer. "You're too pale," she said next, and liberally sponged on a bronzer before she brushed on the blush. Then came the lipstick and my own perfect winged eyeliner.

I studied myself in the mirror when it was done. I looked polished, professional—privileged. I could almost imagine I was me again. But not quite. Time had taken its toll. Whether from the past two months or the past five years, the lines were there, and the shadows.

"We'll take it all," Phoebe said, and everything the artist had used on me was scanned and bagged. Another five hundred dollars, I guessed.

Phoebe led on from there, up and up through floor after floor of high-end designers. I'd always had my favorite labels, but some of them seemed to have fallen out of fashion during the intervening years, and new names had emerged to take their place. Once I could have found my way blindfolded through the store, but now I had to rely on Phoebe to lead me from floor to floor, boutique to boutique. She even came with me into the dressing room. "Oh! To have your figure," she sighed when I stripped down to try on underwear.

"Lots of time for crunches when you're in prison."

"That's what I need." Phoebe flushed as she realized what she'd said. "I mean—um—" she faltered.

I rescued her. "Remember how great Martha Stewart looked when she got out?"

"Yes!" She looked relieved. Prison wasn't so great a barrier if we could bond over celebrity gossip. "We're going to wear this home," she said to the saleslady, nodding at the bra and panty set I was currently modeling. "Pack up the rest for delivery."

Jeans and a sweater were on Phoebe's list, albeit costing about ten times more than at the Gap. "We'll wear these home, too," she said, and, wrinkling her nose, she held out my own clothes to the saleslady. "Get rid of these, would you?"

The sneakers met the same fate after our visit to the shoe department. Kitten heels, stilettos, high-heeled booties. The tally was overwhelming.

Then came the biggest-ticket items: suits and silk blouses and sheath dresses that fit like a second skin. "This is too much," I protested, each time more weakly than before. "I'll never be able to repay this."

"Don't worry. Mark knows a good investment when he sees one."

Phoebe brandished her credit card again—or, rather, Mark's—and the purchases were wrapped up and dispatched with a promise of delivery within the hour.

Mark Ivins & Associates didn't occupy space in a high-rise tower downtown. Its offices were on a tree-lined street on the Upper East Side, only a block away from Central Park. Lonnie pulled up to the curb in front of the limestone facade of a five-story townhouse. A wide set of marble steps led up to ornate double doors, while a second, narrower set of steps led to a separate below-grade office or apartment.

Phoebe took me by the hand and led me up the stairs and through the double doors. Inside was a vast reception hall with marble floors and soaring ceilings and a grand staircase leading to the upper floors. A young Latina woman even lovelier than Phoebe sat at a reception desk at the foot of the stairs. She had bright dark eyes and a mane of thick black hair that cascaded down her back and shoulders. She rose. "This must be Shay," she said with a smile. "How do you do? I'm Luisa."

"Any packages arrive?" Phoebe asked her.

"Yes. They're all downstairs."

"Mark?"

"In his office."

"Buzz him for me, would you? I'm going to get Shay settled in downstairs."

Phoebe pulled me along after her through the hall. The opulence was astounding, and my head swiveled to take it all in. Lacquered floors and red and gold trimmings and crystallized light that made rainbows dance through the air. The space was so heavy-laden with gilt and mirrors that I could almost imagine Louis XIV mincing through it in his high-heeled pumps. Instead a bevy of women were striding through in their own high-heeled pumps, each of them so poised and beautiful that it made me wonder if Mark Ivins used a modeling agency to staff his office.

Phoebe led me through the reception hall. It was wretched excess on the grandest scale, even more so when I considered that this once must have been the private home of some robber-baron merchant or industrialist. All this lavish splendor for a single family who probably spent less than half a year in residence.

She stopped at a richly paneled door and opened it. The door didn't lead to another room—it concealed a small elevator, a glass cylinder like a pneumatic tube in a bank drive-through. As Phoebe stepped into the cylinder, I lurched to a stop. She looked back, puzzled, when I didn't join her. "Oh!" Her hand flew to her mouth. "I'm so sorry! I didn't even think—! We'll take the stairs, of course."

"I'll be all right," I whispered, but I didn't move.

"No, come." She took me by the hand again. This time she led me out the front door and down the steps to the pavement. I glanced down the street. A black SUV was parked at the curb, and I could just make out Lester behind the wheel. Phoebe made a quick right turn and down another set of steps. She stopped at the heavy steel door of the below-stairs space and swiped a keycard through the electronic lock. It buzzed open.

I followed her into a room that was decorated with contemporary art and streamlined furniture in cool tones of gray and blue. It looked like someone's home or the reception area of a professional's office, another lawyer perhaps, or a psychiatrist. There was a desk—modern, glass-topped, with an ergonomic chair—and two flanking couches upholstered in suede, and a potted ficus tree in the corner.

"We keep this apartment for out-of-town witnesses." Phoebe closed the door and handed me the keycard. "Especially witnesses we don't want our adversaries to find out about."

"You mean me?"

"No, well, obviously you're not a witness. It's just that Mark wants you to be comfortable until you're on your feet."

She showed me through the apartment, with arm waves at the top features, like a realtor at an open house. Beyond the lounge was a kitchen and dining area. "We've stocked up on some groceries for you, but here's the number you should call to have anything else delivered that you like. Just tell them Mark's name." Beyond the kitchen were a bedroom and bath. The bed was king-size, with a suede-upholstered headboard and a suede duvet heaped with shopping bags from Saks.

"I'll help you put these away," Phoebe said.

"No, that's all right."

But she was already opening the packages and tearing through the dress bags. I wandered away for a peek at the bathroom—marble tile, rainfall showerhead, and an honest-to-God bidet—and then back out to the dining area. An expanse of French doors opened on the back garden of the property. There were electronic locks here, too. Outside, a teak dining table sat under a wisteria-vined pergola. Daffodils were erupting, just as in the prison yard. I clocked the security cameras aimed at the door and others aimed out over the garden.

A phone rang, and I listened to Phoebe answer in the bedroom. Her tone was low and intimate, and her closing words were a whispered "Me, too." When she came out into the living room, she was beaming. "Good news! The judge put the applications over for sixty days to allow us to conduct discovery into Ned Bartman's dealings with Northstar or the Harrington firm."

"Good."

"Mark says to tell you thanks."

I wasn't fooled by the gratitude. There was no way Ivins didn't already know about reverse auctions. After all, he was the king of shareholder class actions. He wanted to flatter me, and I could guess why.

"I'm sorry I can't have dinner with you tonight," Phoebe said. "Prior engagement. And Mark has a function he has to attend. There're takeout menus somewhere—" She found them on the kitchen counter and held them up. "Just use Mark's name. Oh, and his card!" She dug in her bag and came out with a shiny black credit card. I read the embossed name as I took it from her. *Shay Lambert.*

"Meanwhile, Mark wants you to join him for a drink on the rooftop. He's showing off," she added with a fond smile. "He loves to impress his guests with that view."

I couldn't be any more impressed than I already was. "How do I get there?"

She started to point to a door that was as richly paneled as the one upstairs. The elevator, I guessed, as she caught herself. "Go back in the front door," she said instead. "Use your keycard. Then follow the staircase up. Mark has a private apartment on the fifth floor. For when he works late. One floor up from there gets you to the roof." She picked up her handbag from the dining table. "We've tried to think of everything, but if there's anything you need, anything at all, just give me a call." She opened the door to the elevator and pushed the call button. "Let me give you my number." She stopped with an embarrassed laugh.

"Oh, wait, let me give you your phone first. It's all set up on the company account."

I took the smartphone she handed me and turned it over in my hands. If I'd had such a thing back in February, the cops wouldn't have been nearly so suspicious of me. "Thank you," I said. "You've been very kind."

The elevator arrived, and the glass cylinder slid open. "Oh, by the way," she said, stepping on, "this opens into the gym on the other side, so don't worry if you hear the elevator landing on this floor. You can lock the door on your side." She reached around to demonstrate.

"Okay."

"Good night, then," she called, and the elevator closed and whooshed away.

I closed the paneled door that concealed it, and engaged the lock, then I went to the front door and checked that it was locked. There was a deadbolt there, too, and I threw it, and I did the same with the French doors at the rear of the apartment. There, I thought—I was locked in another cage.

But a golden one this time. I wandered through the rooms, running my hands over the smooth tile and the supple suede. This apartment was even more luxurious than our apartment in Chelsea. The clothes hanging in the closet were even more luxurious than those I used to wear. It was too much. It was all too much. Nothing came for free.

I needed to talk to Mark Ivins and find out his price.

—

I took a long shower under the rainfall. It felt so hedon-istically self-indulgent that I didn't care that my perfect

258

blowout was getting wet. Then I stood naked in front of my new closet with all of my new clothes. How to dress for drinks with Mark Ivins? I had too many options. Again it occurred to me—if I'd had this many changes of clothes back in February, the cops wouldn't have been nearly so suspicious of me.

But it was no use trying to revise the past. What I needed to do now was control the future.

I decided on the same jeans and sweater I'd worn out of Saks, with a pair of ankle boots that made me four inches taller and more powerful. Then I let myself out the door to the street. The black SUV was still there, I noted, but nobody emerged from it as I ran up the steps and into the refuge of Mark Ivins & Associates.

It was after six by then. The reception desk was unstaffed, and most of the crystal and gilt light fixtures were dimmed. My boot heels echoed across the marble tiles to the staircase, where an intricate red-and-gold-patterned rug unspooled upward, held in place on each riser with a gleaming gold stair rod. The second-floor landing gave me a glimpse of a conference room on one side and a law library on the other, both unoccupied. The third floor housed a more conventional office space, with an array of computer workstations and carrels, and a handful of women still at work. The fourth floor showed only a long corridor of closed doors where most of Mark's associates must have had their offices. They gave off a low hum of voices, the drones in the hive.

The fifth-floor landing was the smallest, with one door marked *Private* and the other concealing the elevator. From there a set of narrow, uncarpeted steps led to the roof. I climbed up and opened the door at the top of the stairs. A gust of wind sent my no-longer-perfect blowout streaming behind me. A garden stretched before me, with full-grown trees filigreed in spring blossoms and a cherubic fountain cheerfully burbling and thick-cushioned teak lounge furniture all around. The view was of other rooftops like this one to the north and east, high-rises to the south, and to the west, the great open expanse of Central Park.

"Over here," Ivins called. He was at the edge of the roof, arms and ankles crossed as he leaned back against the glass-panel wall. He wore a different suit from his staid go-to-court suit that morning. This one was a stylish pale silver, the coat cut shorter, the pants sleeker, and he wore it with a vivid turquoise T-shirt.

I walked toward him past a long rectangle of bright green grass so perfectly manicured it must have been cut by hand with scissors. He held a glass in his hand, and he reached for a bottle and poured another glass of the same and held it out to me. "Celebrate with me."

I accepted the glass. "We're celebrating the judge's ruling in Northstar?"

"Yep, and it's all thanks to you."

"There won't be much to celebrate, though," I said, "if you go back empty-handed after sixty days of discovery."

"Oh, we'll find something." He grinned. "Did Phoebe get you squared away?"

I nodded. "She was very kind. And you are very generous. Too generous."

He clinked his glass against mine. "Here's to freedom," he toasted.

"But it isn't, is it? Free."

He shook his head with a sad smile. "You've been working the defense side too long. You've forgotten that there are lawyers who are motivated by anything other than greed. Who do the right thing just because it's the right thing."

I laughed in his face.

His smile turned into a wry grin. "Not buying it, huh?"

"Not for a second. The plaintiffs' bar is in it for the money just as much as the defense bar. The only difference is the defense side is risk-averse. While your side is willing to gamble."

"Oh?" Another gust of wind blew across the rooftop and tossed his hair in a whirl. It was all his, I could see, and thick and silver. "And what am I gambling here?"

"You're gambling that I'll be so grateful for all your help that I'll help you out, too. With the Palmer case."

"I already told you—"

"I know. I didn't believe it then, either."

He regarded me over the rim of his glass as he took a slow swallow. I lifted my own glass and drank. It was a bold red wine, full and dense in my mouth.

"Let's say you're right," he said. "Maybe that is my hope. But it's only a hope. It's not my price. Please understand that."

"Then what *is* your price?"

"Come work for me."

I let out a startled laugh.

"I mean it. Join us. You're still licensed to practice. I checked."

"Did you check the criminal docket? Because you might have noticed that I'll soon be on trial for murder."

"Yes, speaking of that—are you happy with your lawyer?"

I scoffed. "No."

"Then let's substitute new counsel. My treat."

"I heard there was a GoFundMe?"

He waved a dismissive hand. "Only fifty thousand. Consider that your mad money. It's not enough for a real defense. What do you think of Bill Centrello?"

"The preeminent criminal defense lawyer in the country? No, thanks."

Ivins cocked his head. "Okay, explain that to me."

"Apart from the expense? Which would put me in your debt for the rest of my life?" He started to protest, but I spoke over him. "Because I want to steer my own boat. Somebody like Centrello would never allow it."

"Ah." He nodded. "Dev Kapoor, then. He trained with Centrello, but he's younger and more flexible."

I took a sip of wine while I considered it. "That doesn't solve the expense problem."

"Come work for me," he said again. "Pay me back in kind. You're a brilliant lawyer. I knew that even before today. You can handle the Northstar discovery for me. After all, it's thanks to you that we got this far."

"Indentured servitude," I said.

"No different from most of the world's population. They all work for the Man." With a grin, he tapped his turquoise shirt-front. "You'll just be working for this man."

I turned toward the park. The breeze rippled through my hair, and the fragrance of the blossoming trees drifted across the rooftop. I *was* a brilliant lawyer—at least I used to be. That was the question: could I be smart enough now to make this work for me? Ivins was playing me, that much was obvious. I had to figure a way to play him instead. It was jujitsu—I needed to figure out what he viewed as his greatest strength and use it to topple him.

The sun was setting over the park, and I watched it sink while I thought.

His phone pinged, and I looked back as he pulled it out of his pocket and read the text. "Ha!" he said. "Ingram Barrett's lawyers just filed an emergency motion to disqualify me as plaintiffs' counsel in the Palmer case."

"On what ground?"

"On the ground of my apparent personal relationship with a former CDMI lawyer." His mouth stretched into a wide grin. "Just wait till Barrett finds out you're working for me!"

That was what finally decided me. I lifted my glass. "I accept," I said.

His teeth gleamed bright in the fading sun as he clinked his glass against mine.

# Chapter 26

A sibilant hiss greeted Barrett as he entered the courtroom, and instantly he saw that Ivins had packed the gallery with CDMI shareholders. Not the institutional shareholders, of course; not the ones with votes, who mattered. No, these were the young women whose parents gave them a few shares upon their college graduations because they adored the company's labels so much. Then there were the middle-aged men who used to jerk off to Madame's famous poster; they bought their shares out of erotic nostalgia. These were Ivins's typical constituent shareholders, the ones who owned just enough shares to file nuisance lawsuits and become thorns in the company's side.

Ivins was there, of course, working his way through the crowd, glad-handing them like a politician. While Barrett's lawyer, Dick Harrington, was sitting alone at counsel table with his head down. Barrett took a seat beside him. "How's it looking?"

Harrington shook his head and continued reading his notes. This motion wasn't his idea. He didn't think the judge would disqualify Ivins from the Palmer case. He resisted, but Barrett insisted—that was the dynamic of this particular attorney-client relationship. Lawyers made the worst clients, so the saying went, but only because they refused to be buffaloed.

Barrett turned to scan the courtroom. Phil Duvall should have been there and wasn't. Detective Riley shouldn't have been yet was, seated alone in the last row of spectator seats. Barrett immediately got up and made his way back there. "Detective," he said. "I'm surprised to see you here. Considering your case is closed."

Riley looked up through his rheumy eyes. "They're never closed until there's a conviction, Mr. Barrett. And all appeals have been exhausted. Not to mention habeas writs."

"But your work is done. Surely."

"Never hurts to double-check."

Barrett eyed him. Riley was a short-timer, he reminded himself. He was only punching a clock until his pension kicked in. He'd probably come here to kill some time while he pretended to work. It was Cruz who actually worked the case, and since he wasn't here, there couldn't be anything to worry about.

The bailiff cried "All rise," and Barrett returned to his seat as the judge took the bench. Margaret Delacorte. A hatchet-faced fifty-year-old and a legal lightweight who'd managed to parlay her husband's political connections into a lifetime appointment to the federal bench. She'd all but flirted with Mark Ivins in their last appearance on this case, and Barrett braced himself for more of the same.

The original motion to disqualify class counsel, filed the same day Lambert was sprung from jail, was based on nothing more than that. Ivins, having no prior relationship with Lambert, was obviously banking on gaining access to privileged information. But Ivins had changed the landscape when he doubled down in his opposition papers, admitting that he'd not only posted her bail but made her one of the Associates in Mark Ivins & Associates.

That he'd bailed her specifically for that purpose, but only because she was a brilliant and talented lawyer. Not because he was seeking any confidential information. Harrington then amended the motion, arguing the more conventional basis for disqualification: that Lambert had a conflict of interest that had to be imputed to Ivins and the rest of his firm.

Barrett was called first to the stand. He testified that he'd hired Lambert specifically to work on the Palmer case, which she had done exclusively for the one month of her employment. That in the course of her work she'd become familiar with a great deal of confidential and privileged company information. Information that was protected from discovery in the litigation. Information to which Mark Ivins was definitely not entitled.

Barrett was prepared to testify to much more: that on February 1 he discovered her résumé fraud; that on February 2 he instructed the company's director of human resources to fire her; that said director did so that evening; that she subsequently died of a gunshot in an elevator occupied only by herself and Ms. Lambert; and that the police subsequently arrested Ms. Lambert and charged her with murder.

But Ivins stood in objection to Harrington's opening question. "Your Honor, this line of examination has no relevance to the disqualification issue. Moreover, the facts are hotly disputed. Unless Your Honor wishes to try the criminal case and decide the guilt or innocence of Ms. Lambert—"

"I most certainly do not," the judge said. "Moreover, I, along with most of the American public, am already well familiar with the allegations made against Ms. Lambert. Mr. Ivins, your objection is sustained. Mr. Harrington, confine your examination to Rule 1.10 and the subject of privileged information and imputed knowledge."

Harrington gave up without a fight. He had no further questions for Barrett, and Ivins had none at all. Seething, Barrett left the stand and returned to his seat.

Ivins took the stand next. He looked flashy, even in a conservative gray pinstripe. It was his hair. It was too long. Too bright. Like a lion's mane, a totem of his virility. He smiled up at the judge, and she frowned down at him, a thinly disguised effort to hide her blatant infatuation. A young woman, some puppet from Ivins's office, conducted his examination. She read from a script that he'd obviously prepared, with each question simply a cue for his next monologue.

He began by disputing the contention that he had no prior relationship with Ms. Lambert. To the contrary, he declared, he came to know her well when she was a rising star at the Jackson firm. In fact, she bested him in an important case and won his great respect and admiration. He lost track of her over the years but instantly remembered who she was when he read about her arrest and imprisonment; he reviewed the evidence against her and became convinced that she was innocent.

"Object, you idiot," Barrett hissed, and Harrington did. But the puppet was prepared. Since Mr. Ivins's motive in hiring Ms. Lambert was under attack, the young woman argued, it was indeed relevant to know what he learned and came to believe about her.

Objection overruled.

Ivins resumed. He'd made some further inquiries and learned of Ms. Lambert's amazing fortitude. He was told that she was a model prisoner and a valuable assistant in the jail's business office. "And she actually set up a legal aid clinic in the Women's Unit at Valhalla!" he raved. "She went out of her way to help these young women with their legal problems. Anyone else would have been brought low by false imprisonment, but Shay was just so brave. Which isn't surprising when you think how hard she fought to prevent that tragic suicide in the elevator."

Barrett hissed again, and Harrington stood to object on the same grounds of relevance raised by his adversary earlier. The judge, in an effort to appear fair, sustained that objection and instructed Ivins's puppet to confine herself to the Rule 1.10 issues.

The young woman nodded. That was apparently in her script, too. "Prior to posting Ms. Lambert's bail, were you aware that she'd worked on the Palmer case?"

"Not at all. Her name never surfaced in any of the filings or correspondence. It's a big multinational corporation. They must have hundreds of lawsuits going at any given time. There was no reason to suspect she'd worked on Palmer."

"How did you learn the truth?"

"She told me. The moment she got in my car at Valhalla."

"What was your response?"

"I told her that I understood she had a duty of confidentiality, and that we had a duty, too, and would do everything the rules require. And even before her first day of work, we had a Chinese wall in place. The ethical screen the rules require."

He'd hired a professional, an expert in legal ethics, to set up the ethical screen. An office-wide edict went out that no one in the firm have any communications with Ms. Lambert about CDMI or the Palmer case. All the firm's electronic files relating to CDMI or the Palmer case were password-protected, and all the physical files were locked so that Ms. Lambert could not access them. She brought no such files with her, so there was no risk in that regard. And she was assigned an office far removed from anyone working on the Palmer case, so there was not even a risk of casual eavesdropping.

On cross-examination Harrington scored a minor point regarding the relatively small size of Ivins's firm, in terms of both personnel and physical space. Ivins also admitted to a great degree of collegiality and extra-office socializing among himself and his employees. But he refused to admit that any of those circumstances might lead to a breach in the firm's Chinese wall.

"Mr. Ivins, please tell the court exactly what prompted you to hire Ms. Lambert."

"I'm always on the lookout for talented young lawyers. I plan to fully exploit her talents."

"But was that your only motivation? Didn't her previous employment at CDMI factor into your hiring decision in any way?"

Ivins turned a disarming look up at the judge. "I have to admit that it did. You see, I believe that Ms. Lambert has been falsely accused. And I want to do everything I can to help her in her quest for exoneration."

Barrett's stomach pitched at the look on the judge's face. She was buying it, everything Ivins was shoveling at her.

The final witness was the outside ethics expert hired by Ivins to set up the Chinese wall. He testified that he was a member of the New York State Bar; that he served for many years on both the Bar's Committee on Professional Ethics and the Attorney Disciplinary Committee; and that he designed, implemented, and monitored the ethical screen put in place between Shay Lambert and all personnel working on the CDMI matter at Mark Ivins & Associates. It was his opinion that the Ivins ethical screen met and exceeded all requirements and assured the protection of CDMI's privileged information.

Harrington cross-examined him about the fees he charged, but it was a waste of time. There was no jury, and the judge's conscience was beyond being shocked by astronomical expert fees.

That concluded the evidentiary portion of the hearing. The judge heard brief legal arguments from Harrington and Ivins, then issued her foregone conclusion from the bench: the motion to disqualify Mark Ivins & Associates as class counsel in the Palmer litigation was denied.

"I told you," Harrington muttered as he packed up his files.

Barrett didn't linger for any more recriminations. He pushed his way through the crowd of Ivins's groupies clogging the center aisle. Detective Riley was still in the back row on the left, and Barrett did a deliberate about-face in the other direction. And there in the back row on the right was Shay Lambert.

He almost didn't recognize her. Gone was the mousy brown hair in the girlish ponytail. Gone was the cheap beige suit and the prim buttoned-to-the-neck white shirt. Today she wore a sleek black dress, and her hair was long and loose and lit through with a shimmer of golden strands. She looked glamorous and, as she rose to her full height, formidable. She locked eyes with him, and in her cold stare he suddenly saw that it wasn't only exoneration she was bent on. She wanted revenge.

He felt suddenly breathless. He shoved past the last knot of people in the aisle and burst panting through the double doors. Lester Willard was leaning against the wall in the corridor, trying and failing to look inconspicuous. Barrett brushed past a woman by the door and closed in on Lester.

"Sir," Lester said, straightening. "She's in—"

"I *know* she's in there," Barrett snapped. "Where's Culligan?"

"I wouldn't know, sir."

There were certain things Lester made it his business not to know, and Barrett guessed that Culligan's latest bender was one of them. He grabbed the back of Lester's neck and pulled his head down to his level. He spoke into his ear. "You need to grab her. Next chance you get. No more fucking delays."

"Yes, sir. But"—Lester cut a quick glance down the corridor—"she's got security now."

Barrett followed his gaze to the woman by the courtroom door. She had short hair and wore an ill-fitting pantsuit and a pair of soft-soled Rockports masquerading as oxfords. She had to be either a bodyguard or a lesbian lawyer. Or both. "Fuck," he said. Then, "Just the one?"

"So far."

He thought a second. "Unless she's wearing an adult diaper, she's gotta take a leak at least once a day. Stay on Shay. Find your opening."

"Do my best, sir."

—

Lambert's stare sent a chill through Barrett that lasted the rest of the day. He smoked through half a pack on his office balcony while he brooded over it. He tried to reach Culligan at all his numbers, but he didn't pick up at any of them; his assistant tried to cover for him, said he wasn't feeling well and must have turned off his phone, but Barrett knew he was either drunk or deliberately dodging the calls.

Lately Culligan had shown little stomach for the whole operation. Oh, he was fine with it provided everything happened on the other side of the planet. Or—probably more to the point—provided it didn't happen to white people. His attitude changed once it involved Shay. He even tried to argue against the Tony Low operation.

Barrett also tried and failed to reach Phil Duvall. His Manhattan assistant reported that he was in Tours; his Tours assistant reported that he was in Manhattan.

This all started out as a group enterprise. Each of them agreed it was the only way. They even got Madame's blessing on the operation. Then Lucy jumped ship, Duvall feigned ignorance, Madame went even deeper underground. And now Culligan was ghosting him. Barrett stood all alone in the crosshairs of Shay Lambert's revenge.

–

Dread clawed inside his belly like a caged rat. He wondered if it was possible to develop a bleeding ulcer in the course of a single day. He chugged half a bottle of Pepto and left the office before five. At home, he startled the latest maid, thrust his coat and case at her, and trudged wearily up the stairs to the bedroom.

He stopped short. A rustling sound came from Melanie's dressing room, followed by a long, contented "Ohhhh," breathed in a tone he remembered from their first years together. It wasn't possible, he thought, but after today he knew that anything was. His stomach churning, he stole silently across the Aubusson into the adjoining room.

Melanie was there, but not with another man. No, with something nearly as bad. She was preening in front of her floor-length mirror, alone but for the three Melanies smiling back at her, each of them wearing an elaborate ball gown. It was emerald-green silk, with a fitted bodice and a skirt that swirled around her hips and legs like a corkscrew.

She noticed his reflection beside hers. "You caught me," she said with a coquettish smile. "I was going to wait and surprise you on the night of the Gala."

The Met Gala. It hit him, what the gown must mean, and the rat in his belly clawed through his stomach into his guts until his blood ran thick with bile and excreta. The Met Gala was the most exclusive social event in the city, and somehow he'd promised her an invitation. It was nothing but a reflex, a defensive maneuver to ward off her bitter resentment after he failed to get her a ticket to the Graziella runway show. He was a fool to make such a promise, but she was the greater fool to imagine that marrying a lawyer, even one so prominent as he, could ever gain her entrée to that world.

"Send it back," he said. "We're not going."

"What!" The blood drained from her face, turning her skin a sickly white against the green silk.

"We're not going," he said again, and walked away.

"You promised! Barry!"

The crackling noise followed him. It sounded like dry kindling catching the spark. Another minute and it would burst into flame.

"I lied." He loosened his tie as he crossed the Aubusson again to his own dressing room. "Send it back."

"I can't! It's couture! They made it just for me!"

"Tell them you'll list it on eBay. That'll get them to take it back."

"I won't! I'm going to that Gala. With you or without you."

It was one of her favorite games, to dangle hints of all the other men who'd gladly take his place in her life. He had no patience for it tonight. He went into his dressing room and closed the door in her face. He locked it.

She let out an astonished shriek. He went through to his bathroom and closed that door, too, and sank down on the edge of the tub. He pressed a fist against his churning stomach as Lambert's cold dead stare flashed again in his memory. There was something lethal in her pale eyes, and it chilled him all the way down to the cold hard porcelain beneath him.

The sound of breaking glass came from their bedroom. Melanie was throwing things.

A thought came to him, so sudden and unexpected it was like a streak of lightning split the sky. It was something that had never once crossed his mind, but now it seemed so obvious he couldn't believe he'd never thought it before.

Maybe Lucy's death wasn't suicide.

Maybe he'd framed Lambert for a murder she actually did commit.

He saw her again in his memory. The black sheath dress as smooth and glossy as a shark's skin. Her hair and its otherworldly glow. Her pale eyes glittering like shards of glass.

She wanted him dead. He knew that. And if she'd killed once, she could surely do it again.

He pulled out his phone. The number wasn't in his contacts—saving it there would have suggested more of an ongoing relationship than he was willing to admit—but he scrolled through his call log until he found it. He stared at it for a long time while Melanie pounded on the dressing room door. What time was it in KL? Seven a.m.? Though why should he care? When you were about to embark on something like this, the niceties of civilized discourse hardly mattered. His finger hovered over the number.

"Barry, let me in! You bastard!" Melanie howled.

He pressed it.

"Hey, boss," Tony Low answered. "You sent the package?"

Barrett cleared his throat. "Um, no. We're having trouble getting delivery on this end. So we need a plan B."

"Okay."

"You have people over here, right?"

"Sure. Lots. What kinda people you need?"

Barrett searched for a euphemism, a way to extend the package metaphor. "Um, instead of a pickup, a takeout?" He winced as he said it. There was no way anyone could understand what he meant.

Low was silent for a long moment. "Sure, boss," he said finally, with a snicker in his voice. "But that's gonna cost more. A lot more."

He understood.

## Chapter 27

I used to think my life changed in an instant—the instant I lost my job at Jackson Rieders—but in hindsight I knew that wasn't true. The seeds of the Great Recession were sown years before, and the firm had been missing its profit-per-partner benchmarks for some time. The ax that severed my life into Before and After had been swinging for a long time before it landed.

But this time my life really did change in an instant. The instant I walked out of the Women's Unit at Valhalla and into Mark Ivins's car.

Three weeks in, this was my new life.

I woke, early and well rested in my king-size bed, made a cup of coffee in the De'Longhi, and drank it standing at the French doors, where I could watch the first fingers of sunlight creep into the garden. The hyacinths were in bloom in the borders, and I opened the door to drink in their lush, intoxicating scent. But of course they were in bloom. Everything in this garden was forced in a hothouse and not brought here until its moment of perfect beauty, then whisked away when the flowers faded. There was never any awkward in-between phase in Mark's garden. It was much like the women who worked for him. They all seemed to be at the peak of their beauty and were probably pensioned off when their looks started to fade. Nonetheless they all adored him. One of my favorite pastimes was guessing which of them he was sleeping with besides Phoebe. Maybe all of them.

After coffee I dressed in a T-shirt and leggings and went next door to the firm's basement-level gym. Two of my coworkers were already there, spinning to the heavy bass beat of dance music. I greeted them with a nod and mounted the treadmill and watched the morning news while I ran five miles. Phoebe arrived as I was dismounting, and while we spotted each other on the weights, she updated me on all the office gossip, both professional (Mark's settlement with Genco would give him five seats on the reconstituted board of directors; he'd be in control of that company just as he controlled a dozen others) and personal (Mark and his wife were having a rough patch; she had family money, but Mark's net worth had outstripped hers, and that had to change the dynamic of their marriage).

We parted after the requisite reps, and Phoebe got on the treadmill while I went through the elevator and back to my apartment.

Next up in the schedule of my new life: a rain shower, followed by an hour at my desk responding to emails and reviewing pleadings. My office was here in my apartment. This was Mark's solution for maintaining the Chinese wall between me and the Palmer team, but it suited me well. I didn't care to fraternize with the rest of the & Associates; I didn't plan to be with them that long.

I also spent some time poking into the firm's electronic records. Except for the password-protected files, I had full access, and browsing through the various pleadings and correspondence and financial records was an easy way for me to get the lay of the land here. It was also the way I'd uncovered the mystery of how Mark happened to bail me out of jail only minutes before Barrett's people would have: he'd been slipping money to the bail clerk at Valhalla from the first week of my incarceration. He'd known all along that I was in there, but until the clerk tipped him off that my bail was about to be posted by Jack Culligan, there was no reason for him to do anything about it. I didn't blame him for that delay. Obviously he couldn't be sure I'd be an asset to him until he learned that I was a liability to Barrett.

I then spent fifteen minutes on the Internet to see what stories people were dreaming up about me today. It was astounding how famous I'd become. Not infamous, not notorious, but actually famous. As if I'd accomplished something beyond being in the wrong elevator at the wrong time. The irony was that I soon would accomplish something, something very real if my plans came to fruition, but nothing I would ever be celebrated for on the Internet. My fame would be fleeting, which meant I needed to capitalize on it now.

I got dressed in a crisp red suit, summoned Lonnie for a ride downtown, and alerted Alice, who was waiting at my front door when I emerged. She was forty, a faded blonde with a short no-nonsense haircut and a rock-hard body that put my morning exercise regimen to shame. A former state trooper who was once part of the governor's security detail, she was now my bodyguard, hired by Mark the day I told him I was being followed. That was also the day he granted me the use of his car and driver. Now, whenever I left the building, it was in the silver Mercedes with Lonnie at the wheel and Alice riding shotgun. Though not literally. Her weapon of choice was a Glock 17, which she wore in a shoulder holster under her suit jacket. She also wore a coiled wire at her ear, linked to Lonnie in the car.

First stop was a café on Union Square. Alice went in to do a sweep, then gave the all-clear signal to Lonnie, who gave it to me. The reporter was already there waiting; he stood up when I came in, and waved me to the table.

"Morning, thanks for meeting me," he said as I sat down. He leaned forward, elbows on the table, eager to make his pitch even before I picked up the menu.

He was one of four reporters vying for my story. Although I'd made it clear that I could not discuss my case, the murder charge hanging over my head was the obvious hook. But they were each offering a different approach to the story, and I was still deliberating who should get the exclusive. At the moment I was leaning toward the freelancer who dangled a feature story in *Vogue*. A frothy choice, admittedly, but I couldn't help thinking that the photo shoot would be fun.

This one was pitching the social media angle—how the online debate about the case had caught fire and how it might impact the final verdict. He was a little daunted when I told him I'd never dabbled in social media. But he did a quick pivot and decided the irony would be a selling point.

A man stopped by our table on his way out. "Excuse me," he interrupted. "You probably don't remember me." The reporter shook his head, but it was me the man was addressing. "We were on a CLE panel a while back. On multidistrict litigation, I think?"

"Of course." I held out my hand. "It's Don, right? How are you?"

He seemed pleased to be recognized. "I just wanted to say hello. And wish you well."

I thanked him warmly.

"Does that happen often?" the reporter asked after the lawyer left.

"At least once a day. It's amazing, really, how little stigma a murder charge carries."

"It's because your case is so easy to relate to. Everybody dreads being stuck in an elevator. Then throw in a gun and an unstable passenger? It's their worst nightmare."

I finished my spinach-and-mushroom crepe, promised the reporter my decision soon, and left him with the check. Then it was another limo ride, farther downtown, to the offices of the Harrington firm.

Mark had tasked me with finding any evidence that Northstar or its attorneys had conducted a reverse auction and reached a secret deal with Ned Bartman. So far I'd taken the depositions of two of the company's senior executives. Today I'd scheduled the deposition of its CEO, a man named Nelson Ledbetter.

Dick Harrington had sent an underling to the previous depositions, but he was there in person today to defend his client's CEO. Also present was Ned Bartman, Mark's rival for class counsel, along with a young associate from Bartman's office, a nervous-looking boy named Joshua Matson who sat at his boss's elbow and took notes.

Ledbetter was a Houston transplant whose elevated status in the company apparently spared him from having to know anything. In his laconic Texas drawl, he denied knowing whether the company's lawyers had conducted a reverse auction among the firms vying to be class counsel; he denied knowing Ned Bartman or having seen him before today; he denied knowing anyone else in Bartman's firm; he denied knowing whether Northstar had entered into any agreement with Bartman to limit the company's monetary exposure; and he even denied knowing what a reverse auction was.

The other two Northstar executives I'd deposed had been equally unburdened with any knowledge. But that was fine by me. This was a long game I was playing, and I had them on the record now.

As all the players packed up their briefcases to go, I handed my card to the court reporter and ordered an overnight transcript. Then I tucked another card into the pants pocket of young Joshua Matson. On the back I'd written: *Drinks tonight?*

–

Lunch was next on my schedule, this time at the Four Seasons. Nearly every day since I'd been out of Valhalla, I'd had lunch or drinks with lawyers I used to know or wished to meet. I was renewing old acquaintances and making new ones all over town. Everyone I called was curious enough to say yes to my invitation, and as the word got out, I was soon on the receiving end of those invitations. It was more than curiosity; they were fascinated. How could anyone go through what I had and emerge like— this? I had not only survived, I had prevailed. Or so they all predicted.

It was just as Mrs. Casco taught me: wear the face you want the world to see, and that's the way the world will see you.

Today's invitation came from Joel Edders, my old supervising partner at Jackson Rieders, though he'd moved on since then, too. The firm's 2008 layoffs had proved insufficient to right their financial ship, so he'd let himself be poached by another firm in 2009.

He ordered a good wine to celebrate—whether my release from detention or my return to the practice of law wasn't clear. "When this is all over, I hope you'll consider coming to my shop," he said, his glass held high. "It'd be great to work with you again."

I smiled. "When this is all over? You make it sound like beating a murder rap is no harder than passing the bar."

"Equally a snap for you, I bet."

We tussled briefly over the check. I wanted to thank him for telling Mark Ivins about me, and he no doubt wanted to make up for how he'd abandoned me five years ago. I let him win.

–

Next stop was Dev Kapoor's office in midtown. It was on the tenth floor, and as we went up the stairs, I could hear Alice breathing hard behind me. She was in good shape for her age, excellent really, but she was growing weary of the climbs. As was I.

Dev's office was an unprepossessing space. It had utilitarian furniture and nothing but a potted palm and a few framed prints by way of decoration. Dev obviously felt no need to impress. He was a criminal defense lawyer and his clients were all preoccupied with the charges hanging over their heads; any more decor would have been wasted on them.

He came out himself to greet me when I arrived in reception. He was as unprepossessing as his office, a small dark-skinned man, six inches shorter than I was in my four-inch heels. A first-generation American, he had formal manners and a deferential attitude—an unexpected trait in most lawyers and certainly in one who'd enjoyed such a meteoric rise in the defense bar. He was not yet forty and already famous from coast to coast.

"Good news, good news," he said, beaming, as Alice took a seat in the waiting room. He led me down the hall to his conference room. Two other men stood up as I entered. The older one was Paul Schechler, an academic type in tweed whom Dev had hired to analyze CDMI's surveillance videos and HR documents. With him was a young techie named Jon Banoff who was dressed in the techie uniform of logoed T-shirt and Chuck Taylors. Schechler would be the witness on the stand, but Banoff was the one who'd done the work, and he did most of the talking in today's meeting.

His conclusion: the time stamp had been altered on each of the three video clips produced by CDMI as well as on my so-called termination form. He knew that because of something he called second-precision truncation. Before they were tampered with, the time stamps had hundred-nanosecond resolution, he explained, but the software used to manipulate them had truncated the time to second-precision. He couldn't say when the videos were actually recorded, or when the HR form had been completed, but he could say with a reasonable degree of scientific certainty that the time stamps had been manipulated.

His explanation was lengthy and detailed, and I was bored. I already knew the time stamps were altered and didn't really care how so long as the testimony would hold up in court. Dev was clearly elated, though, which told me that he hadn't been sure of my innocence before. Not that it mattered.

A text hit my phone, and I read it under the table. It was from Ned Bartman's young associate, Joshua Matson. *When and where?*

Banoff had written a fifty-page report supporting his conclusion, and Schechler had signed it and for an additional fee was prepared to testify to it. At the end of the meeting, they distributed electronic copies of the report to Dev and me. I immediately forwarded it to Mark Ivins. He'd paid for it, after all.

Dev showed the two men out and returned to the conference room. He was still beaming. "I'll study the report tonight, and if everything looks good, I'll send it to the DA in the morning."

I shook my head. "Not yet."

His smile faltered. "Why wait? Once they see this, they'll dismiss the charges. Within the week, I'd wager."

"Then what?"

"Then?" He seemed to be puzzled by my apparent obtuseness. "Then it will be over."

"Except that it won't. I'll still have this hanging over me. People will be whispering about me and speculating about what really happened for the rest of my life."

"It's not our burden to prove what really happened."

"It is, though," I said. "We have to play the long game, Dev." He deferred to me again, showing only the smallest of frowns as he moved on to the next items on my to-do list. His investigator had traveled to the federal penitentiary in Kansas to interview my half brother Roger. "He said he'd absolutely sign a statement that he never gave or sold you a firearm or even spoke to you in the last twenty years. But only in exchange for fifty thousand dollars. Which of course would render the statement utterly worthless."

"Good old Roger," I muttered. I wasn't surprised.

"The good news is he's not cooperating with the DA, either. He agreed to give them a statement—saying the opposite, I assume—but only in exchange for a pardon."

"There's no risk—?"

"None," Dev assured me. "Even if the DA were willing, the feds would never agree. So the bottom line on the gun is that, yes, your estranged half brother purchased a dozen DIY kits from the same manufacturer as the elevator gun"—*elevator gun* was the euphemism Dev employed to avoid saying *murder weapon*—"but thousands of those kits were sold, and there's no way to source the elevator gun to the kits sold to your brother."

"But also no way to source it to Lucy."

"Yes, but remember—" He checked himself before reminding me yet again about the burden of proof. "Final item," he said, pivoting. "Your husband."

I tensed. "You found him?"

"Not quite. But we learned that he was picked up for possession last month."

"Where?" Dev's investigator had been searching for David in all our old haunts in the Bronx—our apartment building, Cubby's bar, the bodega on the corner, the plasma donation center.

"Outside a club in Tribeca," Dev said. "He gave his address as the Hyatt House in Chelsea, but he'd already checked out by the time the police followed up."

Tribeca and Chelsea. These were his stomping grounds back in our glory days. "Sounds like he came into some money," I said.

Dev nodded.

–

Alice stood up as I returned to the reception area. She opened the outer door to check the public corridor, and her eyes grew suddenly wide. She stepped aside to let a man come through. He wore sunglasses despite the dim light in the corridor, and he ducked his head as he slipped past us.

"What?" I whispered as Alice hustled me to the stairwell. I wondered if Barrett had put a new tail on me.

"Didn't you see who that was?"

"Who?"

"That movie star. Luke Rafferty."

I laughed. "That's why you look so starstruck."

She blushed, and I continued to tease her about it all the way to the ground floor.

I was just stepping into the revolving doors to the street when I spotted a more familiar figure. Lester was parked down the block, in a blue sedan this time, though that did nothing to disguise him. His head grazed the ceiling where he sat behind the wheel. "Alice?" I said.

"I see him." She spoke into her earpiece, and in seconds, Lonnie pulled up and double-parked right out front. The rear door sprang open, and Alice steered me in a crouching run into the backseat. She jumped in after me, and Lonnie took off with a squeal of tires.

I looked back through the rear window as we passed Lester's car. I nodded at him, and he nodded back.

–

I got a text from Mark as we drove north. He'd read the video expert's report and wanted to celebrate. *Great news! Come up for a drink when you get back.*

It hadn't taken long for me to figure out that he was living full-time in his fifth-floor apartment. I saw him one night padding around barefoot while I worked late in the library. From my basement apartment, I often heard him moving about the building. Late at night I heard female voices, too, coming from the fifth floor. Once I recognized Phoebe's laugh. The other giggles came in other voices.

*Just a quick one*, I texted back to Mark. *I have plans tonight.*

*OK. C U @ 6*, he replied.

Lonnie pulled up in front of the office, and Alice did a quick swivel-scan of the street before she opened the car door for me and escorted me down the stairs to my apartment. She hovered by my side while I swiped my keycard through the lock on the door. "I'll be back at seven," she said.

I turned to thank her and came to an abrupt stop. Detective Joe Riley was coming out of the office door one flight up.

"Detective," I called as Alice darted in front of me. I leaned around her. "Did you wish to see me?"

He looked as startled as I felt. He came slowly down the stairs to street level. "I was hoping to grab a minute with your boss." He was wearing the same sad-sack suit he'd worn during my long day in Interview A, and I could only imagine how out of place he must have looked in the grand reception room of Mark Ivins & Associates. "But it seems he's not available."

"Perhaps I could help?" I said. As I came halfway up my own flight of stairs, Alice positioned herself between me and the street. She was on high alert, scanning the parked cars at the curb, scanning the surrounding rooftops.

"Well, uh. I shouldn't really talk to you," Riley said. "Seeing as you're represented by counsel."

I smiled. "That's a rule designed to protect the unwitting. I don't think I'm in any danger."

He hesitated. "Still and all."

"Could you take this inside?" Alice said in a low voice.

That seemed to decide him. He followed me as I turned down the stairs toward my apartment. Alice usually left me at the threshold, but this time she came in and pressed the door shut with her back. She stood sentry there as I led Riley inside.

"Nice digs," he said, his head swiveling to take it in. In a lower voice he said, "What's with the bodyguard?"

I put my briefcase on the kitchen counter. "It seems I'm being followed."

His caterpillar eyebrows crawled upward. "Barrett?" When I didn't answer, he said, "You should have called the police."

"Oh, right. Because my last encounter went so well."

To his credit, he looked away.

I watched him amble a few steps deeper into the apartment before I asked: "Is this the part where you guys ask for a drink of water or to use the bathroom?"

"Hey." He looked back at me, umbrage taken. "*You* invited *me* in."

"I was joking, Detective." Nonetheless, I took out a glass and filled it at the sink and placed it between us on the counter. "Have some water anyway."

He cracked a smile and took the glass.

"What did you want to see Mr. Ivins about?"

"I thought we might compare notes. I assume he's been gathering evidence in his lawsuit against your old company."

"And you want to compare his evidence with—what? Your evidence against me?" I let out a little laugh. "Why, Detective. Are you taking another look at your own case?"

He shrugged. "Just, you know, dotting all the *i*'s."

"Without Detective Cruz?"

"He's busy on an active case."

"And you're not."

He didn't answer. He lifted his glass and studied me over the rim as he took a slow swallow. "I wanted to ask Ivins if he ever came across anything about some charter flights out of Myanmar."

Relief flowed through me like a warm stream. At last. He'd finally looked at the documents in my briefcase. "Those documents are confidential," I said.

"And confusing," he said. "I can't make heads or tails out of 'em."

My relief faded.

"Well. Best be going." He drained the glass and placed it on the counter.

"Bathroom's free." I pointed.

He huffed a laugh and brushed past Alice, who still stood, stone-faced, at the door.

—

I changed out of my suit into a casual summer dress, and at six, I climbed the stairs to Mark's apartment. He hollered for me to come in when I knocked, and I opened the door to the aroma of sizzling beef. Mark had a personal chef named Kevin Ho who was more or less on retainer, and he was in the kitchen tonight, slicing and dicing vegetables on the counter. Mark was nowhere in sight.

I wandered into the living room. The apartment was decorated in the same clean lines and cool grays and blues

289

as my apartment in the basement. It was in stark contrast to the opulent reds and golds and ornate trimmings of his public space. Those rooms were like the mane of a lion or the tail of a peacock, a display to impress—or, really, to intimidate—his visitors. But he didn't need to intimidate anyone in his private space. The people he invited here already knew how formidable he was.

"Be right out," he called from another room. "Fix yourself a drink."

He'd been working. His laptop was open on the coffee table, and a document lay beside it. I skipped the bar and did a quick stealthy skim of the document. It was a draft settlement agreement in the Genco case. One section gave the shareholders he represented the right to appoint five new board members. I flipped a few more pages and confirmed that it was a nine-member board. So Mark would indeed have control of the company.

He came out as I was admiring a small stainless-steel nude on a bookshelf. He was dressed as casually as I was. More so since he was barefoot. "You're right," he said, taking in my empty hands. "We shouldn't have drinks. This calls for champagne." He gathered up his papers and conferred briefly with Kevin in the kitchen. I heard the pop of the cork, and Mark returned bearing two flutes.

"Here's to exoneration," he said, handing me a glass. He was still smiling as he uttered his next words. "Those filthy sons of bitches."

"Mmm." I took a swallow. The champagne danced on my tongue and brought a swoosh of memories: David in a VIP room at a dance club; David toasting me at our wedding reception; David shaking a bottle before he popped the cork and let a geyser of champagne spray over his head—that was the night he got his bonus check, the one that proved to be the last. And there was one final memory: while packing up to steal out of our apartment in the dead of the night, David had found the forgotten magnum at the back of the fridge, left over from the day of my layoff, and chugged it straight from the bottle. I thought of him now, clubbing in Tribeca. Staying in our old neighborhood. Pretending he could ever get that life back.

"After what they tried to do to you, Shay," Mark was saying. "Well, what am I saying? What they actually did—you spent two months in jail, after all—your civil suit against that company is going to be epic."

"Yes. I've been thinking about that."

"I'd be happy to represent you. Believe me."

I gave him a look. "But of course you couldn't."

"Why not?" He spread his arms wide and boastful. "I can handle more than shareholder litigation, you know."

"But you represent the shareholders of CDMI. Whose stock value would take a serious dive if I got a big damages award against the company."

After a beat of silence, he shrugged. "Right."

"It must be hard to remember who your clients are," I said. "When they're only names on a roster."

He bristled a bit at the dig. "That's not true. I'm always acting in their best interests. That's why I filed the Palmer suit. Management's been feeding at the shareholders' trough for too many years. I want to bring them down, Shay. I want to destroy every last motherfucking one of them."

"You're not supposed to discuss that with me," I reminded him. Something was hissing in the kitchen, and another aroma wafted out. The sweet, pungent smell of garlic.

"We could do it. You and me together."

I didn't answer that time. He pulled a sad mouth to show he understood, then changed the subject. "How are you coming on Northstar?"

"I deposed Nelson Ledbetter today."

He cocked his head. "Remind me?"

"CEO."

"Oh, right. Get anything out of him?"

I shook my head. "It was the same as all the other Northstar executives. He never discussed Bartman with anyone at Harrington or anyone inside Northstar. He never met anyone at Bartman's firm. He never discussed with anyone the idea of shopping among potential class counsel for the cheapest settlement. He was appalled at the very notion."

Mark shrugged. "Well, who knows? Maybe it never happened." He grinned. "I might have to win class counsel purely on my merits."

"Let's not give in yet!" I laughed. "I still have some ideas percolating."

"I knew you would. Hey, how about we take this upstairs?"

I hadn't dressed for the outdoors, but he tossed me a suede bomber jacket to put on. He stayed as he was, down to the bare feet. "Kevin, we'll be upstairs," he shouted on our way out.

"You're entertaining tonight?" I asked as we climbed the narrow stairs to the rooftop garden.

"Well, you told me you'd be out." He pretended to be sorrowful. "So I had to find somebody else to fill my lonely night."

Up on the roof, the lights of the city glowed around us like a forest of fireflies. Mark pushed a button on the gas

292

fireplace beside the dining table, and the flames flickered on. I took the chair nearest to the fire, and Mark pulled his in close beside mine. Close enough that I could feel his arm press against mine through the suede sleeve of his jacket.

I didn't pull away. I wasn't worried about his intentions. I knew exactly what his intentions were. He intended to sit back and wait for me to make the first move. That was his established MO. It had become obvious to me in the last three weeks, not only in how he behaved toward me but in how he behaved toward all the other women in the office. He believed himself to be so desirable to women that he never had the burden of initiating the seduction. He could rely on his conquests wanting to conquer him. This was what he considered his greatest strength—his sexual magnetism, his utter irresistibility. I'd thought about it a good deal, especially when I thought about jujitsu. How to use his greatest strength against him. Ideas were percolating.

He refilled my glass as Kevin trotted up the stairs. "Thought you might like some go-withs," Kevin said, flourishing a plate of tiny savory tarts.

"Ah, this is a favorite of mine," Mark said. "Thanks, Kevin." He picked one up as the chef galloped back downstairs. "Try it," he said, and finger-fed it to me. "Good, right?"

"Mmm." It was filled with goat cheese and fennel and melted into a buttery glow on my tongue.

"God!" he burst out unexpectedly. "It kills me to think of what they did to you. And why! That's what's driving me crazy."

I swallowed. "I wish I could tell you."

He popped a tart into his own mouth and looked thoughtful while he chewed. "Interesting phrasing you used there," he said finally. "Like it could be either *I wish I knew* or *I wish I weren't subject to a gag order.* I don't suppose you could tell me which?"

I regarded him for a moment, as if deliberating. "The latter."

"I knew it! God damn it. They're covering up something so heinous that it made that woman kill herself. They couldn't risk anyone finding out what, so they made it look like you killed her."

"Sounds pretty fantastical when you say it."

"But you lived it. They did it to *you*, Shay. The old men who wrote the rules of attorney-client confidentiality— they never imagined a situation like this one."

I looked away. "I'm sorry, Mark. I can't discuss it."

He was silent for a time before he gave up and changed the subject. He wanted to know about the reporters vying for my story and which way I was leaning.

"You know," he mused after I gave him the rundown, "why give the story to any of them? No one could tell it better than you could yourself. You should do a book. I know a few publishers. Work up a pitch, then sit back and wait for the bidding war."

"Only if I'm acquitted."

"You will be. Of course you will. You know—" He was thinking again. "We could collaborate on a book. Yeah!" He sat up excitedly. "How you were framed, and how the two of us exposed it and toppled the evil scum who did it to you. What d'you say?"

"It's too soon to say anything."

He leaned back with a shrug, conceding the point for the moment. "Well, it's also too soon to give an exclusive to anyone else. Whatever you do, make sure you reserve the right to publish your own story."

"That's good advice. Thank you, Mark." I got to my feet. "I'd better head down now."

He looked at his watch and nodded, and he got up and followed me down the stairs. At the fifth-floor landing, he pushed the call button for the elevator. "No, I'll walk," I said. I handed him his jacket and started for the next flight of stairs.

He stopped me with a hand on my arm and a look of genuine concern on his face. "I don't get it, Shay. How can you be so fearless about everything else? The whole fucking state of New York is after you, and you're undaunted. But you can't step inside an elevator."

I took a shaky breath. "I just need a little more time."

"You have to get back on that horse, Shay."

"Soon, Mark," I said as I pulled free and started down the stairs. "I promise."

—

At the second-floor landing I heard a buzz of voices coming from the main conference room. I crossed the hall and poked my head in. A half dozen young men and women were going through stacks of documents spread out over the table. "Sorry," I said when they looked up. "Didn't mean to interrupt."

A skinny boy in a skinny tie shot to his feet. "Hey. You're her, aren't you? Shay Lambert."

I nodded as the others murmured around the table.

"We're working on your document production," another one said.

"Mine?"

"CDMI's."

"Oh." I scanned the piles of paper. These had to be the documents I'd worked on in The Lab. "I'm afraid I'm not allowed to talk to you. Chinese wall? Please excuse me."

I headed down another flight to the main floor. Phoebe was chatting with Luisa at the reception desk, and she gave me a bright smile.

"I see we have some new hires," I said.

She looked blank.

"In the library? Reviewing documents?"

"Oh. Right. No, they're not new hires. They're law students doing an internship."

"Paid?"

"Well, no." She pursed her lips. "But really, it's an honor for them just to be allowed to work here."

–

Joshua Matson was already there when I arrived at the Midtown wine bar. He was waiting at a little round table in the corner; when I came through the door, he rose awkwardly, knocked his glass with his elbow, and dove to right it before it toppled over. He recovered, barely, and held out his hand as I threaded my way toward him. I ignored it and went in for the European kiss on each cheek. When I pulled back, his face was flushed red. With a shy smile, he pulled out a chair for me.

I scooted closer as Alice situated herself in an incon-spicuous spot by the door. "Thanks so much for meeting me, Joshua."

"Call me Josh?"

"Josh," I said with a smile. "I realize this is a little irregular, what with our firms competing for class counsel. But I wanted to get to know you better."

His eyes shone behind his glasses. "Really?"

Not really. I already knew what I needed to know about him. I'd profiled him online. He'd majored in humanities at Oberlin and graduated from Berkeley Law with dreams of practicing good law. A lot of law students started out that way. They thought they'd do civil rights, or environmental law, or death penalty cases. Five years later they were doing tax law and defending polluters. But Josh stuck to his guns and went to work for Ned Bartman, who, like Mark, touted himself as a crusader against corporate malfeasance. The other things I'd learned about Josh? He was twenty-six and had an out-of-shape body, an unfortunate nose, and no social media indication of any woman in his life.

"I read your law review article," I told him. "On whistleblower protections? I was so impressed."

"Oh!" He seemed embarrassed by his obvious pleasure and took a quick gulp of his drink to conceal it. He became even more embarrassed when he realized I didn't yet have a drink. "Oh!" he said again. "What can I get you?"

I asked for a white wine spritzer, and while he went to the bar, I tucked my chair in closer to his. He returned with a glass for me, and I tapped it briefly against his. "Your article. It shows such incredible scholarship," I said. "I know Mark would love to have that kind of intellect on our team."

"Wow. Thanks," he said.

"I was wondering. In the course of your thinking on these issues—did you consider the quandary faced by a potential whistleblower who's a lawyer?"

"How do you mean?"

"The lawyer has an express duty of loyalty to his client. But what if the client's done something that the lawyer feels a moral obligation to report? How do you reconcile those conflicts?"

"Well, the rules are pretty clear," he said. "If the client's about to do something illegal, the lawyer can reveal it. But not if it's already been done."

"What if the bad act's already been done, but the client continues to profit from it? I'm struggling with that."

He blinked a few times behind his smudged lenses. "Um, well—"

"Let's say a lawyer in a law firm—or a corporate law department—discovers something nefarious. Some wrongdoing that really ought to be exposed. But he'd have to breach confidentiality and loyalty to do it. How do you reconcile your duty to do good with your duties as a lawyer?"

His mouth was hanging open. He snapped it shut. "I knew it. You found out something at CDMI. It's why they framed you. To discredit you if you go public."

I sighed and looked away long enough for him to feel certain he'd guessed correctly.

"I wonder if you'd be willing to give that question some thought," I said finally. "And if you come up with anything—anything at all—let me know? I don't expect you to go on the record. Any advice you're willing to give me, I'll absolutely keep to myself." I laid my hand on his knee and felt a muscle jump against my palm. "I wish we had someone like you at Mark Ivins and Associates." I put a wistful tone in my voice. "If you ever want to make a move, Josh, I know Mark would be thrilled."

"Oh." He cleared his throat. "Wow."

"I'm sorry I can't linger." I scooted back my chair. "But could we do this again? Sometime soon?"

"Yes. Any time!"

He lurched to his feet, and I stood and kissed him again on both cheeks. "Good night," I said. "Be good."

It was only eight, but I told Alice I'd be in for the rest of the night, and she took me home and tucked me in.

As soon as she was gone, I slipped out through the French doors to the rear garden and scanned the back of the building. The after-hours security lights gave a dim glow to every floor of the townhouse except the fifth. The lights were ablaze up there, and I could make out Mark's silhouette at his living room window. He was speaking to someone out of sight.

I took the outdoor stairs up to the terrace and slipped my keycard through the lock on the back door. Inside, I stopped and listened, and when I heard no one, I stole up the grand staircase to the second-floor conference room.

I shone my cell phone flashlight over the conference table. I suspected that our unpaid interns hadn't been apprised of the terms of the Chinese wall, and I was right. The CDMI files were supposed to be locked up and password-protected, but here they all were, free for the perusing.

I hurried from stack to stack until I located the files on the Paradis sur Terre asset sales, then I did a quick skim, just long enough to confirm that the sales figures were still artificially inflated. Barrett hadn't backed off from his scheme. He'd already done his worst, and he was seeing it through to the end.

That was all I needed to know. I turned off the light, and as I crept out into the corridor, Mark's voice drifted down the stairs from the fifth-floor landing. I couldn't make out his words, but I knew that tone. He was laughing with the little edge of naughtiness that he seemed to delight in. I wondered what young woman he was entertaining tonight. I wondered if Phoebe minded when it wasn't her.

Then the second voice sounded, and it wasn't a woman at all. It was a man, speaking in a deep laconic drawl, and I knew that voice instantly. I knew because I'd listened to it for two hours straight that very morning. It was Nelson Ledbetter, CEO of Northstar, the man who knew nothing.

I smiled as I crept my way back downstairs. If my long game was on a chessboard, I'd just seen—or, rather, heard—my path to checkmate.

–

So, three weeks in, this was my new life. I had a prestigious position, a luxurious apartment, a fabulous wardrobe, and fifty thousand dollars in GoFundMe cash. What a contrast from my life in Valhalla. In hindsight my time there felt like only a lull in the action. The interval in a two-act play. Now Act Two was under way, and it was time to pick up the pace. I felt like a circus performer who'd hoisted a dozen plates into the air, and they were all spinning on their poles in gyroscopic swirls. I lay awake in bed that night, my mind churning with how to bring each one down and set it carefully into place on my imaginary table.

I was still awake when I heard the low whine of the elevator. My eyes opened, and I counted off the floors as it descended. Four, then three, then two, then the main floor, where it should have stopped. But it didn't. It continued down to the basement.

I slipped out of bed and went into the hall. The elevator opened two ways on this level, so Mark could have been headed for a late-night workout. But it was the doorknob on my side that moved.

It turned slowly until it met the lock and stopped. I felt certain that Mark's keycard opened every lock in the building, but I wasn't worried that he'd use it. I knew he was only checking to see if I'd left the door unlocked. If this might be the night I'd finally give in to my desire.

*Soon, Mark, I promise*, I thought as the elevator whined its way back up to the top.

# Chapter 28

Before this year, Barrett seldom spent any time on his office balcony. He had far too much work to allow any time for rose-sniffing or horizon-gazing or whatever people did outside. To the extent that he enjoyed the balcony at all, it was only for the way it impressed his guests.

Lately, though. Lately he was spending hours each day out on the balcony. Smoking, mostly. He was up to two packs a day and had given up all pretense that this was a temporary setback. But he was also horizon-gazing. On a clear day he liked to imagine he could see the building that housed his old law firm. The building that built him, you could say. Hard work but simpler times. The Code of Professional Responsibility spelled out all the rules that governed the conduct of lawyers in private practice. It was so easy to parse through an ethical dilemma in those days. Simply consult the rules, and if you were still uncertain, anonymously request an opinion from the ethics committee. You got an answer, and you conducted yourself accordingly.

But there were no rules in the corporate world, or perhaps there were too many. Either way, everything was murkier. Maximize shareholder value used to be the guiding principle, but now there were all these other duties. Reduce your carbon footprint and promote diversity and remove the glass ceiling and lean in or lean out or do the hokey-pokey or some such nonsense. It made his head spin.

He hoped that time away might help. He was leaving for Paris tonight. It would be a pseudo-vacation to placate Melanie, who was still in a snit over his failure to deliver on the Met Gala. Marcia had arranged for her to be feted and fitted by the top designers in the city. For Barrett, the trip meant an opportunity to speak to Madame directly about recent events, to confirm her blessing and secure her cover. And the biggest incentive of all: it would place him well away from the scene of the crime when the Lambert problem was finally resolved. An alibi, if you like.

Marcia's voice sounded through the balcony speaker. "Mr. Barrett, your car's here, and your luggage has been sent down."

He took one last drag on his cigarette. "What about my security?"

"It's Colby today, and he's right here."

Barrett stubbed out the butt in the planter box and went through to Marcia's desk. A large Black man wearing the company blazer was standing at attention. Almost all the bodyguards seemed to be Black these days, Barrett thought. It was the same with the cops and the soldiers. If that race war ever happened, he was pretty sure he'd be on the losing side.

Marcia handed him his attaché. Working papers for the plane ride. "You have the first-quarter reports," she said. "Plus the latest draft of the new contract with Luke Rafferty."

"And that, uh, ID badge?"

"It's in there," she said coolly. Marcia gave nothing away. "I hope you and Mrs. Barrett have a wonderful time."

Out on the street the regular driver was loading the bags into the trunk of the company limo. Melanie was taking a separate limo because her luggage wouldn't fit in this one. At least three of her bags would be traveling empty. She planned to fill them with her shopping.

Colby opened the passenger door, and Barrett gave a start when he saw someone else in the backseat. Jack Culligan.

"Hope you don't mind," Culligan said. "I thought we could talk on the way to the airport."

"About damn time," Barrett said, ducking in.

"Yeah." Culligan pushed a button to raise the privacy screen as Colby took his seat beside the driver. "That's what I wanted to talk to you about. I have to apologize for the way I kind of went AWOL on you. Truth is, I've been having a hard time getting my head around all this."

Barrett frowned as he buckled his seatbelt. "Some of us don't have the luxury of time to wallow."

"I know. It's just that Lucy's death, and now with Lambert out—"

"I'm taking care of the Lambert problem." The limo pulled away from the curb.

"How?"

"Tony Low knows somebody. Here. Stateside."

Culligan's forehead creased. "Somebody who—?"

"Yes."

The evening rush hour had ended. Traffic was light as the driver merged onto the highway.

"Gee, I don't know, Barry. It's one thing to manufacture—"

"Manipulate. That's all we did. Besides. What if Lambert actually did it?"

"What?"

"Just because we repackaged the evidence doesn't mean she didn't actually kill Lucy." The more he thought it, the more likely it seemed to him, and the better he felt about everything.

"Huh."

"She could come after me or you next, Jack. We have to neutralize the threat."

Culligan turned to the window and didn't speak for several minutes. Barrett checked his phone and read a text from Melanie. She was waiting for him in the premier members' lounge at the airport. She'd ordered a bottle of Dom.

"It's more than that, though," Culligan said finally. "It's that whole business in Myanmar. I know I went along with it at the time. But the more I think about it… Well, especially after those men drowned in the typhoon."

"Look. I understand," Barrett said. He'd been thinking through these same questions during his hours out on the balcony, and he felt reasonably happy with the answers he'd come up with. Happy enough to share them with Culligan. "Here's the thing, Jack. You have to view everything in context. The context of the prevailing norms in that time and place. Think about it. George Washington owned slaves, but nobody's agitating to take his face off the dollar bill or to rename the capital. Because slavery was a cultural norm. Thomas Jefferson wrote *all men are created equal*, but he owned slaves. Hell, he even fucked his, but he's still revered as one of our founding fathers. Let's face it. This whole damn country was founded on slavery. Because that was the culture of that time and place. Well, guess what?" Barrett was feeling expansive. "In pockets of Asia today, slavery is still part of the culture. Multinational corporations like ours are always being told to respect and comply with local standards and traditions, and that's all we did when we monetized those assets."

Admittedly this was an ex post facto rationalization. When they'd made the decision, all they'd been thinking about was saving the company and thus their jobs. But why was that so wrong? Factory workers were allowed to fight for their jobs, even when violence sometimes erupted. Why not the workers in the executive suite? "Capitalism depends on the exploitation of capital," he said. "And that includes human capital."

Culligan was squinting hard. "I don't know, Barry—"

"It's all just a matter of degree. A sliding scale. At one end you might have the men on those fishing boats, and at the other you have a young lawyer working twenty hours a day in hopes of making partner. They're all being exploited. Minimum-wage workers, unpaid interns, the whole gamut."

"But those men—held captive on a boat in the middle of the ocean for upward of three years—"

"Yes, yes, it's deplorable. But keep in mind—if not for those men on those fishing boats, Americans would have to pay twice as much for pet food. Anyway, most of those people, men and women, would have ended up being trafficked even if they'd never come to work at PsT. It's just a fact of life over there."

"But not over here. And a lot of those girls ended up—"

"No, that was a mistake. Tony admits he dropped the ball there. But to compensate, he's doing this next bit at a discount."

"This next bit being…?"

Barrett didn't answer. "You've still got eyes on her, right?"

Culligan didn't answer, either. "When's it gonna happen?"

"I don't know. I don't know when or who or where. But I know this." Barrett slapped Culligan on the knee as the limo pulled up to the terminal. "We'll all sleep a lot better when it's done."

# Chapter 29

A manila envelope was propped against my front door when I got home late one evening. Alice dove for it, shook it, sniffed it, and took it out into the street to open. She came back and handed it to me. "Just a document. It's harmless."

There was no cover letter or any other indication of the sender. Nothing but a copy of an email from Nelson Ledbetter, CEO of Northstar, to Ned Bartman, Mark's rival for class counsel. In it Ledbetter confirmed *our chat* and alluded to an attachment showing *that little anomaly we discussed*. The attachment wasn't included, but I could guess what it was: a spreadsheet showing the discrepancy in fourth-quarter earnings that Bartman supposedly unearthed all on his own, the discovery he was hanging his hat on for appointment as class counsel. Now we had evidence that he'd been hand-fed the information by Ledbetter.

It had taken three drink-dates with Joshua Matson, and by the last one, I'd had to be a lot less subtle. *It could happen anywhere*, I'd told him. *A young lawyer working third chair on a major lawsuit discovers that his boss made a dirty deal on the side. A deal that could reap him millions of dollars. Does he reveal it to the other side?* But he'd finally come through for me.

When I heard Mark return to the building, I called him with the news. "Come on up," he said, and I went back outside and in the front door and up the four flights of stairs. He was waiting by the open door, barefoot as always after hours, but otherwise fully dressed in white tie and tails. He'd been to a charity do that night, an event chaired by his wife.

"Where'd you get this?" he asked as he read the email.

"Anonymous delivery. Presumably from a whistleblower inside either Bartman's firm or Harrington's."

"Well, what do you know?" He grinned. "An honest-to-God smoking gun. It really happened. They really did a reverse auction."

"We don't have a witness to authenticate it," I pointed out.

He waved a hand. "We don't need one. I'll confront Ledbetter with this email on the stand, and drag out all the lies in his deposition. He'll fess up."

"Then you'll be appointed class counsel."

He spread his arms wide. "Last man standing. Great work, Shay. You really came through for me."

"I need a new assignment. What about the Genco case? I could help Phoebe."

"Nah. That case would be a waste of your talents. Let's keep you on Northstar. Now that we're locked in as class counsel, there'll be plenty for you to do. And if not, I'll think of something else."

"Anything but CDMI," I reminded him.

"Right." A frown crossed his face, but he wiped it away with a smile. "Want to come in? Have a celebratory nightcap?"

"Thanks, but I should head back down. Good night."

I turned and walked very deliberately to the elevator. I could feel him watching me from his doorway as I pushed the call button. The cage arrived, the cylinder opened, but my feet faltered. I did a quick about-face to the stairs.

"No." Mark came at me in three quick strides and took me by the elbow. "You can do it, Shay." He steered me back to the elevator.

"No—"

"You can do anything. You've proved that."

"I'm not ready."

"I'll go with you," he said, and he stepped on and pulled me into the narrow cylinder with him.

The door closed, and when the cage descended, I lurched and stumbled against him, and as he reached to steady me, I flung my arms around his neck and kissed him.

He wasn't surprised. He'd been expecting it, waiting for it, taking it as his due. He didn't accelerate; neither did he resist. When the elevator landed on the basement level, I had to use my keycard to unlock the door, and I had to lead him by the hand into the bedroom.

No one could ever accuse him of making unwelcome workplace advances. "You're sure?" he said before he undressed me, and I could tell it was a practiced bit of his foreplay, a rhetorical question he was certain would be answered in a breathless affirmative. Which was exactly how I answered.

He lay back on the bed and waited for me to straddle him. But it didn't take long for him to give up the charade that I was the one in charge. He flipped me onto my back, and I stared at the ceiling as he rose and thrust above me. He was hinged at the hips, levering up on straight arms and down on bent elbows. The image of a lever rooted in my mind. He was a lever, trying to pry information out of me. When his pace quickened, the image changed, and I thought of an oil pumpjack out on a windswept Texas prairie, drilling deep to tap into my well of knowledge about CDMI and how he might bring it down. Sex was a tool, his greatest one, or so he thought.

What metaphor described my own sexual behavior? That was easy, I thought, as I wrapped my spider arms and legs around him and drew him deeper into my clichéd web.

Afterward, cheek to chest, I murmured, "Stay the night?"

He kissed the top of my head. "I wish. But we have to be discreet. You understand that, don't you?"

He assumed I was smitten. That my ardor would have to be controlled. I gave him the sigh he was waiting for. "Of course. I understand."

He got dressed in his white-tie ensemble, and I clung to him as he padded barefoot to the elevator. His waistcoat and shirt hung open—the mother-of-pearl studs were in his pocket—and I slipped my hands inside, against his skin. "I'm so grateful we had this time, Mark." I lifted my face to his. "I'm so grateful for everything."

He smiled and kissed me again.

"I mean it," I said, breathing against his lips. "I wish I could repay you. I wish I could give you what you want."

He leaned back in the circle of our arms, watching me, waiting for the next part.

"I can't betray an attorney-client confidence or violate my NDA. You know that."

His eyes narrowed; he heard the *but* in my voice and waited for it.

"But," I said. "There's some information I came upon through another source, not through CDMI, and I've reviewed the rules, and I think I can share this much with you. No, I know I can." I rose up on tiptoe to kiss him again.

"What?" he breathed against my lips.

"Four women are being held in the ICE detention center in Elizabeth, New Jersey. One is Thai, one is Cambodian, and the other two are Indonesian. You need to take translators and go there and get statements from each of them. And video it. And do it fast, before they're deported."

Deep puzzled creases carved his forehead. "Why? Who are they?"

"I'll text you their names."

"What do they have to do with CDMI?"

"I can't say anything more. Just do it. Please." I gave him a nudge into the cage and reached around him to push the fifth-floor button. "Good night," I called as the door slid shut. "And thank you!"

When he was gone, I went into the bathroom and used the bidet and stood under the rainfall shower for a long time.

I had one happy thought as I fell asleep that night. I wouldn't have to climb the stairs anymore. At least that much of the pretense could be over.

# Chapter 30

Barrett had a car and driver at his disposal while he was in France, and he also had a body man to open doors and clear paths and generally serve as a factotum. But he dispensed with all of that for his mission today. He took a cab to the Montparnasse station and rode the TGV to Tours. The company had a small satellite office in Tours, but he didn't stop by or alert Yves that he would be in the area. Instead he hired a car and drove himself deep into the château country of the Loire Valley.

Because it wasn't his car, he didn't care about lingering odors, and he allowed himself to smoke as he drove. The deep breathing helped him relax, even if only enough to offset the jitters he got from the nicotine.

His mission today was twofold. The short-term goal was to update Madame on recent developments and get cover for all that had happened and was yet to happen. They needed to circle their wagons. The long-term goal was to demonstrate Phil Duvall's failure to meet the short-term goal and to plant the seeds for a changing of the guard. Or, rather, to fertilize the seedlings he'd already started. This campaign was a long and slow one.

As was this drive. Madame's château was well off the beaten path, and he had to follow a circuitous route through small villages marked off with crumbling walls, past vineyards and forests and meadows of wildflowers dancing in the spring breeze. The *rustique* charm was lost on Barrett. He railed to himself that the chairman of a major international corporation should be resident at that corporation's headquarters. The chairman of a major international corporation shouldn't be living in seclusion under elaborate security measures and with a single gatekeeper. Although—he reconsidered—if the guard did indeed change, if he became that gatekeeper, he thought he could make it work.

When the rental car's GPS told him he was getting close, he pulled off to the side of the road next to a field dotted with golden bales of rolled hay. It looked like a platter of brioche for a giant. He turned the rearview mirror his way and carefully pressed two adhesive strips of mustache onto the skin above his upper lip. He was already wearing a Burberry safari suit identical to one Phil Duvall often wore. Now he added a pith helmet and sunglasses, and when he studied himself in the mirror, he thought he looked like a fool. Exactly like Phil Duvall. He drove on.

A single-track road led up to the gatehouse of Madame's château. It was a two-turreted stone structure with a central arch to drive through. Or, rather, to stop at, since the guard came out and stood directly in the path with his palm out.

Barrett lowered his window and passed out the ID he'd cloned from the company's security files. "*Bonjour*, Monsieur Duvall," the guard said. He returned the ID and stepped aside with a gallant arm wave through the arch. "*Continuez, s'il vous plaît.*"

It was a lucky break: a guard who knew the name and costume better than he knew the face.

The sun dimmed as the lane led through a dense stand of trees, then it brightened again as he emerged into a swoop of manicured lawn that curved around a pond with a fleur-de-lis fountain at its center. Then around another bend and the château came into view.

It was in the classic style, a melding of Gothic and Renaissance architecture, with a steeply pitched roof topped by corbeled chimneys and pierced by gabled dormers, all of it stone-carved with elaborate ornament-ation. At the center was a large round tower topped by a conical roof.

Barrett pulled up beside the arched entry. A maid opened the heavy wooden door as he got out of the car. She was dressed in a white tunic and pants and white soft-soled shoes, and he was a bit disappointed that she wasn't wearing the Halloween version of a French maid's outfit. He stalked toward her in his heavy safari boots as if on the trail of big game. She said something to him, but even though he had some rudimentary French, the only words he recognized were *Bonjour, Monsieur Duvall.*

"English, *s'il vous plaît*," he said.

She bowed to admit him into a cylindrical recep-tion hall. Its curved walls were painted with chinoiserie murals. "You are lucky," she said in slow, careful English. "Madame is having a good day today."

He raised an eyebrow. "Has she been ill?"

She gave him a puzzled look. "You may go up," she said, and pointed toward the stairs.

He realized he was expected to know the way. If he asked for an escort, his cover would be blown. He eyed the carved-stone staircase and followed its curving path up to the gallery above. The mansion was big but not enormous. He ought to be able to find Madame's salon. "*Merci*," he said, and started up the stairs like he was scaling Kilimanjaro.

He congratulated himself as he reached the landing above. His ruse had worked. He'd made it past two separate gate-keepers and was about to have a private audience with Madame. He took off his sunglasses and peeled the mustache from his upper lip. He'd met Madame several times during his early days at the company, and she'd always behaved warmly toward him. Still, she might be angry that he'd arrived without warning and that she'd had no time to prepare her toilette. He decided his best defense would be a good offense. He'd burst in pleading urgency. No time for niceties, he'd convey; a true emergency had compelled his visit.

He headed down the central upstairs corridor. It was lined with mirrors, a scaled-back version of the famous hall in Versailles, and he could picture Madame striding down the corridor as if it were a fashion runway. Doors stood ajar along the hall, giving him a view into each chamber. Each one was empty. He wondered if he was on the right floor. Madame's salon might be another floor up.

Then he heard a strange sound, a rhythmic, high-pitched keening. The wind through one of the chimneys, he thought, except that there wasn't even a breeze stirring outside. Could it be Madame operating some kind of sewing machine? Did she still do that? He cocked his head and calculated the direction and turned that way, down a smaller hallway. The keening grew louder, and he saw a light coming from the room at the end of the hall. He followed it to the doorway.

Inside the room was another maid in the same white uniform. She was spoon-feeding a pale-haired child whose back was to the door. Barrett's jaw dropped in surprise. He'd never heard of a child in Madame's life, let alone a grandchild, but that explained the maids dressed in white; they were actually nursemaids. It might also explain why Madame chose to live this bucolic life. The better to raise a child in.

The maid looked up with a bright smile. "Ah, Monsieur Duvall!" The spoon paused in mid-flight, and the keening grew louder still. "It is nice to see you," she said, her voice raised above the din. "Madame so enjoys your visits."

Barrett came into the room, and the maid stood to greet him. But she stopped abruptly. "Wait. Who are you? You are not Monsieur Duvall!"

He looked from the maid to the child. She was clutching a naked baby doll to her chest and rocking back and forth in her wheelchair. Her hair wasn't blond, it was white, and her face—the face that once graced a hundred magazine covers—was skeletal.

"Madame?" he breathed.

"Get out! Get out at once!" the maid screamed.

He came closer. The woman's eyes were vacant, and a line of orange drool trickled down her chin.

"I shall call security!"

The maid—or, rather, the nurse—hurried to the telephone table across the room. Barrett wondered if he should identify himself, declare his name and position and his right and duty as corporate counsel to meet with the chairman of the board. But he couldn't speak. He could only stare.

"How long—" He stopped. He had to clear his throat. "How long has she been like this?"

The nurse was shouting into the telephone, rapidly and in French. The old woman's distress seemed to grow. Her rocking turned frenetic, her keening turned to screams.

"How did you get in here?" the maid said, apparently relaying the demand from whoever was on the other end of the telephone. "Are you alone?"

"Yes," Barrett answered.

As he said it, he realized it was true. There would be no cover for him. There were no wagons to circle. He was completely alone.

## Chapter 31

The next morning I found Phoebe in a huddle with Luisa at the reception desk. I stopped and raised an eyebrow at their frantic whispers. "What's up?"

"We don't know where Mark is," Phoebe said.

Luisa was wide-eyed. "He left me a note saying, *Clear my calendar today. Cancel everything.*"

"He took Lonnie and the limo," Phoebe said, "and now he's not answering his phone."

"Weird," I said.

We hashed it out: Phoebe would cover the hearing in Mercer; I would handle the conference call in Ralston; Luisa would cancel everything else.

I returned to my office downstairs and logged on to the firm's server and spent thirty minutes learning the Ralston case, then the rest of the morning poking through the entire file on the Genco case. Like the Palmer case against CDMI, it was a derivative action attacking the incumbent management of the company. Under the terms of the soon-to-be-finalized settlement agreement, Mark would appoint five new members of the board, who would then install new management in the executive suite. I studied that mechanism very carefully.

I changed into running tights and a tank top, and at eleven thirty I dialed into the Ralston conference call. I made Mark's excuses and wrested a minor concession from opposing counsel. At noon the call ended, but the line remained open for the hour allotted, and I left my extension open. Anyone watching the switchboard or reviewing the phone logs would assume I was still on the call.

Alice would have been happy to go running with me; she also would have been duty-bound to report my movements to Mark. I slipped out the French doors into the garden, then stopped at the back gate. The alley was clear and the surrounding rooftops empty, so far as I could see. I darted out and sprinted around the corner and flagged down a cab. I took it through Central Park all the way to the river, where I stationed myself near the boat basin café and waited for Nelson Ledbetter to appear.

Something I'd learned over the years when taking depositions: you can often glean as much from the witness's casual off-the-record banter as you can from his actual testimony. One thing I'd learned last week while Nelson Ledbetter shot the breeze with Dick Harrington was that every day at this hour, he left his office at Northstar and took a run along the Hudson River Greenway.

He was a tall man, and I spotted him at fifty yards, his head bobbing high above the pack. I let him pass, and when he was well ahead, I cut out onto the trail and ran to catch up. I gave him a quick backward glance as I overtook him, then I did an exaggerated double take.

"Oh, hello!" I called as I slowed my pace and fell into step beside him. "It's Nelson Ledbetter, right? Shay Lambert. I took your deposition last week?"

He peered at me. His face was red and streaming with sweat. "Oh. Hi," he puffed.

"How've you been?" I asked cheerily, loping along.

"I don't think I'm supposed to talk to you." He could barely talk anyway. "Us being adversaries and all."

I laughed. "But we're not anymore. Mark pulled me off the Northstar case. My work is done, as they say."

Ledbetter seemed to relax at that news, though he was still blowing hard. "Yeah. I heard you found that email."

"You sure didn't make it easy for me, though."

He hesitated.

"But I understand. You had to sell it, right?"

He huffed a laugh.

"Anyway, he just put me on Genco. So now we're not adversaries, we're allies." I winked.

"Oh, so you know about…?"

I nodded. "And thank God. Current management is a shipwreck."

"I got—a good—team lined up," he panted. "We'll—turn it around. By—2015 fiscal year end."

And there it was. My hunch confirmed. All I'd based it on was some cryptic marginalia in the draft settlement agreement, but it all made sense. Mark would be installing new management at Genco, so with the presidency up for grabs, why not offer it to someone who could help him sew up his appointment as class counsel in the Northstar case? He'd made an offer to Ledbetter: conduct a reverse auction with Ned Bartman, leak an incriminating document, and become president of a bigger and better company than Northstar. The whole thing was a setup of Ned Bartman, even if Bartman was already angling to do a reverse auction. It was like framing someone for a crime he actually did commit.

Here was the weapon I'd been hoping for. Ledbetter would probably want to report our little conversation to

Mark, but with Mark incommunicado today, he wouldn't have a chance until after I'd already deployed it.

"Oh, there's my phone," I told Ledbetter, slowing to a trot. "Nice talking to you."

I'd planned that as my exit line, but in fact my phone was buzzing. I fished it out of the pocket on my thigh as Ledbetter saluted and ran on. The call was from the office. I started walking east as I answered, off the Greenway and heading for the city streets.

"Sorry to interrupt your conference call," Luisa said. "I have someone named Joe Riley on the line? He says it's urgent."

At the mention of Riley's name, my heart rate shot up higher than when I was running. The police must have finally deciphered the documents in my briefcase and figured it all out. "Patch him through," I said. At that moment, I spotted Lester Willard. He was watching me from behind the wheel of a blue sedan parked at the curb, facing west on a one-way street going east. I scanned the block for escape routes, but there weren't any. I had a sickening realization that I shouldn't have come here without Alice.

"Ms. Lambert?" Riley said as the call connected.

"Detective." I broke into a run again and sprinted past Lester's car. I headed for the cross street at the end of the block. I heard his car door open behind me.

"It's about your husband."

My breath caught, but I kept on running, slaloming around trash cans and fenced-in sidewalk trees. I kept my eyes peeled for a cab, but in the corner of my vision I saw Lester breaking into a run after me.

"He's in the hospital," Riley said.

A flash of yellow came through the intersection, and I shot my arm straight up. The cabbie swerved to the curb, and I dove into the backseat.

—

Detective Riley was waiting for me at the hospital entrance. "Where's your muscle?" he asked, his eyes searching the street behind me.

I'd intended to call Alice from the cab, but when I didn't see Lester following, I'd thought better of it. Mark didn't need to know that I'd rushed to my husband's bedside any more than he needed to know about my ambush of Nelson Ledbetter. "I gave her the day off," I said.

Riley's shaggy eyebrows met in a frown, and he hustled me off the street and into the hospital lobby. "They've moved him to the sixth floor," he said, leading the way to the elevator bank.

"What happened?"

"Overdose."

I nodded. No surprise there. "But why were you notified?"

"I wasn't." He pushed the call button. "I'm the one who found him." The doors slid open, and I followed him onto the elevator. "Unresponsive. Shallow breathing. Lips and fingers blue. All the signs."

I nodded again. I knew all those signs, too. I'd committed them to memory, just in case.

Riley pushed the button for the sixth floor. "The ER docs pumped him up with naloxone and IV fluids. They say he'll be okay."

I heard the skepticism in his voice. I agreed with it. But I still wasn't following. "You just happened to recognize him?" They'd never even met.

He shook his head. "I've been looking for him. For a while now."

The elevator doors opened on the sixth floor, and he swung his arm out to hold them apart. "Room six-fifteen," he said.

–

David lay flat on his back, so thin under the blue cotton blanket that his body looked like nothing more than a faint swell in a dead-calm sea. A white sheet was turned back in a cuff over the top edge of the blanket and tucked in tight up to each armpit. His eyes were closed, and tubes looped around his ears and into his nostrils. Another tube ran from a needle in his hand to a plastic bag on a pole. An oximeter was clipped to his finger and a blood pressure cuff wrapped around his arm. His chest rose almost imperceptibly with each shallow breath. His skin was gray beneath the stubble of his beard, and his cheekbones jutted out like mountain crags above the hollows in his face.

I crossed the room to the window and leaned against the sill and watched the rise and fall of his chest. It was as if I'd wandered into a stranger's room. I tried to retrieve a memory of him the way he used to be, the way we used to be, and it came to me, our happiest moment—after the first night in our new apartment, when we rose naked to the dawn and stood hand in hand at the window, ready to meet the world, and ready to conquer it. I could see myself so clearly in the memory, I could see all of Manhattan spread out in living color before me, but when I turned to look at David in my mind, he was only a flickering image, as insubstantial as a wisp of cloud.

He seemed barely more solid as I gazed at him in the hospital bed. He was a shell of what he used to be. Or maybe he was always a shell and I'd simply filled him with my own manufactured perfect man. I'd taken Mrs. Casco's advice—*wear the face you want the world to see, and that's who you'll be*—and tried to apply it to David. But it didn't work that way. I'd put the face on him that *I* wanted to see. I'd created an illusion and expected him to become it. Disappointment was inevitable.

"David," I said.

He started at the sound of my voice, but he didn't open his eyes. Tears squeezed out from between his lashes.

"David," I said again.

"I'm sorry," he whispered. "I am so, so sorry."

I didn't speak again, and he finally opened his eyes and moved his gaze through the room until it landed on me by the window. "Don't hate me, Shay, please."

"I don't hate you," I said, and it was true. I didn't feel hate or anger or even disappointment anymore. I looked at him and felt nothing at all.

"It's not my fault," he said, and the tears streamed out of the corners of his eyes and down his temples to drip onto the pillow under his head. "I couldn't help it. I'm not like you, Shay. I'm not strong like you."

"You're right," I agreed. "We're nothing alike."

"I thought it would last forever."

He started to sob, and I knew he wasn't talking about us or our marriage. He was talking about the money Barrett paid him to sell me out.

"How much was it?"

"Thirty thousand," he whispered.

I nearly laughed. Barrett must have been feeling biblical when he settled on that figure. Thirty thousand dollars, thirty pieces of silver. The price of betrayal.

A doctor swept in from the corridor and stopped when she saw me there. "Oh. You the wife?"

I shrugged.

She was a Black woman in her forties with a severe hairstyle and a stern mouth. In quick, terse terms, she laid out David's prognosis. He would need to remain hospitalized until he was stable and his detoxification complete. She could recommend several reputable addiction treatment centers. Fees varied. She left me with a fistful of brochures and a final warning: "He can't do this many more times. The next time might be the last."

"I understand," I said.

She left the room, and a nurse replaced her. There were papers to sign and a medical history to provide, and when David's hand shook too much to write, I signed the papers, and when his voice shook too much to talk, I answered the questions.

A team came in soon after to do another EEG, and I left to give them room to work. I was surprised to find Riley in the corridor outside the room. He was on his feet, leaning against the wall with his arms crossed. His eyes were closed, and he looked like he was sleeping. Asleep on his feet, like an old horse in a stall.

I walked past him to the end of the hall and got my phone out and called Dev Kapoor. He knew what to do even before I told him. "I'll be there as soon as I can round up an ADA and a court reporter," he said. He added: "This would also be a good time to send over the expert video report."

I deliberated for only a moment. "Yes," I decided. It was time to catch all the spinning plates in the air and set them down in their places. "And Dev, those papers we discussed?"

"Printing out as we speak."

A different nurse was fussing with David's IV when I returned to his room, so I took up position next to Riley in the hall.

"By the way," he said. He wasn't asleep after all, though his eyes were still half closed. "I finally figured out those papers in your briefcase."

I closed my own eyes then, with a silent sigh of relief. But all I said was: "Those are confidential business records, Detective."

"Yeah, right," he scoffed. "Is that why you made it so hard on us? It was like some kind of crazy scavenger hunt, with all your little Post-it puzzles."

"Would you have believed me if I flat-out told you?"

He thought a minute and shrugged. "Probably not. Certainly not enough to kick it to the feds. But they have it now."

"Ah."

"The Human Trafficking Prosecution Unit. They can manage all the multi-jurisdictional stuff. Plus I hear they have an informant. Wired up."

"Really?" I wondered who it could be.

"So you won't have to break your precious duty of confidentiality." Riley said the last part with a sneer.

The nurse backed out of David's room, wheeling her cart of equipment, and I headed back in. But I stopped at the door. "I guess I should thank you, Detective. For finding him and bringing him in."

"I got lucky."

I shook my head. "He's the one who got lucky."

–

David was asleep again, or pretending to be, and I sat by the window and waited him out. Dev texted me his ETA, and I confirmed. At four o'clock, Mark Ivins sent me a text and fired off another four in quick succession. When I didn't reply, he started calling at five-minute intervals. I turned my phone off.

David woke at five, and I got up and stood by his bed. "Here's what's going to happen," I told him. "Some lawyers are coming to take your deposition. They're going to ask you about the money and that stack of résumés, and you're going to tell the truth."

He nodded.

"You'll have to stay here a few days. But then you have a choice. You can go into rehab—a good one—and I'll pay for it."

"How?"

"I have fifty thousand dollars, free and clear."

His eyes opened wide.

"If you decide on rehab and complete the program successfully, then we'll find a place together and do our best to work on our marriage. Or—"

He watched me carefully.

"—you can sign the divorce papers my lawyer's bringing over and I'll give you the cash. Fifty thousand. Free and clear."

His eyes fell shut, and his chest rose up and down for a long moment. He turned his face away before he spoke. "I'll take the cash," he said.

I nodded. "Deal."

Dev arrived with a woman from the DA's office. Riley knew her, and the two of them went into a huddle in the corridor while the court reporter set up her machine and Dev went over the proccedings with David. Then Riley and the ADA joined us, and David raised his right hand and told everything that happened the morning of February 2. That there was a knock on our apartment door, and a tall Black man came in holding thirty thousand dollars in cash in one hand and a stack of documents in the other. That there was a second knock later that morning when the police arrived with the search team. And finally that he, David, opened a drawer and told them, *Here. Take a look at this.*

"No further questions," Dev said.

"Nothing from the state," said the ADA, and it was over.

After the others were gone, Dev brought out the divorce papers. David had to sign his own name this time. He managed, and with that stroke of a pen, our marriage was over, too.

–

It was nearly seven when I left the room, and Detective Riley was still in the corridor. "Don't you have any other cases?" I said.

"As a matter of fact, no." He turned and walked with me to the elevator. "This is my last one."

"You're retiring?"

His mouth twisted in a semblance of a smile. "More accurate to say I'm being retired."

"Oh."

"It was supposed to happen a month ago. I lobbied for an extension so I could finish this case."

"What's left to do?"

"I have to fall on my sword."

I gave him a puzzled look as the elevator doors opened. The car was packed, and we rode in silence to the ground floor. But the moment we were alone again and heading for the exit, I said, "What do you mean?"

"My final act will be to write up a CYA for the DA. Admit that we made a mistake when we charged you. With enough mea culpas so the DA can dismiss the charges without getting any egg on his face."

I stopped dead in the lobby. He went three more steps before he realized I wasn't beside him. He turned around and nodded. "We're dismissing the charges against you. And we're charging Ingram Barrett with obstruction and making a false statement. Not that he'll serve a day in the state penitentiary. The federal case will preempt ours."

I let my breath out in a big, slow exhalation. Everything hanging over my head, every burden dragging me down—they were all gone. I had only one more spinning plate to catch before this whole ordeal would be over. I felt lighthearted and a little light-headed, too.

Riley held the door for me. Outside, dusk was settling over the street, but the air was balmy. It was a beautiful May night. "Thank you, Detective," I said. "I owe you for this. For all of this."

"You don't owe me a damn thing. We did screw up. We never sourced the gun to you, and we swallowed Barrett's lies about motive. Gun!"

When he yelled the final word, I thought he was talking about the ghost gun in the elevator, and I was shocked as he rammed against me and knocked me off my feet. A pop sounded, and a light flashed, and the hospital doors behind us shattered into a geyser of twinkling shards of glass.

I landed hard on the sidewalk with Riley sprawled half on top of me. An alarm began to screech in the hospital lobby, and through the fading light I could see a line of smoke curling from the muzzle of a gun. Behind it was a man, small and Asian and running at us with the gun pointed straight at my head. He was only yards away when a big Black man made a flying tackle through the air and slammed him to the ground.

The gun went skittering across the pavement. I wrenched myself out from under Riley and scrambled to my feet. He rolled to his back with his phone out and panted, "Shots fired," as the Black man dug his knee into the other man's spine and wrenched his arms behind his back.

I squinted at them through the dusk. "Lester?" I said.

"Yes, ma'am."

"What are you—?"

"He's been following you for days," he said. "And I've been following him."

Something else went skittering across the pavement. A pair of handcuffs, tossed by Riley to Lester, who grabbed them and snapped them on the other man's wrists.

"NYPD's on the way," Riley called. He was still flat on his back, and I went over to grab him by the hand and haul him up. He got to his feet with a loud groan.

"I guess I owe you now," I said.

He rubbed his shoulder with a wince of pain. "You got that right."

# Chapter 32

I'd always suspected that Mark's keycard opened every lock in the building, so I wasn't surprised when I got home that night and found him sitting at my dining room table. He shot to his feet when I came in. "Where the fuck were you?" As he took in what I was wearing, he added, incredulous, "Running?"

"I went for a long run in the park. I guess I lost track of the time. I needed to think."

"Well, I needed to talk to you. C'mere." He gestured to the laptop open on the table. "You have to see this."

"Okay, just let me grab a shower."

"No. Now," he insisted, and he pointedly pulled out the chair next to his.

He'd spent the day at the ICE facility in Elizabeth, he told me. One of the four women on my list had already been processed out—a euphemism for *deported*—but he was able to interview the other three with the help of the interpreters he took with him. He had videos of all three interviews.

"Watch," he said, and pushed a button on the keyboard.

The video flickered onto the screen. A young Asian woman sat at a table with her hands folded prayerlike in front of her. Mark's voice sounded off-screen, and as the woman answered, another voice could be heard off-screen in a halting translation.

The young woman's name was Peou, and she was from a small village in Cambodia. It was very poor, and there was not enough work and not enough food for her family. She learned that there were jobs in Kampot, and so she walked there, over many days, to a job center near the city. The people there put her on a bus to an airstrip near the coast. Hundreds of people were waiting there, men and women and children, most from Cambodia but others from Thailand and Vietnam. They'd all heard there was good work here, though no one knew what it was. They had to wait a long time until a plane appeared high in the sky. It circled the airstrip slowly, like a vulture, and the people craned their necks and shaded their eyes to watch it. Finally it landed, and the stairs came down, and a fancy lady came out.

She was very pale, with hair nearly as white as her skin. Some people thought she had an American accent, and some thought it was British. She wore clothes like Peou had only ever seen in a magazine.

"Gotta be Lucy Carter-Jones," Mark said.

Another woman walked behind the fancy lady holding an umbrella over her head, and a third woman trailed after them with many bottles of water in her arms. They went into the hangar—*garage*, the translator said first, then corrected herself—and after a few bewildered minutes, the people followed. A platform had been set up inside with two tables in front of it. The fancy lady stood on the platform, and the other two women sat at the tables with big stacks of red and green cards. The fancy lady had a microphone, and she told the people about the jobs they would have. They would make clothes, she told them, in a factory, but a bigger, better factory than they had ever seen. It had air-conditioning, the fancy lady said. So did

333

the rooms where the workers would sleep and the big room where they would eat their meals.

Mark's voice interrupted to tell the interpreter to ask for the name of the facility. But Peou didn't know its name or who owned it.

"Paradis sur Terre," he said to me. "It's gotta be."

I didn't answer.

The fancy lady told the people to line up at the tables, and when their turn came, they answered some questions and were handed either a red card or a green card. If they got a green card, it meant they got a job. Peou got a green card and was told to line up outside at the edge of the airstrip. She was so happy. The people with red cards trudged away with sad faces.

The fancy lady left on her plane, and the workers waited in the sun a long time, wondering what they were waiting for and what they were supposed to do. Finally a cloud of dust appeared at the far end of the airstrip, and a line of buses chugged into view. All the people with green cards were told to get on. Peou was nervous, but she was also very excited about her new job. She thought she would work hard and make much money to send to her family. She thought she would do so well that she would someday get an even better job. Maybe one day she might pass out green and red cards and carry the umbrella for the fancy lady.

She was on the bus for two days. It was hot and crowded and had no facilities. Three times a day it stopped by the roadside so everyone could get off and go into the bushes. They were given bottled water and plastic packets of unfamiliar food to eat. During the second day they drove deep into the jungle on a road so narrow that the leaves brushed the bus windows on both sides. Everything was green and dense and impenetrable. There were many snakes, and when they stopped, Peou was afraid to go very far into the bushes. Once they saw a tiger, its yellow eyes gleaming through the thick leaves.

But at last a clearing appeared in the jungle. Peou pressed her face to the grimy bus window and marveled at all the buildings. They were new and brightly colored, and some were two and even three stories tall.

"Paradis sur Terre," Mark said again. "No question." But still he peered at me for confirmation, and still I didn't respond.

Peou got a job sewing sleeves on shirts. She made many mistakes at first, but her supervisor was kind and told her not to worry, that the cost of her mistakes would be deducted from her account. Her account, she understood, was where the money would be held until she could send it home to her family, but she never understood how it worked. When she asked to send it home, she was told there wasn't enough money in it yet, and when she went to the store to buy soap or toothpaste, she was sometimes told she didn't have enough money for that, either. It was confusing. It wasn't until the second year, after everyone was made to work double shifts, that she was able to send a little money to her father.

On the video Mark interrupted to clarify what she meant by *double shift*. The translation came through: sixteen hours a day, six days a week. This was for a long time.

Then one day last year an airplane came out of the sky, and it was the fancy lady again. Peou had not seen her since that first day in Kampot, and she was very excited and pushed to the front of the crowd to get a close look. The fancy lady looked much older than she had before.

Peou thought she must have been ill, and maybe that was why she hadn't been to visit sooner.

The fancy lady stood on a platform with a microphone and told them—in English, while three different interpreters translated for the workers—that she had some unhappy news but also some very happy news for them. The unhappy news was that this factory would be closing. The happy news was that she'd found new jobs for all of them. Excellent work, far from here. It meant that some families would have to be separated—there was different work for the men and the women and the children— but the children weren't so very young, and it was only temporary, and they would all be so much better off when they were reunited. And here was the most exciting part: airplanes would come to fly them to their new jobs.

Peou had never been on an airplane in her life, and she was very excited as she ran to her room and packed her few belongings. Then the workers assembled at the edge of the airstrip and were given different-colored cards to tell them which plane to get on. Some of the mothers cried when their children got different cards, but the boss men took them inside and explained things to them again, and they came back with their faces down and hugged their children goodbye and waited with their own groups.

Peou was lucky. She got to sit next to one of the tiny oval windows, and she pressed her face against it as the airplane skimmed the top of the teak trees until it rose high above the clouds. When the clouds parted, she saw that they were over the sea, but no one knew which one it was.

No one knew where they landed, either. It was an airstrip, but there were no buildings, not even a hangar, as there was back in Kampot. There were two big trucks waiting in black clouds of diesel smoke, and there were men waiting at the bottom of the airplane stairs when they came down, and they shouted and pushed and said, *Get on, hurry up*, and the women started to cry as they were herded into the trailers. Peou cried, too. She'd heard the stories, and now she realized this would be her story, too.

Mark stopped the video. "You know how it goes from here."

I nodded.

He stood up and thrust his hands in his pockets and paced around the table to the French doors and gazed out into the night garden. "It's CDMI. Obviously. The factory closed, and the traffickers swooped in and sold the workers into slavery, and if I could only prove that management had knowledge that this might happen—"

I cut him off. "What if they had more than knowledge? What if they were the ones who sold them?"

He spun from the window and stared at me.

"Just hypothetically," I said. "To cover up the losses at PsT and defend against your lawsuit and maintain their jobs and comp packages."

His eyes opened wide. He went a full minute without blinking. "If I could prove that?" he said finally. "I could bring down the whole management team. All the way up to Claudine de Martineau."

I nodded. "And you'd recover millions from the D and O carrier. Your shareholder clients would be rolling in equity."

His face was flushed. His eyes were gleaming. He was more aroused at this moment than he'd been in bed last night. "So how do I prove it?"

337

I shook my head sadly. "Not through Peou. She doesn't even know who she was working for or where. I assume the other two women can't help, either?"

He frowned.

"Then I guess you're at a loss," I said.

He pulled his hands from his pockets and stalked toward me with his fists clenched. "Damn it, Shay!" I'd tantalized him, I'd aroused him, and now he was furious that I was denying him his climax. "*You* know how to prove it. Do it, and you not only help me, you help yourself."

"How so?"

He gritted his teeth. "By showing the company's motive for framing you for Carter-Jones."

I shrugged. "I don't need to show a motive. Only that they framed me, and we've already done that. The DA's agreed to dismiss the charges."

"Oh?" Instantly he changed tactics. He came back around the table and dropped to his knees beside my chair. "Shay." He took my hand in his and gently stroked my palm. "Tell me what you know. This can be a game changer for both of us."

"Hmm. More for you than for me, I think." I pulled my hand free and got up and went to the kitchen and poured myself a glass of water.

He came up behind me and gripped my hips. "This can be good for both of us." He pitched his voice low and sexy as he nuzzled my neck. He was deploying his greatest weapon. "We can be quite a team, you and I. I mean, God, we already are." His left hand moved up to squeeze my breast as he brushed his lips against my ear.

I stepped away and regarded him from arm's length as I sipped the water. "If I were going to reveal attorney–client

338

confidential information, not to mention violate my NDA, it would have to be worth my while."

A spark lit in his eyes with the certainty that he'd won. Now we were only negotiating price. "Sure! Just tell me what you want."

"I want you to remove Ingram Barrett as general counsel—"

A look of enormous relief spread over his face. "Of course! That goes without saying."

"—and replace him with me."

His smile froze for a moment before it splintered and fell away. "You're joking."

"Why? You don't think I'm qualified?"

"It's not that—"

"You don't think I've *earned* it?"

"No, of course you have—"

"Then what's the problem, Mark?"

He spread his hands in a gesture of helplessness. "GC's a job for a fifty-five-year-old man. Not a thirty-year-old woman."

"Well. That *is* a problem," I said. I bit out the next words. "Now you fix it."

He stared at me.

"All I'm asking for is a job, Mark. Meanwhile, I'm giving you control of the whole fucking company."

He chewed his lip.

"Five-year contract. At, let's say, half the salary Barrett's been pulling. And I'll throw in a release of the company from all liability for what it did to me. That's worth a few million dollars to the shareholders."

He gave a tentative nod. "What happens after five years?"

"After five years, you'll be begging me to stay. At twice the salary."

"Christ." He barked a laugh. "The balls on you."

"But not undeserved," I said. "After all, I outmaneuvered the great Mark Ivins."

His smile faded.

"Let me print out the employment contract I drafted, and we'll hash out the terms." I put the glass down on the counter. "And then I'll tell you everything you need to know about CDMI management and their involvement in human trafficking." I crossed the room to my desk. "Oh, and Mark?" I added as I sat down at the computer. "If you ever think about double-crossing me on this?"

He sputtered a protest.

"I recorded Nelson Ledbetter admitting that you conspired with him to set up Ned Bartman. And that you're paying him off with a plum position at Genco. I don't think you'd want *that* to get out."

He froze, and I sent him a smile over my shoulder as I pushed *print*.

# Chapter 33

"This is ridiculous," Melanie complained as Barrett helped her into the limo at the airport. "You barely spent a minute with me the whole time we were in Paris, and now you're not even coming home with me?"

"Sorry. Have to go straight to the office."

The porter was still loading her bags in the back as she settled into her seat in a huff. All her bags were full and well over the airline weight limits. The excess-baggage penalties were nothing, though, compared to the cost of the goods inside. Barrett leaned in for a kiss, and she turned her face away so that his lips grazed her ear. She batted him away, and he stepped back and closed her door.

The company limo pulled up behind, and he got in and powered up his phone. He'd been offline for eight hours, but given the speed at which events were moving, it could have been a year. The single minute he'd looked upon Madame felt like a year, too, in his memory of that horror. That was how elastic time was these days.

He called Tony Low first and got an intercept message that the call could not be completed. That could be attributed to local congestion in KL, but it could also mean that Tony had ditched his phone, which he did from time to time. Jack Culligan should know, so Barrett called him next. He got his voicemail. His next call was to Phil Duvall. He'd tried to reach him a few times from Paris, but each time Duvall's assistant reported that he was in conference and couldn't be disturbed. Now she reported that he was out of town.

He held his thumb on the *end call* button for a long time. It was just as he'd feared: he was completely on his own. Everyone else had jumped ship, Lucy and Madame included, in their own way. They'd all left him alone at the helm to navigate around the icebergs and bring the company into port. At the same time that pirates like Mark Ivins were trying to board. It was an impossible task. He didn't know if he could do it.

At Marketplace Tower he left the driver to deal with his luggage and took the elevator to the thirtieth floor. There was some kind of disturbance in the aviary behind the reception desk. The doves weren't cooing, they were squawking and flapping their wings in agitation. He saw why. A Mexican was in there running a squeegee over the glass walls.

Even the unflappable Marcia seemed agitated when she met him in the corridor and took his briefcase from him. "Welcome back, Mr. Barrett," she greeted him with forced heartiness. In a lower voice, she said, "Mr. Gutman is in your office."

"Who?"

"Ms. Carter-Jones's husband? I'm sorry. He was most insistent."

Barrett scowled. "Give him ten minutes. Then make up a call that I have to take."

"Very good."

Elliott Gutman jumped to his feet as Barrett came in. "What the hell's going on, Barry?" he shouted. "Why'd they drop the charges?"

Barrett stopped, his arm extended for a handshake that wouldn't happen. "What are you talking about?"

"The DA dropped the charges against that Lambert woman!"

Barrett's arm fell. "Fuck," he said, then, "Marcia!"

Her reply drifted through the speaker. "Yes, Mr. Barrett."

"Get me whosit—that detective. Wiley."

"Riley. Right away."

"They're calling it suicide," Gutman wailed. "Do you know what that's going to do to my sons? And what about the insurance?"

"Okay, calm down," Barrett said. "Sit down. We'll get to the bottom of this."

The call connected. "Mr. Barrett," the old detective's voice sounded through the Ma Belle speaker. "What can I do for you today?"

"I'll tell you what you can do. You can explain what you're thinking, dismissing the case against Lambert. I mean, what the hell?"

Riley made a noise that sounded suspiciously like a chuckle. "Happens I'm right outside your building. Why don't I come up and explain it to you in person?"

"Fine. You do that," Barrett bit out, and as the call ended, he shouted at Marcia again. "Get Jack Culligan up here."

"It wasn't suicide," Gutman said. "I know that now."

"Of course it wasn't."

"I've been remembering something she said that night, before she went to the office. She said she wouldn't have our boys grow up under a cloud the way she did. Her family—they're fine people, really. I mean, she's got a cousin in the House of Lords! But she always felt that

343

their past cast a shadow over her. The family disgrace, you know. It left a stain. She said she wouldn't allow that to happen to our sons. Her suicide would have cast a terrible shadow over the boys. So I know she wouldn't have done it. She couldn't have."

Barrett stared at him a moment before he grabbed the cigarette pack from his breast pocket and strode to the outer door. The wind was whipping across the balcony, and the saplings in the planter boxes were arching their trunks against it. The plexiglass walls that surrounded the balcony were only three feet tall, and he had to hunker down behind them to keep the flame burning long enough to get the cigarette lit. Inside, Gutman flopped on one of the sofas. Barrett stayed outside, leaning against the stainless-steel ledge and puffing on the cigarette in quick sharp inhalations.

The door from the outer office swung open. "Detective Riley," Marcia announced, and stepped aside to admit the old man. He ambled in, looking around appreciatively. "Mr. Gutman," he said with a nod.

Barrett took one last drag and chucked the butt over the glass wall and down thirty stories to the street. "Detective," he said as he came back inside. He went straight to his desk chair and sat down. Riley took one of the chairs facing the desk, and Gutman, looking pained, got up from the sofa and did the same.

"I've been out of the country," Barrett said. "Elliott brought me up to date on what occurred during my absence, and I have to say, we both have a lot of questions about just what the hell you think you're doing."

"Dismissing the charges against Shay Lambert, you mean."

"Yes." Barrett rolled his eyes at the obviousness of it.

"Yeah, it was bad," Riley said. "Watching our case crumble like that."

"What do you mean?" Gutman said. "You have plenty of evidence against her."

"Yeah, we thought so, too." Riley turned to speak directly to him. "Turns out Mr. Barrett and Mr. Culligan doctored that surveillance video."

"What?" Gutman's eyebrows knitted.

"Get out," Barrett scoffed.

"The time stamps were altered to make it look like Ms. Lambert visited your wife's office that Sunday night. But in fact, that visit occurred on December nineteenth of last year. There's no evidence that she went to your wife's office on the night in question."

"That's ridiculous." Barrett held up a calming hand to Gutman.

"And there's no evidence that your wife terminated Ms. Lambert's employment. The termination documents that Mr. Barrett produced were also tampered with."

Gutman looked to Barrett. "Barry—?"

"He's lying." Barrett pulled off his glasses and chucked them on the desk.

"Then there's the supposed fraudulent résumé found in Ms. Lambert's apartment. Her husband has now admitted that he was paid thirty thousand dollars to plant it there."

"Barry!"

"That's a lie! Marcia!" Barrett roared at the ceiling. "Where the hell is Jack Culligan? He's supposed to be in this meeting."

"I can't locate him, Mr. Barrett," the woman replied.

"Oh, that's because he's in the Metropolitan Correctional Center," Riley said. "Pending sentencing. As part of his plea deal with the government."

"The government?" Gutman looked confused.

"That would be the U.S. government," Riley clarified. "On a charge of conspiracy to engage in human trafficking."

Gutman's jaw dropped at that last word, and Barrett felt the color leave his face like the tide going out.

"He'll get a light sentence, though, in view of his cooperation with the investigation. Specifically"—Riley addressed this comment to Barrett—"the voice recordings he made of his conversations with you."

"You're lying," Barrett bit out, but in his mind he could hear the uptick of a question at the end of his remark.

Riley tilted his head back as if reciting a poem. "'George Washington owned slaves. Thomas Jefferson even fucked his. This whole damn country was founded on slavery.'"

Barrett felt the bottom of his stomach fall to the floor. Culligan. In the limo. With a lead pipe.

Gutman stared at Riley, then swung back to Barrett. "What's he saying?"

"Bullshit. That's what he's saying. It's all bullshit."

"Same charges against you, Mr. Barrett," Riley said. "Plus conspiracy to commit murder. See, the shooter named Tony Low, and Tony Low named you."

Barrett lurched to his feet. "This meeting is over. Get the fuck out of my office."

Riley hauled himself out of his chair, but he wasn't done yet. "Two things happened that weekend, Mr. Gutman. The last weekend of your wife's life. Dozens of women were rescued from sex slavers, and an entire fishing fleet was lost at sea."

Gutman's eyes opened wide at the last bit. Barrett could see him remembering the typhoon and Lucy's reaction to the news.

"Remember her text message? *I can't do this anymore.* The guilt must have been overwhelming. She couldn't live with it any longer."

Gutman blinked furiously. "I don't— What did any of that have to do with Lucy?"

"Those men and women? She sold them to the slavers."

"Marcia!" Barrett roared. "Call Security. I want this son of a bitch out of here!"

Riley held up his hands in mock surrender and headed out the door as Marcia's voice came through the speakers. It sounded tinny and strained. "Umm, Mr. Barrett? Reception just called. There are people here? They say they have a warrant?"

"Oh, right." Riley turned back in the doorway. "That'll be FBI, with a warrant for your arrest." With a parting grin, the detective shuffled away.

Barrett fell back into his chair. Gutman was staring at him. "Ma Belle," Barrett said thickly. "Show me the camera feed in Reception."

The image flickered onto his desktop screen. The receptionist was on her feet, and in front of her stood half a dozen men, some in suits, some in windbreakers. Riley came into the frame and shook hands with some of them. His lips moved. Then he laughed as something streaked across the screen. Then something else.

The doves were loose. They were swooping through Reception, and the men were ducking and laughing while the receptionist crouched under her desk. In the back of the screen the Mexican janitor could be seen tiptoeing around the knot of men and heading for the elevator. He

347

probably thought they were from ICE, and he'd left the aviary door open as he made his escape.

But they weren't from ICE. The back of the wind-breakers said *FBI*.

Barrett groped for the framed photos at the front of his desk and turned them around until they were facing him. Melanie and his children. He stared at them, but they weren't looking at him. They were looking past him, to the trappings of his office, the prestige it brought them. And the money. Of course, the money. He was the job, and the job was him. Without the job, he was nothing, to them or to himself.

"Barry!" Gutman cried as a white dove swooped into the office and dive-bombed his head. He batted at it in a way that reminded Barrett of Melanie batting away his kiss at the airport. The dove flew a figure-eight circuit of the room, landed briefly on the back of the white chesterfield, then darted through the open door to the balcony.

Barrett grabbed his cigarettes. "I need a smoke," he said, and went outside. He flicked a flame from the lighter, but the wind extinguished it at once. He tried again and failed again and finally threw the lighter and the cigarette to the balcony floor.

He'd hire the best criminal defense lawyer in the country. He'd hire Bill Centrello, who would dance circles around those government lawyers. He'd dream up some defense, he'd get the charges knocked down. They'd strike some kind of deal. A fine. Community service.

But Barrett knew he'd never work again. He'd never have value to anyone in this world again. By the time he paid the fine and his legal fees, he'd have negative value.

It was a sobering thought. He was literally worth more dead than alive.

Voices sounded from inside. Men shouting. Marcia, losing all her composure.

He pulled up to his knees on the ledge. He got one foot under him, and the other, and pushed up until he was standing on the narrow strip of stainless steel thirty stories above the city.

A gasp sounded behind him. Marcia was at the door with her knuckles in her mouth, and behind her was Elliott Gutman, his jaw agape with horror.

Barrett spread his arms and launched himself into a swan dive off the wall.

A hundred feet down another dove fluttered past him, and he thought: *We're both free now.*

But in another hundred feet he had a different thought. He thought about that superpower he'd dreamed up, the ability to freeze all action in a scene. He wished he had that power, right this very—

# Chapter 34

The technicians were just putting the final touches on the installation in Reception when the reporter arrived, and I was there to greet him when he stepped off the elevator. I recognized him; I'd read his online bio and most of his recent clips before agreeing to this interview.

"Hello." I held out my hand. "Shay Lambert."

He'd come alone; the *Wall Street Journal* didn't run photographs with its profiles. I had to sacrifice my photo shoot when I chose the *Journal* over *Vogue*, but it was the right call. The investors read the *Journal*, and I worked for them now.

He shook my hand. "Matt Najarian." He was pleasingly paunchy and rumpled, living up to my every expectation of a print journalist. He nodded toward the swarm of people milling around the curtained wall behind the reception desk. "What's going on?"

"The unveiling of our new art installation. Come. Let me introduce you to a few people."

Lester Willard stood at attention on one side of Reception. Alice, in a matching blue blazer, stood on the other side. Between them were most of our Admin employees and a good contingent of the Creatives in from Manhattan. I made the rounds with Najarian in tow. First I introduced him to Nelson Ledbetter, our newly appointed CEO. He'd barely had time to set up his desk at

Genco before the newly appointed board of CDMI lured him away.

"Does he have any background in fashion?" the reporter asked as I steered him through the crowd. It was a setup question. He knew that he didn't.

"His expertise is in finance," I said. "Which is exactly what our shareholders want now."

I pointed out Joe Riley, our new director of corporate security, looking dapper in a well-tailored suit. "Does he have any experience in corporate security?" Najarian asked.

"He's got a long and outstanding record in law enforcement. And obeying and enforcing the law is vital to our new mission here at CDMI."

Next was Cheryl Fitts, the labor and employment lawyer who was recently promoted from staff attorney to director of human resources. The four of us—Nelson, Joe, Cheryl, and I—were the new guard at CDMI. The old guard, the ones who'd ordered and executed the most shameful chapter in the company's history, were all gone, two of them dead and Jack Culligan and Phil Duvall serving sentences in federal penitentiaries.

"Where are the doves?" Najarian looked around the reception area. "I heard there were doves."

"Not anymore," I said. "In light of recent history, keeping any kind of living creature in a cage is not something we wish to associate ourselves with. We've come up with something much more brand-positive. Watch."

A technician called "Go!" and Ledbetter went forward with a pair of oversize scissors. CDMI's new staff photographer crouched in front of him to capture the moment for the company's next annual report. Ledbetter mugged for the camera as he sliced through a wide ceremonial ribbon. The curtain puddled to the floor, and a gasp went up from the audience.

Behind the glass wall where the doves once lived was a holographic diorama featuring a shimmering 3D image of Claudine de Martineau. Her face and body were as they'd been during her prime modeling years, but the dress she wore was from this year's collection of CDMI's premier label, Graziella Atelier. She walked the length of the space and pivoted as if it were a catwalk, then whirled, and as the dress whirled with her, it morphed into a skirted suit from another of our top labels. The audience burst into applause at the seamlessness of the wardrobe change. Claudine took another stroll down the runway, and when she turned again, she was wearing a pair of high-waisted white trousers and a striped French sailor shirt from the JustUs sportswear line. The crowd applauded again.

I turned to the reporter with a smile. "What better brand ambassador than Madame de Martineau herself? And now that she's passed on, this seemed like the best homage possible."

When the hologram spun again, she shimmered into the same white Graziella sheath dress that I was currently wearing. The audience laughed and turned their applause my way. I gave a little wave to the hologram and a bow of acknowledgment to the crowd.

"I guess you're a pretty good brand ambassador yourself," Najarian said.

"I hope to be," I said as champagne corks began to pop. "Want to come back?"

Lester shadowed me as I headed out of Reception. "It's okay, Lester," I said over my shoulder. "We'll be in my office."

He nodded and stood down like the good soldier he was.

I led the reporter down the corridor to my corner office. He let out a low whistle as he came in. "A lot of glass," he said, turning a slow revolution through the room.

"Transparency," I said. "That's our new watchword." He looked out at the balcony. "Is that where—"

I gave a short nod. "Can I get you anything?"

"No, thanks."

"Please, have a seat." I waved to one of the visitor chairs as I took my own seat in the high-backed leather chair behind the desk.

"I see you have a virtual assistant." The reporter nodded at the Ma Belle speaker on my desk.

I brightened. "Yes. It's a wonderful tool. Our R and D people have been doing amazing work with robotics, too. Garment manufacturing is the perfect application for robotics. Before long, sweatshops will be a thing of the past."

"Displacing a lot of workers."

I shook my head. "Relieving them of demeaning drudgery. Look, when mechanized farm equipment came along, it displaced a huge population of agricultural workers. But nobody's arguing that we should go back to toiling in the fields. Because other jobs came along to fill the gap. Better jobs, with more meaningful work. Nobody has to be a field slave anymore. And someday soon nobody will have to make clothes in a sweatshop, either. That's the way forward."

I could see he was growing restless with my sermonizing, but I went on anyway. This was the story the company needed to get out there. No more exploitation of labor. No more minimum-wage workers. No more unpaid interns. It was a new day at CDMI.

He let me wax on for a few more minutes before he cleared his throat and changed the subject. "Our readers are more interested in how you personally were exploited. You spent two months in jail for a crime you didn't commit."

I sighed. It was inevitable that the interview would take this turn. "Yes, and to answer your next question, yes, it was awful."

"How did you manage to get through it?"

"An ordeal like that helps you discover just how deep your inner resources are. I had a wonderful mentor when I was a girl. Gina Casco," I said, and spelled it for him. "She taught me how to visualize what I wanted to be and make it come true. I wanted to be strong in jail. I wanted to be a survivor. And so I was."

He jotted that down and asked his next question without looking up. "It must be awful, having to come to work here every day. On that elevator."

I took a sharp breath and slowly let it out. "Well. Let me say first that it's an honor and a privilege to come to work here every day. I wouldn't have it any other way. But as for the elevator? Yes, that's difficult. I mean"—I let my voice falter a bit—"that poor woman."

He arched an eyebrow. "Poor woman? The one who sold almost two thousand human beings?"

"On orders from above, not that that's any excuse. Obviously. But she had enough innate decency that she couldn't live with herself afterward. And that makes me sad for her."

"But not for—" Najarian waved toward the balcony.

"No," I said tightly. "Not for him."

354

He cupped his chin in his hand and gave me a long, probing look. "Can we go back to that day? February second? Describe how it happened."

I half-spun in my chair. "I'd rather not."

"It's not something you like to remember. I understand. But you must realize. There are some people who will always wonder what really happened in that elevator."

"Do you?" I parried. "Wonder?"

"Oh, well—" He gave a shrug.

"There were only two possibilities, right? Murder or suicide. And one of them was eliminated by both the police and the district attorney. Do you know the legal term *stare decisis*?"

He shrugged again.

"Already decided," I said. "Whatever question there was has been settled. Lucy killed herself."

"But some people—"

"Let me tell you about our new worldwide labor standards."

He sighed, and with a resigned nod, he scribbled some notes while I held forth about the company's global initiatives into fair labor practices.

The interview—in fairness, by that point it was a diatribe—wound down after an hour. He pocketed his notepad and thanked me for my time, and I buzzed my assistant to show him out.

After he was gone, I strolled out onto my balcony. The potted trees wore autumn colors now, and the air was crisp with the promise of fall. From here I could see thirty stories down to the miniature cars snarled in a traffic jam at the intersection. But the blare of their horns was too faint to register, and the smell of their exhaust would never reach me up here. It was a bright clear day and I could see the skyline of Manhattan, the spires and crags of the buildings that housed the biggest and best law firms in the world. Once I wouldn't consider working anywhere else, but no more. Now those law firms worked for me.

Still, there was a shadow over my mood, cast by that reporter asking about the incident. His question triggered a flash of images and sensations that cut like lasers through my brain. I felt faint with hunger again and almost delirious with exhaustion. I felt the rage that burned inside me as I stared into Lucy's wild animal eyes. I felt the chill of the cold metal trigger against my index finger, I heard the reverberating roar of the gunshot, and I smelled the spicy metallic zing of the gun smoke. My eyes squeezed shut as the flood of memories threatened to swamp me.

*No.* I shook the images from my mind. I didn't want to revisit that scene ever again. *Visualize*, I remembered, and so I visualized myself where I'd rather be—here, at work. I went back inside and closed the door.

"Jingjing?" I said to my office ceiling. "Get me Yves in Tours."

# Epilogue

Digital voice recording automatically made by the Ma Belle virtual assistant program, February 2, 2014, at 9:02 p.m., via mobile app registered to Lucy Carter-Jones, and automatically saved to a remote server on a cloud farm in Virginia:

*I know what you did.*

[long silence]

*What—? What just happened? What did you do?*

*I didn't do anything. The power went out.*

*Oh, God. Push the alarm.*

*I already did. Hello? Security guard? Can you hear me?*

*Nobody's answering. Why isn't anyone answering?*

*Looks like we're stuck. Locked in a cage. Now you know how that feels.*

*Don't.*

*Eighteen hundred people. Sold. Locked up. Shipped off like cargo. You did that.*

*Please. Don't.*

*How can you sleep at night? How can you get up in the morning? How can you live with yourself after what you did?*

*Stop. Please.*

*[Sounds of weeping]*

*I can't.*

*Can't what?*

*Live with myself. I can't. After those girls—those men on those boats—*

*You put them there. You.*

*It's like a curse. My family curse. Generation after generation. It has to end. I—I came here tonight to kill myself.*

*Oh, sure. Then why are you still breathing?*

*I—I couldn't do it. I have a family. I have children.*

*They had families, too. All those people you sold.*

*They can't know about this. My children. They have to be free from this curse. Which means they can never know. No one can ever know.*

*What? Oh my God—what is that? Put that away! What are you doing?*

*I can't have you walk out of here knowing what you know. I can't have you telling anyone about it.*

*No, Lucy, you don't want to do this. No!*

[Sounds of grunts and gasps, followed by a blast and a thud]

[Silence]

[Sound of three electronic beeps]

*911. What's your emergency?*

# Acknowledgments

Myriad thanks to Jennifer Weltz, who does everything an agent is supposed to, brilliantly, but who also sparks some of my best ideas and saves me from most of my worst. I'm always grateful, even when I grouse. Thanks also to Ariana Philips, Maddie Ticknor, and all the other great talent at Jean V. Naggar Literary Agency.

It's a pleasure and a privilege to work with Sara Nelson, my editor, who first read this novel while holed up in her house during a hurricane and still managed to put together the deal that brought me to Harper. I'm so grateful to Sara and all the rest of her team, including especially Mary Gaule.

Many thanks to Heather Drucker for all her efforts on behalf of this book. When I first learned that Heather would be the publicist for *The Cage*, multiple people told me she was the best in the business, and now I know that they were right.

Much love and gratitude to Alison, Jordan, John, and Will, who always promptly answer my most off-the-wall research questions and do so without judgment, at least as expressed to me.

Finally, much love to my one and only, who's the world's worst beta reader (seriously, everything I write can't be the best thing ever) but a pretty darn good husband.